I0627378

THE EVER RISING
BOOK THREE

FATE BOUND BY BLOOD

CHANTEL BURNHAM

EVER RISING BOOKS LLC

First paperback edition August 29th, 2025

ISBN: 978-1-962158-04-6

Imprint: Ever Rising Books LLC

Book Cover by My Lan Khuc Valle

Also by Chantel Burnham

The Ever Rising Series
Magic Feared and Furious
Misfortune Gilded in Greed

Content Warning

This book contains descriptions that may be upsetting to certain readers, including: discrimination, kidnapping and captivity, trafficking, violence, and cruelty to mythical animals.

For my grandma, Sherron Robison
Thank you for your listening ear, your generosity, and your great
examples of love, forgiveness, and resilience.
I love you.

PROLOGUE

The mega yacht rocked in the white-capped waves of the tropical storm, despite being docked in its sheltered cove off the Mexican coast. But the rolling breakers didn't bother the man sitting in the creaking library aboard the swaying vessel. Smoke curled from the cigarette resting in his limp hand as he looked over an email on his tablet. Raindrops burst against the windows, occasional forks of lightning casting the dim room in silver. Taking a puff, he stretched out his long, thin arms, smoothing his slicked-back, prematurely graying blond hair. He exhaled a cloud of smoke from a mouth that was too big for his face—a mouth that was his best asset for schmoozing customers.

The cell phone on the desk beside him rang. He answered with a sigh.

"Yes?" After a moment, the man sat up, clutching the phone closer to his ear. "They're coming? And you're sure?" he asked. He listened for several seconds, then a low whistle escaped through his parted lips. "And HAMMA? They're not aware of . . . No? Excellent."

He stood and began walking up and down the length of the room, his pale cheeks flushing with color as he paced back and forth, puffing smoke from his cigarette.

"You've done well. I'll alert the captain immediately. We can't count on them doing the *entire* job for us, though they've done it before." He laughed, then paused. "We need a contingency plan to extract it ourselves. Yes? Excellent." He paused, then smiled, his wide mouth revealing straight, too-white capped teeth. "Keep on them, let me know exactly what their plan is. Very good."

He ended the call, and as he sat down at his desk with a contented sigh, he pushed an intercom button on his desktop.

"Captain, meet me down in my library. We need to chart a new course."

PART I
THE DESERT

CHAPTER ONE

The teenage boy struggled to keep his head above the water. Waving his arms, he called for help in a weak voice as his head breached the surface for a split second before going under the water again.

Blowing my whistle, I stood at the edge of the pool. The Nevada sun beat down on my shoulders as I studied the chlorine-blue water, energy zipping through my veins.

Okay, Cordy. Take it easy. I exhaled. *No showing off.*

Taking a shallow breath, I dove into the pool, my body slicing through the water as if I were flying through the air. The teenager sank to the concrete bottom, his arms suspended over his head, no longer thrashing around. Despite my reminder to hold myself back, I reached his side in two unnaturally quick strokes. Wrapping my arms around his chest, I dragged his body through the water.

The boy's head lolled as we broke the surface, and I suppressed an eye roll as I stroked toward the side of the pool. There, a crowd of my fellow teenage lifeguards-in-training were waiting to take him from me. They pulled him up by his arms and laid him out as I boosted myself up onto the sun-scorched concrete. I crouched over his still form, crystalline water drizzling from my long, naturally silver hair onto his bare chest.

When the teenager didn't move, I glanced up at Mrs. Stewart—a short woman from the Red Cross—to see if I should start chest compressions.

The woman sighed. "Luke."

The boy lying on the concrete snapped his eyes open and grinned at me, squinting at the blinding desert sun.

"What? I'm waiting for my mouth to mouth," he teased with a wink.

"I think maybe Allie should do that," I said, glancing over my shoulder to where Luke's girlfriend was glowering at us from underneath an umbrella. She had come to watch her boyfriend on the last day of training, and didn't take kindly to anyone touching, talking to, or even looking at her boyfriend. And I thought my last relationship had been toxic.

Behind me, someone started clapping. I turned to see Mr. Anderson—a thin, older man with a wiry gray mustache and a cowboy hat covering his thick head of black hair—moving toward us, his clipboard under one arm as he clapped. "Very impressive, Cordelia," Mr. Anderson said, smiling.

I peeled my heavy, wet hair off my neck and flung it over my sunkissed shoulder, droplets trickling down my arm. I wished I had tied up my hair before coming to training.

"Thanks," I replied with a smile, despite my discomfort at his exuberance.

Mr. Anderson, who was also the high school swim coach, was in charge of scheduling the lifeguards during the summer. "I wouldn't be surprised if you just set some kind of record for fastest retrieval," he exclaimed. "Very good!"

I cringed inwardly at the admiration in his voice, but nodded to him in thanks. I grit my teeth, mentally kicking myself. Why could I not hold myself back while in public?

"Now I want to remind you, Luke," Mr. Anderson called, raising his voice, "and all of you, that most times, drowning isn't what you see in the movies. Remember the video we watched?"

"Nice 'drowning,' Luke," Travis called as he tossed Luke a towel.

"Yeah, you looked like you were doing water ballet," Joshua teased. The rest of us laughed as the boys helped their buddy up off the pool deck.

Mrs. Stewart looked up from writing something on her clipboard. She was in charge of holding the training for all the teens that were going to be lifeguarding for both pools in Moapa Valley. She looked around at all of us, making sure we were paying attention. "Now, everyone, your tests are tomorrow in Vegas at three o'clock, so don't be late. Make sure to take one of these cards with the address. We will go over all the first aid and skills you've been learning for the last few weeks, and you'll receive your scores next week. Very good everyone."

The coach clapped, calling a general "good job," as people began gathering their things. I gnawed my lip as I stared at the card I had taken from the clipboard being passed around, wondering how I would get to Vegas for my test. I would have to find some excuse to tell my mother. Maybe I could catch a ride with someone.

Luke caught my eye and gave me a wink, and I was about to laugh, but at that moment, Allie marched past me, flashing me a dirty look as she reached Luke. She grabbed his arm, whispering to him in low tones.

Chagrined, my eye caught Joshua's, who had been staring at me rather openly, and I gave him a polite smile.

I'd known Joshua had a crush on me ever since I moved here last year. I would catch him staring, only for him to turn away, face red. At first I was worried he knew something, but I shook that thought away. He'd lived in this podunk town his whole life, he wouldn't know about me. Or about anything like me.

Joshua was cute and fairly popular, if a little shy of me, but I'd told myself that it was for the best. I had been avoiding people for the last year, so I never encouraged flirting. The kids at school probably all thought I was the emo new girl that was too good for this place. Honestly, sometimes I wished that was the case.

Had I not had a hard year recovering, I would've found this place beautiful. While it was very different from what I was used to, it would've been a perfect place to enjoy myself, despite the dry heat. But my mother thought it was best I kept to myself, and I had agreed with her.

Until recently.

Ever since we'd moved here, my mother had encouraged me to keep a low profile. I was happy to oblige for the first nine months of our lives here, especially after what had happened to me back in Maine.

I had been afraid of people after the incident. After Noah. I was ashamed to admit, I had even been afraid of the water.

But after months had passed, and no major incident had occurred, I was starting to feel the effects of our quarantined lifestyle. My mother didn't understand, she was only concerned with keeping me safe. But I was almost seventeen: I needed friends and social interaction again. Part of the reason I'd begun training was because I'd convinced myself that it would actually be safer to have some friends, to divert suspicion. Besides, I felt after what I'd been through, I could take care of myself.

I made a face at Joshua to show my sheepishness at Allie's reaction, and he nodded in agreement, wincing. His gaze lingered on me a little too long for comfort, so I turned away from the group, grabbed my towel from its place on a lounger, and wiped it over my hair as I looked out over the rippling pool.

Underneath the blistering sun that made me feel like I was drying out like a piece of jerky, I was loath to leave the pool without taking one last dip, but I had to remind myself that I needed time to get rid of evidence that I'd been swimming. As this tiny pool didn't have facilities, it was always an ordeal to shower off so I didn't go home smelling like chlorine. It'd be game over if my mother ever found out.

I moved to gather up my bag but the coach stepped in my way, stopping me.

"Cordelia, may I speak with you?" he asked, his expression friendly.

"Sure," I replied, nonchalant, though my stomach tied itself in knots. I knew I shouldn't have shown off, but I couldn't help it, being in the pool brought out that side of me: the side I was supposed to be hiding.

We stepped aside, letting the other two girls and the rest of the boys walk past toward the changing stalls.

"I was wondering, why haven't you joined the swim team?" the coach asked, his tone politely curious. I suppressed the dismay rising inside me with a small laugh.

"Oh, I don't much like competition," I lied. "I screw up under too much pressure."

If he tried to talk to my mother about this at all, it would come out that I was training to be a lifeguard. And that would get me grounded for the rest of my life.

Mrs. Stewart passed, giving me a smile, and I bit my lip as I looked at the coach.

He cleared his throat, eyes narrowing as I met his gaze again. "I dunno, you seem to be doing rather well under the pressure here. In fact, you seem like you're flourishing. We really could use your speed on the team. You're a natural in the water."

I smiled, a wistful pang cutting through me. I wanted to join the swim team more than I could say, but I knew I never could. Sitting near the water watching others swim was one thing. Competing in water sports, in view of everyone, was something else entirely.

"I've never been interested in joining the swim team," I said with a shrug. "But I thought I could put my talents to good use and earn some money, at least," I said.

He put a fist on his hip, pushing back his cowboy hat, and stared me down. I tried not to squirm under his gaze.

"Sorry," I prompted, hoping it would end the conversation. "It's just not my thing." If he believed I didn't *want* to do it, and not that I *wasn't allowed* to do it, then maybe he wouldn't talk to my mom at all. I could only hope.

Mr. Anderson huffed out a sigh. "Alright," he relented. "But if you change your mind, I'd love to get you involved before the school year starts."

"Okay. Thanks," I replied with a grateful smile, edging away before he could protest again. I darted to my bag and slung it over my shoulder. I gave a quick glance behind me to see if I'd left anything behind, and I noticed that the group of boys waiting by the changing room were watching me. Smiling, I waved good-bye and headed out the gate.

As I walked across the parking lot, I could feel the liquid already wicking away from my damp hair. I was amazed at the severity of the heat even in late May. I made a beeline toward my ATV that I had parked in what little shade could be had in the middle of the Mojave Desert. The four-wheeler was pretty beaten up, and that was the reason my mother had bought it for me: it was cheaper than a car, and it was street legal enough that I could get around, but not really go anywhere. We were in hiding, after all, and she needed to know I was safe. Especially because of what I was.

But I was sick of hiding, by playing by my mother's rules. I felt as if my life was sprinting by me, and this job was a necessity for me, therefore it was a necessity to lie to my mother.

I had even come up with a clever ruse as to where I was disappearing to for hours: I told my mother that I had gotten a job at the local feather factory, where turkey feathers from the wild turkeys that practically owned this town were gathered and cleaned to be sold to craft stores. I didn't have to worry about her finding out that the factory shut down years ago; she had less contact with people in this town than I did. And there was no risk of her stopping by like she would if I had told her I was working at a fast food place. I would be safe to work, earn a little money, and be near the water for several hours every day.

I was on the verge of successfully thwarting my mother's plans of keeping me high and dry.

Guilt shot through me at my deceit, but she had forced my hand. I contemplated my life before we moved here as I searched my bag for my keys. I hadn't always been a hermit, and I wasn't used to being one. Back in Maine, I had been fairly popular, with a large group of friends and notoriety at my old high school. And though I didn't go into the ocean with my friends on beach trips, I had lived a life full of weekend hangouts, high school football games, clubs, and other extracurricular activities.

Here in Nevada, I was a recluse. No outdoor activities, especially not in this desert, no friends, no clubs, no parties, no online presence. And definitely no swimming. My mother had moved us to one of the driest places in the country and forbade me from even touching a puddle that came during the monsoons.

We didn't take trips to the lake anymore, or the pool, not even to a hot tub. Back in Maine, day trips to lakes and water parks had been a common, almost mandatory, part of our lives. Now we had nothing, and I was willing to do whatever it took to not be afraid anymore; I would get some of my previous life back. At least the parts that made life worth living.

As I pulled the keys out of my backpack, I heard someone calling my name. I turned, surprised to see Joshua hurrying after me.

"Hey, Cor!" he called again, jogging over.

"Oh, hi," I said, anxiety twisting in my belly. Joshua was probably the nicest and most timid of his group of friends, and though I was friendly enough with the guys in the halls of the high school,

I'd never hung out with them. Joshua was cute, if you went for the big-blue-eyes-and-blond-hair type.

I used to. With Noah. I shook away the memories threatening to slink to the forefront of my mind and focused on the just-as-attractive-as-my-ex guy standing before me.

This heat had pasted Joshua's normally floppy hair to his forehead, but his blue eyes were as sharp as ever.

"Hey, I was wondering," he began, his expression casual, but I could hear the quaver in his voice, "a bunch of us are going to the The Scoopery later tonight, do you, I dunno, want to come along? With me?"

I looked down, fiddling with the straps on my backpack, nearly dropping it. Face flaming, I ran a tongue over my lips, flustered at how uncool I was acting. Rusty, I guess.

"Oh. Um, really?" The thought scared but intrigued me. I was pretty desperate to get out, but I was still feeling cautious. When I'd first moved here, I'd been asked out quite a few times, but I had immediately turned them all down, and word quickly got around that I didn't socialize. Since I'd been staying away from people for so long, I had felt sure that all my high school peers thought me a freak by now. In a way, they would be right.

"Yeah, I . . . uh, wanted to know if you wanted to go with me." Joshua looked like he was holding his breath.

"Why?" I asked, feeling bemused. "Not that I don't want to go, it's just . . . I thought you guys thought, I dunno, that maybe I was a little weird," I finished with a breathless laugh.

"Why would we think that?" he asked, his own laugh a little nervous.

"Well, because I keep to myself," I prompted. "I stay quiet. Don't you guys think I'm stuck up?" It was a thought that constantly plagued me, that these country kids thought I was some big city snob who was too good for a place like this.

The real reason was that I was afraid of them, and what they could do.

But people would read other people's intentions however they would.

Joshua shook his head, and I could see him relaxing. "No, no way. You're new here. Well, new-ish. It can be hard to break into a crowd that's known each other since they were little." He gave me a nice smile, and I allowed myself to smile back. "It's okay to be shy, no one thinks of you like that. At least I don't."

Pleasure curled in my stomach. He wasn't making fun of my insecurities, nor was he indulging them. My mother always indulged my fears, and it was refreshing to have someone contradict me. He was so nice. And he *was* actually cute. I tried to push my ex's face out of my mind, my scar twinging.

Joshua wasn't Noah.

"So, you want to come with me?" he asked again, his smile more relaxed now.

"Okay, yeah," I said, my smile widening. "That could be fun." Telling my mother wouldn't be, though.

"Okay, great," Joshua said, getting awkward again. "I'll, uh, pick you up around six."

I nodded, giving him my phone number, which he had to retype into his phone several times because his fingers were shaking. His nervousness made my stomach twist. I hadn't been on a date in a while. What would I talk about? I couldn't talk much about myself or where I was from—that had to stay secret. However, I didn't dwell too much on that. This wasn't a "real" date, it was more of a group hangout. I could handle that. It would be a good way to jump back into the social aspect of trying to be a normal teen.

We waved good-bye, and Joshua jogged away, looking as relieved to be leaving as I felt watching him go. I would try to not be so awkward tonight, and I hoped Joshua would do the same. I pulled out a water bottle from my bag and poured it over the black seat of my four-wheeler, hoping to cool it a bit so it didn't cook my skin as I drove. Already my silvery hair was no longer dripping wet as I climbed onto the ATV.

Instead of heading home to shower off the evidence of my covert pool activities, I drove to a secret place up in the Moapa Valley canyon hills, where I kept a few gallon jugs of water and a bottle of shampoo hidden underneath a ragged wooden pallet. I killed the engine and, still in my swimsuit, used the shampoo and jugs of water to wash my hair and body, clearing away the smell of chlorine.

By the end of the "shower," I had emptied two of the jugs. I put them on my ATV to fill up back at home when my mom wasn't looking. I then waited a good while in the canyon, taking turns in the shade and sunlight to allow myself to air dry. I'd say one thing for this desert sun: it gave me a better tan than I'd ever had back in Maine. Once my hair and swimsuit were sufficiently dry, I changed into the clothes I had in my bag.

I wasn't worried about being seen while I dressed. I would hear any other ATVs coming, and no one would willingly *walk* this far out into the middle of sunbaked nowhere.

Dressed and dried, I stowed away my secret shower supplies back under the pallet and started my ATV to head toward home.

Chapter Two

Driving back across town, I crossed the railroad tracks—where a slow-moving train passed twice a day—and drove down the long worn road to the outskirts of town. I turned into the winding dirt driveway that led up toward my house. The house was nothing out of the ordinary, the same dusty red stucco of the desert that stretched for miles around, but it was what I had been calling home for a year. It sat on a small plateau beneath four palm trees, tucked away behind the hills. We were fairly far outside of town, to avoid nosy neighbors.

I heard muffled music thrumming from the house as I parked the ATV beside my mother's beat-up truck. Hurrying inside to the blissful AC, I ran up the stairs to my room to hide my backpack containing my swimsuit before ambling back downstairs.

I walked past the living room, where my mother was dressed in her white bikini to keep cool, dusting the shutters over the living room window while she sang along with the blaring radio.

"Mom, I'm home," I called over the music.

"Hi, hon! How was work?" she trilled, looking over her shoulder at me as I passed by. She had been reluctant to let me get a job in the first place, as she always assured me we had plenty of money. Not that I knew where we got the money from, as my mom didn't have a job, but I was able to convince her it would be good for me, preparing me for the real world and whatnot.

"I'll be finishing up with training soon, then I'll get my real hours," I replied honestly, padding into the kitchen. I threw open the refrigerator and peered inside. Grapes, carrots, tortillas, and leftover fajitas were all that were available for a quick snack, though nothing really appealed to me. I settled for a cluster of grapes and plopped myself on the couch, enjoying the crisp, cold sweetness of each grape as I burst it with my teeth.

"I was thinking of making lasagna for dinner tonight. Is that okay with you?" Mom asked, turning down the radio.

I took a deep breath. Just get it over with. Maybe she'd react positively.

"Um, this guy from school, Joshua, asked me out to dinner tonight," I said, hiding my wince behind another mouthful of grapes.

My mother whipped around, her eyes wide, clasping the ocean-blue stone necklace at her throat, the one I never saw off her. She always grabbed at it when she was angry or worried. Before she could explode with a flurry of questions, I held up a hand. "Not even really dinner. It's just at The Scoopery with a bunch of his friends. It's not a *real* date."

My mom turned off the radio entirely, and I groaned as she set down her duster. No music meant *business*. I scooted over as she came to sit on the couch beside me.

"Joshua. Do I know him?" she asked, her tone a little accusatory.

I wanted to give the snarky reply that she didn't know *anyone*, because she never went out, but I kept my tongue in check.

"No, probably not," was the reply I settled with.

A beautiful woman, my mother took the breath of almost every man that had ever laid eyes on her, which is how she claimed she was able to catch the attention of my "enchanting" father, who had also been extremely beautiful. She was fit, willowy, and graceful, as if moving was a joy to her. She had long raven black hair and warm olive skin that I'd failed to inherit. I tended toward my father's Icelandic skin tone, according to her.

My mom bit the inside of her cheeks, and I watched her, anxious as I tried to mentally prepare for any arguments she would throw at me. She always said she had wanted to go into law; she was excellent at convincing people why they should or shouldn't do something.

I, however, had not inherited that trait either, and so had to watch in envy as my mother waltzed her way out of difficult situations, where the same situation would leave me floundering. Thankfully, I had learned ways to avoid being wiled by her arguments, and could hold my own against her.

"Mom, it's just hanging out," I repeated. "We're just going to *hang out* with a group, is all. It's not like it's one-on-one, and it's just around town. A very public, popular place."

I could see the wheels in her mind turning, thinking of every horrible scenario that could possibly occur with me being out unchaperoned. I know she still hated my last boyfriend, Noah, and probably all males for a while, for what happened back in Maine. I did too. But I had learned my lesson, and I was going to keep Joshua at arm's length.

"Mom, please, I need friends. I need to get *out*," I plead. "We've been hiding for a year, and nothing has happened. I'll be perfectly fine. Besides, Joshua is really sweet, and kind of scared of me," I added, laughing. My mom smiled, but her eyes remained sad.

"What time?" she asked.

"Six." I glanced at the clock. It was almost five. If my mom put up a struggle, I had an hour to convince her. My mother crossed her arms, her fingers drumming along her bicep, which meant she was coming up with a list of excuses.

"Honey, what if some water gets dumped on you, or your sweat causes you to, you know . . . *break out*?" she asked, her tone that wavering quality that told me even she didn't believe her reasoning.

I leaned my head back, a growl rumbling in the back of my throat.

"Mom, you *know* that isn't how it works!" I said, pushing myself off the couch to my feet. I was tired of her fear and how it rubbed off on me so easily. "We're hundreds of miles from the nearest body of saltwater! We shouldn't have to be afraid, or cut out all water from our lives because of *him*!"

We glared at each other.

It was a low blow bringing up my father, but I wanted to show her I wasn't afraid of discussing it. It wasn't fair that I should be punished because I was what my father made me. I wasn't as fragile as she thought; my demands to know about my father when I was eleven should've been proof of that. I was the one affected, I had told her I should know the truth.

After months of my eleven-year-old self asking many harassing questions and her coming to realize I wouldn't stop asking, she told me about my dad. Sometimes, at times like this when I brought him up, I wondered if she regretted telling me of her and my father's meeting.

It had been a romantic, chance meeting while my mother had been on a family vacation to Bar Harbor, Maine, when she was seventeen. My mother had described my father as one of the most handsome men she'd ever laid eyes on. When she learned that I was the result of that summer fling, she told me she was resolved to find my father and live happily ever after. She moved to Bar Harbor when she became a legal adult.

She never talked about how her family felt about her having me and leaving them, and I suspected it was a painful parting, because I'd never met any of my grandparents or aunts or uncles, and she never talked about them. Growing up, it was just her and me, best friends.

And there on the seashore I grew up until I was almost sixteen, the both of us hoping for a glimpse of my mythical father—especially once my selkie heritage started making an appearance.

Of course, after she told me the story, I had been even more skeptical of his reappearance than my mother. Sure, he rose up out of the sea once, but that didn't mean he'd do it again. Her beauty was no doubt the reason he'd deemed to choose her in the first place, but he'd had his fun; he wasn't coming back. He might not have realized that there was a reason to come back. After all, the consequences of their meeting didn't fully come to fruition, we could say, until nine months later. A new responsibility for my young, abandoned, confused mother.

But what did selkies know of human responsibilities?

Though my mother probably still daydreamed, I knew she wasn't stupid. She had just been a naïve, headstrong teenager, tricked by moonlight and a handsome stranger, but she learned quickly enough that the world wasn't a romance novel or a chick flick. I feared, however, that she would always hope.

I, on the other hand, wasn't so romantically inclined. At least not anymore.

I thought I had loved Noah back in Maine, and that had turned out to be a very bitter lesson for me to learn: I couldn't trust anyone lightly with my secret. A secret my father, a magical creature, had foisted upon me, successfully messing up any chances I had for a normal life. I couldn't even hide behind normal physical features, as my silver hair, another gift from dear old Dad, stood out in public.

When I was younger, we simply told people my hair didn't hold pigmentation because of a medical condition, but as I got older, and gray hair on a teenager became more mainstream, people just assumed it was dyed, and I didn't bother to correct them. I got a few funny looks occasionally, but nothing more than that; no news crews descending upon us, no angry villagers with pitchforks.

I grabbed my mother's hand, and she squeezed mine back. "Mom, please, I need to get out. So do you." My mom had been on fewer dates than I had, if that were possible. Even back in Maine, she never brought anyone home to meet me. I'd just figured she was pining for my father.

"We can't stay afraid forever. And you're young, you can't wait around for *him* forever, and I can't change who I am, but I have learned to be cautious. I can't continue living like this. Please."

I looked up to see my mother's eyes glistening, and I felt slightly guilty, but not enough to drop the subject. I knew her tricks. She bit her lip, opened her mouth, then closed it. She looked down at our hands, a few drops landing onto her knuckles.

"Mom?" I asked, uncertain. I didn't mean to make her cry. I was just trying to state my case. Usually she would bristle if she didn't agree with me, and the argument would go on for hours.

She wiped her eyes with the back of her hand and looked up at me, her nose pink, eyes watery. "I'm sorry. I just wanted you safe, and there are things that aren't . . . I'm just afraid. You know? I can't lose you."

"Mom, you're not going to lose me, it's a hang out," I said, leaning my head on her shoulder. "But I know what you mean. I'll be careful. I promise."

She nodded and cleared her throat, wiping the tears off the back of her hand onto the couch cushion. She raised our clasped hands and kissed the base of my thumb. We sat in silence for several moments, then, taking a chance, I took a breath.

"So, can I go hang out tonight?"

My mom gave me a misty smile, and when I clapped my hands together and made an exaggerated pleading motion, she laughed and softly kissed my forehead. "Yes, fine! You can go. It'll be nice to have the house quiet for once." She sniffled, but gave me a warm smile. "However, I am reserving the right to do mom things and meet him first before you leave."

"Oh, Mom," I complained, but I cast her a teasing smile.

"I insist, young lady. We'll invite him in so I can meet him properly." She gave me a stern look before it softened into a laugh.

"Fine." I considered her for a moment, then reached out and wrapped my arms around her shoulders. "Thank you, Mom. Love you."

She planted a kiss on my temple, gave me a squeeze, then released me. "You'd better go get ready."

"Yes, since I'll need forty-five minutes to prep myself," I said, rolling my eyes in mock annoyance. I moved to the stairs, then paused at the banister and said, "Mom, you should probably put some real clothes on. Otherwise he'll want to take *you* out instead."

My mom looked down at her bikini with a laugh as she stood up from the couch. "You really think so?" she asked, fluttering her eyelashes at me as she kicked up a leg behind her in a coy pose.

"You know it," I laughed, charging up the stairs.

I changed into shorts and a casual t-shirt, not wanting to seem overeager to impress a bunch of locals at one of the few hangouts in town. I tied my long—and still slightly damp—silvery hair into a braid then wrapped it up into a bun on the crown of my head.

My phone buzzed in my pocket. A text from Joshua, asking for my address. I gave him directions, as our house was fairly hidden, then smiled when he sent back a smiley face with a, "See you soon!"

I tucked my phone back into my pocket, and my hand grazed the puckered welt that I could feel beneath my shirt.

Unbidden, my mind went to the darker thoughts that always threatened. Would Joshua be happy to see me if he knew what I really was? What would my peers do if they all knew about my real self?

Probably try to kill me. Wouldn't be the first time.

I pulled my hand from my side and shook away the memory that was dangerously close to surfacing, quickly casting my thoughts to my father instead, and the conversation I'd just had with my mother.

When I learned about my father, I had done as much research as I could on the subject of selkies, but there wasn't much to be had, except for myths about mortal men stealing the sealskins of the female selkies to make them human, and then marrying them. The stories usually ended up sad, not only for the selkies, who were often held hostage, but for the humans too. Most often in the myths, after living her life as a human and having many children, the female selkie would find her sealskin hidden in the attic or the basement, would put it on, and would return to the sea, abandoning her human family—her children. I couldn't imagine what I would do if my mother ever abandoned me to be with a secret family, a whole life, I didn't even know about. But those stories didn't match my experience. I didn't fully turn into a seal. I didn't shed a sealskin.

While I could control the change in fresh water—choosing whether or not to change into my father's side—I couldn't fight or control the change if I was submerged in seawater. I had never been able to take off my seal skin. I didn't even know how to, so I assumed the stories to be metaphorical, written by mortals who had never really seen a selkie before.

But notwithstanding all my weirdness and a few physical quirks, I looked like a normal sixteen-year-old girl, despite my gray hair and somewhat freakishly large eyes, another quirk inherited from my father. The only trait I seemed to have inherited from my mother was her willowy, lithe frame.

I was pretty enough, on a good day at least, but if boys found out what I really, truly was, no one would ever think me attractive. They would think me a monster.

The painful memories of the night we left Maine resurfaced in my mind. Bracing myself for the ache that accompanied seeing it, I yanked up my shirt and stared at the three inch, angry red scar that slashed near my navel. My mother had sewn it up herself. She'd said the scar, along with Noah, would fade.

Noah's hateful, handsome face danced across my memory. I had been so stupid to think myself forever in love with him. I had wanted to share this secret with him, to have this hidden part of myself revealed, twining ourselves closer in love, having this side of me not just be mine, but *our* private secret.

I squeezed my eyes shut at the influx of regret at my stupidity. I had been so excited. I had taken him to a secluded, hard-to-reach cove that I often visited to go swimming alone, sharing with him my secret beach in the dead of night.

We had gone into the sea together, something I'd never done. I didn't swim in the ocean with my friends, so he was excited. Probably because he thought something else was going to happen.

His happiness soon turned to horror, however.

I had been so naïve to think he would understand. And not just understand, but accept me for what I was, wholeheartedly.

Not only did he not understand, he had tried to kill me.

I shook my head, opening my eyes as pain raced through my heart, unable to tear my eyes away from the vivid weal that signified my misjudgement. Noah had pulled out his pocket knife and had tried to stab me in my stomach when he saw my transformation. I had twisted away at the last second, but he'd still gotten me in the side.

I'd fled the cove into the open sea, bleeding and heartbroken, as Noah's shouts of terror and disgust reverberated inside my head. I'd swum home, pulling myself up on shore of our private beach as I called for my mother. She hurriedly helped me dry off as I told her through my tears what had happened.

She'd packed us up that night, and we were gone by noon the next day. We'd left a lot of our furniture and unneeded items behind in the only home I'd ever known.

Aching sadness enveloped me as I remembered our old house back in Maine.

It had been a large, but cozy shingle-style home overlooking the sea, with separate rooms dedicated to books, art supplies, and dozens of musical instruments that my mother had collected over the years. Before she had me, she had traveled all over the world with her family, and was proficient in most of the instruments she collected.

Now, everything was shoved into the spare room, spilling into our bedrooms and the living room. Music, art, and reading had kept us sane during the long, secluded desert days. My mom especially mourned the loss of our enormous kitchen.

Back in Maine, neighbors popped in whenever they wanted, and my mother would feed them all. Now our kitchen was a tiny square that held a range, a fridge, two tiny countertops, with barely enough room for a table for four. Not that we were inviting anyone over anymore. Our socializing days were done.

Because of me, and what my father had made me. But mostly because of what I had done.

But I hoped to change that. I cast my mind back to my date tonight, the flurries in my stomach returning as I thought about actually socializing again. I knew better now, and I was not going to blow it.

I hoped my mother wouldn't make a big deal of Joshua's arrival. I just wanted to have him say hi and then both of us get out without any problems, or worse: a lecture from my mom about how he needed to keep me safe. Like I could be anything but safe in this dust-bowl town.

With that cynical thought, I left the bathroom and went downstairs. I saw my mother had put on some shorts and a loose t-shirt, her hair tied up off her neck.

I flopped onto the couch and watched my mom pluck out tunes on a beautiful old guitar she said she had found at a rummage sale, her silky voice almost lulling me to sleep. At my mother's urging, I picked up my flute, which I had been taking lessons for since I was eight, and I accompanied her to several songs, occasionally changing out instruments while I waited for Joshua.

As the music filled the house and nostalgia of my previous life sang through the instruments, for a time, it almost felt like nothing had changed.

Chapter Three

When it was almost six, the doorbell rang. Before my mother could beat me to it, I jumped off the couch and flung open the door.

Joshua stood on the porch in jeans and a button-down shirt, his hair slicked back, his cologne applied with a heavy hand. He looked good.

"You look great," he said, his face going pink. I was almost touched by how genuine he was; I was wearing an old band shirt of my mom's, shorts, and no makeup. I desperately wished I could wear makeup again, but it only accentuated my abnormally large eyes, and I didn't need attention drawn to them.

"Shall we go?" he asked, grinning and pointing with a thumb over his shoulder to the truck idling behind him.

"Yeah." I smiled.

"Who's your friend, Cordy?" my mom asked in her pointed way, coming up behind me. I could feel her eyes drilling into us both.

Dang it. I would just have to make this quick.

"Mom, this is Joshua, Joshua, this is my mom," I sighed.

Joshua's eyes nearly bugged out of his head as he stared with round, innocent baby blues at my towering, gorgeous mother. I wasn't offended. Everyone reacted that way the first time seeing my mother, who took it all in stride like a pro.

"Nice to meet you, Joshua," my mother said, holding out a hand.

He took it silently, then recovered himself. "It's nice to meet you, Ms. Jones."

"Just Calli, please. You're just going to The Scoopery, then?"

Joshua laughed, smoothing his shirt nervously. "I promise I'll keep her out of trouble," Joshua said, not looking at my mother, but giving me a small wink.

My mother's expression softened. "I'd greatly appreciate that," my mother said, giving me a meaningful look. I could tell she liked Joshua already. He was gallant, polite, and, even though he didn't know it, he said exactly what my mom wanted to hear, without her having to coax the promise out of him with a lecture.

"Okay, well, have fun you two!" my mother called after us as we started down the gravel drive toward Joshua's truck.

He opened my door, his face still pink, and I hopped up into the cab. He shut the door and got in on his side, pulling out of the driveway. We were silent for a moment, as Joshua was still regaining his composure.

"Your mom is kinda hot," he said, his voice wavering a moment as he pulled onto the main road. He then gasped, as if he didn't realize he'd said it out loud.

"Yep," I replied, watching out the window as we passed the public pool, my throat feeling drier than usual as I watched it slip behind us.

"So are you, yeah. You are too, really pretty," he said, the words stumbling over each other as they came out of his mouth.

I laughed as his face blushed a splotchy pink. "Thanks. You look nice too." We fell silent.

Don't be awkward, Cordy. I took a breath.

"So, how many siblings do you have?" I asked, shifting in my seat so I was focused on him.

Joshua's face lit up as he glanced at me. "Four. I have a little brother and three little sisters who are triplets."

"Triplets? Seriously?" I asked, my mouth dropping open.

Joshua laughed at my expression. "Yeah. They're seven years old, and I had no idea how much trouble three little girls could get into. And my brother, he's ten, and a little daredevil."

He continued to complain about his siblings, but the smile never left his face as he spoke about them. A shot of jealousy lanced through me. I was an only child, but I'd always wanted sisters.

We laughed and talked until Joshua interrupted his own anecdote with a loud, "Oh, there they are!"

We pulled into the parking lot of the local creamery and diner. I saw several people I recognized from school waiting outside the front door, and I frowned.

They weren't Joshua's normal friends; they were the most popular kids in our grade. These were not the sort to step foot in a place like The Scoopery, even if it was one of only like two places in Overton.

"That's not who we're meeting up with, is it?" I asked, feeling a little incredulous, as well as uneasy. I didn't like where this was heading. Joshua nodded, looking excited and nervous.

"Where's Luke and Brent and Travis and your other friends?" I demanded. "I thought that's who we were meeting up with." At least I could see myself having fun with those other guys.

"Well, Angelina invited me to come hang out with them tonight," Joshua said, turning to look at me. His eyes were wide with excitement. Or was it fear? "Please, just follow my lead. I've wanted to be a part of their group for a long time, and they finally invited me. Please don't ruin it for me."

The uneasy feeling increased as he parked the truck and turned off the engine. He turned to me. "Please. Getting into their group is like, huge, and they asked me to hang out with them tonight."

"Are you kidding me?" I asked, anger mixing with several other emotions. Sure, I acted timid and quiet, but I wasn't afraid of speaking my mind. Joshua had kept this little plan from me. I thought I was going to be hanging out with a bunch of laid-back teens who didn't care about being seen in a place that was overrun with families and kids, and I was totally fine with that. Joshua's friends were fun, funny, and cool. These types looked down on those who acted hick, which I found ironic, seeing as these people lived in a pretty big farming community.

I was also nervous, because these teens were exactly like the friends I'd had back in Maine; the ones not afraid to bend—or break—the rules in order to have a good time. The type Noah had been.

"Why do you need these people? You've got like, twenty friends at school," I pointed out.

"These people can get you into society," he explained in a hushed tone, as if I were slow.

"*Society*?" I snorted. "What, are you from the eighteen hundreds?"

"Please," he urged, looking almost frantic. "They're super rich and can get us into all sorts of cool concerts and stuff. I bet Angelina even knows where Grayson First lives in Vegas. Her family probably knows all the celebrities!"

I huffed out a sigh as I stared out at the group. While I didn't know any of these kids, I knew Joshua was a pretty upstanding guy. I'd once seen him help Mrs. Ferguson gather up the papers she'd dropped everywhere, while his friends watched her struggle to gather the fallen flyers for the school dance. She'd patted Joshua's cheek in thanks, which had all the boys in our grade patting Joshua's cheek for two weeks straight whenever they passed him in the hall. Joshua had just laughed it off. Maybe these guys weren't so bad, if Joshua was hanging out with them. Perhaps I was making some snap judgments of them, which wasn't fair.

I frowned. Joshua looked so pathetic, watching me with wide eyes, holding his breath, and I couldn't help myself. I was desperate to get out, and I wanted to make friends, too. I swallowed my reservations. Maybe it would be worth the risk.

"Fine," I said in an exhale.

Joshua's expression brightened as he unbuckled his seatbelt, hopped out of the truck, and came over to open my door. "Thank you! It will be fun, you'll see! Okay, be cool!" he said as I stepped out. I gave him an incredulous look. I knew how to be cool, even if I was a little rusty. Joshua, however, needed to worry about himself. He was so full of excited energy I was half afraid he was going to give them all a big wave as we approached the group.

Angelina, the obvious alpha of the crowd, was looking fashionably up-to-date in every aspect, complete with dumb brute boyfriend, Franco, hanging off her hip. I'd seen him around at school. He was notorious for pranking—aka bullying—other kids in the hallways at school and elsewhere. His signature move was picking people up and throwing them into dumpsters or oleander bushes.

Angelina turned toward us as we neared and gave us a smile. She had waist-length caramel beach waves, light bronze skin, and stood just a little shorter than my own five foot ten. She had moved in a few months after I did, and rose quickly in the ranks of popularity. Angelina was surrounded by eight of her adoring friends, whose names I couldn't remember.

"Josh, you made it," Angelina said, gracefully sweeping her wavy tresses off her shoulder. "And you brought a date."

"Yeah, this is Cordelia, I hope that's okay," Johsua said coolly, smiling in a self-assured way. Angelina glanced at me, then shrugged. "Sure, I guess," she said.

I felt my smile stiffen. They didn't know I was coming? I turned to look at Joshua's profile, but he avoided my eyes. Coward.

Well, I wasn't going to act awkward about this. I wanted to show them that I belonged anywhere.

"Hi, I'm Cordelia," I said, giving them a smile. The group nodded at me in a brief greeting, then I gave a short, smiling exhale.

"Well, shall we go in?" I asked, looking toward the diner entrance, holding my breath.

Everyone exchanged looks and then began to giggle.

I clenched my jaw, my unease shooting up another notch. I figured it was a long shot that we'd actually be going in. Ice cream shops weren't cool enough for these kind of people. And not only was I going to be "that weird girl" for the rest of the night, I was unsure what the plan was. The lake? My mom would kill me if she found out I went there. No one looked like they were dressed for a night on the beach. So what were they up to? I tried to keep my nerves from showing. They didn't know about me. There was no way.

"We were just meeting here," Angelina said, laughing. "We're all heading to Vegas."

"Las Vegas?" I blurted, and I glanced at Joshua. His casual demeanor was slowly slipping and he began fidgeting. I figured he was fine hanging out with these cool new friends in town, but heading to Vegas, without telling his parents? That might break him.

"*Oh*, I don't know if we can go to Vegas, we told our parents we were just hanging out in town," I started, and Joshua made a strangled *shhhhing* noise, and then quickly laughed.

"Of course we're going to Vegas, Cor. Why would we hang out here?" Joshua said, in a very loud, false bravado. "It's so lame."

I frowned at Joshua.

Angelina smiled at him and then turned to the others to discuss carpooling and who would drive. Joshua turned to me, his eyes wide in warning.

"What are you trying to do?" he murmured frantically.

"Be cool, *Josh*," I reminded him. I sobered, suddenly realizing something. "Did you know about this?" A nervous feeling began creeping into my stomach.

He looked away.

"Joshua, did you know we were going to Vegas, and you lied to me?" *Again*, I thought.

He looked at me, his expression almost scared, then looked away.

"Joshua." My heart pounded in my throat. There was no way he knew.

He shook out his shoulders, trying to regain his composure, and he turned to me, face pleading.

"Yes, okay? I knew we were going to Vegas."

"Why didn't you tell me? And why invite me?" Anxiety tumbled in my stomach, but I shook it away. Joshua didn't have the means to hurt me. I didn't look it, but I was very strong, and if he somehow magically knew what I was, I could easily escape an attack.

I'd done it before.

But in all seriousness, I was curious. It took guts to lie to get someone to come out with you. It didn't seem like something he would do: lie and run the risk of blowing it with a potential girlfriend. Not that I considered myself girlfriend material. Not at the moment.

"I like you, okay?" he said, blushing. "And . . . I just wanted to hang out with you. And Angelina asked me to come, and I thought that you would like to make some friends. I knew you were shy, and since I'm making these new friends, I thought that, well, you could join me."

I narrowed my eyes, trying to ignore the sweet sentiment. "But you still lied."

"I know," Joshua said, his tone contrite as he stared into my eyes. "I'm sorry. I didn't know if you'd come with me if you knew who we would be hanging out with; they're like, the *it* crowd, and I was afraid you'd say no to Vegas, too."

"Joshua, we can't go to Vegas," I whispered, hoping he would agree with me. While the thought was alluring for me, as a night on the town sounded amazing, I was still wary, and I knew my mom would not like it if she found out. She'd probably lock me away forever and I'd never get to socialize with anyone ever again.

But it wasn't Joshua's fault I was so anxious; he didn't know my past and my fears. "It's an hour away. What are we going to do there? Gamble?"

"Of course not," Joshua said, his brow wrinkled in thought. "We can walk down the Strip or something."

"The Strip? Are you kidding me?" Had he even seen the temperature outside lately? "Do you really think that's why Angelina and her friends are going there?"

"Fremont Street?" he asked hopefully. "Or maybe a show?"

"I doubt that very much," I snapped.

"Shhhh!" Joshua said as Angelina turned back to us.

"Josh, are you and Cordelia okay driving down by yourselves? All of our cars are full."

"Sure, no prob," Joshua replied.

"Great. Let's head out. We'll meet in the lobby at The Lucky Clover." Her eyes flicked over me, as if confused as to why I was there.

"Great," Joshua said, saluting Angelina and steering me back to the parking lot. I couldn't let him go to Vegas. I couldn't let myself go to Vegas, no matter how much I wanted to go. I didn't want to think about the conniption my mother would go into if she learned about this. Without permission, with this group of people, people she saw as the epitome of danger.

When we reached the passenger door, I planted my feet, stopping us short, and I turned to him.

"Okay, you can get out of this, right now. We can ditch them and I will go on a real date with you; limited time offer."

My heart hammered, and something in my gut told me Vegas was trouble. I tossed that thought away; there was no danger in Vegas, besides the high crime rate. There was no ocean there to reveal me, but I didn't feel like going with Angelina and her group. I didn't know them as well as I knew Joshua and his friends.

Joshua bit his lip in thought as he hesitated, but then he shook his head. "Are you kidding? We're not ditching them."

"Why not?" I worried that I would have to go so far as to say I'd make out with him if we blew them off.

"You don't just *ditch* Angelina!" he said, as if explaining the obvious. "It's a miracle she invited me! She's rich, and I've heard they do really fun things in Vegas! I can't bail on her invitation, it's social suicide! Please! I don't want to be there alone," Joshua pleaded. "I need a friend there with me."

I had a feeling inviting Joshua to go to Vegas with them was part of some sort of initiation. He was a sweet, naïve boy trying to climb a social ladder; I understood that. I had been a socialite myself back in Maine. But my eyes were opened quickly and painfully. High schoolers were idiots who thought they were invincible, that nothing bad could ever happen to them. They were wrong. And it seemed like I was the only one who knew that. But even *I* felt the pull to go be reckless, be stupid, be free. Even if just for one night, to feel alive again.

Joshua's expression grew more frantic as the cars began to pull away.

I sighed. The idiot. He would be eaten alive if he went alone, and, despite him lying to me and my own better judgment, I was extremely curious as to what was going on. Besides, if things got weird, I could easily ditch out and get a Tryp home.

"Okay, okay, I'll come. *But*," I said fiercely, my teeth flashing as Joshua's face brightened, "Don't shush me anymore." Despite my annoyance, my heart beat in anxious anticipation.

"Sorry. I promise," Joshua said solemnly, raising his hand in pledge. Then his face broke into a smile. "Let's go!"

"What about your parents?" I asked as I hopped into my side of his truck. For me, it would be just one more lie in my belt that I was keeping from my mother.

"I'll call them and tell them we went to someone's house and hung out there. My curfew is eleven-thirty." He buckled his seatbelt and revved the engine.

I looked at the clock on the dashboard. It was six now We had five hours to try and stay out of trouble.

Chapter Four

We made the usually hour-long drive in under forty-five minutes. Joshua drove like a demon, despite the summer traffic; clearly he wanted to spend as much time as he could in Vegas before his curfew. If he even kept his curfew. I was sure that if he stayed long enough with these morons, he would soon decide having a curfew was beneath him.

My mom hadn't bothered with a curfew back in Maine, and I hadn't needed one here. What could I do that was dangerous in the scorching desert? Well, besides head off on an unplanned trip to Vegas, I supposed, but she wouldn't find out about this.

The only sound in the truck was the AC blowing. Annoyance lapped against my mind. I shouldn't have agreed to come, but my desperation for a social life was stronger. Joshua was quiet too, probably because he was trying to reassure himself that this wasn't a dumb idea.

Using the GPS in Joshua's phone, since mine was an ancient flip phone, I was able to guide us through crazy downtown toward the casino Angelina had told us about, The Lucky Clover, which, according to the map, was near the Bellagio. We parked quite a ways away from the casino because the parking was insane, which meant weaving through the summer crowds while the heat beat in on us from both the sky and the blacktop.

The Bellagio came into sight, the iconic fountains out front shooting gallons of water into the parched air accompanied by blaring music. I could feel the chlorinated mist tingling on my skin. Though it felt vastly different from an actual sea breeze, I would take what I could get. I had to resist the urge to stop and stare at the glistening oasis in this withered desert, knowing that if I did, I probably wouldn't be able to stop myself from jumping into the shimmering water.

After some searching, we found a rather unremarkable casino that was tucked away behind some of its grander neighbors. The casino was a square building only about twelve stories high, with a large neon four-leaf clover sprouting out of the roof.

We were greeted by two doormen dressed in green uniforms, complete with buckled shoes and green top hats. I didn't envy the heat the two men must've been enduring. They opened the doors as we approached.

Cool air gushed over us, cigarette smoke irritating my lungs and making my eyes water as we entered. I was particularly sensitive to pollution, and Vegas was replete with smokers, car exhaust, and other, more unpleasant, smells that assaulted my senses. It was very different from the sand and barren desert around our house.

An Irish pub song blared from the speakers, welcoming us into the colorful interior of the gambling den. A fountain in the middle of the lobby depicted a portly leprechaun cast in bronze. The ludicrous-looking creature was wearing a gigantic grin and was cast mid-jig on top of a large cauldron of gold. Water spouted from his hands, mouth, and top hat, which he was tipping off to the side. The carpet was a gaudy gold color with cartoonish four-leaf clovers printed on it.

Arches opened up in four different directions, leading to different areas of chaotic gambling. Watching those who were sitting at the machines, it made me wonder what Angelina and her posse were planning on doing here; they were too young to be allowed to gamble. Unless they all had fake IDs.

We waited off to the side of the lobby for Angelina and her crew, and I threatened Joshua that if they didn't show in ten minutes, I would leave. To my dismay, Angelina appeared not long after, her crowd in tow, which was much larger now than it had been when we'd left The Scoopery.

"You made it," she said, coming up to us. She introduced us to the group of ten newcomers as friends she had here in the city.

"So, where are we headed? The buffet?" Joshua asked once all the introductions were made, with less bravado than I'm sure he wanted.

Again, the group laughed, and Angelina tossed her hair with a superior smile. "Follow me."

She led us through the crowd to a desk where two tall women, also dressed as leprechauns, complete with mini hats and green kerchiefs around their necks, were answering phones. Angelina flashed a card at them, then gestured to the rest of us behind her.

"They're with me. I reserved a private room for the evening."

"Yes, of course, Miss Montgomery. Come this way."

My heart began to pound with curious anticipation as I followed the group through one of the arches.

The air was thick with smoke, the dings from slot machines, and the chatter of hundreds of gamblers, people from all walks of life coming together to try their luck against the machines. We wound our way toward the back of the casino, where we stopped in front of several doors guarded by scowling security. The casino worker flashed her security badge and slid it through a card reader on the door. A light blinked green, and with a nod, the rough guards stepped aside.

"Come along," the green-clad woman said, gesturing to us to follow her through the door. Angelina's friends hurried after her, chattering happily. Joshua and I, however, paused for a moment before Joshua took a deep breath, and, trying to look like he belonged, marched through the door.

What were *we doing*? I thought, frowning. Though nervousness fluttered in my belly, I was now also extremely curious. I tried to reassure myself that there was no way these people living in a place as remote as Moapa Valley, Nevada, could know about me. As a precaution, I quickly typed a cry for help with my location to my mom as I slowly followed behind. I didn't press send, but tucked my phone back into my pocket.

We piled into an ornate elevator, and rode up to level seven, Angelina's friends chattering happily around me.

The doors opened to reveal an elaborately decorated corridor, nothing like the gaudy leprechauns and clovers downstairs. Instead, polished marble floors reflected the brightly lit hallway. The air up here was cleaner, and much, much cooler than downstairs.

"This way, if you please." The worker gestured to a heavy wooden door down the hall emblazoned with a shiny gold number seven-seventeen. I quickly and secretly added that detail to the text to my mother before slipping my phone away again.

We entered into a spacious room with a soaring ceiling, decorated with lush carpets, crown molding, and oversized decorative urns. Off to one side of the room, a buffet was being laid out with more food than all of us combined could eat: sushi, a salad bar, roasts, potatoes, fresh-made rolls, seafood, chicken, pasta, and an wide variety of desserts.

The rest of the room was dedicated to a roulette table, tables for poker, blackjack, craps, and a few slot machines. My mouth fell open as I realized that wasn't all. On the far side of the room, I could see a mini bowling alley with two lanes, half of a basketball court, and a room that split off from the main room that was a fully-stocked arcade, complete with pool table and air hockey.

Joshua and I stood gaping at the array of entertainment before us as the rest of the group piled into the room, some breaking off toward the buffet, some heading to the poker table.

I leaned into Joshua. "How much will it cost us to spend even five minutes here?" I asked, my heart dropping. I only had about fifteen bucks on me. The buffet alone would probably cost twenty. Joshua merely shook his head, drinking in the sights.

Angelina came up to us.

"Well, what do you think?" she asked, smiling.

"I think . . . I might not have enough money to be here," I replied, because Joshua was still looking punch-drunk.

Angelina laughed, tucking a strand of hair behind her ear. "Oh, it doesn't cost you anything. My dad owns half of the Clover, so I get to come here whenever I want with my friends. We also have a pool and spa area you can use. We rent out swimsuits if you forgot them."

I stifled a smirk at Joshua's glazed expression, but my stomach twisted. This was definitely more than I could have ever expected, but it also felt too good to be true.

Angelina gave us a smile and beckoned us further into the room, but I reached out and tapped her shoulder to get her attention. "Hey, look."

She turned around and stared at me, politely curious. "Sorry, this is so amazing, but I feel bad about being here when I wasn't invited, so . . ." I ignored the angry pinching from Joshua, and I moved my arm away. "I mean, it looks like so much fun, but I feel like you were too polite to say no—"

Angelina held up a hand, giving an uncomfortable laugh. "No, no, it's totally fine. I'm sorry if I made you feel that way. I mean, I will admit I wasn't expecting you—"

I shot a glare at Joshua, who had come back to Earth long enough to look embarrassed.

"—But honestly, it's fine." Angelina gave me a genuine smile. "You just moved here right? I was new here once too, it can be hard to break into a new friend group, so I'm glad you came. I promise I'm not as snobby as I seem at school." She gave a self-deprecating laugh. "It was hard for me, getting used to this place. So I know what it's like."

I wanted to point out that I had actually moved to Moapa Valley before she had, but decided to keep my mouth shut. I knew what she was talking about, though: how hard it was to acclimate to a small town. Even Bar Harbor, which was hardly more populous than Moapa Valley, had its summer crowds.

Angelina continued, "So don't be embarrassed about being here." Angelina gave me a smile that I returned. "That's why I invited Joshua," Angelina continued, glancing at Joshua, who flashed us a toothy grin. "He was in a lot of my classes last year, and I wanted to get to know him better. And you seem nice, so don't even worry about it. Come on!"

I looked between Joshua standing beside me and Angelina's retreating form, and something clicked. I grabbed Joshua's arm.

"Angelina likes you!" I hissed. "That's why she invited you! And then you invited me, so now she's probably mad at me!"

"No, no way," Joshua said, shaking his head. "She has a boyfriend. There's no way. Did she seem at all mad or jealous to you?"

My shoulders relaxed. "Well, no. She seems surprisingly nice." Maybe I wasn't in for some jealousy-fueled-girl-hate directed at me. If she really was as snobby as I had imagined, she probably would've been spitting venom at my coming without an invitation, especially if she really did like Joshua.

Joshua clapped his hands to get my attention, then rubbed them excitedly. "So, want to take a chance against me at bowling?" he asked.

I gave him a cautious smile.

It was one of the best nights I'd ever had.

Once I relaxed and got to talking with Angelina's friends, I realized they were nicer than I had thought. I supposed maybe I had been a little judgmental of them.

The food was incredible, and I ate as much sushi and ice cream as I could hold. Specialty virgin drinks were served every so often, and I filled up on piña coladas and strawberry daiquiris.

For the first half of the night I played bowling and arcade games with Joshua, both of us being too timid to approach the gambling tables. Angelina's friends didn't seem to mind that they were underage, and shouts of joy or despair could be heard every so often throughout the room.

I wondered why such lavish rooms were not open to the public, but I heard Angelina explain to Joshua that most of the money the casino earned came from the exclusive clientele that ordered these special rooms. The wealthy, her father discovered, preferred a more refined way to gamble, and so they paid more for swankier accommodations, while the common folk played down in the main casino. It was a new business plan that her father had come up with, and, according to Angelina, it was working very well.

"So, why do you live in Moapa Valley, and not here in Vegas?" Joshua asked.

Angelina rolled her eyes. "Dad was worried about the crime. He figured the valley was much safer." She laughed, turning to me. "Hey, let's go try some poker, or the roulette table," she said. Joshua followed nervously, but I stayed put at the pool table. When they realized I wasn't following, they came back.

"Sorry, I don't want to lose all my money," I said with a chagrined smile. "I'm, uh, saving up." I actually didn't want to have to explain it to my mom when hulking men arrived at our house to collect when I inevitably lost more money than I had on me. The House always wins, so they say.

"Well, then, it's your lucky night." Angelina smiled. "The casino provides a certain number of chips to you, and once they're all gone, then you're done, and if you win, you get to keep it all."

"Seriously?" I asked, now understanding why so many of the kids were at the gambling tables. No risk, all reward.

"Yeah." She laughed at my incredulous expression. "My dad doesn't allow underage kids to use their own money up here. He knows we come here, but he doesn't want to be responsible for angry parents knocking down his door, so he told me that my friends could have a certain number of chips each evening. Spend them how you will. Like carnival tickets."

"Come on, Cor, let's at least try it out!" Joshua cajoled.

"I don't know how to play poker," I admitted. "At all."

"How about roulette, then? It's easy. Come on, I'll show you," Angelina offered. I allowed Angelina to lead me to the roulette table, where four other kids were playing.

We began to play, and soon, I began to realize I had more luck than I first imagined. At first, I had lost all but two of my chips, but then, very slowly, I began winning it all back, and then some.

"What is your strategy?" Joshua called over the cheers and moans as I won again, raking in a hefty pile of chips.

"I thought it was a game of chance!" I grinned as Angelina laughed.

"If you keep going, you'll break the bank!" Joshua predicted, but I shook my head.

"No, I'm bound to lose sometime, and it will be everything I have," I said, my own heart pounding with excitement.

"Well, if you're going to lose anyway, do something daring," Joshua called.

I nodded. "Might as well."

Taking more than half of my winnings, I put them on a random number. As the ball rolled, I saw I was going to lose. The ball just missed my slot

"Well, I guess that's it for me," I laughed, staring at my sad pile of chips.

Angelina shrugged. "Eh, might as well play the rest. You'll be able to get more chips the next time you come anyway, and you didn't lose anything, right?"

I shared a smile with Joshua at her mention of, "next time." "Which do you suggest?" I asked, and she studied the board as the spinner called for bets to be placed.

"I'd place it all on that one. A single number is the highest risk."

Shrugging, I pushed the rest of my chips on the square, and a moment later, the spinner called final bets. The ball jumped, rolling around the ball track and clattering against the spinning wheel. My mouth dropped open as the ball tumbled to a stop into my pocket number, earning a cheer from those at the table. I had just won back more than double what I'd lost.

"Wow," Joshua hooted as Angelina squealed in delight. "Maybe stop betting now," Joshua advised, who had only won a handful of chips.

I didn't know anything about the denominations on the variety of colored chips as I scooped them up into my arms, Angelina helpfully gathering up any that fell from my cradled limbs. Three hundred dollars worth, perhaps?

"And I really can keep this?" I asked.

"Yup," Angelina said, nearly dropping a few chips.

"Excellent," I breathed. I was sure my paychecks from lifeguarding would need supplementing.

We reached the counter where the chips would be cashed, and as I tried to help the man organize them by color, I heard Angelina whispering to herself. After a moment she gasped.

"Oh my gosh, Cordelia," Angelina squealed as the man behind the desk began taking chips from the stacks. "You won almost four thousand dollars!"

I stopped in my tracks, turning to look at her, mouth hanging open. She laughed as I rasped, "You're kidding, right?"

Angelina shook her head, but instead of looking annoyed, she genuinely looked pleased for me.

"I can't take all of this," I said, stepping away, but Angelina and Joshua stopped me.

"Why not? It's a casino," Angelina laughed. "Besides, this is chump change compared to what we get from downstairs alone, not to mention the patrons that use these special rooms. They drop ten grand just for antes. Trust me, what you won isn't even a drop in the bucket. Take it, you won it! I'm so glad!"

As I watched Angelina urge me to take the money, the idea suddenly came to me that Angelina was more of a people pleaser than I first thought. Perhaps she wasn't as confident as I first imagined, and brought people here so that she would feel validated. I mean, if her father was a big business tycoon, perhaps she didn't get the attention she needed at home, and therefore brought droves of her friends to impress them with her father's casino.

I watched in amazement as my cash was loaded into a duffel bag and stored in a locker for safekeeping until the evening was over.

Angelina explained that any winnings would be delivered by guard to our houses, so we wouldn't have to worry about lugging huge bags of cash around Vegas.

I grimaced. So there *would* be hulking men showing up at my house. My mom would have so many questions. "Um, would it be possible for them to take it to your house? And I could pick it up later?" I asked, blushing. "I don't want my mom placing me in solitary confinement for gambling."

Angelina laughed and agreed.

As we went back to play a game of pool, my spirits rose. Despite the extravagance around me, for the first time in ages, I felt normal.

Chapter Five

"Crap, my mom is going to kill me," Joshua laughed as our group made our way down the sidewalk, Joshua's curfew well behind us. "But it was totally worth it."

The evening air was still unbearably hot, despite the sun having been down for hours. Now that the fun had dwindled down, I noticed I was starting to feel sick.

Probably all the sushi I ate, I thought with a grimace. *And I probably shouldn't have eaten any of that last round of food they brought out before we left.*

"Have you ever broken a rule in your life, nerd?" Angelina's hulking boyfriend, Franco, chuckled, giving Joshua a push.

Joshua shook his head. "First offense."

"Then your parents will go easy on you," Franco continued. "The first time is always the softest. Once you start doing it more often, that's when they go hard on you."

I followed along, laughing at the jokes, but the heat made me feel like I was being pressed down by a great boulder. I fell to the back of the group despite my efforts to keep up. Ahead of me, the others began roughhousing. The main offender being Franco, who was pretending to shove people into the traffic of the Strip.

Dizziness began to envelop me. I assumed it was mostly because of the heat and overeating at this late hour. Perhaps being shut up for so long and then being thrust into huge crowds made me more susceptible to catching germs, and I had no doubt that germs were plentiful in a casino. The thought made me visibly cringe.

We were passing the Bellagio fountains when I noticed our group stop around me. I had been so focused on just putting one foot in front of the other, it was nice to stop for a second. Everyone had paused to watch the fountains spray color into the air as music thrummed in time to the jetting water. I didn't realize how bad I felt until the group stopped, and I felt myself sway on the spot. I gripped the railing in front of me, taking a deep breath, then looked up when I heard Franco say, "Hey." He was watching me, his face illuminated by the flashing lights.

"You're not looking so good, Cor," he said over the noise of the music and crowds, sounding thoughtful. I saw him share a sly glance with one of the other boys his size, but it didn't register that it should've been a warning.

"I'm fine," I replied weakly, knowing I was not fooling anyone. In fact, I felt like I was going to pass out any moment.

"Nah, it must be the heat. You're wilting like a flower out here," he asserted to me. Then, speaking louder to the group, he hooted, "I think this one needs a drink!"

Arms suddenly wrapped around my waist, and I felt myself being hoisted into the air, hands on the small of my back, shoulders, and legs. A cacophony of shouting and laughing erupted around me as I was lifted toward the railing surrounding the Bellagio fountains.

Before I could even attempt to slip out of their grasp, they moved to heave me over the side. At the last second, they corrected, still gripping me tightly so I wouldn't actually fall into the water. My stomach did a somersault as vertigo clutched me, and I could only gurgle incoherently. Water, lights, and shouting voices were a disorienting swirl around me, and I didn't know which way was up or down.

"Whoa, you almost fell," Franco called in a singsong voice. "Oh no! Oops!" Franco shouted, feigning dropping me again, my stomach convulsing. Wild laughter ensued.

"Put me down!" I gasped, trying to hold back my churning stomach. I didn't want to think about the mortification I would feel if I barfed all over two of the most popular guys in school. To put it in Joshua's words, it would be social suicide.

I weakly slapped at their hands, trying to show my distress as I was lowered over the railing again, the laughter swelling. I could hear Joshua and Angelina shouting at Franco to put me down.

"Oh noooo, I hope you don't—Ahh!" Franco's laugh turned into a genuine shout of alarm as the hands holding me slipped. My view tilted, I felt myself falling, and water rushed up toward me.

I heard screaming a split second before I plunged into the warm water. I allowed myself to sink, and under the surface, I regurgitated all of the snacks I had eaten that evening.

Instant relief washed over me as the water cooled my heated body, and the sick feeling went away as I lightened my stomach.

I pushed the soiled water away from me, grateful for the coverage of nightfall so hopefully the contents of my stomach wouldn't be noticed. I stayed under the water as the last remains of the food in my stomach came up, and I took a deep breath, the water passing through me as if it were air, the cool wetness soothing my dry throat and skin, though I could taste the acrid chlorine on my tongue.

As I relished the sweetness of the water on my parched body, I started with a jolt, realizing that people were probably wondering why I was taking so long coming up for air. Worried that I would cause a panic, I found the ground with my feet and hastily stood.

My head broke the surface of the water, and I took a theatric gasp of air for dramatic effect. The height of the water came up to about my chin, and I pretended to cough and hack, wiping water away from my eyes.

"*Cordelia*! Are you okay?" I heard Angelina and Joshua shout. I looked up to see not just those from my friend group, but *everyone* along the balcony staring down at me, with more people gathering from the street to see the commotion. And most onlookers were pulling out their phones.

Dread filled my stomach, and I whipped my hands up to cover my face under the guise of wiping away water, hoping the darkness of the night and the reflections of the water would hide anything of my identity, in case this got put up on the internet. I turned away, glancing out over the water, trying to think. While throwing up had made me feel like a new woman, I was still in big trouble; I'd heard getting into the Bellagio fountains was a big no-no.

"Here! Reach up! Come on!" Franco and Joshua called, reaching their hands down toward me. I swam over to the wall and gave a halfhearted leap, but there was no way I would be able to reach. I saw some rocks barely poking up from the surface near the wall, and I clambered up onto them, water streaming from my clothes. With a groan, I realized my phone was still in my pocket. It was just an old flip phone so that I could stay off the grid but still contact my mother. If she found out how it had gotten ruined . . .

"Come on, *hurry*!" Franco gave one last passive attempt at grabbing my hand, then ducked away, shouting, "Abort! Let's get out of here!"

"*Hey*!" I bellowed, but Franco and the rest of the group, no doubt afraid of getting caught, disappeared from view, all except Joshua, who was still reaching for me. After several precarious jumps, I was able to grip his hand. With his help, I was able to clamber up and over the railing.

"You okay?" Joshua asked with a wince, rubbing his arms, as I wiped a hand down my dripping face to keep it obscured. As I nodded, trying to calm my heart at that very near miss of being discovered, I saw Angelina hurrying back toward us through the muttering crowd.

"Cordelia! I'm so sorry about that!" Angelina cried, stopping before us. "I was trying to stop them from leaving, the jerks, but they're gone."

"What do we do? Do we just leave?" Joshua asked, anxiety coloring his tone. He turned away from a woman filming him on her phone, a panicked look on his face.

Angelina surveyed the crowd that had gathered, also ducking her head. "Uh, yeah, we don't want to deal with security. Let's just get out of here."

We dashed through the crowd, water squelching out of my tennis shoes, leaving a perfect trail for anyone to follow. For once, I was glad of the heat; my watery footprints would evaporate in no time.

We ran down the sidewalk and dodged into the crowds. When the Bellagio was out of sight, we slowed and Angelina turned to us.

"I'm so sorry, Cordelia!" she moaned. "That complete jerk! He always does this. He thinks he can just pick anyone up and harass them with no consequences."

I pulled out my phone and tried to turn it on. It remained black.

"Oh no, is your phone ruined?" Angelina asked, her expression mortified.

I shook the cell phone around, water audibly sloshing inside it, and nodded.

"I'm so sorry! I'll buy you a new one," Angelina began, then paused. "Actually, I might make that idiot buy you one." She considered for a moment, then shook her head. "No, he's too dumb, he won't do it. He never takes responsibility for anything."

"Sounds like a gem," I muttered as we walked down the street. I got some weird looks from those passing by because of my drenched clothing, but I could feel myself starting to dry.

"I'm really sorry, Cordelia," she repeated. "He's . . ." she paused, visibly weighing her words. "He takes a little getting used to."

Her tone made it seem like *she* was still trying to get used to him, too. I wanted to say she should dump him if she didn't like him, but decided against it.

As we waited for my clothes to dry, we wandered down the Strip. The blazing neon lights, the city sounds, and laughing with Angelina and Joshua helped me ignore the chafing of my wet clothes. Soon, I was dry enough, and Joshua suggested we head toward where we'd parked.

"Oh no! If that idiot drove off without me, so help me," Angelina cried as we neared where we had parked. She pulled out her phone and began swiping her screen.

"We can give you a ride," Joshua offered, but at that moment Angelina squealed out in anger.

"He *did* leave me! That jerk! He knew I could get a ride home from one of my dad's chauffeurs. He texted saying he didn't want to get an earful from me on the ride home, so he just left! Oooh, that moron!" she seethed.

"We can give you a ride back," Joshua offered again, but Angelina shook her head.

"No, don't bother," she sighed, slipping the phone back into her pocket. "I can head back to the casino and get a ride from there."

"You sure?" I asked, and she nodded.

"Yeah. No offense, but my dad sends me home in limos, so . . ." She shrugged, giving us a shy smile.

"Dang. Can we get a ride with you?" Joshua joked. "No, just kidding."

"Maybe next time," Angelina promised. "Well, I better head to the casino, and you guys better get home."

"My parents are going to freak," Joshua said again, this time shaking his head.

"What about yours, Cordelia?" Angelina asked, turning to me. "Are you in trouble?"

"Nah. My mom has never given me a curfew."

"Lucky," Joshua muttered.

"Okay. Well, drive safe," Angelina replied. "And Cordelia, I'll get you a new phone."

After a few minutes of me rejecting her offer of buying me a new phone, I finally relented. With a promise to get my new phone to me soon, we said our good-byes, and Joshua and I headed toward the crowded parking lot.

Once Angelina was out of sight, Joshua whooped and jumped into the air with a fist pump. I laughed, feeling some of his exuberance rubbing off on me

"Wasn't that *amazing*?" Joshua exclaimed, hopping along beside me. I laughed at his excited energy. He kept pumping his arms like he had been all pent up and was now released. "See, that is what I meant when I said 'society.' And you made fun of me!"

I rolled my eyes. "Okay, fine, I was wrong. That was pretty cool."

"And Angelina is so down-to-earth for a gajillionaire," Joshua continued. I nodded in agreement.

"So we're going to hang out with her again, right?" Joshua asked, coming to a stop outside the truck door and unlocking it.

"If she invites us again," I grinned. "Then heck yes." I would just make sure not to eat so much next time to keep the barfing to a minimum.

I walked through the front door, my heart soaring with happiness for the first time in months, when I stopped dead in my tracks.

My mother was sitting on a kitchen chair that she had pulled into the entryway, so she would be framed in the doorway right when I walked in. She was still dressed in her bikini, if a bikini could be counted as dressed, with her arms folded tightly across her chest.

"What?" I asked. I didn't have a curfew, I had to remind myself. I looked down at my phone, which was banged up pretty good. Before coming inside, I had thrown my phone down on the ground to give a different excuse as to why my phone was dead. I had also been worried she would be able to smell the chlorine on me, but I had thought I could hurry inside and shower before having to talk to her. I was dry now, and Joshua did have a pretty large bundle of strong-smelling car fresheners called "Thundersmoke" hanging from his rearview mirror. I hoped it was enough to cover any smell of chlorine left on me.

I looked back up and met my mother's eye, determined that I'd tell the truth about what happened, but with a few details tweaked.

"You really thought you could sneak around me?" she demanded, and for a moment, I was afraid she had found out about the lifeguard thing.

"What do you mean?" I asked, hoping she'd tell me what she knew before I said anything else.

"I went to The Scoopery and you weren't there," she accused.

"*What*?" I gasped. "You went to *spy* on me on my date?"

"No!" she denied a little too forcefully. "I went to go get a scoop of ice cream and right when I walked in I forgot you were going there with your friends—"

I snorted. I didn't know how she kept a straight face while telling *that* complete lie. It was my first time going out in a year, to the only ice cream parlor in this tiny town, there was no way she would have "forgotten" that detail.

"—And I didn't see you there, at all," she finished coolly. "So, where did you go?"

I knew saying I went to Vegas would get me into trouble, but not as much trouble as she was obviously expecting me to have gotten into. Like going to the lake. I would rather tell her the truth about Vegas than get the topic of water up on her radar again. I was still hoping to do the lifeguard thing, after all. I couldn't spoil that chance with a lie now. If I wound too many webs, I would eventually get caught in them.

She might forbid me from seeing Joshua again after this betrayal, but it was something I had to risk. I cared too much about lifeguarding.

I sighed and leaned against the front door.

"Mom, I honestly thought we were going to The Scoopery. But once we arrived, a group of his newer friends said they were going to Vegas. I didn't want Joshua to do something stupid, so I went with them, to keep an eye on him—"

"And who was keeping an eye on *you*?" she interrupted.

"—and then we stayed out late, and I actually had fun. I didn't do anything dangerous," I finished quickly. At least not on purpose, I didn't.

My mother's jaw was moving back and forth, and I braced for the storm.

"You went to Las. Vegas. Without TELLING ME?" she thundered.

"Yes."

"Why?" she demanded. "Do you understand how worried I was? You couldn't have called? Texted?"

"Joshua begged me not to." My mother made an indignant, blustering noise, and I spoke over her to get my explanation out. "He said that he was afraid you'd call his parents and rat him out, or that you'd demand I come home." That part was true. He had asked me not to as we were getting onto the on-ramp. He had been terrified that his evening would end before it had a chance to begin. "I didn't want to disappoint him. He's one of the few people I know who are really nice."

My mother glared at me, the tendons standing out in her neck. I thought she was going to start really yelling at me and begin barring up what freedoms I had, but instead, to my surprise, she deflated, her shoulders slumping, her arms uncrossing.

"I understand," she said, her voice low. "You've been lonely, you've been stuck in this hot, horrible wasteland, and you've been hurting, because of me." She bit her lip, brow furrowed.

I paused for a moment. "I'm sorry, Mom. It's just . . . why did we move here?" I asked. It was a question I always asked when the topic was broached. My mother never gave a satisfactory response, only the same, worn-out one she'd always given me: to keep me safe. We could've moved anywhere in the US that didn't have access to saltwater, and I would've been perfectly fine. We could still enjoy the water, enjoy our lives. Instead, we were stuck here, drying out and wasting away in this place, forgotten by everyone.

"Don't you have family and friends wondering where you went? How come they never visit?" I asked. I never got direct answers from my mother about her family, either. She would clam up for days afterward if I asked direct questions about her parents or siblings. However, my boldness at defying her wishes of late made me feel more courageous, and I didn't care if she got mad. In fact, it might even stop the interrogation about tonight. She moved us here, where I had to lie and cheat to get some fun and water back into my life, so it wasn't entirely my fault that I'd had to take matters into my own hands. She was driving me to this.

My mom bit her lip again, this time looking on the verge of exploding.

"What? What won't you tell me?" I asked, my voice wavering. "We used to tell each other everything."

Her eyes filled with tears and she looked away. I softened, realizing the fight wouldn't come, at least not tonight.

"Mom, what's wrong?" I asked.

"Nothing. Go to bed, hon, I'm just tired, and I was really worried. That's all."

I knew that wasn't all, but she wasn't pushing me for details, and I didn't want to push my luck, so I bid her a quiet goodnight and climbed the stairs to my room.

Guilt surged through me. I didn't like lying to my mother, but sometimes I wondered if she blamed me for having to move here, for my own good.

After jumping in a quick shower to scrub off the disgusting fountain water, I brushed my teeth and climbed into bed, pushing my sheets and blankets off so I lay uncovered. Cold air gushed from the vents, chilling my wet head, and I soon fell asleep, dreaming about the sea.

Chapter Six

My mother avoided me as much as she could after my night in Vegas. As she always did when her family was brought up. I was still afraid of getting caught in my several lies, so I was more than happy for the coolness between us. Because my phone was dead, I had emailed the coach via my laptop and told him of my plight, and that he'd have to contact me through email about lifeguarding.

The day after my night out, I caught a ride back to Vegas with Joshua for our Red Cross tests. They said we'd get our results within a week, but I knew I had aced it the moment I'd finished, and I bought a legit Red Cross swimsuit while I was there.

When the email for the certification came two days later, I wasn't surprised to see my name on the list, but was happy to see Joshua had passed as well. I couldn't wait to start work on Monday.

Another big surprise came when I saw Angelina in the grocery store that same evening I'd received my certification. I had gone to pick up a few things for dinner before my mother came home from running an errand, and Angelina gave me a brand-spanking-new phone. The best on the market.

I had sputtered that I couldn't accept it, but she'd waved me away, saying it was all her fault mine was dead, and she didn't mind buying me a *real* phone. "No offense," she had said with a small smile, "but I didn't know they still made flip phones."

I had gone home, grinning from ear to ear, and even the still-cool looks from my mother, who had come home late from wherever she'd been, couldn't make me feel bad. We hadn't been talking much, so my mom didn't even realize I didn't have my old phone. Now I would just have to find a way to hide my new one from her until the perfect moment.

Monday couldn't come soon enough. I had to hide out for the rest of the week, pretending I was at my fake job while I waited for my real job to begin. Thankfully, the adventure I'd had in Vegas with Joshua and Angelina turned into an easy friendship, and I now had friends' houses I could hide out at.

Angelina was an only child and was alone most of the time, as her parents were often handling business at the casino.

We played nerdy video games and watched a lot of movies in Angelina's empty house, and I could feel part of my soul healing. I hadn't realized how much I'd craved doing normal, stupid teenager things, instead of constantly worrying about my genetics. Sometimes, to my disgust, Franco and a few of Angelina's other friends would come over. I noticed that once her friends arrived, Angelina seemed to dumb herself down, like she was afraid of being found out that she was actually smart.

However, I understood. Everyone had secrets, trying to hide sides of themselves that may be deemed unsavory, so I never mentioned anything to her.

Finally, Monday morning came.

I relished the daydreams I had as I slipped on my red lifeguard swimsuit before dressing in regular clothes. I pulled my thick, silver hair up into a ponytail, and, packing away my whistle and towel in my backpack, I left my house for the pool.

I'd only been seated in the lifeguard chair for a few moments before the doors opened, and kids and parents came rushing in, arms full of towels, sunblock, floaty toys, and umbrellas, desperate to escape the skin-crackling heat. My chest fluttered with pride and excitement as I started the newest chapter of breaking free from my self-isolation and my mother's fears.

When my third week of lifeguarding came around, I was starting to tire of the job.

The first two weeks were a cinch. I sat under an umbrella, watching kids and parents play in the water, blowing my whistle at those splashing too roughly or who refused to walk around the pool. Nothing major had happened other than a patron getting a bee sting. I had to admit, I thought that being a lifeguard would be much more exciting than this.

I now cringed at the ridiculous fantasies I'd had of myself while training for the real thing; how I would gallantly save a drowning swimmer every other day and be hailed as the town hero. Or a patron at the pool would secretly be a talent scout, and would offer me a position on the US Olympic team. They'd been fun scenarios to imagine, but now had begun to shrivel under the bright rays of the Nevada sun.

I supposed it was good that I *wasn't* saving the whole incompetent town from drowning at my day job, otherwise my mother would hear about it.

While the absurd daydreams had kept me sane as I trained for my certification, the job was actually more boring than the certification had been. The only thing that kept me from quitting was free use of the pool after patrons had left. It certainly wasn't the paycheck.

I started to realize that lifeguarding wasn't my oasis in this desert anymore. It was my new friends, especially Joshua and Angelina. We hung out every chance we could; we had even been back to Vegas twice in the last three weeks. Each visit had been as fun as the first, despite Franco's obnoxious presence: he always seemed to manage to cause some kind of scene that drew attention from strangers, which I did not need. Angelina had promised to get tickets for a show this Friday, and I was hoping I could convince her to leave Franco home.

But I still had my job to do before that time, so I slipped on my guard swimsuit with a little less enthusiasm than I had the past couple of weeks.

When the pool opened, exhaustion flooded my body as I saw the same rowdy kids who didn't listen to the whistle push their way through the doors and run toward the edge of the pool. The heat was already weakening me, especially since the pool looked so blue and inviting. Taunting me. The chaos of screaming kids around me seemed to sap my strength even more, though my shift had only just started. It was going to be a long day.

After an hour of waiting and watching in the shade, I took my turn on the lifeguard tower, switching with Joshua. He gave me an apologetic look as he climbed down. "Good luck with that bunch," he said, giving me a bracing touch on my shoulder as he nodded toward the shouting kids.

"Thanks," I groaned.

I climbed up onto the tower, resigning myself to another hot, dry day. I sipped continually from my warming water bottle, but it couldn't shake the dryness in my throat. My whistle chirped every five minutes at the same group of boys, whose roughhousing only grew rougher and rougher as the afternoon wore on.

I was just about to stand and go over to give the group a final warning when one of the boys climbed out of the pool, then turned and ran to jump back in with a front flip. At the last second, he slipped. Half spinning, half falling in, I saw him hit his head against the edge of the concrete as he fell into the water. He sank out of sight, and didn't come back up.

No one in the noisy, churning pool noticed except me and his friends, who were laughing at his failed attempt. I, however, knew it was no laughing matter. He had hit the edge hard. Hard enough to daze him, possibly even knock him out.

My whistle shrilled. Ripping off my old baseball cap, I dove off the stand into the water, whistle still trilling as I plunged.

The noise of the crowds muted to nearly nothing as I hit the water and stroked toward the sinking preteen. He wasn't moving, stunned by the blow, a thin ribbon of blood trailing upward from his head. After three clenching heartbeats, his arms started flailing sluggishly. The water churned above us, suspended legs dangling in the water.

Watching the kid's strength fade as I neared, something hot and malicious erupted within me. Thoughts, excited and wild, wondered what it would be like to pull him deeper and simply watch as he struggled, relishing as I observed the life ease out of him.

Startled by my heated fascination to keep him under the water, I stopped short, just a few inches away from the floundering, semi-unconscious kid, my eyes wide as I watched him. I shook my head, hoping the feeling would leave, but the yearning was still electric inside me. I was afraid that if I touched him, instead of pulling him upward, I would push him further down into the depths.

Disgust and horror rose within me. What kind of monster was I? Never before had I felt something like this, and I had done mock rescues for training; I had been swimming with friends before I moved here. Never had I felt such wicked, cruel desires. The desire to drown. To kill. I fought the urge to vomit at the strong craving of depravity: I had someone to *help*. I got this job to *help* people.

The thought broke me out of my bloodlust, and, fighting the bone-chilling urge to keep him under the surface with me, I gave the bottom of the concrete pool such a vicious kick that pain ripped across my toes.

The yearning was tempered even further by the pain, so much so that I was not afraid of touching the boy. I scooped the kid up as I erupted from the floor, and in a stroke so powerful I had to physically stop myself from launching clean out of the water, we surfaced. The noise suddenly turned back on. The kid gasped as we broke upward, and his wail interrupted the fun around us.

A woman—I assumed it was the kid's mother—began screaming, and people were scrambling about the pool, trying to figure out what was going on.

I had been under the water for no more than fifteen seconds, although it had felt like fifteen minutes. When I'd broken the surface with the boy, the other lifeguards were still trying to clear the pool. I had prevented a disaster before it ever began, but I had also almost caused a tragedy, and no one but myself knew it. They would think me a hero, when I was truly a villain.

I felt hollow, dirty, and sickened at the thought.

Everyone around me cleared away as I brought the sobbing, struggling boy toward the side, blood trailing down his forehead and over one eyebrow. Adrenaline was still surging through me as I handed the boy up, my heartbeat crashing against my rib cage. I pulled myself up onto the concrete as the kid was hurried off to his mother, who was sobbing uncontrollably as she clutched her son, the other lifeguards trying to get him free enough to check his injury.

The rays of the sun beating down on me felt cold, my skin prickling with chills, the noise around me seeming muffled. Again, nausea churned in my belly, and I had to hold back the urge to be sick. Now that the situation was over, the bloodlust and adrenaline drained from me completely, leaving me clammy and trembling.

Someone was patting my shoulder, and I finally looked up to see Joshua, who was shaking me. "Cordelia, you're bleeding! Can you hear me? You're bleeding!" He looked over his shoulder, calling toward another lifeguard that was trying to empty the pool of patrons. "She's in shock. Someone get a towel!"

"No, the kid is bleeding. On his head. Do we need an ambulance?" I replied, my tone void of emotion, my brain feeling slow and stupid.

"No, Cordelia, your foot is bleeding."

Reacting like I was moving through syrup, I looked down at my foot, where pink water trailed from the torn skin across my toes, puddling at my feet.

"Someone get the other first aid kit!" Joshua called, placing a beach towel around my shoulders and leading me toward a bench near the entrance.

I wanted to reply that I was fine, it didn't even hurt, but I didn't. I wasn't fine.

I was sat down and left alone for a moment, clutching the towel to my shivering body. I wanted to cry, but I was too numb. Joshua returned with another towel that he wrapped around the broken skin on my toes.

"How is the kid?" I asked, my voice wavering.

"We think he's okay. It looks like a small abrasion on his forehead, but they called an ambulance anyway. You might need to go with them; that foot looks bad. What did you do, run a cheese grater over it?"

I grimaced at the mental image, then shook my head, my damp, silver tresses flopping limply. "I must've bashed it on the pool's edge when I dove in," I lied. The truth was too awful to think about.

"Dang. That looks painful. Stay here; I'll be back."

He left me alone again. I tried to ignore the crowd of people who were watching me curiously as I sat on my bench in the corner. The lifeguards would clear the pool because of the blood in the water, maybe even shut the pool down for the rest of the day.

After sitting in a daze of muffled voices and blurred vision for who knows how long, a medic came and checked out my foot. I gave monotone responses to his questions, he bandaged my foot, then left.

I didn't know what was going on with the kid at all, but my stomach writhed at the thought that I'd hurt him. Did my hesitation under the water, while probably saving his life, also cause some complications?

A few minutes later, the coach came into view. It must've been serious enough that someone called the supervisor here. I shivered. The coach crouched down to my level and gave me a soft pat on my towel-covered knee.

"Hey, are you okay?"

"How's the kid?" I asked again, my voice hollow.

"He's doing fine, they're treating the bump on his head. How are *you*?" He glanced at my foot, and I tucked it under my seat.

"Fine." I was coming out of my shock, but the cold disgust at myself remained.

"It's perfectly normal to feel disturbed or upset after your first rescue. You did really good; the kid is going to be okay."

I scoffed so softly that I don't think he heard because he continued, "It can be a scary thing, but you did so great. Your quick reaction avoided any lasting damage, and the boy will be okay. You'll be okay."

Tears welled in my eyes.

There was so much that was not okay. I didn't know what was wrong with me or why. I couldn't explain it to myself, and I certainly couldn't explain it to anyone else. What kind of person had the urge to *drown* someone? I knew I was only half-human, but I thought that the human part was strong enough to overpower any selkie-animal urges I had. Did being half selkie make me some kind of murderous freak?

I jolted as the next words the coach spoke entered my brain.

"We used your phone to call your mother, and she's on her way down here to pick you up."

Panic flared up in me. My cover was blown. She knew about my lies. About the lifeguarding. She knew I'd been in the water.

My heart sank. I was in for it now. I exhaled, steeling myself for her arrival.

Well, at least my mom would be happy about one thing: I was quitting lifeguarding. I wasn't going to risk my newest horrible secret getting out. I wouldn't even tell my mother about what had happened. If I did, she would probably have me committed somewhere. Being half-selkie was bad enough that my mother had to give up her life, now she had a potential murderer on her hands.

The moment came too soon when my mother rushed through the pool entrance, her face ashen, her eyes wide with fear and anger. She had a whispered conversation with the coach, then came and helped me to my feet. I left with her, feeling lower than the ground.

She got me in the car, telling me we'd pick up my ATV later, and drove us home, the desert landscape a dusty blur through my tears. The whole ride, she was quiet. A part of me wished she would just start yelling already. I deserved it. I knew that. I had betrayed her trust, I had lied countless times to her. I had gone in the water, and now, unbeknownst to her, I had almost put someone in danger when I was supposed to be rescuing them. What's worse, I would have blown our cover while revealing myself as a full-fledged monster. I clenched my eyes shut. More than ever before, I didn't want to be me.

Chapter Seven

W e pulled to a stop in our gravel driveway, and still my mom
didn't say anything. She helped me out of the car, me limp-
ing on my injured foot, and we went into the house. She sat me down
on a kitchen chair, and, noticing that I was shivering under my damp
towel, began to fix me a cup of hot cocoa, putting the tea kettle on
the stove to heat. I stared at her ramrod-straight back and wondered
at her silent, unforgiving form. We sat in silence for several moments
until I couldn't take it anymore.

"Just yell at me, Mom. Just do it," I said, resigned. She turned
to face me, empty mug in hand, her eyes filled with tears. My own
eyes stung at her tender expression.

"Honey, I don't want to yell at you. I'm so *proud* of you. You
rescued someone." She traced a finger around the rim of the mug,
working her jaw. "I understand why you did everything you did.
Why you took that job without telling me." I ducked my head and I
heard her take a deep breath. "But now, I have to ask you some very
important questions."

My stomach sank. I didn't want her asking about the rescue. I didn't want her to know that anything was amiss.

"How . . ." She paused, then turned to the stove and lifted off the kettle that had just begun to shrill. In that moment, I was suddenly back at the busy pool, my lifeguarding whistle trilling, the child sinking beneath the surface, unnoticed by almost all but myself. A surge of those awful feelings surfaced again, as in my mind's eye I saw the struggling form of the kid. I shuddered, turning my head away from my mother, who still had her back to me. More tears seeped out of my eyes. What was I going to do?

"Sweetie." A hand rested on my head and I jumped. Wiping away the tears, I turned back toward her. She ran her hand over my forehead, brushing the tangled silver hair out of my face. She sat down, setting the mug of steaming chocolate before me, and looked me in the eye.

"Cordelia, you have to tell me, how did you feel when you went to pull him out of the water? Tell me everything."

Panic compressed my heart. Did she know? Did she know the horrible, gruesome things that I felt? Did she know something about selkies that I didn't?

I shook my head. "I felt fine. I *am* fine," I lied, trying in vain to hide the tremble in my voice.

"Honey, there is no way you're fine," my mother said, her voice gentle, but with a hint of that all-knowing-mom-power.

"*Yes, I am,*" I insisted, standing and flinging the towel off my shoulders. "I'm going to my room."

As I stormed out of the kitchen, ignoring the pain in my foot, my mother called, "Honey, you can't be fine after *wanting* to drown someone!"

I stopped dead, the air whooshing out of my lungs, my knees buckling beneath me, and I grabbed the banister to keep me from collapsing to the floor.

No, it wasn't possible.

I turned, my stomach twisting so painfully I thought my insides would burst.

"W-what are you talking about?" I choked. I would not cry now. I might vomit, though.

My mother pulled me into the living room and onto the couch beside her.

"Sweetheart, I just want you to know, before we go any further, why I moved us here." She took a deep breath, her eyes closed for a moment. "I moved us here to protect you, because there are things that you—"

"No, you did not move me here for that," I replied, getting angry now. I felt relieved to be discussing a different topic, glad for the excuse to discuss anything but what happened at the pool. Still, horror curdled my stomach. How did she know? Did someone see me at the pool and tell her?

At least talking about why we moved here gave me an excuse to get angry. And yell.

"You know perfectly well that you wanted me to be away from saltwater because I have no power over choosing if I transform in the ocean," I continued, my voice rising. "You know that I can remain in my human form in fresh, even chlorinated water! *You know that*! So don't you tell me that you moved me to this dry wasteland for my safety, we could have easily stayed near lakes and been perfectly fine!"

"No, no, no, honey," my mother urged. "It was fresh water that I was more afraid of for you."

I paused, my heart battering against my ribs like stormy waves against a rocky shore.

"What . . . ? Why?" I rasped.

My mother sighed, her expression pained, her voice slow, like it was difficult for her to speak. "It's time for me to tell you where you came from."

"I know, I know," I interrupted, my stomach still feeling sick, not sure I wanted to hear what my mother had to say. "My father rose from the sea as a human, but he was really a selkie, and you had me."

"Yes, that's true, but you don't know where *I* came from," she said.

I paused, staring at her with a blank expression. That was true, I technically didn't know where she lived with her family, but what did that have to do with anything?

"Honey, I came from a relatively unknown part of what is now Greece," my mother began, taking a bracing breath.

"Okay . . . so I'm half-Greek—" I began, but my mother shook her head, holding up a hand to stop me.

"Honey, you don't understand. I'm not Greek. I'm not . . . human."

I stared again. I tilted my head, then let out a humorless laugh. It came out as more of a gagging noise. When my mom didn't smile with me, my skin went cold. "You—you're serious?"

She nodded, her mouth pulled tight.

"So . . . what are you, then?" I gaped.

"Ever heard of a naiad?" my mother asked, trying to smile, but it faltered before it reached her eyes.

I didn't know how to respond. Yes. I'd heard of naiads, back when I had learned Greek mythology in middle school. But, was my mother saying that *she* was . . .

My mother took a deep breath and began speaking like she was admitting something unpleasant. "I grew up and lived for decades—no, centuries—in a lake. I lived there with my sisters. Naiads are notorious for drowning those that wade into our lair. We drown for sport, and because we're so long-lived, it didn't bother us. As long as we had a place to call home, magically tethered to our mother lake, we could live indefinitely; maybe forever, I don't know." She exhaled, and took another deep breath, not looking at me.

"I don't know how long I've lived. Living in that lake, the years blended together. Endlessly. Then when he came," my mom said, her voice growing softer, her eyes going distant, her hand straying to the necklace around her neck, "he seemed to snap all of us out of ourselves. He . . . changed us, somehow . . ." She tapered off, falling silent. I frowned as I trailed my eyes over her faraway expression. She couldn't be talking about my dad.

"Who?"

"Hmm?" She jerked her head toward me. "What?"

"Who snapped you all out of yourselves?" My frown deepened. Was my mom *blushing*?

"N-no one. Just a man, a powerful one." She exhaled. "After that, my seven sisters and I began to notice humans, and that the people began to change. They carried odd things in their clothing that we didn't understand, like pocket watches, and guns, and other wonders. We realized that the world was moving on without us, and we wanted to see it. We could leave our lake. Out of the water, the webbing on our hands and feet disappeared, our hair dried, and we were able to survey the land above the waves.

"We traveled the world over the next decades, using all the gold and money from those we'd drowned over the centuries, learning new things: music, art, literature as we traveled across Europe, Asia, and Africa, seeing the marvels of modern human life. We traveled to the US after a time. We learned some scary things along the way, but it taught us how to protect ourselves." Again, she reached up and touched the stone necklace at her throat. The one she always wore. I had always assumed my father had given it to her.

My mother took a deep breath, running the backside of her hand underneath her eye, clearing away the remaining tears there. "One place we liked going very much was the seaside. Seawater is very exotic and alluring to us. And the wonders that boardwalks are!" She glanced at me, and I nodded. Boardwalks were some of my favorite places too. But that was before. Before everything changed.

My mother continued. "We adored those parks along the coasts as we experienced the food, the music, the dancing, making us one with the people. We learned how to almost become human. We even enjoyed hanging out with humans. Some people even taught me how to ride a bike about a year before you were born." She gave a soft laugh that turned into a faraway look. "We would have to return home every so often and stay in our lake for a few weeks to recharge, but we began to stay out in the world more than our watery home.

"We didn't drown as many people after we began traveling, but there was still that pull, especially when we were in our mother lake.

"I met your father one summer when we were visiting the US again. He was so handsome, so charismatic. I didn't know he was a selkie. That's another thing we did," my mother said, wincing sheepishly. "Seducing men was another of our enjoyments. It's also how naiads enlarge their family groups. But having a naiad child is rare. When I found out I was pregnant, all of my sisters were so jealous." She let out a choked laugh, her eyes distant. "They fawned over me, caring for me back in our mother lake to await your arrival. And when you were born a girl, we celebrated." She fell silent, her far-off expression tinged with a bittersweet look.

"Why?" I asked, and she jumped as if she'd forgotten I was there. "Why were you excited I was a girl?"

She licked her lips, closing her eyes for a brief moment. "Females are the only carrier of the naiad 'gene,' if that's what you want to call it. All males born to naiads are human; females are born naiads."

"So, if you were so happy, why did you leave?" I asked, aghast. I had aunts that had celebrated my birth. My mother had a family that loved her.

My mother's face registered deep sorrow and pain, and she closed her eyes tight, her breathing labored.

"It was only after you were born that I learned your father was a selkie. He didn't know I was a naiad beforehand, either. We both thought the other was human." She reached up and ran a thumb over the stones around her throat. "This necklace I wear protects me from those that would hunt me for my magic. I never had to get you one, because you don't seem to need one to hide your magic; your signature is very different, very subtle. Most magical beings wouldn't recognize it for what it is. I suppose your father had a relic as well, because I felt no magic on him. Had each of us known what the other was . . ."

"Why? What?" I asked, confused. She looked at me as if annoyed I wasn't following.

"Honey, when humans have relations with most mythical creatures, like selkies, the child is either a selkie or a human, one or the other. But because I'm a naiad, and your father is a selkie, the magic in both our blood clashed in you, and you became both of us. That is why you don't turn completely into a seal when you change, as true selkies do, and why you can breathe underwater, which selkies cannot. You became half me, half your father."

"So . . . what?" I pressed.

My mother looked up at me, her eyes burning. Her next words were spoken as if they were weighed down with stones. "It is greatly looked down upon for mythics of other kinds to procreate with each other. It creates . . . magical hybrids, which are taboo in all mythical society."

I swallowed, my heart thumping uncomfortably in my throat, not sure I wanted to hear anymore, but the words came out anyway.

"Why?" I breathed.

My mother shook her head, her eyes still closed, tears seeping from under her lashes. "Hybrids are unpredictable. They can have magic that is new or strange. As such, they are shunned and feared. But no one really knows what hybrids are capable of, because . . . they're always killed off when they're young."

Horror gripped me. People like me were killed off? "So, wait, I'm . . ." I stopped. I couldn't articulate the thoughts rushing through my head. I was a hybrid. Taboo. Dangerous. Too dangerous to leave alive.

"My sisters called you an abomination," my mom continued, sobbing openly now. "I was so excited to have a child, my sisters were so envious . . . until you were born, and we discovered what you were. Then they wanted to destroy you. Wanted *me* to destroy you. I refused. And because I refused, they cut me off from my mother lake."

Pain at the injustice my mother endured, as well as the horror of family wanting me dead, cut through me, but I tried to wrap my head around something else she had said. "Wait, what does that mean, cutting you off?"

"I no longer have access to my mother lake, or them, or the Ever—" she choked, clapping a hand over her mouth to cover a squeak.

"The Ever?"

My mother shook her head. "I just mean, every single thing I love." She began crying again as I frowned at her, but more pressing questions surged through me.

"How is that possible?" I asked, staring in awe at my mother.

"Magic," my mother said, her voice thick.

"You can use magic?" I asked, incredulous. Did that mean I could potentially use magic? Why didn't she use it to help us hide or seal up my wounds?

My mother calmed for a moment, wiping her eyes. "No, not necessarily. Naiads aren't like humans that can work magical spells, such as casting a fireball. As magical creatures, we do have a few magical talents, and combining wills to banish someone from the water and make them mortal is one of them. It's like an instinct. Most magical creatures have magical capabilities that pertain to their species. That's another reason why hybrids are so feared. They can break the bounds of those magical capabilities."

She sighed, looking over at my frowning face. I was having a hard time following. My mother had never once mentioned magic. I mean, I knew I was part selkie, and that other magical creatures existed.

I think I even saw a fairy once, under a full moon in Germany during a vacation with my mom when I was thirteen. I saw the pink glow from a window of our rental house in the Bavarian Alps, but by the time I'd run out there, it had vanished. A tiny fairy ring of mushrooms that looked like dainty parasols was visible in the grass the next morning.

I had never really considered the scope of it all. I thought we had lived such a normal life because my mom was human and didn't know much about the magical world.

Because my mother had never explained *anything* to me.

"It's hard to explain, which is why I never told you all this before," my mom said, her eyes welling with tears again. "Once my sisters severed the bond between our home lake and me, I started aging, though very, *very* slowly. I can't breathe underwater anymore, though I can hold my breath longer than any human. Hours. I can't swim as well as I used to, either. I'm still excellent, but I don't fly through the water anymore.

"And they tried to banish you with me; you were a monster in their eyes, one that had to be gone, immediately. Along with me. But for some reason it didn't take. It angered my sisters, but there was nothing they could do, and I had to flee." With an anguished wail, she covered her face with her hands, her shoulders trembling.

I sat, immobile, staring at nothing, wanting to ignore the thousand thoughts that were buzzing through my mind. My mother's unnaturally musical sobs were nearly driving me crazy, and so I was grateful when she stopped crying and looked up at me with puffy eyes, hiccuping slightly.

"So, I bought a little house near where I had met your father, hoping I'd run into him, to let him know about you. Selkies are usually interested to know if their children became like them or not. I do not know how your father would've reacted to you, but he was a good man; I think he would've accepted you. But, your father never showed, so you grew up there. Then the accident happened, and I had to move you away, to keep us both safe." She stopped speaking, and the silence felt like the shutting of a door.

I understood that she wanted to keep me safe . . .

"But why *here*?" I demanded. This place, while I could appreciate its beauty, still didn't feel like home, where the sun pounded on you constantly without the refreshing coolness of water, where we were almost unable to breathe in the heat.

"It's the last place anyone would look for us," she replied, head bowed. "And . . . no water to endanger . . . others."

I couldn't argue with that. My head still buzzed with questions, but I blurted out the one that stood in the forefront of my mind.

"So, I'm not even a little bit human?" I rasped.

My mom gave me an anguished look, then shook her head with a soft, "No."

Her answer hit me like a meteor. I'd been living among them like I was one of them. I thought I *had* been one of them. Now to realize I was never who I thought I was . . .

A sharp pain knifed through my heart, leaving me gasping. Not only was I a freak to other humans, I was a freak to other magical beings.

Not full selkie, not full naiad. Not one bit human.

I put my head in my hands, my throat closing up.

"Oh, honey."

I felt my mom move closer beside me, and I lifted my head, shifting away.

"Wait, so the reason I wanted to drown that kid . . . was because of my naiad side?"

My mom nodded again, her eyes swollen from crying. "Like I said, it's inherent in our nature. Thankfully for me, it was dampened when I was severed from my home lake, but, since my sisters couldn't do it for you . . ." She exhaled, long and slow. "That's why, when I noticed odd things in you about your selkie side in Maine, I was so worried about the freshwater side of you coming out, and that you might kill someone. Maybe even try to kill me, because of your hybridness."

"But I've swum hundreds of times," I said, trying to keep the truth from sinking in that I was actually dangerous, that even my mother had been afraid of me. It couldn't be true, I was normal! I wasn't a danger! "With tons of people, and I've never had that urge before." I looked at my mother, pleading silently that she would calm my fears, tell me something to give me hope.

My mom put a hand out toward me, but I shied away again.

"I think seeing someone *really* drowning must have triggered you," she said, her voice ragged. "Had I known what you were up to . . ."

"Would you have told me the truth about myself?" I asked, ignoring the sharp stinging in my foot as I stood, whirling to face her.

My mom didn't reply, didn't even look at me.

So no.

"You would have stayed silent and put even more restrictions on me to stop me from going into the water?" I breathed.

She was silent again.

A yes.

I clenched my hands into fists, my knuckles popping, my voice shaking. "So you would have just let me go on thinking a lie about myself until something truly horrible happened? I could have taken precautions for myself if I'd known the truth."

"Honey, I fear there's no way . . . now that you have had your first taste . . ." She threw her hands up helplessly. "The urges will only get stronger. You won't be able to overcome them like you did today . . . this side of you has shown itself. You won't be able to contain it."

"And you honestly thought ignorance would protect us?"

"I knew you'd get upset," my mom said, this time she was pleading. Her pathetic excuse enraged me even more as she continued. "And I was thinking that maybe you wouldn't believe me, really believe me, that you would have these urges. I didn't want you to test your limits, to test it out to see what it felt—"

I cut her off with a gag. "You really think I would've drowned someone just to see what it felt like?" I sputtered, the hurt and disgust squeezing my lungs. Remembrance about the malicious, breathless feeling I had when I was under the water, watching the boy struggle made me choke. I never wanted to feel that predatory feeling again.

"Yes, of course! *I* would have!" she declared.

"Well, I'm *nothing* like you," I snapped. She physically recoiled, leaning away from me, her face twisting into a broken look. "I will overcome this horrible urge. I care about people, and I don't want to be a murderer!"

After a moment, she cleared her throat. "I just didn't want you to be upset." Her voice shook, and she didn't meet my eye. Her avoidance put my teeth on edge. How could she have done this to me? The one hope that I'd been holding on to was that one day I'd be able to go back into the water, once things had calmed down. Now I never would without being a danger to others.

"I think I would've been even more upset if I actually *killed* someone, and went on thinking I was some sort of monster, and not knowing it wasn't *me* being a monster on purpose, but it was just my genes!" I shouted, my knuckles aching from clenching them so hard. "I was going crazy, thinking I was secretly some psychotic mass murderer who had been dormant!" Which, now, I realized wasn't far from the truth.

I clapped a hand over my mouth.

"*Well, now that you do know about it, we can learn to deal with it,*" my mom said in her soothing voice, trying to calm me. But I didn't want to be calmed. The icky feeling inside me wasn't going away, and now that I learned that *this*, this disgusting urge to murder was a part of me—and that part wasn't even human—meant these feelings, this horrible truth, was never going to go away. I would feel sick and disgusted and alone for the rest of my life.

"There is no 'we,'" I spat. "It's all been about you. You didn't tell me you were a naiad, because it was inconvenient for you to talk about the truth, because it would hurt *you* to talk about your stupid family. You haven't cared about the weight *I'm* carrying! I'm half-selkie, half-naiad! You don't care about what I've been going through! Back in Maine, with Noah trying to kill me because of what I am! And today! The fact that *I* almost killed someone doesn't seem to faze you. You don't care at all!"

"Honey, yes I do!" my mom shot back, her voice tearful. "I just . . . *I'm new at this*! I don't know how to protect you in the human world! If we were at my home lake, we would just submerge to the bottom and not come up for a few decades until everyone that knows about you was dead, then we could make a clean start of it! But we can't! I'm still trying to figure out how to make it in this world! A world without water. A world without my sisters." She started crying again. "You don't know what I've sacrificed for you!"

My blood turned glacial at her words. She would rather be with her sisters? Those naiads that would rather see me dead than be allowed to exist as a hybrid?

But my mother didn't seem to know what she had said, or if she did, she didn't bother to correct herself. She just ignored me and continued to cry, her throaty wail making it hard to think.

"Even though they banished you and thought me an abomination because I was *different*?" I snarled over her weeping. "Some family."

I didn't feel any pity at her tears; the anger surging inside me burned away any sympathy. The realization that she wanted to go back to the water and be with her family more than she wanted to live on dry ground with me, her freak daughter, was too much for me.

Turning, I grabbed my shoes, and, despite my aching foot, marched out the door into the desert.

Chapter Eight

I spent the rest of the afternoon marching around the desert hills, stewing about the danger I had put hundreds of people in because of my ignorance. Ignorance wouldn't have saved me against the law or against the horrors of my own conscience. If I had drowned someone, I would've been culpable without any idea as to why I had these urges, and probably would've gone mad.

What hurt even more than my mother's earth-shattering lies was the fact that my mom, my best friend, was sick of being with me. I was the reason she had been banished, the reason we moved here, the reason she wasn't traveling the world with her sisters. The reason she'd lost a part of herself. And now, she wanted to go back. The thing was, once I became of age, and she didn't have me with her anymore, she would probably be welcomed back to the lake. My own mother would leave me.

I didn't know what to do with that realization.

I stayed out in the desert until night fell, and then, afraid of being attacked by coyotes or mountain lions, I went back to the house. I slipped into the dark kitchen, drank several glasses of water, and went straight upstairs to my room without checking whether my mom was still awake or not.

I got into bed, but didn't fall asleep for hours, sadness creeping into my soul. I had nowhere to go, and no one who understood me.

I emailed the coach early the next morning to tell him that I quit, effective immediately. Then I left the house before my mom got up. I had to walk to the pool to pick up my ATV that we had left in the parking lot yesterday. After filling up the tank at the gas station and buying several jugs of water, some sunscreen, and a hat, I spent the rest of the day zooming around the desert. Unfortunately, the machine was old, and I couldn't get it up to a sufficient speed for adrenaline to burn out all my anger.

As the sun neared the distant mountains, I drove to the caves in a cliff wall I had discovered months ago. I parked and climbed up into the bowl of one of the shallow cavities. I leaned back against the warm red sandstone, hidden from the desert sun, and contemplated the mess that was my life.

My phone rang, but I didn't bother pulling it out of my pocket. I felt too numb. If my mother was worried, I didn't care. Let her have a taste of what it was like being me, worried and confused all the time. When the phone rang twice more in quick succession, I sat up, scooting so that my legs were dangling out of the cave lip, and I pulled it out, irritated. I was ready to answer, shout a few words, then hang up, but I saw that it wasn't my mother calling. Taking a deep breath, I answered.

"Hi, Angie," I said, trying to make my voice as perky as I could.

"*Cor*! How are you doing? Are you okay?" she said in a rush, "Joshua told me what happened yesterday at the pool, and he said that you quit! Is everything okay?"

My throat grew tight, the rocks in the red sand below me growing blurry as tears welled up in my eyes. I was quiet for a moment, and Angie, softer this time, asked, "Cor? What's wrong?"

I shook my head, trying to clear the tears from my voice, but when I spoke, my voice cracked. "Nothing. I mean, I . . . I was just really shaken, you know?"

"Oh, Cor, of course you were," Angelina replied, and the tears escaped my lashes and spilled down my cheeks. "I'm so sorry, that must've been so scary!"

I cried harder. She would never understand how scary it truly was.

"Joshua has been really worried too! Everyone was when he told us. I'm sorry." She paused for a moment, then asked, "Where are you? Can I come over? Or you can come here to my house, we can hang out and watch movies or something?"

I took a deep breath and wiped the trails from my face. "Thanks, but . . . I kind of want to be alone right now."

The line was quiet for a moment, then Angelina asked, "Are you sure you're okay?"

"Yeah, just . . . feeling weird and sad." I picked up some pebbles from the cave floor and tossed them out to the ground below. "I need to . . . sort some things out."

"Okay. Just know, you can call me any time, okay?"

Swallowing, I replied, "Thanks for understanding. You're a really good friend."

"You're one of my best friends, Cor," she whispered, her voice cracking. "Just . . . call me if you need anything, okay?"

"I will, thanks. Talk to you later."

I put my phone down beside me on the cave floor, staring out into the sky as the sun began to set. Guilt filled my chest. My friends didn't deserve to be shut out, but at the same time, my confusion was difficult to get over. I didn't know how I would act around them, not being one of them. Suddenly, the crushing loneliness felt worse than anything else. I placed a hand over my mouth, an anguished sob rising in my chest. I'd never felt so alone, because even with what happened back in Maine, I'd had my mom. Now I had no one who truly understood me.

My phone rang again, making me jump. I scrambled to not drop it out of the cave as I cleared my voice. "Hi, Joshua," I whispered.

"Where are you, Cordy?" he asked, his tone gentle but firm.

"No, really, I'm fine," I protested, cursing the tears in my voice.

"Where are you? Please? Angelina sounded really worried. I'll come and get you."

"No, you don't have to," I lied. He must have heard the yearning, wistful tone under my false bravado, because he just said, "Cordelia."

I sniffed, and my determination to be alone crumbled. With a choked voice, I tried explaining to him where I was, with an admonishment that, "It might be pretty hard to find."

"Don't worry, I think I know where you're talking about. I'll be right there."

Half an hour later, I heard a dirt bike roaring over the dunes. I waved so that Joshua would see me, and he pulled up to the cliff wall and parked. He clambered up into the cave and sat beside me, our legs dangling in the open air. With a tentative look, he wrapped an arm around me. I leaned my head against his shoulder, relieved that no tears came.

Though he couldn't know why I was upset—and he would definitely freak out if I told him the truth—I couldn't help but melt a little at his touch as he sat there, quiet. For me. He was probably bursting with questions, yet he didn't press me. He was a pillar of comfort that didn't demand I explain myself.

We sat in silence, watching the sinking sun turn the air a rosy pink around us as it disappeared behind the barren Nevada mountains. A hot, dry breeze made my hair dance, the fine, pearly-gray strands tickling my face. Bats began swooping in the sky as pink deepened to purple, the desert hushing with the onset of night.

After a while, I pulled away and looked at Joshua. "Thank you," I murmured.

"We were really worried. You were so shaken at the pool, I knew something was wrong. Are you okay?" he asked, his face watchful.

I nodded from side to side. "Fine."

Though I was still pissed at my mom and confused about who I was, my loneliness and sadness had mostly abated. His face pinched in a frown.

"You don't have to pretend with me, Cordy," Joshua said, catching a strand of my silver hair that was drifting in the breeze, tucking it behind my ear. "If something scared you, I want to be here for you. I care about you, and I . . . I really like you."

My breath hitched in my chest in that funny way I had forgotten about. His face, reflecting the softening light and watching me with those wide blue eyes awakened a part of my heart that Noah had closed up.

"I like you too, Josh," I admitted, biting my lip shyly, my heart beginning to pound.

A strange, almost fearful look passed over Joshua's face, and then in the space of a breath he slipped an arm around my waist. I met him halfway, recognizing the signs, and our lips met. He wrapped both arms around me, pulling me close, and I placed my hands on his chest, where I could feel his heart dancing to the same quick step as mine.

Kissing Joshua was very different than it had been with Noah. Noah's kisses had always felt confident, almost insufferably so. Joshua's kiss was breathless and urgent, scared of what could happen when he took that leap.

I pulled him closer, my heart quickening at the almost excruciating feeling Joshua had in his touch, like he was simultaneously afraid of touching me and afraid of letting me go. His hand slid up the back of my neck into my hair, pressing me closer.

The jangling of his phone made him jump and instantly pull away. He fumbled for his phone, answering with an almost angry, "Hello?" I placed a hand to my flushed face, my emotions a swirl of confusion, joy, and annoyance. What was so important that he'd had to answer the phone right then?

He was quiet, then barked, "No," and his face darkened. After a few moments of listening, he said, "Okay. *Okay!*"

He hung up without saying good-bye, then turned to me.

"I have to go. Family problem."

"Okay, yeah, of course," I said, still trying to calm my pulsing heart.

Joshua met my gaze. "You'll be okay?"

I smiled and nodded, though inside I was frowning. What were his thoughts about what had just passed between us? I was suddenly self-conscious. Was I that rusty at kissing?

While his expression conveyed that he wanted to kiss me again, he merely brushed my cheek with his hand before quickly turning away and scaling out of the cave and down to his bike. With a deafening roar, his dirt bike came to life and, spraying sand, he sped away. He cast one glance back at me before the sandy hills swallowed him from view. I exhaled, watching the empty horizon where he'd disappeared, my heart thumping in a way it hadn't for a long time.

I sat in the cave until it was almost dark, then climbed down and hurried home, where I intended to lock myself in my room to avoid my mom. But there was no need, as my mom wasn't home. I watched a movie until I heard her truck pull up. I hurriedly clicked off the TV and was halfway up the stairs when she came in through the front door. I heard her pause, a small gasp escaping her as she no doubt saw me on the stairs.

"Cordy," I heard her say behind me, her tone stunned. I came to a standstill on the stairs, keeping my back to her.

"Surprised to see me here?" I snapped, tightening my grip on the banister.

"N-no, I just . . ."

I whipped around to see my mother pulling the trench coat she was wearing around her more closely. I narrowed my eyes at the bizarre attire, but I didn't care enough to ask.

"I'm glad you're home," she said, her voice timid.

"I'm not."

My mom sighed. "I know you're still mad, and I don't blame you—"

"Really? Because I thought you did blame me—that I was the reason you had to leave your *real* family." I knew I was being dramatic, but I wanted her to know that I hadn't forgotten her hurtful words.

"Honey—"

"*No.*" I stomped up the rest of the stairs and slammed my door.

I spent the remainder of the week riding the dunes. Zooming around the desert was equal parts disconcerting and comforting.

While I ignored the tentative texts from my mom, I readily replied to Joshua and Angie. It was only after my mother threatened to call the police if I didn't tell her I was okay, that I began to reply to her with one-word answers, still refusing her pleas for me to come home.

I didn't tell Angie of my kiss with Joshua. It was personal, and had opened something inside me that I thought was closed forever. It wasn't a gossiping point. Not to me. And I still didn't know how I felt. While kissing Joshua had been wonderful, it had only added to my confusion, as it had made me feel human. *Normal.* I grit my teeth at the thought. Would I ever *not* feel confused?

As I pulled to a stop at the top of a dune—the dry wind whipping my face as I took in the view of the towering red cliffs before me—tears filled my eyes. If I was the combination of two aquatic mythical creatures, then why did I love human life on land so much?

That was one part I missed from my old life: traveling around the world with my mother.

I really was a freak of nature. I revved the engine and barreled down the sandy hill.

On Saturday night, after a day of riding to Valley of Fire and climbing the rocks there, I came back into town as dusk was falling. I hated the idea of going back to the house before midnight, so I drove my ATV into Overton, to see what could be seen. If they hadn't closed down the movie theater before we'd moved here, I would've gone to see a movie on their one screen. The tiny building with the large CLOSED sign sat sad and decrepit as I drove past, onward to the only market in town to get into some air conditioning, my skin hot from being in the sun for so long. Maybe I'd buy myself something sweet. I deserved a treat after the week I'd been through.

I wandered the aisles while soft rock played over the PA system, occasionally interrupted by an employee calling another to an aisle or to check a register.

As I was considering whether I should buy two boxes of cookies or three, someone called my name.

I turned to see Angelina and her mom, who was pushing a semi-full shopping cart, come to a stop at the entrance of the aisle I was in.

"Hi!" Angelina called, smiling. She turned, said something to her mom, who nodded and moved on past my aisle while Angelina came toward me. I quickly stuffed the three packages of choco-late-coconut-shortbread cookies back into their place and turned back to Angelina as she came up to me.

"Hey, how have you been?" she asked, smiling. "We missed you at our get-together yesterday, and I've missed playing with you online. I hope you're feeling better."

I grimaced inwardly at my hermit-like behavior. Though I had still been texting both Joshua and Angelina, I had basically closed myself off to in-person interactions over the last week. I still didn't feel much like being around humans, a creature I'd believed myself to be—at least partially—my whole life until a week ago. Now that Angelina was standing right in front of me, the awkwardness hit me with full force. How did humans normally stand? Was I holding my arms weird? What did humans do with their hands while standing still?

"Yeah, I'm doing better now. How are you?" I asked, giving her a weak smile.

"I'm doing great! Actually, I'm glad I ran into you! I was going to text you, but, no need!" Angelina said, and she looked ready to burst, her grin sweetening my sour mood.

"Yeah?" I asked, my curiosity piqued.

"For my seventeenth birthday, my parents are taking me to California for two weeks before school starts. We're going to go to all the major amusement parks and the beach and a ton of stuff, and they're letting me invite my friends. My parents are footing the bill, of course. Can you come?" she asked, breathless.

I stood staring at her, speechless for a moment. She considered me a close enough friend to ask me to go on her birthday trip? While it was true that we had gotten closer over the last few weeks, I imagined she would only invite her really good friends to such a lavish trip. She *had* called me her best friend, but it hadn't really sunk in because I had been so down in the dumps when it happened.

Now, the realization hit me hard. I was her best friend. The icy lump that had been my heart softened. I stifled the tears that threatened to come to my eyes. How embarrassing would it be if I started blubbering right here in the snack aisle?

I pushed away the negative thoughts of what Angelina would think if she knew what I really was. She and Joshua were different. And while I would probably never trust anyone with my secret ever again, I could still have friends. I could accept that low of a bar right now. Especially since I couldn't even talk to my mother. Knowing I had a good friend and an I-didn't-know-what-Joshua-was-to-me-yet was truly comforting.

"Really?" I asked, my smile becoming more genuine.

Angelina nodded, grinning. "It wouldn't be the same without you. I'm inviting the other guys, too, and Joshua, but all my other friends are such idiots that it would be nice to have you there, someone who can actually hold a conversation with me, and who shares my love of nerdy games," she giggled, and I laughed too.

"So, can you come?" she asked, eyes wide with the question.

I bit my lip, thinking hard. I would've loved to, but my mother would never let me go. California. The ocean. Whenever I stepped into saltwater, I couldn't help my selkie transformation.

Even I realized the dangers of being near the ocean. My desire to enter the water might be too great to resist, despite the peril. But still, the fact that I could hang out with friends, live in the moment, enjoy my life; away from my mom, out of the intense, dry heat—

"I'd love to," I said, before I had considered every angle. I needed a getaway, something to take my mind off of the knotted ball of confusion my life had become.

Angelina gave a hushed squeal and danced on the spot. "Yes! I'm so excited!" She grabbed my hands. "It's going to be so much fun!"

I was smiling now, too, and my heart felt a lot lighter at Angelina's unbridled excitement.

"Me too! Thank you so much for inviting me!" I said, giving Angelina a hug. She squeezed me back.

"Of course! It's going to be amazing!" she said as we broke apart, and I saw her wipe away a tear. She gave an embarrassed laugh and shook her head. "I'm so excited!"

Angelina's mom poked her head around the corner. "Angie? I'm ready to check out now."

"Okay," Angelina called over her shoulder. She turned back to me. "I'll text you! See you later!"

"Bye!" I said as she turned and practically skipped down the aisle and out of sight.

Smiling, I left the cookies where they were on the shelf, no longer needing the comfort food, and exited the store. Jumping onto my ATV, I stared at the pink wispy clouds above me, darkness leeching their color as the last rays of the sun disappeared behind the purple, craggy mountains.

I was determined to go to California, no matter what.

PART II
THE COAST

Chapter Nine

The Nevada desert seemed almost beautiful to me as I packed my bag for California. Of course my mother didn't know I was going to California. She thought I was going on a school band trip to southern Utah: still in the desert, still away from water. I already knew how to play the flute, so when I told her I had joined band, she didn't question it. In fact, she'd been strangely supportive, probably trying to get back on my good side.

It had taken all my wits—and the help of Joshua, Angelina, her mother, and Franco, amazingly—to pull off the elaborate lie. I had to provide band trip release forms, permission slips, fake itinerary, and Franco to play the part of Mr. Murphy when my mom called to make sure everything was okay. I'd glared at her when she asked if they needed another chaperone, and she quickly backed off. I'd felt guilty for concocting such an elaborate lie just so I could get away for a while, but I figured she'd lied to me all my life, I could lie to her for a few weeks more. Besides, some time apart would be good for us. My mother obviously felt the same, as she had agreed without much convincing.

With a strained good-bye to my mother, and the requisite promise to call her every night, I loaded up in the twelve-seater van, taking a seat beside Angelina. As I settled into my seat, while Franco and Joshua loaded my bags, Angelina turned to me, whispering under the nearly deafening chatter of the other teens around us.

"Hey, so, since we've been through so much together, I got us these." She pulled out a small velvet drawstring bag. Inside was a pair of bracelets. They were slender braids of silver, each with a large shimmering pearl dangling from it. "I thought we could have friendship bracelets," she said, smiling cautiously as she stared at me.

"Oh, wow, Angelina. Really? They're so beautiful!" I ran a finger over one of the pearls, smiling.

"Well, we're partners in crime now, I figure we should have matching accessories," she laughed.

"Thank you so much," I said, taking one of the bracelets from her. My pearl was slightly pinker than hers, but they were identical in every other way.

"I even told my mom I needed to buy a clarinet to pretend I'm in band," Angelina giggled. "She bought me one without question!"

We laughed and clinked our friendship bracelets together as the engine started, and off we went to California, leaving my guilt behind with the skin-chapping heat.

Five and a half hours later, we pulled up to the Hotel Joya Del Mar on Venice Beach.

Though I was nervous about staying directly on the beach, I was excited to see the theme parks. I realized I would have to come up with some excuse as to why I couldn't swim in the ocean. I would just make sure to stay away from Franco. I knew he would ignore any of my excuses and throw me into the surf the first chance he got.

The moment we stepped out of the van, and as I took in the expanse of the ocean—the familiar blues deepening in hue the further they went out—something cracked inside me. I stared in longing at the sun reflecting off the glittering waves.

While I now knew I was part naiad, I also knew that the selkie side of me was more dominant, and the smell of the sea called to me like a comforting lullaby. I'd watched ocean documentaries back in Nevada in an attempt to quench my desire to see the ocean, but it couldn't compare to actually being here.

"Cor, are you crying?" Franco called, laughing.

"No, the salty air is hurting my eyes," I lied, wiping the tears away from my face.

"Really?" Angelina asked, looking concerned.

"I'll be fine, I'm just not used to it. And, that's why I can't swim in the ocean, it makes me sick," I said, thinking fast.

"Wait, are you saying you're *allergic* to the ocean?" Franco snorted, his expression twisted up in scorn.

"Yeah, it . . . makes me swell up, and I can't breathe," I replied, hoping they would believe the ridiculous lie and not ask too many questions. Franco and the others chortled at me while Angelina frowned.

"Oh, Cordelia, I'm so sorry. If I'd known, I wouldn't have gotten a hotel so close to the beach!" she said, her tone anguished.

So close? We were practically standing in the crashing waves. I could feel the salty sea breeze dancing along my skin, and I had to stop myself from sighing aloud in yearning. However, regret squirmed in my belly for making Angelina and Joshua stress.

"No, no, don't worry, I only swell up if I go into the water, so I won't be able to swim, but I'll be fine once I get used to the air. I'm so excited to be here!" I said, smiling and turning to look at the hotel. "This is so beautiful!"

"Are you sure you can't come swimming?" Angelina asked, putting a comforting hand on my shoulder.

"Yeah. I'm sorry," I shrugged.

Franco immediately began poking fun at me, pretending to swell up and drown while everyone but Angelina and Joshua laughed.

"Well, don't worry about it," Angelina said, perking up. "We're planning on starting off with a few lazy beach days before going to the studio adventure park, but we're renting bikes for the week, so we can go on the bike path and the Santa Monica Pier," she said, pointing off to the right, where I could see the long pier jutting into the water, the top of a ferris wheel a monument of fun far across the sand. "And then there's Venice Beach proper—we have tons of stuff planned." Angelina put a hand on my shoulder. "You won't even miss swimming in the ocean."

Angelina always knew what to say to make me feel better, however, as I glanced back at the crashing waves, I knew *not* missing the ocean would be impossible. That massive expanse of blue was going to be a constant, shimmering temptation in the back of my mind. I smiled gratefully at her as we clinked our friendship bracelets again before we gathered up our luggage and entered the hotel.

I instantly fell in love with the place.

The crystal chandeliers and sweeping tiled staircases made it feel like an elegant mansion, while still giving off "beach house" vibes with its teak furniture and live potted plants everywhere. And, of course, lots of windows to see the ocean. It was so breathtaking that I forgot to feel guilty about lying to my mom. Or at least I could lie to myself that I didn't feel guilty.

My room faced the ocean, and I felt my heart constrict a little tighter every time I looked out at it. But even I wasn't stupid enough to go into the ocean in front of people, no matter how loud the siren song. I would just have to be careful to steer clear of Franco.

After an amazing breakfast the morning after our arrival, we all rode our bikes along the path that ran along the beach. Franco and the boys were desperate to hit up the skate park to learn some new skateboard tricks by watching the regulars as they skated across their concrete domain.

While the boys and a few of the girls went skateboarding, the rest of us perused the flea markets and shops. I had determined that I would come clean about the trip once I got home. I wanted to prove to her that I could be trusted to not act too stupidly about what I was while out of her sight, and maybe I'd even throw it back in her face at how it doesn't feel good to be lied to, for good measure. But to do that, I realized I would have to buy my mother a very big apology gift.

I was standing at a stall, debating between an intricate music box or some very boho jewelry my mother would love, when someone yanked hard on my purse. I whipped around, clamping down on my bag, as a teenager in a dark hoodie jerked on the purse again.

"*Hey*!" I shouted, panicked as he wrenched hard again, and I struggled to keep my purse from slipping free. As I strained back on the straps, the thief lunged forward and punched me hard in the arm, trying to force me to drop my bag.

"Ow!" Pain blazed up my arm where he'd slammed his fist into my bicep. "Stop! *Help*!" I screamed, hoping to attract the attention of those around me. Angelina, who was a few stalls down, screamed and ran toward me. Several people rushed the thief, shouting. The teen, realizing he wasn't going to get my purse from me and have time to escape, released my strap and ducked into the crowd. A few people halfheartedly chased after him, but stopped when they realized the kid was gone. Angelina hurried to my side, her face pale.

"Cor! Are you okay?" Angelina squealed.

Wincing, I rubbed my injured arm. He must've been wearing a ring or something, because the skin where he had slugged me was torn and bleeding. I grimaced.

"Yeah, I'm fine," I said, giving a weak smile. "I'm just glad he didn't get my purse. I'll make sure to keep a good hand on it from now on." Though I'd left some of my money at the hotel, I'd brought the majority of it with me, knowing we were going to the shops.

"Me too! Dang, if only Franco had been with us, that kid wouldn't have gotten away!" Angelina fumed, looking over the heads of the crowds. "That's so scary! I wish we could call someone, but since they didn't get your purse, I don't think there's much we can do."

Her phone beeped at that moment, and, giving me a bracing look, she looked at her text. "It's Franco. He said they're all hungry, and they want to meet us at a restaurant near where they're skate-boarding." Angelina looked up at me. "You sure you're okay?"

I smiled, rubbing my arm again, the stinging slowly fading, the bleeding already stopped. "Yeah, fine. Let's get the others and go."

Wrapping her arm around my elbow, Angelina and I waded through the crowds, chatting and laughing, but making sure to keep our purses in front of us, and soon the almost-purse-snatching incident faded from my mind.

Chapter Ten

Staying away from the ocean waves was harder than I had anticipated, especially with the peer pressure. Angelina tried to coax me to come into the ocean whenever they all went swimming or surfing, suggesting I take Benadryl or get a shot from the doctor, but I was able to wave her off.

While the others swam, I would sit in the sand far from the dangers of the splashing surf, trying to focus on reading and sunbathing, but the foaming crests battered against my mind, a relentless itch. I wasn't able to stay outside for long before the urge to throw myself into the waves became too much. When that happened, I would retreat back inside the hotel to swim in the pool or get a massage.

At night, we'd go to the pier, ride the rides, eat the vendor food, and just enjoy being young and alive.

However, despite the fun and happiness I'd craved, my eyes always strayed to the ocean, the crashing waves an endless summon, often putting a somber turn on my mood.

I'd thought I would be strong enough to resist, to just enjoy the sight of the sea, but I realized being in the desert for so long had weakened all my resolve. The call was too strong.

On the second day of our trip, I broke and began making my plan.

I knew I had to be smart about my trip into the sea. Obviously I would go in the middle of the night, but the pier was always so busy I wasn't sure I'd be able to go unseen even after dark. I spent the next couple of days fretting, all of the ideas I'd come up with falling to bits. The California coast was just too busy.

Then, Mother Nature threw me a lifeline. The day before we would start going to the amusement parks, I could sense a thunderstorm brewing, unseen, on the horizon.

I nearly cried as I felt the pressure in the air change, the smell of lightning on the breeze. My senses were verified by a quick check on the weather. Rain and thunder for the next two days. Bad weather would drive people from the pier and beach, leaving it mostly barren, save for the few crazies that would be out on the beach in the middle of the night, in the middle of a storm. Like me. I knew this was my only chance. I could go into the ocean, and no one would be the wiser.

True to my senses and the weather app, it began storming midafternoon as we were playing beach volleyball just outside the hotel.

"Oh no!" Angelina cried as lightning forked in the air over the water with an ominous rumble, causing her to miss the volleyball that was spinning over the net toward her.

I felt a raindrop plop on my shoulder, and I looked up, closing my eyes in silent thanks.

We all turned toward the open ocean, watching the thunderclouds boiling toward us. Rain began to deluge down, and, as a group, we abandoned the volleyball net, running for the hotel.

"Oh, I hope it won't be raining tomorrow!" Angelina cried as we hurried through the doors, shaking rain from our clothes.

"Don't worry, we'll still be able to go to the park. Some rides might be shut down, but only until the rain stops," Franco assured her, pulling her close. I cringed, not being able to stomach the idea of someone like Franco kissing me. Even though he really helped me out with this whole charade, he was still a bully, and a proud bully at that.

My mind strayed to Joshua and the kiss we'd shared as my eyes found him among the others. He wasn't looking at me, or at Angelina and Franco. I still didn't know what he was feeling, and we hadn't been able to talk, but part of me wondered if he was avoiding me, if maybe he regretted kissing me, as it made our friendship awkward. I shook the thought away. I had much bigger things to deal with at the moment.

My mind was so filled with my plans for going into the ocean, I barely paid attention as everyone decided we should eat dinner. During the meal, it was discussed that since it was raining anyway, we might as well turn in early so that we'd be able to get to the park as early as possible.

After dinner, we all bade each other goodnight and turned in.

My hands shook as I locked my door, gathered a few towels, some fresh underclothes, and slipped off my bracelet, setting it on the bedside table so it wouldn't get lost. I also decided to slip my phone into my purse in case I needed a flashlight. Once everything was gathered and set by the door, I went to stand in front of my window, watching the rain blur out the dark gray ocean and stormy heavens.

My nightly call to my mother did nothing to ease my anticipation. After telling her our secret phrase so she knew I was truly safe, I kept the conversation light, fabricating short stories about what had happened today during the "band trip," and what the plan was for the morrow. After promising to call again the next night, I hung up. My jitters were getting stronger with every passing second. Glancing at the clock, I realized it was only seven-thirty. With a groan, I turned off my lights and sat down by the rain-streaked window to wait for the cover of night.

When one-thirty a.m. finally passed, I couldn't wait any longer.

Gathering my plastic bag, I slipped out of my room, down the stairs, and out onto the beach.

The rain was coming down in sheets as I unhooked one of the bikes we had rented for the week. I pedaled down the bike path toward the pier, the beach appearing empty through the murk of the storm. While the lightning was a little daunting as I biked toward my destination, I knew I'd be safer once I got into deep water.

Anticipation for the ocean and nervousness at possibly getting mugged grated at the back of my mind, causing me to pedal as fast as I could toward the pier. As I approached, I saw the wharf was devoid of most people, though the bars were lighted and full of those enjoying the late hour with friends. I hoped the rain would deter anyone from coming onto the beach and under the pier.

Once I got to the pier, I stayed in the shadows of the wooden wharf as I lugged the bike across the rain-flooded sand. If I left it near the bike trail, I was afraid someone would swipe it. The steady rain washed away any sweat that was forming on my skin, and I gasped in relief when I finally reached the waterline.

For a second, I was afraid of finding vagrants under the pier, but at the moment, it thankfully appeared vacant. Though rain dripped down on me from cracks in the wood above, it was much drier under the pier.

After propping my bike against a piling as close to the water as I could without fear of it getting washed away, I straightened and took a deep breath.

I stared at the waves hissing up on the soaked sand, the rain drumming on the wharf overhead, and anticipation surged in my chest. Was this really about to happen? After so long? After so much fear?

In one breath, I stripped off my pants, leaving my panties and t-shirt on. I stuffed my pants into the plastic bag hanging from the handlebars so they wouldn't get sandy, and turned back to the water. The hairs all over my body were standing on end, goosebumps of longing prickling along my skin. With painful breathlessness, I took a step into the cool, foaming surf.

An intense sensation of static electricity began shooting up through my feet and into my legs as I waded up to my waist, and without any more hesitation, I dove into the salty swell.

The transformation was slower than I was used to, probably because it had been so long since I'd taken my selkie form. I could feel the tickly feeling of the seal coat sprouting from my legs as they fused together, morphing into the back flippers of what looked like a harbor seal from the waist down. After a few more moments of uncomfortable change, the itchy pain subsided, and I floated under the stormy waves, savoring the feeling of the saltwater on my skin.

I opened my eyes, and in the darkness and murk of the polluted water under the pier, I could see the ocean floor a few feet below. My underwear, now torn and ruined, was slowly sinking to the sandy bottom. I scooped them up and tossed them up and out of the water onto the shore without my face breaking the surface.

I hovered, silent, suspended in my watery heaven. And with a bracing breath of seawater, I looked at my hands, curious to see my selkie-naiad body with new eyes. Though I had a furry webbing between the fingers, they were still usable as hands, with opposable thumbs. I'd forgotten how odd, yet velvety, the webbing between my fingers felt.

Starting from the wrist on my left arm, silvery fur dotted with brown spots ran up my arm to my shoulder like a furry tattoo sleeve, where it circled behind my neck to my left shoulder blade, and then the narrow strip of fur curved inward to run down my spine, meeting up with the slick fur that formed my tail at the waist. Other than a few tiny patches of fur dotting my body, the rest was my own skin. I'd never truly appreciated how shocking the contrast of my silver gray, spotted pelt against my human—well, naiad—skin was. It was no wonder Noah freaked out when he saw me transform. That didn't mean I forgave him for trying to kill me, but I now understood I was quite a sight. I looked like a silvery, furry mermaid with the flippers of a seal instead of the tail of a fish.

I was amazed that it never occurred to me that I wasn't half-human, because so many details seemed obvious to me now. Not being able to shed a coat, my mermaid-esque form. I could breathe underwater, transformed or not, which was useful, I realized as muffled thunder rumbled through the water.

My ability to breathe underwater, more than anything, should've tipped me off that I wasn't just half-selkie, but I never imagined my mother lying to me about all that I was. She'd never held back once she finally told me about my father.

I shook my head. I didn't want to think about my mom and her issues and lies.

This was *my* time.

I knew it was a serious possibility that I would get lost in the ocean depths and forget to get out and back to the hotel before the sun came up, so I had to be extra mindful of the time.

With a flick of my flippers, I shot out of the murky water under the pier and into the cleaner, darker water of the open ocean. My eyesight was just as acute in the dark water as it had always been, and I could easily spot the sea creatures of the night. In fact, I wasn't afraid of sharks at all. I didn't know if it was because of my mother's genes, my father's, or a mix of both, but I could easily outswim sharks and other predators. Not that they ever bothered me. In fact, most creatures seemed to avoid me, so my freakish speed was only ever used for fun.

I didn't feel like darting about at the moment, though. I drowsed in the water, eyes closed, enjoying the ebbs and flows of the storm-tossed sea currents. After several minutes of relaxing, I dove down to the ocean floor. Disgust and anger bubbled inside me at the amount of trash that littered the bottom. Was it really so hard to use a garbage can?

I angrily began gathering up the beer cans and plastic bottles swaying on the seafloor, stuffing them into the plastic bags I found, determined to take the bags of garbage with me when I went back to the shore. However, the farther I went out, the less litter I found, and I was able to forget some of my anger and play among the kelp and outcroppings of rocks. It was dark, but I had no problem seeing in the gloom. As I glided along, only dropping down if I saw something intriguing, my thoughts turned to myself, and my situation.

It was my first time transforming since I'd learned the truth about myself, about all of what I was.

Some—no—*all*, considered me a freak of nature, maybe even dangerous, but it hit me that I was utterly unique. It didn't matter that I wasn't human, naiad, or selkie. I was still me. I was a marvel. Something new. Even if no one else knew, I knew who I was. Who I truly was. I was a good "person," for lack of a better word. I wasn't intentionally vicious, and I didn't want to be. I tried to be kind. That was a good start. It didn't matter if people didn't know me very well. *I* knew me. And I had friends that liked me for my personality, and that was what I'd been most honest and open about. Sure, they didn't know my other skin, but they knew what was inside of me, and that was what mattered.

And, if they proved trustworthy of my secret, maybe I'd let them know one day. Far, *far* in the future. I wasn't so enamored with my new friends that I forgot how easily a person could turn on you. People you'd known your whole life. Noah had taught me that. But I had to realize that not everyone was Noah. No, I knew there were people out there who would accept me, they would just take a while to find. But first, and more importantly, I had to accept myself.

As I glided along the dark sea, I finally felt at peace with who I was. I realized I could live a semi-normal life. Maybe marriage was out of the question for me, now that I realized I wasn't even human, but maybe, after high school, I could search the world for others like me: hybrid outcasts, and those that accept them. Maybe I could learn more about who I was, and where I belonged in this world.

A huge weight seemed to lift from my heart. The fight I'd had with my mother had put questions and doubts into my soul about myself.

I was never able to fully process what had happened back in Maine, fear driving my need for survival over anything else. But now I could; I could sort through Maine, I could sort through being non-human. And though the truth my mother had kept from me had shocked me, it didn't really change who I was as a person.

Sure, I would have to be more careful while I was in fresh water, but if I could fight the urge to drown on my very first compulsion back at the pool, I could definitely handle it now, knowing what to look for in myself. I wouldn't become the monster others expected me to be.

Feeling heartened, I smiled and darted further into the ocean.

As I swam, I occasionally heard the engine of a boat passing overhead, someone out late-night fishing in the stormy weather, but the noise didn't bother me. In fact, the sound fueled the desire in my blood to push myself into high speed. I quelled the feeling for now, but I promised myself I would do this again tomorrow night, to get myself racing around the ocean. At the moment, I was content to glide along the currents, luxuriating in my own unique skin, feeling at peace for the first time since Maine.

As I swam along, something glinted in the sand below me, and I dove down to take a closer look. The pressure didn't bother me as I sank to the bottom, searching between the corals and rocks.

I was just inspecting a small, chipped bowling statue when something heavy fell across my shoulders. Startled, I looked up to see a nylon net being lowered around me. Adrenaline spiked through me, and I batted at the mesh, wriggling away. I darted a ways away, and saw the outline of a boat far above me. For a moment, I was terrified that someone was trying to catch me, but then I took several deep breaths, trying to calm myself.

No one could possibly know I was here. It was just some fisherman that happened to drop a net where I was. If they had radar, they probably thought I was a fish.

The thought instantly made me nervous again. I would look like a pretty big, strangely shaped fish, and they would pursue me if I stayed out here any longer.

Though reluctant, I quickly headed back to the shore, stopping only to grab the bags of trash I had gathered. Though those in the boat above thought I was just a fish, I felt jittery about someone hunting me. I looked back and saw the fishing boat trolling the net, following behind me.

They were definitely tracking me, a large catch they didn't want to let escape. Time to get out of the water. I swam faster toward the beach. I didn't go as fast as I could, because I didn't want to raise intrigue, so I serpentined around until I was out of sight of the boat's silhouette, then made a break for the beach. Soon the sloping shore came into view, the water getting warmer and more trash-lined.

I zipped toward the pier, eager to leave the sticky situation behind. I would be back tomorrow night, I reminded myself.

I swam through the pier pylons holding up the wharf, and soon my hands hit sand. I cautiously broke the surface and glanced at the open ocean through the barnacled pillars behind me. I could barely see the boat in the distance in the softening rain, and there was no way they'd be able to see me. I was safe.

Exhaling in relief, I started pulling myself up onto the shore. Through the darkness, I could see my towels there on the bike near the water's edge. I had made sure to place them very close by, because it was hard for me to move on dry land when I was in this form, and I would have to get most of the seawater off myself before I could get my legs back. Getting mostly dry was one way, although washing off in fresh water was fastest. Using my back flippers and my hands, I pulled myself up onto the firmer, wet sand, headed for my towels.

From behind the pylon where my towels sat, the dark shape of a man materialized.

"Don't move," a voice commanded.

Heart nearly bursting with fear, I backpedaled, trying to twist myself back into the waves, when I heard a voice calling, "She's heading back into the water!" as I splashed back toward the surf, but two more men materialized from behind the pillars, standing in the shallows, cutting off my retreat. Through the blinding lights that appeared above me, the men raised what looked like guns, but I didn't care. If I could get most of my body in the water, I could slip past the men who were stumbling about in the dark chaos of flailing flashlight beams and crashing waves, and escape.

More men appeared from the shore, and all converged on me, shouting instructions and commands as I floundered in the shallows of the beach. I could hardly breathe as my bike was pushed over and the men surrounded me. I had to get into the water!

Something heavy stomped on my shoulder, pinning me down. My face slammed into the sandy shallows, submerging my head as my arms were forced behind my back and something cold and metallic clicked around my wrists. I flailed, hitting a pair of legs with my flippers. I heard muffled shouts as I felt someone fall on top of me.

All sound muted beneath the water as my face was pressed harder into the sand, the silt kicked up in the water tickling my closed eyelids. After a moment, I was lifted from the water, gasping at the sand I had swallowed. I blinked the grit and water from my eyes as I was lifted and carried to a group of black skiffs a short distance from the pier. I flexed my tail, trying to slap and squirm free, but more hands restrained me. I could see one or two more boats filled with men in black military-looking uniforms. Fear gripped me. These were no common thugs.

I thought I heard some people shouting a ways down the beach, their voices carried on the wind. I started screaming, hoping whoever it was that was shouting would hear me, or at least the men would get scared and drop me. Instead, a rag was shoved into my mouth and I was hurriedly dumped into the sodden bottom of the boat. Men piled in around me while someone commanded, "Go, go!"

I wriggled, and several boots pinned me to the floor by my hips and tail. Heart thundering in my chest, I looked between the men around me, but no one gave me another glance as the boat was shoved off the beach. With a roar, the motor started, and we blazed over the waves out to the open sea.

I tried bucking against the boots holding me down, but I was wedged in such a way that I couldn't budge. Fear threatened to subdue me, but the animal instinct of escaping danger blazed up in me. If I could get overboard, I could easily get away.

I worked at the rag in my mouth. Once I had my mouth free, I would have very strong teeth at my disposal for helping in my getaway.

While I worked on getting my gag out, questions and fears pinged around my mind: Who were these people, how did they know, and what were they going to do with me?

Chapter Eleven

The trip in the motorboat felt like an eternity as the terrible unknown stretched before me. Escape was an arm's reach away, but my hands were tied. I was able to get my gag out, but I couldn't reach any close shins with my teeth.

The rain had died down, and there was so much seawater in the bottom of the boat that I had no hope of getting my legs back anytime soon. Even the thought of being naked didn't bother me if it meant I could get free, but I had no chance of getting into the water.

Finally, the motor slowed, and the hull of an immense ship blocked out the sky. The words *Elusive Fortune* were scrawled in large letters across the side of the battleship-esque bow.

The motorboat stopped—with me still gaping at the size of the ship above us—and I was unloaded onto what looked like a mini loading dock inside the side of the ship. I flapped my tail and flailed my arms as hard as I could while the men had me suspended in the air, hoping I could get them to drop me in the water, but to no avail. The men were burly and knew their footing on a rocking ship.

To my left, the lights of the coast were barely discernible in the dark, and to my right, the vast, overwhelming blackness of the ocean spanned on forever. I'd forgotten how utterly abyssal the open ocean looked at night. It seemed an omen to my future. I was quickly heaved away from the dock edge and through a door.

I was carried down a hallway and shouldered into a sparsely decorated room, where I was placed into a galvanized steel tub filled with seawater, barely big enough for me to comfortably fit my tail in all the way. The men left immediately, shutting the door behind them.

The moment they were out of sight, slipped my cuffed hands under my tail and heaved myself out of the tub, landing on the floor with a heavy thud and a flood of water. I crawled toward the door, my flippers galumphing against the wooden floor. I reached up and twisted the knob, but it was locked. Disappointed but not deterred, I looked around the room. There was a port window that looked like it would be a tight squeeze. I would need my legs to reach that high.

Looking around for a blanket or curtains, anything to dry me off, I saw a woven rug under a chair in the corner. It would have to do. I clambered forward and grabbed the rug, tugging it free from the chair legs. Wincing at the pain in my shoulders from the rough capture, I scrubbed the nonslip side of the rug over my fur. I didn't need to be perfectly dry, but enough that the magic in me didn't think I was submerging in seawater.

As I continually flipped the rug for dry sections, wishing for sun to help the process, I could feel a slow tingling starting in the points of my long flippers. I continued rubbing the rug, my heart pummeling against my chest, and soon the tingles raced up from where my ankles should be and into my calves. My fur began to fade painfully slowly, skin peering through the silvery patches. Just as the tingling reached a crescendo throughout my entire tail, the door opened.

"No!" I screamed as the same men as before paused in the doorway for a split second upon seeing me half-transformed on the floor before setting upon me. I was picked up, bucking and slapping, but in that moment I was more worried about keeping the heavy rug wrapped around my waist as my fur completely faded. They held my ankles so tight that I could feel bruises forming as I flailed, but the men didn't even pant as they carried my wriggling body up two flights of stairs and down an ornate hallway before hauling me through the double doors into a luxurious library.

Books were stacked all along the walls, and in the middle of the room was a large marble desk. In front of the desk was another metal tub of seawater, larger and more ornate than the one downstairs.

I thrashed, trying to get the men to drop me before we got to the water, but they only tightened their grip as they lugged me to the clawfoot tub and dropped me inside it. The tingling erupted across my body, and my flippers returned immediately. The man ripped the sodden rug from me, and water sloshed all over the floor as they held down my wrists, unlocked my handcuffs, and used them and another pair to cuff my hands to two steel loops welded to the sides of the metal tub.

As the handcuffs clicked shut, I grit back the tears burning in my eyes, not wanting to show weakness in front of my captors. A slow clapping sounded off to the right, and a smarmy voice said, "Wonderful show, my dear. What a transformation! That was a delight." I whipped my head toward the sound, where a man stood in a doorway that led out of the library into another room. I immediately hated him, whoever he was.

His blond hair was streaked with gray and slicked back with copious amounts of gel. His pale blue eyes were hard, and he smelled like cigarettes. He was wearing a flashy satin robe, parted to reveal his bare, white chest. Beneath the robe was a pair of white pajama pants with red hearts printed all over them. He was barefoot.

The man's attention turned from me to the two men, where he barked, "You idiots couldn't even move a can of paint without getting it everywhere. Get someone to come clean this water up before the floor warps. Then tell Oliver to prep the accommodations." He waved the two men away as he moved behind the desk and stared at me, his expression appraising.

"Well, well, well, my dear. Welcome to my ship. My name is Parker Colton. And my, my. Aren't you a pretty thing?" the man asked as he sat down at the desk.

"And aren't you a *slimy* thing," I snarled, shuddering. His voice felt like a paintbrush dipped in oil was being smeared all over me.

"Aha. It talks." Parker seemed pleased.

I glared back at him. I wasn't going to give him any information, not even my name.

"So." He pulled my purse from out of a drawer and plopped it down onto the desk. "Cordelia, is it?" he asked with an arched brow.

I didn't reply, but fear rippled down my spine. They'd obviously been keeping tabs on me at the beach; how long had they been watching me before that?

With a shudder, I realized that maybe my mother had been right to be afraid of people coming after us. I had always thought that she was being a little over-paranoid: no one believed in creatures like me.

At least not enough people to do anything about it. I was obviously very wrong.

A sudden hope sprung in my chest as I watched him slip the cash from my wallet into his desk drawer. If he had my purse, he had my phone! If I could get to it, I could call for help. I glanced down at my hands in the cuffs. These would be a problem. Maybe he would unlock my hands for a while, and if he left me alone in here, even for a minute, I could grab my phone.

Not wanting the man to know how fearful yet hopeful I felt, I put on an aggressive face, and sat quietly in my tub. Maybe he would get bored and leave.

"Come, come, dear. Do be cooperative. Let's be friendly about all this." Parker pulled a lighter and a box of cigarettes from his drawer and, selecting one, propped it in his mouth. "We will be in each other's company for some time." He began to flick the lighter, hand cupped around the flame. I made a disgusted noise, and he looked up.

"Do you mind?" he asked around his cigarette.

"Yes, I do mind," I snapped, flexing my fists against the cold metal cuffs. I felt annoyed at myself for replying, but sitting in a cloud of smoke would only make this night a thousand times worse. Parker shrugged.

"Anything that makes you comfortable." He tossed the unlit cigarette and lighter onto his desk and leaned back into his chair.

"How about letting me go? That would make me very comfortable," I retorted.

The man laughed a laugh as oily as his hair. Shaking his head, he said, "Oh, I couldn't do that. There are a lot of people who would pay good money for you. I know HAMMA has been tracking you for at least a year now, trying to get you in their crosshairs." He grinned at me, the delighted expression sending a wave of shivers across my skin. "In fact, they won't be too pleased that I poached you out from underneath them. From what I hear, they were spending beaucoup bucks trying to get to you. The fact that I beat them to the prize will make them furious." He chortled, as if pleased at the thought, then he fell silent, and I stared at him in bemused amazement.

Someone else was looking for me? Who was Hamma? And how did they know about me? From Noah? He was the only person besides my mother who knew what I was . . . Had he talked?

After a moment, Parker continued, talking more to himself than to me. "If HAMMA hadn't finally acted, I wouldn't have caught you in time for the convention. I mean, HAMMA would definitely pay big money to get you back. And it would save me a trip . . ." His face twisted in consideration, but then he shook his head. "Eh, but their money pales in comparison to the buyers overseas. Besides, HAMMA had their shot and they squandered it."

"Hamma?" I asked before I could stop myself. I had planned to keep quiet as I tried to mull over an escape, letting him talk himself hoarse, but the questions were building up inside me.

Parker looked up at me with a distracted expression. "Oh, of course you wouldn't know HAMMA. They are HAMMA, after all. Very good at what they do, I guess." He flashed a pleased smile. "But I'm even better."

Annoyed at his evasion, but trying to keep calm, I said, "Look, I don't know what you're talking about, but you can't do this, whatever you're trying to do. It's illegal."

He chuckled. "You're sweet to think that bothers me."

I glared at him, and he smiled back, a smile that turned into a belly laugh.

"Oh, I can see the questions inside your eyes. You're dying to know how I even knew about you, let alone caught you, am I right?" He looked ready to burst, as if he couldn't wait to share everything.

I looked away, gritting my teeth at how easy my face was to read.

Parker leaned forward. "HAMMA needs to hire better cyber security experts. Imagine my interest when I learned that an organization that trades in magical creatures was basically emptying out its bank accounts for a single mark. It had to be something special, and so I *had* to help myself to the chase."

I exhaled. "Well, you only won the chase because you were lucky. Those nets you put down were useless, and I would've gotten away if you hadn't followed me back to the beach."

"Oh, honey," he replied with a smirk. "Why do you think I dropped those nets? It wasn't to ensnare you."

I stared at him, comprehension dousing me like a bucket of ice water.

"You were . . . driving me. Toward the beach."

"That's the ticket," he said, winking. "There was no way we could catch a water creature in its own element, they're typically too fast. But if we scared you back onto land, we could catch you there."

"But . . . but how did you know where to drive me? How did you know exactly where I had put my towels?" I asked, my voice cracking.

Parker smiled. He gestured to the scabbing, mottled green and brown bruise clearly visible on my bicep. "You remember that purse snatcher that almost stole your purse a few days ago?" he asked with a sly smile. "He may have been working for me, and he may have brought me the means to track you." He held up a small tablet. "Blood tracking is nothing new in the magical world. And fancy tech gadgets like these have made magic more accessible than ever for those not great at wielding it. I'm glad we caught you when we did, the blood tracking spell almost ran out, as the sample we got was limited."

My heart sank, realizing I was out of my depth. I didn't know anything about magic. Those tracking me were more advanced than I thought. This man, and those like him, had magic and tech on their side. Parker continued with his explanation. "I've been following HAMMA for some time, picking up the slack when they make a blunder. My guy collected a sample of your blood. Then we just waited until you were alone. The waiting paid off. Who goes to the beach at two a.m. unless they're trying not to be seen? Then we set our trap. Isn't it thrilling?"

"Who are you?" I bit out. Parker slid his index finger down his cheek and across his lower lip, considering my question.

"You could call me an aficionado for everything rare and valuable."

"You're a collector?" I asked, unimpressed.

"For the simpleminded, yes, that would be an adequate explanation." He leaned forward. "I *collect* rare specimens and sell them to the highest bidder. I've commissioned digs, searches, hunts, and occasionally kidnappings." He gave me a narrow smile. "In fact, this boat," he said, leaning back into his chair and gesturing to the room, "Was a gift from a dear customer of mine, Abdul Salamah, when I sold him a particularly interesting artifact found on a dig in Nicaragua. He said he was buying a brand new, bigger yacht anyway, and gave this to me as a bonus. In fact," he laughed, "he was so pleased that he said—"

"Look, I can tell you like to hear yourself talk, but my friends are going to notice me missing, and will come looking for me." I wasn't sure my friends would be able to find him on this boat way out at sea, but I wanted him to know people would notice me gone.

Parker hooted, slapping the surface of his desk. "Oh, I know they're going to come looking for you. They'll want their 'Unknown Aquatic Species' back."

I stared at him stupidly. "What are you talking about?"

"You haven't caught on yet?" he asked, a sly smile curling his thin lips.

I didn't reply. My mind was in such a whirl, much of what he was saying wasn't registering.

"Don't you find it strange that a very rich friend just started inviting you to things? Started showering you with gifts, extravagant activities, and secret trips? That she got you away from your family, to be vulnerable, after giving you a good time and getting your guard down? Classic M.O. of HAMMA when capturing sentient myths. They buddy them up, make them feel safe and among friends, then they attack when they're off guard. It's safer for them that way, so they don't get blasted with unexpected magical attacks."

I stared at him, my mouth going dry as what he was saying clicked into place. "So, you're saying my friends . . . They're HAM-MA?" Angelina? Were Joshua and Franco and everyone else in on this too? Dizziness blurred my vision as I took several deep breaths. They had set me up, pretending to be my friends. Had none of it been real?

Parker gestured at me with finger guns, clicking his tongue. "Sorry, toots, but you got played. Didn't your mother teach you about protecting your secret?"

"But—I've never shown them, or even told them what I am!" I snapped. He was wrong, my friends weren't trying to capture me . . .

"I'm sure you've shown them somehow. Or they got a sample of your DNA that would prove what you are. Or rather, aren't. You're not human at all, are you?"

My mouth went dry as my mind flashed back to all the cups and forks and towels I'd used at the casino that my friends—HAMMA—could've gathered . . . they certainly would have my DNA, but . . . I wasn't human at all . . . Would that even show up on a test?

"How do you know all this?" I croaked. "How could you know all of this was going on?"

Parker smiled. "I have my ways."

"What if I wasn't a magical creature? They would've spent money on some random girl," I argued, trying to keep his lies out of my mind. My friends weren't mythical animal hunters. Again, my mind flashed to Noah. He'd been my boyfriend for years, and he had turned on me the second he saw what I was. I'd known these people for only a few months . . . why couldn't they be hunting me? If someone came asking Noah directly about what he saw, he would definitely tell them everything. His own ego wouldn't even consider the possibility that he was insane.

I gripped the sides of my tub, focusing on not passing out. I had learned nothing from Noah! Shame curled in my stomach. My mother had been right to be afraid.

"HAMMA makes sure," Parker replied, cutting through my thoughts. "They wouldn't have continued hanging out with you or brought you on this trip if they weren't. Although, they need to change up their strategy, because they've lost more magical creatures to me than they've caught. I don't spend months buttering up my prey, just to lose it to someone who was waiting in the shadows. They never learn." He shook his head, as if annoyed, then fixed me with a stare. "It's a good strategy, keeps down expensive hospital visits. But the execution is shoddy." He paused, his expression shrewd as he looked me up and down, confusion lighting his face. "Interesting. I've *never* heard of a pinniped mermaid before. You couldn't be the full selkie that HAMMA thought. A subspecies? Or . . ." He paused, resting his chin on his knuckles as he scrutinized me. I glared back, not saying a word.

At that moment, shouting erupted in the hallway behind the closed library door. Parker pushed a button as gunshots rang out, and my heart leapt, thinking maybe I was being rescued somehow, but then Angelina's mother, Angelina, a nervous Joshua, Franco, two girls I'd recognized from Vegas trips but who hadn't come on the California trip, and two boys I didn't know burst into the room. Franco and another enormous guy I'd never seen before were holding two of Parker's uniformed men hostage, guns pressed to their temples.

"Parker Colton. I should've known," Angelina's mother snarled, pointing a shaky finger at him.

"Ah, Regina. How nice to see you, though I wish you wouldn't shoot your guns inside my ship," Parker said, his tone a gentle rebuke. "Care for some refreshment?"

"Shut up and give us back our asset," Regina said, eyeing me with a greedy look in her eye. There was no compassion, no acknowledgement in her expression that I was anything but a commodity to her.

I looked from Regina toward Angelina and Joshua, and they at least had the decency to look ashamed, not meeting my eye. Franco sneered at me, shouldering his way further into the room, pressing the gun harder into his hostage's temple.

The others stared at me with interest, whispering to each other. I tugged at my shackled hands, uncomfortable and infuriated at feeling like some exhibit at a zoo.

"I'm sorry, Regina," Parker was saying, "I can't do that. You know very well that I caught her fair and square. But welcome aboard," he stated, looking amused. "Ah, I see you have some of my men with you."

"They were very easy to take down," Regina sneered. "You need to give them more combat training. Franco and Richard were able to subdue them within seconds."

"No, I'm not talking about them," Parker said with a small nod to the group.

In one swift movement, Franco and Richard pivoted, releasing their captured crewmen, and pointed their guns at Regina and Angelina.

Angelina screamed as she, Regina, Joshua, and the three other HAMMA agents were surrounded on all sides by Franco, Richard, and the two men they'd been holding "hostage."

"I managed to train them pretty well, I think," Parker replied as Regina glared back at him through the mess of guns.

"You . . . you work for him?" Angelina asked, gaping at Franco, who smirked back. I felt my own mouth drop open. If anything, the fact that Franco was a competent agent was almost more surprising than anything else that had happened tonight.

"How . . . how?" Joshua sputtered.

"You thought I was too stupid to be a double agent, huh?" Franco smirked. "But I've been giving Parker info all along. And I've been disrupting your plans."

"The Bellagio fountains in Vegas," Angelina whispered hoarsely, comprehension dawning on her slack face. "I thought you were just being dumb!"

"Nope." Franco grinned.

There was stunned silence for a few heartbeats, then Parker clapped his hands. "So how did you all get here? I do love a good story." When no one said anything, Parker clicked his tongue. "Come, come, no need to be shy. You made a valiant effort! No shame in that."

Regina tossed her hair back, nostrils flaring in anger, but to my surprise she began sharing. I thought for sure she wouldn't want to give Parker the satisfaction of knowing the details of her failure. Unless . . . I looked to Angelina and Joshua, who were also watching her with amazed expressions. What was she up to?

"Our alarm went off when the asset left her room, alerting us that she was on the move. *Angelina*," Regina said, glaring at Angelina, who hung her head in shame, "was still asleep, and the asset eluded us. She wasn't wearing the tracker we gave her," Regina said, casting me a disdainful glance, and I felt as though ice water had been poured over me as my mind went to the friendship bracelet that Angelina had given me. And here I thought I'd been a considerate friend by taking it off before my swim so it wouldn't get ruined! I whipped my head to stare at Angelina, and again, she avoided looking in my direction. I clenched my jaw, my mind unable to comprehend that someone could be so vile. It suddenly became difficult to breathe.

"However, we were able to track the asset's location via her phone. After we'd captured some of your men that were still on the beach, we were able to locate your ship."

Parker shrugged. "Well, I'm glad they could accommodate you, and I suppose I'm glad you're here. Better that you know now that I have the asset than having to run all over California wondering where she went. Isn't that thoughtful of me? Also," Parker said, holding up a finger as he began rooting inside my purse. He pulled out my phone, the phone that Angelina had bought, which was yet another trap to not only befriend me, but to track me. "You said it was this phone that you followed?" Parker asked. Regina stood stiff and silent.

To my horror, Parker threw the phone down onto the ground and smashed it with a golf club that he seemed to whip out of nowhere. There went my one chance at rescue. My devastated gasp was drowned out as Regina pulled a pistol out of the back of her jeans and pointed it at Parker. Franco and Richard moved closer, shouting about a weapon, and shoving Angelina, Joshua, and the other HAMMA agents to their knees. Parker held up a hand to quiet his men, completely unaffected by the gun pointed at his heart.

I hadn't realized how scary Angelina's mom was—if she even was her real mom. Parker didn't look at all surprised at the gun in his face. In fact, he smiled, as if he'd been hoping she'd pull out a weapon.

"Listen, Regina, can we speak alone? Send the kiddies off to the pool deck. Franco and Richard can serve refreshments while they wait, and let's you and I have a chat. Okay? I have a proposition for you."

Regina was stock still for a moment, then her shoulders loosened as she lowered the gun, but only slightly. "Angelina, take the others upstairs."

"But, Mom, shouldn't we—" Angelina began as she got unsteadily to her feet.

Without turning around, Regina cut her off with a clipped, "Did you hear me?"

Parker cleared his throat. "Franco, tell Oliver to show the kids the Special Poolside Lounge, and then to come ensure no one interrupts us," Parker commanded, gesturing to Franco, who quickly took the gun from Regina's hand and ushered the others out. Angelina and Joshua cast me a quick glance before disappearing through the door, leaving Regina and Parker alone with me in the library.

"Would you care for a drink, Regina?" Parker asked, moving to pull out the chair on the other side of the desk. Regina threw herself into the seat. Neither person seemed to acknowledge that I was still there. It was like they didn't care if I heard their conversation: I wasn't a human, they didn't consider me a threat.

"You must be exhausted," Parker condoled, going to a cabinet that was disguised as a row of books. He opened it up to reveal bottles of alcohol nestled in velvet-lined racks. "Running around for people who don't even appreciate the hard work you put into this venture. Honestly, when was the last time you got a raise?" he asked, pulling out a bottle of clear liquid and two crystal-cut glasses. Shutting the cabinet, he turned back to Regina, who was lounging in her chair with poised grace.

Regina didn't reply, but watched Parker silently as he poured the drinks. She accepted the glass he poured for her and considered the drink with pursed lips.

"You said you had a proposition, Parker. Let's hear it." Locking eyes with him, she downed the entire contents of the glass without a wince, then held it out for more. With a smile quirking at his lips, Parker poured her another generous amount.

"I was hoping you'd accept an offer to come work for me. You're rather high up in HAMMA's ranks. They'd *never* suspect you to betray them," he said with a wink.

"What's that supposed to mean?" Regina snapped.

Parker was silent for a moment, then replied, "Mendoza."

Regina's face went slack, and Parker's smile widened as he continued, "So, you'd be the perfect person to work on the inside, giving me the information I need to get to their creatures before they do. You could be my connection, my ace up my sleeve. I know your talents. I know we can profit like never before."

Regina laughed humorlessly through her nose. "How many other HAMMA operatives have you offered this proposition to?" she asked, this time sipping her drink with coyness.

"None," Parker said, leaning forward in his chair. "I became particularly interested in this case, not only because of the exorbitant amount of money HAMMA has thrown out just to capture this creature, but because I learned you were involved in the extraction."

I saw Regina cast Parker a quick, surprised look, then the same guarded expression fell once more, hiding any information that her face might tell.

"As you said," Regina said, her voice tired, "they'd never suspect me to become a traitor, because I wouldn't. HAMMA is my life, you should know that. It's why we broke up in the first place. If I didn't do it for you *then*, why would I do it for you now?"

"Because," Parker said, settling back into his chair, "although you're more beautiful than ever, I see that you are tired. Tired of HAMMA, who you thought was so wonderful, so worthwhile to give your life to, not paying the bills as you thought it would. You've grown wiser, I see it in you. Sure, extractions like this allow you to live in luxury for a few months, but these types of jobs are few and far between. They only use you when your talents, or rather, the resources you possess, like your daughter, can be exploited. I'm sure that's tough on you, and your child."

Regina puffed up like a bullfrog, her eyes hard. Parker continued with the same syrupy slowness, unaffected by her heated expression.

"If you worked for me, I'd utilize you at every opportunity. I know your talents, and I wouldn't use you just because your daughter can be used as a ploy. Plus, I can pay you three times what *HAMMA*," he cast her a knowing look, "pays you on extractions such as these. What you're receiving now as benefits of your work?" He ran a finger around the rim of his glass and looked in her eyes. "Fool's gold. It's just enough to keep the peons enticed, to think they'll be seeing more from the profits. But we both know that they never will."

When Regina didn't reply, Parker stood, his movements slow as he came over to Regina's side, sliding up onto the desktop, where he towered over Regina, who had stiffened at his closeness.

"I also know you, Regina. I haven't stopped thinking about you."

Regina met his eye, and he leaned ever so slightly forward as she raised her face toward his .

"Ugh, do you mind handing me a bucket so I can throw up?" I drawled. "You guys are worse than a soap opera." Even *I* knew that Parker was laying it on more thickly than he needed to I was surprised that Regina had bought into his act as much as she had.

Both jumped at the sound of my voice, having forgotten I was there. They shifted away from each other, Regina looking embarrassed while Parker simply looked annoyed.

"So," Regina said, clearing her throat, her cool attitude returned. "You wish me to be your inside woman, and in return, I would get what?"

"Split profits, fifty-fifty." Parker said, straightening his posture as he remained perched on his desk. "Which will be far and away more than what you make now. You wouldn't have to bother with all those 'trickle-down' policies HAMMA has placed on you, despite the perks of being on extravagant extraction missions. Not to mention, as HAMMA scares off a lot of big buyers with their clumsy tactics, my clients are willing to pay a premium for professionalism. Plus the benefits are amazing." He ran a slow finger over his bottom lip, eyes locked on Regina.

Regina pursed her lips again, unable to stop the blush from rising in her cheeks.

"Say I do it," Regina said, exhaling. "What do I do if HAMMA catches on? Am I out on my ear?"

"No, of course not. We'll lose opportunities, sure, but you'll have a lot of information about HAMMA, their future raids and assets—and their buyers—so we can undercut any future deals. Either way, having you in my corner is a win for me, and a win for you. Bonus is, your daughter doesn't have to be used in such a way anymore. My employees' families receive ample attention and benefits as well."

Regina heaved a theatrical sigh. "I just can't go back empty-handed to HAMMA," she finally said. "Besides, they'll track you down to take back the asset," she said, gesturing to me with a flick of her hair. I narrowed my eyes at the pair of them, but neither were paying attention to me. So they were all just a bunch of backstabbing liars and thieves, trying to get the upper hand. I'd fallen into a pit of vipers, and I wasn't sure I'd be getting out unscathed.

"Oh, I'm aware they'll try," Parker continued. "But I've yet to be stolen from. Another reason I'm a superior employer."

Regina sighed again. "I'm still not convinced that working for you would be in my best interest. HAMMA has been my life, and," she paused, looking up at Parker with dewy eyes, "yes, things have changed—I'm not seeing the benefits as I once did—but I'm afraid of betraying them. And yet, I can't keep going on like this." Her voice wavered, as if holding back emotions. "My daughter is utilized more than I am. More and more creatures are captured by young adults."

Parker nodded. "It's a young person's game at HAMMA."

She looked up at him. "What would you have me doing?"

Before he could answer, he shifted forward on his desk and pulled a buzzing cell phone out of his pocket. Putting it to his ear, he replied, "Yes?"

He was silent for several moments, then nodded. "Excellent. Punch it. I've got it handled here, but I'll need assistance moving her out."

He put down the phone, and looked at Regina. "Sorry, a storm's coming." Without warning, Regina stood and threw a punch at Parker, who deflected it as if expecting it. Regina leapt sideways and kicked the chair at Parker. He sidestepped it and lunged at her, tackling her and pinning her to the desk. A lamp and desk ornaments went flying as they scuffled, and finally Parker had Regina's face pressed flat against the desktop, Regina's hands twisted behind her back, with Parker putting pressure on them so she couldn't move.

"I figured you were stalling, waiting for backup, but I didn't realize your organization had such an army at your disposal," Parker said, panting.

"You really expected me to fall for your lies?" Regina snarled, her voice muffled from her face being forced against the marble desk. She kicked out at him. "I know what to expect from your 'offers.'"

"You *have* grown up," Parker said, sounding impressed. "I can't manipulate you like I once could. Oh well. You'll still be useful to me."

At that moment, the boat engines roared to life, and in the next moment, I could feel the boat speeding over the ocean, the water in my tub sloshing. Parker laughed as Regina struggled against his grip, and I watched them in silent fascination. Parker was a lot stronger than he appeared.

"The backup you called for doesn't have as much finesse as you thought. My men saw them coming from a mile away. My men let *you* onboard, because we knew you had some of my operatives, and I needed leverage myself. But your organization is young, still learning the rules of the game." He pinned her harder as she tried to kick out at him, and he leaned close to her ear. "I've been doing this much longer than you have, darling. But to stop you from doing something stupid, I'll just have to hold you here until I've finished with the sale of *my* very unique creature." He got off her back, making sure to keep her arms pinned, and called toward the closed door, "Oliver, come take her away."

The door opened, and a blond behemoth shouldered through the doorway, taking Regina from Parker's grip.

"I'm sorry, my dear," Parker said, shaking his head back and smoothing his hair that had become mussed during the tussle. "Don't worry, no harm will come to you and the others that have trespassed on my ship, who, by the way, are already in the brig. You'll join them. I'll let you out when we get back to the States." He stared at Regina's enraged face, and he put on a pout. "I'm sorry you refused to make this work. We could've worked well together."

"You slimy—" Regina began, but was cut off as she was wrenched through the door. Regina continued to rage as she was marched down the hall, out of earshot.

"Phew," Parker said, picking up a few of the items that had fallen off his desk. "Well, we're underway. I'll have someone come to take you down to your accommodations," he said, and for a moment I didn't realize he was talking to me. "Have a nice evening."

Without another word, Parker left the room before I could come up with a biting comment, leaving me alone in the tub. I leaned my head against the back of the tub and closed my eyes, my wrists aching to the bone against the metallic handcuffs.

I felt a headache coming on from everything that had happened and everything I had learned in so short a time. But the ache was nothing compared to the pain radiating around my heart.

Everything Joshua and Angelina had done and said were lies. Lies to entrap me and use me. I had been right. They weren't anything at all like Noah. They were worse.

The worst a person could get, taking me far from home, far from my mother, far from safety, all under the guise of being an understanding, compassionate pair of friends. The betrayal cut me so deep I couldn't focus. I didn't know what my future held, but in my gut I knew it was going to be a horror show.

I tried to cry. I *wanted* to cry, but my eyes were just as dry as the Nevada desert, a place I never thought I'd miss—a place I'd probably never see again. I choked on a laughing sob. My mother wouldn't believe it if she knew I was missing the desert.

I stilled.

I'd never see my mother again.

What would she think when I never returned?

Though I didn't want to think it, the bitter thought came unbidden, that maybe now my mother would get what she wanted: to be able to run back to her real family, her real life, finally free.

That is, unless these people somehow learned I was a hybrid, and tracked my mother down too.

Both thoughts filled me with horror. Guilt and despair warred within me as any remaining hope of reconciling with my mother crumbled to dust.

Chapter Twelve

I sat numb in the tub, trying not to think about my future. Exhaustion prickled at my eyes. I just wanted to sleep, and maybe wake up from this.

The door opened, interrupting my worries, and several men stepped into the room. They unlocked my wrists from the tub, then hastily cuffed them together, but not before I had landed a solid punch on the nearest face. I was hoisted, sopping and slippery, through the hall and down several flights of stairs. I considered struggling, but it would only get me a painful meeting with the floor. I had no chance of escaping, and I wasn't in the mood to be seriously manhandled.

They eased me through a final door into a considerable room that was lined with cages of all sizes. Most were empty. I felt a slight spark of joy in seeing Angelina, Regina, Joshua, and the others crammed into a cage just large enough to hold them all comfortably. The irony curled a vicious smile across my face as I passed them.

In one of the other cages, I saw a pure white dog lying curled up in the corner. Instead of paws, it had the hooves like a deer. It watched with wide eyes as we entered the room. Another cage held a snake that, instead of scales, was covered in turquoise and scarlet feathers, and the third held a small humanoid with ragged clothing, shaggy hair, and a tiny pointed hat. The cages occupied with animals seemed to shimmer with an odd, colorful film, like that of a soap bubble.

I was taken to a sizable cage at the end of the room, beside the one filled with my so-called friends. Both of the larger cells lacked the same shimmery barrier I had noticed on the animal cages. I was settled on the bench inside my cell, and the men left me. With horror, I realized I would soon dry out, and then I would be sitting here, in full view of everyone, without any underwear on. When I was fighting for my escape, my nakedness was at the bottom of my priority list, but now, just sitting exposed like some living display made heat flare across my face.

A few minutes later, the men came back inside, lugging the empty clawfoot tub into the room, followed by several men with water-filled buckets. One man held a gun on me as they opened my cage, and I snorted. I was outnumbered, could barely move in my current form, and was still handcuffed. The men set the tub inside, filled it with the buckets of seawater, then uncuffed me and plopped me back into the tub. After taking off my cuffs, they didn't bother shackling me to the tub again, for which I was grateful. I did manage to give them a few blows with my tail as they hurried out of my cage, slamming and locking the door behind them. Then all us prisoners were left alone.

The HAMMA members all talked among themselves, sometimes casting me angry or worried looks. Angelina and Joshua refused to look in my direction.

The caged animals remained quiet, unnaturally so. Each time one awoke up from their respective naps, they would always watch me with cautious, sometimes aggressive eyes. I didn't know any of the species by name, and I was pleased to overhear that the HAMMA people didn't seem to know either, except for the snake, which Regina called a feathered serpent from Central America.

As I was pulling my eyes away from the vibrant feathers of the snake, I noticed Regina's hand was stretched toward the shimmering cages, her face hardened in concentration. After a moment, she sat back, looking frustrated. Her eyes then flicked to me, and she repeated the action, reaching a hand out toward me, face contorted. After a moment, a puzzled expression entered her face and she lowered her hand, studying me with a frown until someone asked her a quiet question and she looked away.

Despite the late hour and all the horrifying excitement, I felt wide awake. How could I sleep with mere bars separating me from those traitors?

One by one, everyone inside the cell next to mine fell asleep on the mats and blankets they'd been given. I stayed awake, wondering what I could possibly do to escape. My thoughts turned to my mother again, and this time I had to fight back tears. She never mentioned HAMMA as a threat we had to be careful of, so she probably didn't know they existed. Unless that was another piece of information she'd failed to share with me. I had been annoyed at how afraid she was of people coming for me after Noah's attack. I knew my ex wasn't smart enough to send people after me. I was sure people would think him nuts if he'd tried. I'd been wrong, apparently.

I'd been wrong about everything. I had thought that, with a few exceptions, most everyone was relatively good and honest. I realized now, knowing my mother was a naiad and having lived for centuries, she'd seen more of the world than I had. She knew human nature better than I ever would.

A wave of anguish rose up inside me. I'd never felt like this, so alone. I couldn't connect to humans in any way, knowing they would either attack me or sell me to the highest bidder, and I couldn't trust other magical beings to not kill me on sight because I wasn't "normal," whatever that looked like.

My good feelings from coming to terms with what I was just a few hours ago were gone, left in the depths of the sea. I was special and utterly unique alright, and that made me nothing but a target. Everyone saw me for what I was, not who I was. Tears dripped down my face, and I occasionally glanced toward my sleeping prison mates, making sure none of them saw my weakness. My pride wouldn't allow them to see how much their betrayal had hurt me. It would only give them power.

I was splashing my tub water on my face to cool my heated cheeks when I heard someone hiss at me. I whipped my head toward the sound, and saw Angelina, who had stepped over her sleeping friends, and was now pressed against the bars, looking at me with wide eyes.

"What?" I snapped, and she winced, shushing me.

"Don't wake everyone up," she implored.

"Oh, why not?" I bit back. "You don't want them to know you're talking to the *asset*?"

Angelina looked down at her hand. "I . . . I didn't think . . ." She paused, working her lower lip, then looked up at me, and anger coursed through me as tears glistened in her eyes. She was the one crying? "When they sent us on this extraction, I . . . I wasn't expecting a creature so—"

"Human-like?" I cut in. Angelina nodded, looking away.

"Well, I'm not human, so you're off the hook on feeling guilty about your part in all this." I shifted away from her.

"No, you don't understand. I . . . Once I realized it was someone who looked and acted human, and then I got to know you . . . I started feeling uneasy about this whole thing. I don't care what anyone says, you're just as much a person as I am. I didn't want this to happen."

"And yet you carried on with the plans anyway, didn't you," I snarled, turning back to her, causing the water in my tub to slosh over the edge.

"You don't understand; it wasn't my choice!" Angelina pleaded in a whisper. "I had no control! No matter how much I wanted them not to, I couldn't stop them hunting you!"

"But you could've said something to *me*!" I rasped, not quite able to hide the hurt from my voice, despite how angry I was.

"I wanted to," she said, her voice low. "Many times. But I didn't know when or how. I was afraid. Afraid you'd run away and we'd never see each other again, and—"

"You'd be blamed for losing your asset," I supplied.

"No, I was afraid of losing my friend!"

"Well, now some rich gazillionaire is going to put me on display in his house somewhere in the south of France, so you failed either way. And honestly, I won't mind as long as I don't have to see your face again."

"You don't understand—"

"You keep saying that," I interrupted, "but I understand more than you know. Like you said, I have every feeling you do. But you're right, we are not the same. I would never search out and capture creatures for profit."

"We don't do it for profit!" Angelina said, her voice wavering, her knuckles tightening against the bars. "We capture animals from those who wish to do them harm and release them into the wild," she chanted, as if reciting it from memory. Her expression then turned sickened. "At least, that's how it starts out . . ."

I laughed, loud and derisive as I stared at my flippers poking out of the water. "That is such BS. Then why capture me?" I snapped my eyes to meet hers, making her jump. "I *was* free. Either you're lying, or you've been duped, because any organization that goes after animals that are already free isn't doing it to free them; they're doing it to benefit themselves. Wake up."

Angelina fell silent, and I wanted to let her stew, but I couldn't help laying on one last layer of guilt.

"You were my best friend, you know," I said, stretching the truth a little. I didn't know her well enough to fully replace the friends I'd had back in Maine, but at least in Moapa Valley she had been. Now, I realized, all her hobbies were probably mirror images of mine so that she would have more in common with me, helping her to earn my trust. It had worked. I clenched my jaw. "I trusted you. I was even stupid enough to think about sharing this side of me with you one day. And Joshua . . ." I broke off, glancing at Joshua's still form. I had been stupid enough to think that Joshua might have become my boyfriend. But that was over now. How did I attract such trash men? They either freak out when they learn what I am and try to kill me, or they'd been planning to kidnap me all along.

"How long have you been members of HAMMA?" I snapped. I was sick of lies; the ones I'd told, and the ones that had been told to me. They caused nothing but pain and heartache. If I'd just been honest, about everything . . . this might not have happened. I was learning, and now, I wanted truths. Even the hard-to-hear ones. Maybe I could learn something useful. Angelina seemed guilty enough to answer my questions. I would use her as she had used me.

"All my life," Angelina replied. She glanced behind her, where Joshua was sleeping. "Joshua's family is relatively new to the organization, and everyone else here has been members for years."

"What even is HAMMA?"

Angelina paused, then said, "When you first join, they tell you that they are a group that respects magic and creatures of magic that the rest of the world doesn't know about, and they protect them, and rescue them if they are in danger." It was said so smoothly that I knew it was another memorized line, but at the same time, she looked a little sick as she said it.

"'Respects?'" I snorted. "If you respected me at all, you wouldn't be telling me the lines they've been feeding you. You'd tell me the truth."

Angelina was silent again.

"So, that casino in Vegas, is it owned by HAMMA?" I asked.

Angelina nodded. "It's where HAMMA's higher-ups go to schmooze potential clients and collectors, as well as to relax. They also own another casino in Vegas, but we use the Clover to draw out magical creatures."

"Let me guess, that roulette game at the casino was rigged to let me win?" I asked, my mind going back to that night. I'd felt so free, so reckless, yet so untouchable.

Angelina nodded. "It's called the Pleasure Island tactic. We solidify their trust by making them feel lucky and invincible." She paused, then sighed. "I didn't choose this life, you know. I just . . . grew up with it, learning that magical creatures were for us to protect. The philosophy changes once you get past a certain stage. As my mom and I got higher up in the community, we were taught creatures are to be used for our benefit. We just learned about the switch a few years ago. I didn't like it, or understand the sudden shift, but HAMMA kept my mom and me well cared for. The members lower down in the pyramid collect the animals and magical relics, thinking they're doing magickind a service, and turn the items over to the higher ups. Most everyone thinks the creatures are returned to their habitats, but now that we've gotten higher in the organization, we learn that almost everything gathered is sold or kept by the leaders. And those, like me, who have been in it for a while, get to go on the more in-depth raids, where we get to live in luxury during the undercover ops. Joshua was brought in because there aren't that many members in the Valley, and they needed manpower. I didn't agree, but I went along with it. I guess I was just used to it. Until I met you, I'd never come across a human-like entity before. Usually it's been creatures like firemanders and animals that grant luck or safety, or whose organs have healing properties. Nothing like you."

"So how did you find me?" I demanded, shifting in my tub.

"HAMMA heard of the episode in Maine. They're constantly trolling for stories like that. They talked to your ex-boyfriend, and learned about how some sort of mermaid creature attacked him."

I rolled my eyes. Of course Noah had said that *I* had attacked *him*. It gave him an acceptable reason for stabbing me, and not just because he was a stupid brute.

"They got your old Maine address and your photo from him, and with a bit of magic and some belongings you'd left behind, they were able to track you to Moapa Valley. My mother and I were contacted by HAMMA, informing us that we would be moving to Logandale for this raid. My mother is an expert at finding mythical animals, and we've moved all over the country, assisting on difficult extractions. They also contacted the HAMMA members in Vegas for their support, and this ruse was designed to draw you out." Angelina glanced up at me, then looked away again. "Our overseers seemed really excited about you, but they didn't say why. They never really tell us details. They knew you'd be overly cautious after what happened in Maine, so they told us to wait, on HAMMA's dime, until you started opening up again. After that, it was all about establishing trust."

"Las Vegas? My new cell phone? The times we hung out?" *The kiss*? I thought, my heart aching as I saw Joshua sit up from where he'd been sleeping, staring at us. He got to his feet and moved toward us as I continued. "None of it was real, I was just being handled. Although, it seemed a funny tactic back in Vegas to earn my trust by throwing me into a fountain."

"That was all Franco. We . . . actually had a plan to grab you outside the Bellagio that first night in Vegas. The last round of food you were given at the casino had been laced with tranquilizers, which had started to kick in, but then Franco messed it all up. We had planned many ways to grab you during the trips to Vegas, but Franco always made some kind of scene that prevented us. I just thought it was because he was so stupid. He even convinced us that we should milk HAMMA for all it's worth, and drag this 'vacation' out for as long as possible. It was his suggestion to get a free trip to California out of it and take you there. I should've known to be suspicious when he started making sense. We had no idea he was working for someone else. I didn't think he had it in him. Apparently he's actually pretty smart."

"I wasn't comfortable with it either, when I learned our target was you," Joshua broke in, stepping over the last snoring guy to come sit next to Angelina. My teeth were immediately put on edge at his approach. "Neither of us were."

"I'm so sorry to cause you discomfort," I snapped, my heart aching as I considered the safety I'd felt during our kiss. My face flamed as shame gripped me. "I can't believe I actually *liked* you, you jerk. Both of you!"

"You were becoming our friend too!" Joshua pressed. "I wanted to tell you so many times, but . . ."

"But, what? You got tongue-tied? You certainly weren't when we kissed," I bit back. Joshua ducked his head, and Angelina looked away in embarrassment.

I looked between the two of them, Angelina's reaction revealing a horrible truth. "You told her, didn't you?" I gasped, my face burning. "You told everyone in your organization that you kissed the freak of nature!"

"No! Cord—" Joshua began.

"That's why you ran," I continued, my voice breaking. "You were so eager to get away from me after the kiss because you were so disgusted—"

"No, I promise you, that wasn't it!" Joshua implored, his hand jerkily reaching out to me through the bars. "It was—"

"Well, it doesn't matter," I snapped, my stomach hurting, my fists aching from being clenched for so long. "It wasn't anything special, and neither was your friendship. You can justify your actions however you want; I will never forgive you."

"You don't understand—" Joshua began.

"That's what Angelina keeps saying," I snarled. "I may not be human, thankfully, but I understand English perfectly, thank you."

"*No*," Joshua snapped, then lowered his voice again so I could barely hear him. "It's dangerous for us to go against HAMMA. It isn't safe for our families for us to speak openly. HAMMA says they act harshly to protect their members, but really, it's scare tactics.

"If we had warned you, my siblings and my parents would've been taken away, maybe killed." His voice cracked, and he went quiet for a moment. He took a deep breath. "A few years ago, my little sister was nearly killed by a mythical animal that was in our yard. It moved so quickly, I don't even know what kind it was. HAMMA arrived just in time to save her, and my family immediately joined the cause. But the longer we stayed in, the more HAMMA's true nature began to show. They will do *anything* to capture every magical creature. The fact that this guy beat them to the punch is amazing, but it's still dumb to go against HAMMA," Joshua said, looking at Angelina, who nodded.

"Oh, so you two are in danger? Well, better that *freak* than you, right?" I mocked, looking up in time to see Joshua share a pained expression with Angelina. "And since you were new to the organization, is that why you wanted to start hanging out with Angelina? On our first date, you said you were trying to get into her 'crowd.' Was it because she was HAMMA, and you were new?"

Joshua cast his eyes away from mine. "It was actually just part of the ruse to get you to trust us."

"Wow. Did you even want to become a lifeguard on your own? Or was it just because I was there?"

"No, I did, actually." His imploring eyes met mine again. "And then we became friends—"

"*Don't you dare* call yourselves my friends!" I snarled, annoyed that tears choked my words a little. I turned away, heat rushing through my veins as I glared at nothing, their lies reverberating inside my skull, chilling my heart. They tried talking to me some more, but I resolutely ignored them. They soon fell silent as people in their cell began waking up.

I was too angry to actually sleep, but I closed my eyes, trying to tune out my neighbors and the nightmare that was now my life. I remembered feeling like my life was a catastrophe when I discovered I was part naiad just a few weeks ago, and I almost laughed aloud. I'd had no idea what the word "catastrophe" meant until tonight. And if my current life trajectory was any indicator, my future was only going to get worse.

Chapter Thirteen

I jolted awake as a door opened with a clang, and laughing voices echoed around the brig. I blearily sat up in my tub, my back aching, as three uniformed men bearing trays and containers on a cart entered the room. I didn't know what time it was, but I knew I had only been in this cage a few hours.

"Feeding time at the zoo!" one of the men called, while the other two laughed. All three looked only a few years older than me, which somehow made me feel worse. Was everyone my age so easily corrupted? One young staffer stood guard with a drawn gun while sandwiches were roughly thrust into the HAMMA cell by another uniformed employee, who was basically the height and width of a lamppost.

The third worker was moving along the magical animal cages, using an odd-looking device that opened a hole in the iridescent barrier, big enough for food to be slipped through the bars. However, the animals cowered far away from the man as he worked, it seemed as though the magical barriers were unnecessary.

"Ahhh, my favorite attraction," Mr. Lamppost said, coming to a stop at my cell. "The seals." He pulled a large, dead fish out of a container and held it up through the bars at me.

"Arf, arf! C'mon, do some tricks for me!" he coaxed, his cold eyes drilling into me. The other two workers laughed, coming up behind him to watch. I stared at him, careful to keep my expression deadpan.

"Arf, arf, arf!" He hurled the fish at me, and I didn't have time or the space to dodge it as it hit my shoulder with a wet slap. The three men burst into laughter. Biting the inside of my cheeks to keep from yelling, I picked up the large fish and flung it back at them, but it hit the bars and plopped to the floor. I turned away, determined to ignore them when a second fish clipped me hard against my chin. I gasped, pain flaring across my jaw as the fish fell into my tub, scales littering the water. The men laughed harder.

"Leave her alone!" Joshua raged, and I turned to see him standing, pressed up against the cell bars as he glared at the workers.

"Or what? You'll tattle on us?" Mr. Lamppost teased as he threw another fish at Joshua, who ducked away as the fish clanged against the bars.

"Dang, we should've brought a beach ball so she could balance it on her nose," one of them snorted, turning back to me.

"I've got something even better," Mr. Lamppost snickered. "I bought them while on shore." He pulled out a pack of firecrackers. "Let's make this a real show."

Dread welled up in me as he pulled out a lighter and began opening the firecracker pack. One of the men kept looking over his shoulder, a semi-worried look on his face as the other two pulled out the small explosives and began lighting them.

The first few fireworks they threw into my cell, I was able to quickly fish out of the water, only burning my hands—the water doing nothing to extinguish the fuses—and throw back toward the gleeful guards before the firecrackers exploded. The guards ducked away as the explosives went off, then came back to stand at my cell, chortling.

"Hey, man, wait until it's about to explode, then throw it at her," came a voice from the HAMMA cell. I turned to glare at who spoke, and saw one of the male HAMMA prisoners who had come onboard with Regina watching me with a smirk. Angelina slapped the man hard on the shoulder, but the damage was done. The skinny guard guffawed in agreement and eagerly pulled out more fireworks. I was tempted to hurl myself out of the tub to get out of the line of fire, but I realized that if I did, then I wouldn't be able to get back into the tall, clawfoot tub, and I would dry out, and be naked in front of everyone.

I wouldn't let myself be humiliated that way.

The first belated firework came in, exploding just as it hit the water near my elbow. Sharp heat danced along my skin as the water roiled and splashed, and I cried out.

"Stop it!" I heard Angelina shout. Her pleas went ignored as more fireworks were lit, paused, then thrown. Another firework landed on my collarbone as a second one landed in the water near my tail. Biting pain flared where the firecrackers had erupted. The sharp smell of gunpowder and smoke filled my nose, making my head hurt as my skin throbbed.

"Stop! Stop it!" I raged, as another firework landed in my hair. I managed to brush it off just as it combusted, burning my hands. I splashed water on my head, hoping to douse any possible ignition in my hair.

"Light the rest all at once, see what happens," one of the guards sneered, and I looked through my sopping hair toward their evil smiles, my stomach sinking.

A fish came hurtling at the guards, smacking one of my tormentors hard across the face, and we all turned to see Joshua standing at the bars again.

"*Leave her alone*!" Joshua bellowed.

All three men abandoned their fireworks and marched up to Joshua, who aimed a punch at one of the workers the moment he came within range. Joshua landed a fair blow, but then Mr. Lamppost grabbed Joshua's arm and pulled him tight against the bars. Angelina jumped to Joshua's aid, trying to knock the man's grip away, but she was shoved back by the second worker. Regina tried to hold Angelina back, shouting for her to not get involved or cause trouble. Undeterred, Angelina leapt forward again, pressing herself against the bars to claw at the men's skin until Joshua was released. Both Angelina and Joshua staggered backward, the two groups glaring at each other, panting.

"Just leave her alone, you cowards!" Joshua growled, nursing his bruised wrist.

At that moment, the gigantic man Parker had called "Oliver" entered, his expression stormy.

"What is going on here?" he demanded. The three workers fell silent, avoiding everyone's gaze.

Joshua pointed at the three men. "They were—"

The blow came out of nowhere as the nearest HAMMA thug punched Joshua in the gut, no doubt to silence him. With a strangled gasp, Joshua fell sideways. Angelina shrieked and dropped down beside him, cradling his head as he coughed. No one else from the HAMMA cell spoke up.

Rage welled up inside me. Not only would no one else stand up for me, but those that tried were silenced. But I wouldn't be, and I was ready for some payback. I took up where Joshua left off, pointing at the three workers.

"Those three were throwing fireworks at me," I accused, holding up a blackened stub of a firecracker as proof. "And that guy was encouraging them." I pointed to the HAMMA brute that had punched Joshua.

"*What?*" Oliver raged at the three cowering men, shoving through them to my cell with a furious, "There better not be a scratch on her!"

He stood in front of my cell, visually inspecting me as I lay in the tub. Thankfully there wasn't a hint of creepiness in his look. It was calculating and analytical. His eyes lingered on the red marks on my arm, neck, and hands. He then turned away from me, his body tense. The three men tried to appear calm, but fear painted their faces.

"You three are confined to your bunks," Oliver barked. "We'll be in Osaka soon. I'll be reporting your behavior to Mr. Colton, and he will decide if we're going to kick you off the ship. You better pray he'll decide to wait till we've docked. Now get out of here!" The three men scurried from the brig like rats escaping a cat, leaving Oliver standing alone, breathing heavily as he watched them go. After making sure everything else was in order, Oliver left too, taking the food cart with him and leaving us all alone.

I exhaled, rubbing at the stinging burns on my skin, glowering. Only now after the workers were gone did I realize I hadn't received any real food.

"You shouldn't have gotten involved," I heard Regina whisper to Angelina over the murmur of everyone else in their cell. I glanced over at them. Regina was hissing at a defiant-looking Angelina. "We're going to get in trouble soon enough, we don't need you to add more to it—"

"Oh, shut up, Mom," Angelina snapped.

The brig fell silent as Regina reeled back, eyes wide. "*Excuse me?* You do *not* talk to me like that, young lady!"

"Or what?" Angelina bit back. "I told you I didn't feel right about trapping Cordelia, but you didn't care! You never care! You always do what HAMMA says. You don't care about anything I say or how I feel!"

My mind immediately went back to the argument I'd had with my own mother. My heart ached. I had said those same words to her, but the circumstances could not have been more different. At least my mother had been trying to protect me. Angelina's mother was using her.

"Don't you be ungrateful, Angelina," Regina said, her tone irate. "HAMMA has given us everything we have! This is our livelihood!"

"But at what cost?" Angelina shouted back. "We're not the good guys! I've known that for a few years now! If anything, that leprekin and their crew are the good—" There were gasps as Regina raged, "*Don't you dare say that!* Don't you say another word, Angie, or I'll have to report you." Regina glanced around the cell. "No one reports anything without my say so. I will handle this."

Angelina snapped her mouth shut, but stared daggers at her mother, then turned and sat apart from everyone. After a saddened look toward me, Joshua hurried over to Angelina's side and put an arm around her. I tore my eyes away from the pair to see Regina glaring over at me. I stared unflinchingly back until she turned away.

A few hours later, Oliver came back inside the brig, munching a protein bar, followed by three different men and one woman. The men were laden with soaking wet towels, while the woman carried a measuring tape. At Oliver's commands, the men lifted me out of the tub and the woman took my measurements. I made her job as difficult as I could, flapping and writhing until she was finished. I was then wrapped in the sea-soaked towels and set on the small bench in my cell. Before I could even think about removing the towels and launching myself toward the open door, my arms were chained to the walls above my head. They then chained my tail to the bench. Not a word was said to me as they worked. Once they were satisfied I wouldn't be able to move or take off my towels in any way, I was left alone.

My stomach clenched. This Parker guy didn't seem to miss a beat. He must have understood that I couldn't get my legs back until I was nearly dry, or washed clean of the seawater. I didn't know what he needed my measurments for, but whatever Parker was up to, it didn't bode well for me.

I knew our destination, Osaka, but I'd never been there, and I didn't know what we'd be doing, so I couldn't even devise some sort of loose escape plan. Plus the language barrier would make it difficult to find help. My mother knew a lot of languages; she probably even knew some Japanese. She had tried to teach me some languages over the years, but I'd struggled to pick them up and had grown discouraged.

Parker's goons checked on me every once in a while, but my towels were never rewetted. After several hours, my arms aching and my body screaming for a good stretch, the men returned. They stripped me from the still-damp towels, returned me to my tub, which was unfortunately a nice change from the chained bench, and left without a whisper of what they were up to. But I had my suspicions.

Although this bleak tub in a glorified animal cage appeared to be the bottom of the barrel as far as accommodations go, I had a sinking feeling that whatever Parker was planning, I would soon miss this place.

PART III

JAPAN

Chapter Fourteen

The next few days passed in relative boredom and annoyance as I tried to ignore my supposedly apologetic next-door neighbors. I had been steeling myself for weeks of having to ignore them, and of the cramped conditions of my tub, when I overheard some of the new workers assigned to feed us, feedings now routinely overseen by the imposing Oliver—who was constantly munching protein bars—that we would be arriving in Osaka tomorrow.

Apparently Parker had integrated magical upgrades into the boat so that it could travel at incredible speeds. A confusing concoction of gratitude, anger, and fear burbled within me over this knowledge. At least I wouldn't be spending weeks cooped up in this tub.

I was thankfully fed sandwiches—the same as everyone else—when the food cart came around, and I was surprised when they also changed out my tub water every day. It wasn't fun sitting in my own waste. The HAMMA people were blessed with bathroom breaks, albeit one at a time, and that seemed like a dream to me: to be able to get up and walk around, even just for five minutes. I'd tried asking the workers every time they brought food if they could just bring me some towels and pants so I could get my legs back, even if just for a few hours, but my requests were ignored.

On the fifth day since my incarceration, I felt the boat's engines whine down to a low rumble. I didn't have long to wonder if we'd arrived at our final destination when Parker entered the hold, dressed in a well-tailored suit, his hair elaborately coiffed into a modern pompadour style, his fingernails buffed, his shoes so shiny I could almost see my reflection.

Oliver and Franco followed him, carrying towels and wheeling in a wheelchair. I glared at Franco as he cast me a sneer. I hadn't seen his hulking form since that fateful night, and I wasn't happy to see it now. He was now dressed in a crisp yacht uniform in Parker's colors of navy blue and gold, his hair slicked back. He looked totally different from the bullying teenager I was used to, except for the smug expression on his face. That hadn't changed at all.

"Are you ready, my dear?" Parker asked, clasping his hands together.

"To punch you in the face? Been ready," I replied. Angelina and Joshua snorted.

"Ha ha. Still have your attitude, I see," Parker said, flashing me a smile, then sobering. "Well, let me see if I can reign it in a little." He came up to the bars and squared himself off toward me. "We're heading into the city in a bit. And since I don't want you to hurt yourself, I want you to understand something." He gestured toward the wheelchair. "We'll be wheeling you out of here, with you behaving like a little angel. You *will* behave yourself on deck, on the wharf, in the city, and out in public, do you understand me?"

I smiled. If he couldn't control me, maybe he wouldn't be able to take me anywhere. "I understand that what you're hoping I'll do is going to be impossible. The second I see other people, I start screaming," I bluffed.

He shook his head, chuckling softly through his nose, and stepped closer to the bars.

"You'll be wrapped in saltwater-soaked towels, with a blanket on top, and wheeled about. Now, unless I'm mistaken, which I'm not, the towels will keep you in your selkie form for quite some time. Therefore, you can't get away. You'll come willingly. And if you had any daydreams about a daring escape, let me paint you a scenario." He cleared his throat, then smoothed his hand in an arc before him, as if smearing the air with color. "You scream for help, you rip off the towels, showing your flipper tail. The seal girl. A crowd of thousands, all suddenly privy to your little secret. Can you picture it? You flopping out onto the street in the middle of a country that has all the latest technology. Your face, what you are, spread around the world in *seconds*.

"If you thought you had no hope of escape from me now, which you don't, of course," he chuckled, "just imagine trying to escape from *anyone* when the whole world knows about you. Everyone would be after you. You would never rest."

My stomach dropped to my flippers as my heart crashed against my ribs.

"People would think it's a hoax," I rasped, cursing my wavering voice. "That I'm just wearing a latex tail."

He shrugged. "Maybe. But it would be easily verifiable, once people got up close. And if you're out there long enough, you might even transform in front of everyone. Either way, do you *really* want to risk it?"

I swallowed hard. He was right. If even a handful of outsiders who didn't already know about magical creatures saw me and learned I wasn't a hoax, I would be hunted for the rest of my life. And they wouldn't only be after me, but others like me.

"So," Parker said, his voice chipper, "I suggest you sit nice, don't struggle, and you won't have anything to fear. I certainly don't want our secret to get out to the public. I want only the elitest of the elite to know about you. Which is exactly who we're going to meet. So, you ready?"

I didn't reply, I just sat, numb. Even if I could escape the wheelchair, Parker was flanked by his hulking goons. I wouldn't be able to get far.

The door was opened, and I was quickly wrapped in soaking wet, salty towels and placed onto the wheelchair, where a tarp-lined blanket was tucked around me. Parker took the honor of pushing me, and as I was wheeled toward the door, I couldn't help but glance at Angelina and Joshua. Their faces were pinched with worry. I cast them a narrow look before I was pushed out of sight, hoping to give them one last dose of guilt for what they'd done to me. I didn't know if I'd ever see them again, but I wanted them to remember.

We rode an ornate elevator up, and I was wheeled out onto the main deck. I was so busy gulping in the fresh air that I almost didn't notice the skyline of Osaka as it burst into view. A gasp escaped me as I looked out. From our vantage point, we could see the port of Osaka and the magnificent cityscape beyond. The city was a series of waterways that threaded through the spires of skyscrapers. The sun was heading toward the horizon, already casting the city into shadow. I'd always wanted to travel to Japan. My mother and I had planned to come here on one of our summer trips. But that had been before Noah.

I'd been to cities larger than Osaka, but I'd never felt smaller or more alone, though I couldn't deny the beauty of the place all the same. I'd never seen a city with so many canals and rivers, all rushing to the sea.

"If you look over there," Parker pointed, his tone jovial, as if he was taking a favored niece on a special outing, "it's that adventure park you weren't able to visit back in California with your 'friends.' I'd forgotten they had one here. Isn't that something?"

I stared at the distant, barely visible rollercoasters with a clenched jaw. "If I'm on my best behavior, will you take me?" I asked with a dead expression. He merely laughed in a way that oddly reminded me of Santa Claus. It was too jovial and refined, and I hated it immediately.

I was wheeled down the gangplank and onto solid ground, where a large, wheelchair-accessible van idled, waiting to take us to our destination.

They loaded me into the van and secured my wheels so I wouldn't bump around. The large vehicle lurched as the driver—a young man with bright red hair poking out from under his uniform cap—started off toward the center of the city.

Had my situation been different, I would have enjoyed watching all the sights pass by my window; bridges that spanned black waterways reflecting a rainbow of sparkling lights, bikes weaving through traffic as thousands of people hustled about their business, and the hint of old Japanese architecture mixed with the new, with parks and gardens interspersed between the skyscrapers and streets. I tried to get lost in the sights, even for just a little while, and forget that I'd been kidnapped and was on my way to be sold.

But I just couldn't.

After over an hour of driving, mostly taking back roads that were either clogged with people or so convoluted that the driver could only go a few miles an hour, the van pulled around an massive, square building. The sky was darkening, the clouds splashed with orange and pink as we drove into the parking lot behind the building.

The wide, four-story building was covered in tinted glass that reflected the multi-hued clouds. There was a large dirt field off to one side, filled with covered trailers, delivery trucks, and moving vans, but beside the few cars parked in the parking spaces, the paved lot was empty. The streets around us still bustled with people, but it appeared everyone who worked in this office building was done for the day.

The van pulled up to the side of the building out of view of the street, and after typing a few buttons on a black box set away from the wall, the grinding of gears echoed in the quiet. Ahead of us, a section of wall lifted revealing a ramp that led downward under the building. We were swallowed up by concrete and steel, and the door closed behind us as we descended into an underground parking lot. A road branched off to lower levels, but the driver pulled up to a set of double doors that opened as Parker stepped out of the van. My wheelchair was lowered, and Parker again took control of my chair as we entered a hallway that housed a pair of elevators made of such a shiny chrome that I could see the circles under my eyes as we passed.

We exited through another set of doorways to reveal that the gi-normous building was actually one cavernous, open-concept room. There were a few shallow stairs leading to higher or lower landings throughout the room, and several balconies going up multiple stories to encircle and overlook the empty space of the main floor, but that was it. The only other doors were ones that led off from the gigantic room.

The vast space itself was bustling with activity as people set up stages, booths, cages filled with animals, and tables full of merchandise.

Above us, the ceiling soared up four stories. The centerpiece of the ceiling was an expansive golden tree, hanging upside down, roots curling along the ceiling, branches reaching out over the room, glittering with lightbulbs and shards of crystal.

No one gave us a second glance as we weaved through the workers putting up the final pieces of stages and curtains.

"Ah, here we are." Parker wheeled me over toward the many doors that lined one wall of the conference hall. Several Japanese women sat behind a table nearby.

"Colton, Parker. I called a few days ago and reserved makeup and costume?" Parker said, and one of the cosmeticians, a middle-aged woman with a pixie cut, consulted a clipboard.

"Ah, yes. Ayami, Haruko," she called, gesturing for two young women to come over. The older woman spoke quickly to them in Japanese, and they bowed and gestured for us to follow them to one of the doors. Inside was a bathroom, complete with shower, toilet room, and vanity with curling irons, makeup station, and different goos and potions for skin and hair.

"Excellent. Before we begin," Parker said to the two women, his voice loud as though the two women were deaf or slow, "I would like a word with the young lady alone?"

"Of course," the taller woman replied in perfect English, her expression a bit hard. "Just call us when you're ready."

"Thank you." He waited until the door was shut, then turned to me. "You'll be getting your legs back now. No one knows what you are, and I want to keep it that way. Until the perfect moment, that is."

My heart, though broken, began to beat in anxiety.

"So, you will shower, which will bring your legs back, I imagine, and then these women will get you all dressed up. I'll be waiting right outside. Don't try anything."

"Why am I getting dressed up as if I were a human? I thought you wanted to show everyone here what I was."

Parker laughed through his nose, shaking his head. "Dear, I'm nothing if not a showman. Patience. My plan will be revealed soon. Now, into the shower."

"If you want me showered before next week, you should probably help me," I replied, my voice dull. I felt dead inside, hopeless. I was in a city of strangers, in a world and community no one knew existed. Maybe if I got my legs back, I could make a break for it, but for that, I needed to play a part.

"Right-o. Here we go."

He pushed the wheelchair as close to the shower as it could go, then busied himself untying and unwrapping me from the towels and blankets that had kept me trapped in my selkie form. I considered punching him while he was bent over me, but quickly discarded it. I needed my legs back if I wanted any chance of escape, and to do that, I needed his help.

When I was free and could slide off the chair, he tipped the wheelchair a bit to help me plop onto the tiled floor of the shower.

"Soap, shampoo, and conditioner there," Parker said, pointing at bottles lining the shelf. "Here, let me get the water for you," he said when he saw I was unable to reach the knob from my position on the floor, my flippers sore from being cramped in the tub for nearly a week. The water, glacial and powerful, hit my shirt, and I let out a gasp as I writhed away from the icy stream.

"Sorry," he quipped, flashing me a cheeky smile. He turned the dial up a bit, but I had no choice but to stay under the freezing water until it warmed up.

"Get out," I snapped, as the telltale volts began to cramp around my abdomen where skin and fur collided.

"Of course." He slowly closed the shower door, eyes peering through the crack until the very last, and then I heard the bathroom door shut, and I was alone.

I wasn't expecting to cry, but at the sound of the door shutting, and me being alone for the first time in five days, the anxiety, betrayal, and loneliness hit me deep in my gut, and the tears ran with the shower water.

Between gasps from both the upheaval of emotions and the cramps I felt in my muscles, I began to scrub at my flippers and webbed hands with a bar of soap, washing away the crusted saltiness, causing the spasms to intensify.

After a few uncomfortable moments, I had my legs back, albeit sore and achy. I got to my feet, mindful of my shaky legs on the soapy floor, and quickly washed away my tears before starting on my hair with copious amounts of shampoo and conditioner.

The feeling of being clean for the first time in nearly a week, and having my legs back, helped calm me and clear my thoughts.

I was stuck here. There was no way I was going to get past Parker, especially if he saw me as a flight risk. I would have to be smarter. I knew he was arrogant; if I acted beaten down and submissive, it was possible he would relax and I could take advantage of one of his larger lapses due to his overconfidence in my compliance. I couldn't lay it on too thick, but I wouldn't be as blatantly defiant. I would remain vigilant for opportunities, but I would have to play this sick game of his, and act for the big show. There was no other choice.

Not yet, at least.

Chapter Fifteen

I stayed under the hot shower stream until I heard the door open again and a woman called, "Hello?"

I turned off the water, and was just wondering about how I would get a towel when a fluffy white bathrobe was handed to me over the shower door.

"Thank you," I replied, taking it. Inhaling the scent of clean laundry, I slipped it on. I felt better, more confident and hopeful now that I was back in my everyday skin. And clean. It was amazing how things felt different when you didn't smell like an open sewer next to a fishing dock on a hot day.

I was about to step out of the shower, but I paused. Would these women help me? Or were they part of the same crime world that Parker was?

I exhaled. No, I wouldn't say anything; I couldn't trust any of them. I would have to go along with this, at least for this evening, to get off Parker's radar. But I would keep my eyes open, and take this time to observe.

If I could somehow slip out of the building during the evening, all I needed was to jump into the nearest river. This city was flooded with rivers. It was possible. I could swim for hours, and no one would be able to track me. Parker had mentioned on the night he had captured me that his blood-tracking device had almost been depleted, something about the amount of blood being minimal. Parker had yet to get more blood from me, and I could only hope the spell had expired by now.

Making sure the robe was tied tight around me, I stepped out of the shower, where two Japanese women stood.

"Hello," I said, keeping my voice shy.

"Hello," both women responded, the shorter woman's accent more pronounced than her taller companion.

"I'm Ayami. This is Haruko," the short woman said. Haruko handed me a pile of clothes: undergarments, a pair of shorts, and a t-shirt. Haruko gestured toward a screen off to one side of the room.

"Please, get dressed."

I slipped behind the screen and quickly donned the clothes, feeling more and more calm, my mind forming plans. I wouldn't know which one to use, but having multiple plans and then going with what the situation called for seemed best. When I stepped out from behind the screen, Haruko descended on me, bearing a tape measure. After she took my measurements, Ayami swiveled the chair in front of the vanity toward me. "Come sit, please."

I took a seat, and the women immediately got to work. Haruko focused on blow drying my hair and curling it, while Ayami began applying makeup to my face, accentuating my enormous eyes and puckered lips. Haruko began spraying so much hairspray into my face that I had to keep my eyes shut for the majority of the time.

"There, done," Haruko said after nearly an hour of different brushes dusting my face and feeling my hair being snipped, tugged, and pinned. "Now to dress you."

I opened my eyes and gasped at the reflection. I turned my head back and forth, studying my reflection, not sure I liked what I saw. Whoever was staring back, it wasn't me. For one thing, she didn't look sixteen: she looked twenty-five. And sexy, in that Hollywood Hills type of way.

My silvery hair was done up in a half ponytail. The hair that was gathered in the ponytail had been teased so much it stood several inches above my head, while curled bangs swooped down and framed both sides of my face. The rest of my hair fell in beach curls down my back. My eye makeup was smoky and made my eyes look freakishly large, my cheekbones stark as mountain peaks, and my lips were a shade of red so dark it was nearly black.

Bewitching.

Mysterious.

Expensive.

I hadn't noticed that Ayami had left, but she returned bearing a vibrant blue mermaid gown that glittered with crystal beading around the entire bodice and speckled the floor length skirts.

"He ordered it special, but only gave us a handful of days to make it." She gestured for me to stand. Grimacing, I slid into the dress. When all the buttons and straps were in place, I looked in the mirror at the stranger reflected back. So this is what Parker had taken my measurements for.

I had to hand it to these women, they had a knack for working quickly, to precision. The dress hugged my curves perfectly, and the irony that the gown was mermaid style was not lost on me.

"You look stunning. Parker will be pleased with his date," Ayami said, giving me a wink. I wanted to vomit on the dress for spite. The fact that they thought I was with Parker romantically made me want to rip my hair out, but Haruko had used so much hairspray, it was practically bulletproof.

"Is he waiting out there for me?" I asked, hoping he was distracted, maybe giving me a chance to sneak away.

"Oh yes, he's eager to see you," Ayami said, mistaking my hopeful questioning as excitement.

With a resigned sigh, I allowed them to lead me out of the room, where Parker was sitting beside the door, flanked by Oliver and Franco. When Parker saw me, he stood up suddenly and turned to me with a raised brow. I noticed he too had cleaned up more while they were getting me ready. He was now wearing a tux and bow tie.

"Well, well, *well*," Parker said, his eyes raking down my dress. "This will work out even better than I'd hoped. You certainly are eye-catching," he said, stepping over to me. Taking my hand, he bent to kiss it, but I yanked my hand away in alarm.

"I'm a minor, remember?" I snapped. Parker smiled, taking my hand. Though I pulled in vain against his grip, he kissed it anyway, keeping eye contact with me before finally breaking away and straightening.

"Don't flatter yourself," he replied with an amused smile. "While you are stunning, I don't go for non-humans."

When I shifted away from him, rubbing the back of my hand against the scratchy beads of my dress, he laughed. "Won't do any good to wipe it off now. Did you know kisses are a potent magical device? They can bind or break certain spells, depending on the will of the sorcerer, but surely you knew that from children's storybooks.

They got the idea from somewhere. It's a bit archaic, but it's the easiest magic to perform. I'm no sorcerer, but I do know a few magic tricks.

"You see, we now have a bond between us," he said, grinning. "You have to follow wherever I go, until I kiss your hand again to break the bond. Observe." He turned on his toes and marched five paces away. When he got about three paces away, my hand was yanked as though I had a rope tied to it, and I was towed forward, nearly running into him as he stopped and turned about suddenly. He smiled as I tried to back up a step, but the invisible tether kept me from pulling back.

"Ah, excellent," he drawled, clasping his hands together.

I struggled to pull a few steps farther from him, but he clicked his tongue.

"So, be good, or I'll take you out to the busy street, dump saltwater on you, and let the world deal with you."

"Oh yeah?" I challenged, fighting—and unfortunately winning—against the voice in my head that shouted at me to act submissive. "And lose out on a massive payday? I'm not betting on it."

Parker gave me a cold, sly smile. "I'm not opposed to 'liquidating' some of my assets, little lady. Especially if they insist on being more trouble than they're worth."

I glared at him, inwardly gritting my teeth. He was unflappable.

"Where are you going to get seawater around here?" I snapped.

"Allow me to show you." He turned and began walking away so quickly I was almost yanked off my feet again.

While I had been in the bathroom, the rest of the convention hall had finished being set up. There were now people, who were dressed like Parker and me, adding the final touches to their booths and stages filled with animals and merchandise.

We wound through the crowd until we came to a stage near the back center of the room, where a considerable saltwater tank stood.

I stared at it with widening eyes.

Parker smiled. "I knew from the moment I heard about you that you were going to be my crowning jewel for the convention. I was afraid HAMMA wasn't going to sweep you out in the open and away from protection until after the convention, and I would have to go in myself and take you, but thankfully they brought you away just in time for me to snag you. I ordered this tank five months ago. Isn't it lovely?"

I gaped at the monstrosity as my mind whirled. Five months?

If multiple groups of people had known about me while I'd been trying to hide in the middle of the desert, where could I go to truly hide if I ever escaped? My hopes of returning to a normal life were slowly dwindling.

"I said, 'Isn't it lovely?'" Parker demanded, pulling my attention back to my waking nightmare. The tank was cylindrical, about ten feet in diameter, eight feet in height. The bottom was full of short stalks of kelp, with a large, flat rock submerged in the middle of the tank, most likely there so that I could rest and "sun" myself. Like some sort of animal on display.

It finally sunk in. I would be nothing more than a beast in a cage to be ogled at by the highest bidder. I turned to look at Parker in horror.

"Do you like it?" he asked, his face smug.

Without thinking, I raised my fist and propelled it into Parker's face.

I hit something solid, but it wasn't Parker's pompous, punchable face. My knuckles crumpled against an invisible barrier that stood about half an inch away from Parker's skin. Pain lanced up my arm, and several of my knuckles popped with the impact. With a strangled cry, I turned, holding my throbbing hand while Parker clicked his tongue. He reached out and yanked my chin toward him, looking at my pain-pinched features.

"Oh, sweetie. I hate to have the merchandise damaged, but you did need to learn for yourself that you oughtn't try to attack me. It's useless. Let me see the damage," Parker said, and without waiting, grabbed my hand, raising it to the light. I cried out as my knuckles and wrist twinged with heated pain.

"You put quite some force behind that punch. If I wasn't magically protected, I wouldn't be as impressed." He handed me back my hand and gave me a stern look. "I'm going to let that pass, but as I said before, any other cute exhibitions like that, and I will make good on my threats."

"Yeah right," I snarled, turning my wrist slowly, making sure nothing was broken. "There's no way you'd miss out on a one-hundred-thousand-dollar prize."

Parker gave a delighted laugh. "Oh my darling, you *greatly* underestimate yourself. Please," he chortled. "I don't even leave the house for a hundred grand. No, I'm expecting the first and *lowest* bid of the convention to be at least five million."

I stared up at him, my mouth agape, forgetting the pain in my hand for a brief moment.

I tried to speak, but my mouth had gone dry. I swallowed several times before rasping out, "People would really blow that much money on an oddity like me?"

He gave me a small pat on the back. "You're one of a kind, dear. And once everyone here knows it, the bids won't stop coming. The magical collector community is full of eccentrics. Rich, covetous eccentrics," he said with relish.

At least five million? My mind reeled. However, I had a ray of hope. If he had that much money, and more, at stake, there was no way he would risk the world knowing about me. His threats were completely empty.

"However," Parker said, again seeming to read my thoughts. "I'm also nothing if not spiteful. I'm not above showing you to the world, and then selling you. Do you want to be responsible for blowing the whistle on every magical creature in existence? If I'm not mistaken, most magical beings like their anonymity. That's why they're so hard to catch, and they wouldn't look kindly on someone who so carelessly revealed themselves to humans. Magical creatures, along with everyone else, would hunt you down. So don't test me."

His words about other magical creatures frightened me, especially since there was another element to his threat that he was unaware of—my taboo hybrid status—but at the same time, I still felt like he was bluffing. Nothing was more important to him than money. And while I conceded that he would enjoy the notoriety of revealing me to the entire world, he was still a businessman at heart. So while I would tread carefully for now, I didn't allow his words to scare me into complete submission. If I saw a chance to escape, I was taking it.

"Now, enough gloomy thoughts. Let us enjoy the evening." He shook back his cuff and looked at the gold watch on his wrist. "It's nearly seven. Should be starting soon." He lowered his arm and rubbed his hands together, his cheeks flushing as he looked around the room with wide, happy eyes. Disgust twisted my stomach. He was like a child on Christmas morning.

"Well, well, if my eyes aren't deceiving me," Parker said, sounding thoughtful as he stared into the crowd. "Houston Banwell. I didn't think I'd be seeing him here. He's been out of touch with our circles of late. No one really knows what he's been up to, not even me, which is surprising," he chortled. "But I'm glad he's here. I think you'll intrigue him. Especially once he sees you in the tank—"

"So, why'd you doll me up if you're just going to stick me in that tank?" I asked, cutting off his rambling thoughts. I didn't need a recap on every rich A-hole who was going to be throwing millions of dollars at Parker for me.

"Ah, a good salesman piques the interest of his customers before he pulls out the merchandise."

I rolled my eyes as Parker stared around superiorly. People began arriving in droves through the front doors, as well as from the elevators that led to the first level of the parking lot. The room began to flood with people from all around the world. And all looked exceedingly wealthy. I saw more diamonds, gold, and endangered animal furs here than on a red carpet. Waiters began to circulate the crowd with platters of hors d'oeuvres and glasses of champagne.

"It's time," Parker said as the crowds swelled. "Come along, pet." This time, instead of hauling me through the crowd, he turned to me and offered me his arm. I gave him a snide look, but he just smiled, took my hand, and placed it in the crook of his elbow. I glared at him.

"Remember, play nice," Parker warned out of the corner of his mouth. "Okay. Ready to schmooze," he breathed to himself as he brushed his bow tie, and I struggled against the despair threatening to envelope me. Swaggering forward, he led my defeated form through the crowd. I couldn't get away from Parker because of his stupid kiss spell, and I couldn't scream or make a scene, because everyone here was an enemy.

It was possible that my bad behavior would turn away possible buyers, but I had a feeling it would just make people see me even more as an animal, not a person.

I was alone in a sea of monsters.

Chapter Sixteen

Parker's plan was, frankly, brilliant.

He first led me to a table where a Filipino woman was selling medications. Magical medications. She had pills and tinctures for everything and anything: from lotions claiming to completely erase wrinkles that were made from the oil of mushrooms picked from a fairy ring on a new moon, to chewable tablets that put you to sleep for just two hours, but gave you the equivalent of a full night's rest. "For the hard-working businessman that wants to get ahead," the label said.

The lowest priced items started at thousands of dollars. I glanced over the items on the table, marveling at the variety of labeled materials from all over the world: yowie fur; gbahali teeth; karkadann blood and horn; delicate, fiery rarog feathers; ananse venom; and more that I didn't have time to read; all the ingredients you could ever need to make your own potions or talismans at home. I stared in wonder at the range of this modern apothecary, as Parker made his announcement to those crowded around the table.

"Ladies and gentlemen," Parker called with a flourish of his raised arms, "I'm Parker Colton. Some of you may remember me from years past having brought you new and exciting finds."

I noticed that several of the people turned to look at him with interest and recognition.

"Well, this year, I have something exceptionally exclusive to share. Something that has never been seen before in the known world. I would like to invite you to my stage at ten p.m. when I will be revealing my find, after which bids will be opened. Bidding will last for the full three days of the conference."

Several people appraised Parker with interest, while others turned away before he'd even finished talking, interested more in what was immediately before them than what could be seen in a few hours from now.

"For my companion here," Parker said, eyeing those that had lost interest in what he was saying, but gesturing to me, "is not what she appears. And if you would like to see her true form, I invite you to my stage. Again, ten p.m."

Nodding to those who had been listening, he placed his hand on the small of my back and guided me out of the crowd to the next booth to make his announcement again. I stopped listening to his presentation. It was essentially the same every time, and the responses of each group was mostly positive and intrigued.

I was more interested in the incredible variety of mythical beings and products available; interested, and horrified.

I saw a Japanese couple selling tech such as cell phones and tablets that boasted two months of battery life without needing a charge and reached Wifi signals from anywhere on earth. They had a display of the devices being made in real time by dwarves who were sitting in cages set just higher than the booths.

Other people were simply selling mythical creatures. There were cages filled with everything from tiny bears to multicolored humanoid beings, to a variety of birds, to tanks of water much smaller than mine filled with strange fish, sea life, odd plants, or octopuses with too many arms.

One booth that intrigued Parker was an immense reinforced cage that held a hulking, green-gray humanoid with two horns jutting from the crown of its skull and curved fangs protruding from its mouth. The towering creature leered back at those ogling it. Parker called it an oni, recently captured, and going for an astronomical price. Apparently, according to Parker, the oni hadn't been seen in over eighty years.

Parker was in a foul mood for several moments as he stared at the oni, who was glaring back, complaining that he had competition for the rarest item of the convention. His temper cooled, however, as he surveyed me in my beautiful gown and perfectly manicured appearance.

"I know you're much more special than any old oni. There are hundreds of them, just underground and hard to get to. But you . . . you're one of a kind," he purred. My lip curled in revulsion as his mood visibly lightened.

Other booths were smoky, with fires going on behind the counters, where exotic foods from mythical plants and creatures were being cooked. I felt sick, knowing that people were consuming magical creatures like me.

Another stage held glass cases full of curios. I saw countless books, stones that glowed softly, cursed bottles of alcohol, varying pieces of magical jewelry, bones of long-dead creatures, arcane statues, enchanted weapons, boxes that claimed to hold items far too large for said containers, magical candles; the mythical objects seemed endless.

During our tour, I also saw several magicians performing trivial feats of magic, just enough to entertain. I felt more and more sick the further we progressed around the crowded conference room. I was finally seeing more of the magical world, but they were all trapped, just like me. What did this mean for the future of the magical community?

Finally, nine-thirty rolled around, and Parker—glee dancing across his flushed face—said it was time to head back and prepare for my big reveal. I had tried several times to escape during his announcements, even going so far as trying to get Parker to "kiss" my hand as I'd yawned and stretched, bumping the back of my hand against his wide mouth in the process. However, I'd forgotten about the barrier, and my hand was immediately deflected. Parker had known what I was up to right away, and he had merely given me a smug grin. It was worth the try, but I was still upset that I had tried to touch the slimy man's oversized lips.

By the time ten p.m. had nearly rolled around, I was resigned to my fate. For now, I had to show these pompous elites who I was. I still had three days to plan an escape. But escape or no, the thought of having hundreds of eyes on me, seeing the real me, made my skin crawl.

We made our way back to our stage, and Parker turned to me as I eyed the monstrous tank with dread. "Now, my dear I had this dress made special for this occasion. This dress tears away here." He ran a finger across my abdomen, just under my bust line. I knocked his hand away with a soft snarl, my hand bouncing against the protective barrier.

"Tsk, tsk, temper," he warned, waggling his finger at me. I glared back.

"Keep your hands to yourself, then," I snapped.

"I have to show you the workings of your dress," he replied with a raised eyebrow.

"You can do that without feeling me up," I growled.

"You must have a high opinion of yourself if you think I'm interested in a base creature such as you." He grimaced. I desperately wanted to show him how I felt by throwing another punch at him, even if he did have a protective barrier. However, he didn't touch me again as he pointed to the tank.

"You'll be jumping into the pool, feet first, mind you, from that ladder behind the tank there. Your cue is, 'She's the only one of her kind in the world,' and I'll turn and point to you. That's when you jump. We'll be attaching the back of your dress onto a hook that is welded on the top of the ladder, so your dress will tear away as you fall. I want people to see your transformation."

I stared at him. "You're going to strip me down in front of hundreds of people?"

"Don't get your panties in a twist, you'll have *those* on underneath, so I suggest you relax. People *need* to see your transformation. It's what will sell the whole thing," he said with relish, and I glared at him. He saw my expression and laughed.

"And don't worry, your bodice will stay on, safeguarding your modesty," he said, rolling his eyes with a chuckle. "There are clients' kids here; I don't need to get a reputation of that sort."

I snorted. "I'll just be exposed in every other way."

"Yes, exactly." He paused, frowning. "Though that scar I saw is a little bit of a blight, it doesn't totally ruin the effect. I hope."

I bit the insides of my cheeks as my hand automatically went to rest over the knife scar that was currently hidden by my dress. "I'm sorry any trauma I've experienced will bring down my price," I said through clenched teeth.

Parker waved away my snarky apology as if I had just accidentally bumped into him. "We'll just make the best of it, and hope nobody notices," he said with a sigh. "Hopefully your pretty face and amazing transformation will draw away their attention. I made sure the women used special, magically enhanced makeup and hair products so that you'll remain pretty while in the water. They said it lasts two weeks before magically vanishing."

I rolled my eyes, my heart fluttering. "Of course you did. We wouldn't want my mascara to run."

He nodded knowingly, then turned. "Also, you're going to be televised, but just onto the two large screens there," he pointed to two screens on either side of the tank. "It's an internal system, so that everyone here, and only here, can see." As Parker had been explaining everything, the first of a large crowd began to gather. "Ah, we have an audience already. Excellent." He glanced at his watch. "Ten minutes to go. Go get on the ladder. And you better not jump in until I say so, or you will regret it."

Though I had been considering jumping in early and disrupting his plans before he even mentioned it, I thought better of it now. I needed to act more compliant, but it was proving harder than I thought whenever I saw his smug face. I kicked myself for undermining my own plan to put him in a good mood by pretending to be resigned and hopeless. I needed to do better. I didn't want him getting wise to any future attempts I'd be making.

He shepherded me to the ladder. I kicked off my heels, giving Parker a look that said I wasn't climbing that ladder wearing them, and then started upward. I felt Parker hook something on the end of my dress, then kiss my hand before he stepped off the ladder and hurried to the front of the tank to greet the crowds. I stood on the narrow platform that had been welded to the top of the ladder, awaiting my cue, heart pounding.

I rubbed the back of my hand against my dress, my breath hitching; Parker had just released my magical tether to him. I glanced around, then I grit my teeth; there was no way I would be able to make it to a door, half the convention center had eyes on me. And both Oliver and Franco had taken up residence at the bottom of the ladder, blocking any possible escape.

"Ladies and Gentlemen!" Parker called into a microphone as a spotlight zeroed in on him. The dull roar of the crowd immediately silenced like someone had hit a giant mute button. "Friends! We have just a few more minutes before my presentation, and so I would like to give you a little backstory on how I came across this one-of-a-kind marvel."

I tried to keep my legs steady as I stared over the gathering crowd. Everyone was listening raptly to the made-up nonsense of how Parker had found me. My stomach twisted as I saw that almost all the guests had gathered around my tank or the projection screens. I couldn't breathe as I stared out over the numberless horde. I was about to be exposed for what I was to the most dangerous people in the world. I couldn't run now, and once I was in the water, the walls were tall enough that there was no getting out until someone fished me out.

It will be okay. I have to keep Parker happy, I chanted to myself. *He will screw up eventually. He has to.*

"Behold!" Parker shouted suddenly, and I was blinded by spotlights coming from three different directions. The crowd's murmurs of curiosity reverberated in my chest.

"She is the only one in the *entire* world." He turned and held up both hands, presenting me to the crowd.

That was my cue. Hoping I was making a good decision to play his game, I took a bracing breath and leaped off the platform.

I felt my dress rip away from the bodice, the cold air hitting my skin a split second before I plunged into the icy saltwater. Volts shot up and down my legs as the bubbles rose up around me. I could no longer hear what was going on outside my tank, but I saw the crowd rush the tank as my body convulsed, and fur began sprouting, my legs fusing, my feet transforming to flippers.

The transformation was complete in fewer than ten seconds, and I watched as the crowd went crazy. I could even hear the din as it bounced off the glass and reverberated in the water.

My secret was out now.

Parker caught my eye, and he gestured for me to position myself on the underwater rock, to pose and preen.

Keep him in a good mood, I kept telling myself. *Keep him in a good mood. He'll mess up when I put him off his guard.*

Clearing the hair out of my face, I flitted toward the rock. It was smooth, and I realized it was actually made of some sort of plastic. It made sense. A rock this size would've been way too heavy to move without the help of a crane. I sat on the rock in an iconic mermaid pose, and stared out at the boisterous crowds. Relieved that the water stifled most of the sound, I watched as Parker kept the people back, no doubt wanting to stop them from pressing their faces up against the glass and smudging it like children at an aquarium.

"Ladies and gentlemen, please," Parker's magnified voice, which I could hear even through the glass and over the muffled roar of the crowd, shouted into the microphone, unable to keep the elation from his voice. "She will be available for viewing for the remainder of the convention. My associate here will take your bids so everyone will have a chance at this lovely marvel. However, put your bids in quickly, because all offers will be final by the end of the conference."

As I situated myself upon the rock, anxiously brushing my flippers against the sandy bottom, I stared at the excited, jabbering crowd. There was a line forming to sign up for the auction, while others stared, speaking with companions and pointing at me, obviously talking about my features; my drawbacks, my blemishes, my assets.

Shame, fear, loneliness, as well as anger, hit me with the force of storm-driven waves against a cliff side. These people saw me as nothing more than an exotic pet, like some colorful tropical bird.

I second-guessed my determination to play along with Parker. These types of people had connections, money, and influence to find me should I ever escape. And now they knew about me.

I shook my head, fighting back tears, though no tears would ruin the makeup on my face.

I felt stupid: I should've struggled instead of showing myself. I should've laid down in the middle of the crowds and refused to get up. So what if they all thought I was some wild animal? Why hadn't

I made a run for it when Parker took off my tether? What had I had to lose?

I took several deep breaths, not wanting to blubber in front of everyone here. I could still find a way to escape, there was time, and now I had some idea of what to expect here. And then, I could disappear.

I would have to hide somewhere remote, out in the wilderness. I could do it. My animal instincts were enough to help me survive. I would bring my mother with me, so I wouldn't be alone. If I ever got out, and if she ever forgave me. And this time, I would remain in exile. My mother had been right. Only now, I wasn't safe anywhere. There was nothing else for me in the world. I couldn't trust anyone, especially not humans.

My heart sank with every new thought.

I would have to live alone. No normal life for me. Only hiding and fear.

I sat in thought for the remainder of the night, sometimes hiding behind the rock when I felt too overwhelmed by those leering at me through the glass.

The hours crawled by, and Parker stayed by my tank all night, speaking with those who had questions. He ignored my gestures for him to come to me to tell me the time, or when this stupid thing ended for the night.

I was floating on the surface, dozing, when the announcement finally came that all final purchases needed to be made, because the building was closing for the night, to reopen tomorrow night at seven p.m.

Parker, no doubt worried about someone breaking into the conference center and stealing his one-of-a-kind gold mine during the night, rigged a small netted seat on a winch to come down and scoop me out of the water and lift me over the top of the tank. I was then placed into my wheelchair again, draped with wet towels, tarp, and blanket.

As Parker was answering a few more last-minute questions to a crowd of adoring fans, I was wheeled to the side of the tank near the parking garage doors. Parker called Oliver over to him to take some names down, and after a cursory glance at me, he hurried over to Parker's side. I leaned back into my wheelchair, exhausted. I considered trying to wheel myself away, but it would be fruitless.

I closed my eyes, my tummy cramping in hunger, when my wheelchair was suddenly jerked to the side, nearly tipping me over the arm. I looked back in alarm to see a man in a mask backpedaling while wheeling back the chair. I was so stunned that I didn't cry out, just watched dumbly as the man pulled me clear of the tank, about-faced me sharply, and began booking it toward the parking lot doors.

Was this man an ally or enemy? It was possible he was taking me to a worse fate than my current one, which would be truly terrible, but I had no way of knowing. I didn't know if I was rooting for him to get away with me, or if I should alert Parker of my second kidnapping.

"HEY!" I heard Parker yowl behind us, and the man picked up speed, going full tilt toward the double swinging doors.

I heard a strangled *fwump* of a body hitting something solid a millisecond before my chair tipped, sending me sprawling free from the chair. I flew forward and hit the corner of the double door frame, my head zinging. Through the pain and dancing stars, I saw Oliver wrestling with the masked man, a crowd of people surging toward us. I must have blacked out for just a second, because when I opened my eyes again, Parker's unpleasant face was inches from mine. I gagged, and Parker produced a light from his phone, shining it in my eyes.

Squinting, I looked away from the brightness to see that we were surrounded by clamoring people, and Parker's usually unctuous expression was harsh. He looked paler than usual.

He glanced up and away from me. "Oliver! Hand that scoundrel over to Franco to be taken care of, and you accompany me back with her. Quickly!"

I couldn't see through the crowd until it parted and Oliver shouldered through to scoop me up and set me into my chair. He proceeded to rearrange my wet towels and blankets. I clutched my throbbing head with both hands and curled into my chest, trying to hide my tears of pain.

People tried to waylay Parker with questions as he got me to the parking lot, but he stoutly refused any information, afraid of any other attempts to spirit me away, and told anyone who tried to stop him that they would have to speak with him tomorrow. He hurried us to our awaiting van, telling the redheaded driver to navigate as though we had a tail. On our way back toward the yacht, we took back roads and made quick, random turns down side streets, Parker obviously afraid of being followed and cornered.

During the entire ride, I hadn't seen even a hint of a crack of an opening for a possible escape. My headache had dimmed, but I was so exhausted emotionally and physically that I knew it would've been useless. Parker kept a keen eye on me the whole trip. He took my hand and held it tightly as if worried I would disappear, though I struggled against his grip. He even reapplied the magical tether on me, though I wondered if using that magic wore him out, because he was getting irritable and grumpy, and I could see the fatigue in his eyes.

As I looked at Parker's wan face, I felt determined to use that knowledge to my advantage; magic wasn't his strong suit. After nearly two hours of doubling back and forth, we arrived back at the yacht, where I was hurried onto the ship and back into my cell with no problems.

Back in my tub, I was fed better than I had been in the five days I'd been in Parker's possession, no doubt because Parker was pleased with the reception he'd been shown, and he felt sorry for his little injured pet. Food and water helped my headache, and Oliver, who supposedly had been an orthopedic surgeon before having his license revoked and turning to a life of crime, gave me a checkup and pronounced me fine save for the goose egg on the back of my head.

A relieved Parker ordered someone to stand guard outside the brig's door. With a quick word for Oliver to check up on Franco and then report any findings about my masked assailant, Parker gave a melodramatic yawn and stretch, declaring he was exhausted and was going to bed.

Before he left, I asked for some clothing, but Parker ignored me. As he waltzed out of the room, I glared after him. I knew he was using my half-selkie form as an extra precaution against losing me: it was difficult moving a half-blubbery seal-girl on dry land, after all.

The caged HAMMA crew was asleep when we entered, but woke up and watched as I was loaded back into my cage. The fatigue finally caught up to me as I sat in my tub, and I had no desire to deal with the curious, worried looks Angelina and Joshua tried to bait me with. After finishing my meal, I settled as comfortably as I could into my tub and immediately fell asleep.

Chapter Seventeen

"Cordelia. Hey, *psst*! Wake up!" Angelina's voice broke through my troubled dreams. I groaned, but my name came again. I came fully awake but didn't open my eyes, hoping to fall back asleep. Or that they'd stop.

"Cordelia, wake up! I have something important to tell you. Cordelia!"

I shifted away with gritted teeth, trying to convey that I was ignoring her. Maybe this was a new tactic to torture me. Sleep was the only escape from this nightmare I had, of course they would try to take it away.

"Cordelia, please!" Joshua's voice whispered, then he whistled to get my attention. My eyes shot open as I clenched my teeth, and I sat up in my tub, glaring at both of them. My entire body ached from the cramped position I had fallen asleep in, and my stomach rumbled with hunger. I felt like I'd only gotten a few minutes of sleep. Whatever these traitors had to say, it'd better be life-or-death type of important. Rubbing my puffy eyes, I glowered over at my former friends, who were pressed up against the bars, looking at me.

"*What*?" I hissed.

"I just want you to know, there might be more trouble coming your way," Angelina said, sharing a concerned look with Joshua, who nodded.

"Oh really? *Trouble*? Oh dear me," I drawled, stretching my neck with a grimace. "Is that really all you woke me up for?"

"I'm being serious," Angelina said, her tone annoyed.

I rolled my eyes as I tried to rub out the knotted muscles at the base of my skull. "And why is that?"

I looked into their cage, wondering why she wasn't afraid of her mother overhearing her giving the "asset" warnings, but her mother wasn't there. The other HAMMA members were snoozing, but I was positive they were only pretending to sleep. Ever since Regina told the other HAMMA members to keep quiet about Angelina and Joshua's behavior, neither of them seemed worried about the others listening in anymore.

"This morning, Parker found the stealthy tracking device my mother had planted in Parker's office the night you were taken," Angelina said. "He's having a talk with her. He's pretty upset. He's probably interrogating her about how much info our operation director, the guy that was pretending to be my dad back in Vegas, has."

"That guy was *pretending* to be your dad?" I asked, incredulous. I'd talked to that man a few times back in Moapa Valley when I started hanging out at Angelina's house, before this whole mess happened. We'd eaten dinner at the same table. Just another lie.

"Um, yeah. We've learned that people tend to trust full-family dynamics better than single-parent families . . ." she replied, grimacing at her own words.

"And you didn't find anything weird about that at all? Anything unsavory about this whole charade of pretending to be a family to kidnap people? It didn't give you even a little pause?" I raged, the fiery blood pounding through me causing a headache to throb above my eye.

"Of course it did, but, well, I was used to it . . ."

"And now that you're in this cage just like me you've grown a conscience. How convenient," I replied, blinking through my tired vision. Everything looked blurry from lack of sleep. Angelina shifted uncomfortably, biting the inside of her cheek, and Joshua took over.

"Hey, we just wanted to warn you that there might be a fire-fight should HAMMA find Parker's boat, or the convention that Parker is taking you to."

"I doubt they'll find the convention hall," I replied, rolling my shoulders and stretching my arms across my chest. "You haven't been as *lucky* as I have to actually see the city, but Osaka is huge."

"You could help us," Joshua pressed. "Give us information about where the convention is, and then we could break you out—"

"So that I could be in HAMMA's custody? No thank you, I'll find a way out of this myself. I don't trust either of you to even lend me so much as a pencil."

Angelina and Joshua fell silent, though Angelina's eyes, bright with unshed tears, watched me while Joshua picked at some peeling linoleum on the floor.

"You've just been buddying me up so that I'll tell you everything, and you can be the heroes to your sketchy little club," I accused, stretching my hip so much it spasmed.

"No, that's not true!" Angelina burst out. "We're . . . really, *really* sorry. We didn't mean to—"

"Get attached?" I droned, too tired to hold on to the anger slipping out of me.

"Cordelia, stop it!" Joshua barked as Angelina began crying.

"Oh, did I hurt your feelings?" I asked, hating that I felt a little bad, but I couldn't stop myself from continuing to rub it in. "Not that I believe you actually have any real feelings at all."

"Cordelia," Angelina said between her tears. "I know you're upset, but please, we want to be your friends, and we promise we will help you get away for real, from everyone—"

"So, you two are planning on betraying HAMMA?" a snide voice interrupted, making us all jump. "Parker's always looking for new talent."

I turned toward the door of the brig just as Franco stepped into view, smirking at us as he leaned against the doorframe, continuing, "I can put a good word in for you, though I'd say you're a little late to do anything useful for that freak of nature."

"Oh shut up, Franco," Angelina said, her voice a little shrill.

"You're not my real girlfriend, Angelina. I don't have to pretend to listen to you anymore," Franco shot back. "But you . . ." He narrowed his eyes at her, "I can't have two prisoners talking about a jail break, especially since you're talking about stealing from Parker, even if there's no way you'd succeed. Parker is always two steps ahead."

"That's not what I heard," Angelina shot back. "My mom got the upper hand on him, despite your betrayal, you stupid hypocrite."

I snorted at the irony of her words.

Franco's expression hardened. "Well, he's going to make sure that freak is steal-proof, even if HAMMA does try something, which I doubt. This freak of nature is going to stay put."

"Stop calling her that!" Joshua shouted suddenly, and Franco turned his attention to Joshua.

"Well, look who's the hypocrite now. Defending the thing that you were working so hard to capture," Franco chuckled.

"Only because HAMMA threatened my family," Joshua huffed. I thought back to how Joshua had spoken about his family. I knew how much he loved them. It made sense he would want to protect them.

"Oh I know. HAMMA is not very nice to their defectors, are they?" Franco taunted. "If you keep talking about breaking out, I might just tell Parker to let HAMMA know about your defection, and we'll let them deal with your family. I just hope your family won't regret your decisions."

"Don't you *dare* talk about my family," Joshua snapped, leaping to his feet. Though he wasn't as tall or beefy as Franco, Joshua was still muscly, and fairly tall himself.

"Or you'll what?" Franco asked. "I'm not afraid of a teen like you."

I frowned at that. Franco wasn't a teen? That made sense as to why he was so huge and older looking, but still, he acted like a stupid teenage boy.

"So shut up," Franco continued, "or your family will be the ones to pay the price for you running your mouth."

Joshua, who's face had gone white at Franco's thinly veiled threat, was now clenching his fists, as if struggling to keep from doing something stupid. Whatever he was trying, it didn't work. When

Franco, satisfied he'd silenced them both, turned around to leave the brig, Joshua bent down, picking up an old banana peel from his breakfast, and threw it through the bars at Franco's retreating back. The peel hit Franco in the back of the head, and Franco halted for several seconds before slowly turning around, a feral smile on his face.

"Finally. An excuse."

Before Joshua could stumble away from the bars, Franco had lunged forward and grabbed Joshua's shirt, pulling him tight against the cold steel, snarling into Joshua's face. "I hope you've enjoyed having teeth," Franco sneered. Angelina was hitting and screaming at Franco to let Joshua go, as Joshua stared back at Franco, fear contorting his face. Franco raised a threatening arm, obviously delighting in the tension.

A flurry of fear erupted in me as I stared at the pair of them. Parker and his henchmen weren't afraid of breaking the law in any capacity, I'm sure they wouldn't even blink at murder.

Everyone inside the HAMMA cell was no longer pretending to sleep, but sitting up, watching the tension build. I knew it was just moments before the bloodbath began and Franco started beating on Joshua, and maybe even Angelina. As angry I was at the two of them—and trusted them as far as I could throw them—maybe, *maybe*, they were telling me the truth, and were really on my side. Either way, it would be to my advantage to let them think I trusted them, even just a little bit.

Angelina got a good hit to Franco's face, and Franco shoved Angelina, who went spinning to the floor, before he turned back to Joshua and gave him a wide grin, cocking back his meaty fist.

My mind reeled. I needed to do something to catch Franco off guard.

Without thinking, I burst out laughing, making it as loud and derisive as I could.

The mounting tension broke, and everyone turned to look at me chortling inside my tub. I shook my head and stared, grinning through my fear, at Franco. "And you people think that *I'm* the dumb animal. This is exactly like watching gorillas at the zoo. Except gorillas are actually intelligent." My heart thudded against my throat. I had no idea what I was doing or saying, I was just uttering nonsense, anything to get Franco's mind off of punching Joshua's face into an unrecognizable pulp.

Franco made a noise like an angry bulldog as he swiveled his head to look at me. I continued provoking him, my own anger rising with each word.

"It's actually incredible that you think you're such a big man, Franco. You always did pick on those smaller and weaker than yourself. What, are you scared that you'll lose against anyone your size with half a brain? That tracks for you cowards that work for Parker." I tittered. "In fact, since you love beating up on helpless people, maybe you should beat me up!" I called, then paused, pretending to think. "Of course, Parker did have to have a whole *army* of men to capture *me*, one teenage girl, so maybe *you're* the helpless one." My snort of derision was genuine as the irony hit me. I locked eyes with him. His expression had turned cold and hard, but I continued to press him. "Come on, Franco, come over here, show me you're not a puny weakling by beating me up, since I'm such a big threat! Unless you don't think you can take me?" I taunted, latent fury fueling my words, just saying anything to get Franco's full attention on me, perhaps giving Joshua a chance to free himself from Franco's grip. Franco visibly swelled even larger as my implications hit him, and I bit back a grin of delight. *"Come on, coward! Show us what a real man you are and try to attack me, you idiotic brute!"* I jeered. Cold shivers rushed over my skin as Franco knocked Joshua away and turned fully to face me, his enraged expression oddly slack. "That's it, *come on, you pathetic sissy!"* I called.

Franco stomped up to my cell, his face contorted in a snarl as he glared at me through the bars. "When we move you to the conference, I'm going to personally make sure you suffer," he seethed, his face turning red. I honestly did laugh at that one. Like Parker would ever let him hurt me.

"Oh, I'm so scared," I gasped, clapping my hands up to my cheeks in mock terror. "Why wait for tonight?" I snapped, turning from taunting to anger as rage boiled to the surface of my skin. *"Come on, show me what you got right now!"* I shouted, more goosebumps thrilling across my skin in waves.

He rammed against the bars, trying to get them to budge. I laughed again over the clanging.

I had started the name-calling to try to take the attention off of Joshua and Angelina, who had now scrambled back to safety, but now I couldn't stop. My fury was building, something deep inside me was screaming to be released, and whipping Franco into a frenzy was the only release I had.

"Maybe if you reach for me, you can get at me," I taunted with a wicked laugh, watching him start to swell with rage. *"Come on, you brute! Reach!"*

He lunged toward me, pressing his face into the bars, both his arms outstretched as though hoping he could strangle me.

"Wow, you really think you can hurt me through those bars?" I snorted. Franco continued trying to reach for me, and I barked out a genuine laugh at his insane expression. "Oh, you're so adorable, you big oaf. I don't think you'll be able to reach me through those bars. *Try breaking them*," I drawled. "*Show me how strong you really are, I'm sure an ape man like you could do it! Or are you a stupid, widdle weakling? Come on, show me you can do it! Break those bars!*"

Franco, wild eyed, let out a roar and began trying to pry the bars apart, grunting like an angry elephant. I stared in amazement at him. One of the bars creaked ominously, and for the first time since I'd gotten his attention, I felt pinpricks of fear as I stared into his feral eyes and bulging muscles as they strained against the unmoving—yet groaning—metal.

"Stop that!" I demanded, a flicker of fear in my chest, the heated rage now cold across my skin, but Franco continued to attempt prying the bars apart, a manic look in his face. "Stop! Stop it!" I shouted.

"FRANCO!" a voice bellowed out, and we all physically jumped. Franco released the creaking bars, panting, and whipped toward the sound of his name. The glazed, furious look faded from his expression as he noticed his boss. Parker stood in the doorway, dressed in yoga clothes, watching us. Fury was etched in every taut angle of Parker's body as he glared at Franco. "What the hell are you doing?"

"I—I—I was—I don't—" Franco stammered, staring at his palms, the skin striped red and white from his colossal grip on the metal bars. "I don't know," he quavered, suddenly looking small against Parker's building rage.

"He was threatening me," I inserted, pointing at Franco. Franco paled, swallowing hard.

"Why?" Parker demanded.

"I don't—She was taunting me, and I—"

"She was . . . taunting you?" Parker asked slowly. "You were really trying to hurt her because she was *taunting* you?" he hissed, stepping forward till he was nose to nose with Franco. "With everything going on today, I do not have time to deal with this, Franco!" Parker shouted. I imagined Parker was still trying to get it out from Angelina's mother how much damage she'd caused with her tracking device. "If I find even a scratch on her . . ." he seethed, looking toward me.

"But I didn't even touch her," Franco protested, looking more like a worried schoolboy as he gestured toward the bars. "How could I?"

"Maybe not physically. Emotionally, yes," I insisted loudly.

"I don't want her excited or distressed any more than necessary!" Parker thundered.

I rolled my eyes at that.

After a moment, seeing I was unhurt, Parker closed his eyes, pinching his nose between his thumb and forefinger for a brief moment before, in one lightning quick movement, he turned and drove his fist up into Franco's stomach. Franco brayed like a wounded rhino and doubled over, his mouth flapping open and shut like a caught fish.

Parker leaned over the wheezing Franco, whispering in his ear loud enough for everyone to hear. "The only reason I'm not killing you here and now is because you've done good work so far. I wouldn't have caught her without you. But so help me, if I see you anywhere near her, or this brig, for the rest of our time here, I will end your existence. Do you hear me?" When Franco nodded, still struggling to inhale, Parker shoved him over. "Now get out of here. You're relieved from accompanying me to the conference this evening. Tell Gabriel to be ready to join me tonight. Now get out of my sight!" Parker shouted over his shoulder, "Adrian, Nando! Get in here!"

Franco, coughing and inhaling raggedly, stumbled to his feet and staggered out of the brig as two more uniforms entered.

"Today of all days," Parker fumed. "One of my best men has gone crazy, and I might be raided. Why is this happening to me now? Ugh, I might need to move," he muttered to himself. "I can't just move the boat, this prime docking permit took weeks and thousands to get," he murmured, his tone whiny. "Ugh, okay, okay. You," he said, pointing to one of the uniforms. "Call Oliver, tell him to bring Regina down here and lock her back up for the time being. And tell him to stay down here to keep things quiet. I have some calls to make."

He left the room as one of the sailors pulled out a radio and re-layed Parker's message. Several minutes later, a smug-looking Regina, sporting a now-bruised face, was brought into the hold. Angelina gasped as her mother was thrust back inside the cell.

"Mom! What happened?"

"Oh, nothing much." Regina waved her away from inspecting the growing bruises on her face. "What happened here?" she asked, grabbing Angelina's wrists and studying her scraped, raw palms from where she fell.

"Franco happened," Angelina replied.

"But only because they were planning on breaking the M.A. out," one of the other HAMMA agents inside the cell piped up. I didn't know his name; he wasn't part of the group that had come with us to California.

"What?" Regina asked, whipping to look at him. The other three HAMMA agents nodded, glaring at Joshua and Angelina.

"Yeah, they said they were planning on betraying HAMMA, and were going to get the asset out, and they said—"

"Not another word, Steven," Regina snapped.

"But they're traitors!" Steven insisted, wiping away the sweat on his forehead. "And they almost got us all killed—"

"You're all still alive, aren't you?" Regina declared, glaring around at everyone. "Besides, it's not for you to decide what constitutes traitorous behavior, or what happens to traitors. I, not you, will report everything that has happened, do you understand? I don't want to have this conversation again." Her voice dropped so that I could barely hear her. "We'll be having a conversation with the director face-to-face soon. Everything will be revealed then. So keep quiet."

"You mean a HAMMA raid here?" Steven whispered, and Regina tried to shush him before the words got out, but it was too late. Regina closed her eyes with a low exhale. "Please shut up, Steven," Regina whispered.

The cell fell silent, and Regina helped Angelina wrap up her hands as best as they could. Once they finished, Angelina tried to get her mother to share more details about what had happened to her, trying to tend to the bruises on her face, but Regina waved her off. As Angelina argued with her mother, Joshua turned toward me, eyes locking on mine.

"Thank you," Joshua mouthed.

I quickly broke the eye contact, uncomfortable at the feeling of camaraderie that had passed between us over such a horrible event. I shook it away and considered everything that had happened.

I'd never been a snitch before my time in this boat, but if it helped keep me and my two possible allies safe, I would do it again. I hated that I was almost overjoyed that Franco had been punished and put out of commission, and that I had been the cause.

I wasn't a violent person, at least I'd believed I wasn't before almost drowning a kid several weeks ago. I had done things I never thought I'd do, and I would have to do a lot more just to get out of this mess. I just didn't want it to change me. I didn't want to have to become a monster just to regain my freedom. I quickly turned my thoughts to something else, afraid of what possible horrible things I'd have to do to escape, and if I'd be brave enough—or desperate enough—to take certain roads.

I considered the group in silence as they settled back down, everyone quieting. I again wondered if everything Angelina and Joshua had said had been a ploy to win my trust, and that maybe Regina was in on it, but they had risked their families and their own personal well-being to stand up for me. And Joshua's glance of thanks had looked genuine. Something inside me—instinct, maybe—told me that though I had to be more careful about being burned again, perhaps those two truly didn't mean me any more harm.

However, there would be no way for me to really figure that out or not. For one, I wasn't going to trust them with any personal information, and two, I had bigger problems. One being the convention again tonight.

With a HAMMA raid possibly looming, Parker was sure to be more vigilant than ever. It would be impossible to escape while I was in my tank, and I would be in my seal form at all times. I tried to consider escape plans with an ever-watchful Parker and my seal tail as factors, but hunger and scantiness of sleep was making concentrating on anything difficult. I tried dozing, but the tension in the air, the headache from before, and my cramping stomach made even *that* escape impossible.

Several hours later, Parker came back inside the hold, not at all dressed like he was headed for the conference—instead wearing a tracksuit—my wheelchair and several armed men accompanying him. With a nod from Parker, guns were trained on those in the neighboring cell as their door was opened. Two men filed inside the cell. Screaming erupted inside as one man pulled Angelina up and dragged her out of the cage, while the other man shoved Regina back. Regina clawed at him like a wild beast, despite the multiple guns aimed at her. She was knocked to the floor, and the second man slipped out the door to safety. When the cell door was slammed and locked, Regina threw herself against the cell bars, her bruised and battered face twisted in a snarl. "You bastard!" Regina raged at an unaffected Parker. "What are you doing to her?"

Parker came up beside a newly handcuffed Angelina and placed a hand on her neck, forcing her to look at her mother.

"Taking her as insurance. Now, listen to me, Regina. *Regina!* Shut up and listen to me," Parker barked. Regina stopped her spewing obscenities to stare daggers at him. "If your HAMMA people do show up, and they destroy my yacht, hurt my men, or steal *anything* from me, I will find out, and I will kill your daughter. Do you understand?"

Regina shook at the bars. "*You—*"

"Bastard. Yes, I know." He cast the stricken Regina a steely look. "Heed my words, Regina, and your daughter will live. Let's go." With a click of his fingers, my cell was opened, and once again I was tucked into towels and tarps and wheeled from the cell.

"Don't you dare hurt my baby, or I'll search the world for you, Parker," Regina snarled. "There won't be any place you'll be able to hide."

Parker turned back to glance at her, a superior smile playing about his thin lips. "Darling, HAMMA has been looking for me for years. What chance do you think you have? Now, don't fret. When this convention is all over, you can be reunited, and I can go on my merry way. I just don't want any interference from HAMMA in any way. Remember, no harm to anything of mine, and I'll not harm anything of yours. Those bruises you received during our little interview don't count." Without a backward glance, Parker turned and strode out of the room. I was wheeled after him, and Angelina, flanked by several men, was marched out behind us.

Chapter Eighteen

Parker was nothing if not consistently paranoid. For over two hours, we drove through different parts of the city to allay Parker's fears about being tailed from the ship. I couldn't even enjoy the sights of the city, my stomach was squirming with so much anxiety at what was going to happen to me. Parker wouldn't say a word as to what we were doing.

Finally, Oliver turned down a calm street in a less busy, less flashy district of Osaka, and pulled into an underground parking garage of a nondescript office building. The small fleet of cars full of Parker's henchmen followed in rapid succession. I assumed Angelina would be following us soon with her contingent of guards.

I was wheeled into an elevator, where Parker pulled out a key card and slid it into the slot, entering a code on the keypad beside the buttons. The elevator carried us to the top floor, where the doors opened onto a sterile hallway with four doors leading off of it. Oliver opened the first door on the right, and we entered into a large room, just as barren and bleak as the hallway. The only features inside were the lights and two heavy doors that each had a square, barred peeper window. Opening one of the doors revealed a smaller room with no windows, just hard floors and a metal bench.

"Ah, yes, this will do quite nicely," Parker said, stepping into the cell and spinning in place as if taking in a richly furnished space. "These accommodations are the best I could get in such short notice, I had to call in a few favors. If I'd had more time, we would've been living like kings. However, it's only for a couple more days. I suppose I'll survive." Parker turned to face us as Oliver pushed my wheelchair into the cell-like room.

"Once they get your tub and all the luggage unloaded, we can settle you in. Thankfully my room down the hall is much more comfortably decorated," Parker said, giving a contented sigh. "Yes, I feel much, much better. No one knows where we are so they won't be able to get in here and take you away from me." He gave me a generous smile.

"What a weight off," I murmured, too tired and lethargic to come up with a more sarcastic remark.

"I'll say," Parker replied. Behind us, the outer door opened, and a shackled Angelina came in. "Ah, yes, put her in the other cell. Very good," Parker directed. Angelina passed out of sight, and a few moments later, I heard the other door shut and lock.

"Excellent. Oliver, I'll trust you to oversee the setting up of her tub? And remember, don't feed her. I don't want her stomach poking out before the convention tonight." He gave an enormous yawn. "I'm going to go catch a few winks, I haven't been able to sleep much today, and I'm beat—"

"Wait, you're not going to feed me?" I gasped. "I haven't eaten since last night!"

I had looked at the clock in the car when we pulled into the underground garage, and it had said two-thirty p.m. I wasn't going to last the rest of the day and all evening without eating *something*.

"It will put off any potential buyers if they think I'm selling a *chunky* one-of-a-kind wonder," Parker chuckled, then turned to Oliver. "Once everything is set up here, leave four men here, and send the rest back to the ship. Make sure they all follow the safety and evasion protocols. You'll set up guard changes. Don't disturb me unless there's any news from the ship worth waking me for." Motioning finger guns at my incredulous expression, he turned and sauntered out of the room.

"Have you ever *seen* a seal? They're supposed to be chubby!" I shouted after him. With a growl, I sat back into my wheelchair, Oliver standing beside me as we waited for my tub to arrive. I heard a crinkling above me, and watched as Oliver pulled out another of his protein bars and began munching it while we waited. My stomach groaned like an angry whale at the sight of the chocolate-covered bar, and I looked away, biting my lip to hold back stinging tears.

In short order my tub and fresh saltwater arrived, and then I was left alone, hearing the distinctive sound of a locking door shutting behind the retreating men.

I tried to sleep some more to block out my hunger and maybe regain some energy, but quiet clunking and scratching from the wall I shared with Angelina was putting my teeth on edge. Finally, after hearing a particularly loud thunk and a muffled gasp of pain, I turned toward the wall with a snarl.

"What are you doing over there?" I demanded.

The whimpers of pain behind the stark white wall stopped, and after a brief pause, I heard Angelina's sheepish reply, "I tried to kick the door open."

"Seriously?" I asked, holding back a laugh.

"That door is really strong."

"You'd probably have more luck trying to kick through the wall," I replied with a snort.

"I . . . tried that. They're painted steel, not drywall."

"Hmm. These people really did think of everything," I responded. "And your guards aren't telling you to cut it out?" I asked, glancing toward the barred window in the door. From my vantage point, I could only see the ceiling in the other room, but I assumed we had guards stationed outside our individual doors.

"I can see out the tiny window, and there's no one out there right now. But they'll be back soon, I'm sure. Can't let their investment get away, now can they?" Angelina replied bitterly.

"Doesn't feel good, does it?" I snapped.

"I wasn't talking about me," Angelina replied. We both fell silent, then Angelina's voice came again. "Cor, I really am sorry. Joshua is too." She paused, then I heard a bitter laugh through the wall. "Can you believe that we had even discussed telling you about all this and smuggling you out to safety? Joshua was so determined to fight for you. We even planned a day to do it, just before the trip to California. I was nervous, but Joshua was resolved. He was so brave." I could hear the admiration in her voice even through the wall. "But, that night that you two . . . kissed . . . Joshua's phone rang, right?"

My face flamed. "He told you all the gory details, did he?" I said through gritted teeth. "Did he tell you he was relieved we were interrupted because it felt like he was kissing a mackerel or something?"

"No, Cordelia . . . that phone call was his parents. They had found out about our plans, maybe they had read our texts or overheard us or something, I don't know, and they had called him, wondering where he was. They were worried he had done what we had planned, that he had told you who we were and what we were planning. They told him to come home immediately, because they were terrified of what HAMMA would do to not just him, but his little brother and sisters as well. They were so scared. He'd been chomping at the bit to tell you. But HAMMA's means of . . . persuasion . . . are very effective." Her voice was bitter. "They even have videos of what happens to traitors and magic users. Joshua came over to my house after his parents showed him one of the videos that HAMMA had given them as a warning. He couldn't stop crying." Angelina's voice broke, and she fell silent.

I exhaled. Joshua had been jittery and nervous that night we'd kissed. And when he'd answered the phone, he had seemed genuinely angry and annoyed. It wasn't totally implausible that Angelina was telling me the truth.

"We should've done more for you, Cor," Angelina's broken voice came through the wall, and tears pricked my eyes.

Something banged on both doors simultaneously, making me jump and Angelina yelp, and someone shouted, "Hey, keep quiet in there!"

"What, are we going to wake your precious Parker, or something?" Angelina shouted back.

Two men's voices laughed. "No, Parker's room is soundproof so he can ignore annoying sob stories like yours, but we can't. So shut up!"

We all fell silent, and I spent the remainder of the afternoon switching between dwelling on Angelina's words and thinking of means of escape. But both felt impossible; my mind was so muddled I couldn't think straight.

No wonder starvation and sleep deprivation were means of torture. You couldn't concentrate on much when you were suffering from both. If Parker insisted on starving me, and having me "sleep" in this tub, he wouldn't need to worry about me escaping at all. Maybe he knew that. It didn't help that soon after, the guards outside our rooms started blasting the most annoying synth music I'd ever heard.

By the time Parker came to get me for the evening, I was fuming.

Outside my door, I heard muffled yelling, and the music was quickly turned off. In the blissful silence I heard Parker calling, "—and don't let me hear that stupid stuff playing in here ever again."

I instantly felt revolted that Parker and I shared a common opinion about something. My door unlocked, and Parker, in his tux, waved Oliver inside with the wheelchair.

"Hurry up, no time to waste," Parker said, looking at his luxury watch.

Despite being submerged in water for hours yesterday, my hair and makeup still looked magically fresh, as if I'd just walked out of the beauty salon. Whatever products those women had used really had worked their magic.

I glowered as I was wrapped into my towels; the hunger, my impossible situation, and my sour mood battering around in my perfectly primped head. The last thing I wanted to do was go sit in a tank for another six hours and be ogled at by the rich and heartless while they dined on things more exotic and expensive than caviar and white truffles. I was loaded into my chair again, and this time Parker didn't bother pushing my wheelchair: the novelty had worn off.

Instead, I was handed off to Oliver as Parker sauntered ahead to the parking lot, his other guard trailing behind him, leaving Oliver alone with me to roll toward the van. When I saw the van idling, waiting for us, dread curled alongside the hunger in the pit of my stomach.

Another night of humiliating exhibition. Only this time I was starving, exhausted, and at my wits' end.

I sat back into the seat, arms folded, my renewed anger flooding through me. "That idiot should know that if I'm going to survive the night," I said to no one in particular, a shiver running across my skin, "he needs to *feed me!*"

The wheelchair stopped moving suddenly, and something crinkled above me. I glanced up in time to see Oliver pull a protein bar from his coat pocket.

He lowered the glossy, black-wrapped bar and placed it in my hand, his eyes a bit glazed. My fingers curled around the thick bar, reading the words printed on it. *Apex Alpha Peanut Butter Chocolate Power Protein Bar.* Bewildered, I looked back up at Oliver, who was shaking his head slightly, frowning.

"OLIVER!" Parker shouted, making me jump. I looked over to see Parker standing beside the van, glaring at our stalled position several paces away. Parker's eyes fell on the bar in my hand. "What did I say? I told you specifically not to give her anything to eat! Animals only need one meal a day, and I will not have her turn into a blimp!" Parker marched over to me and snagged the protein bar out of my hand. "Honestly, she may try to win you over with that pretty face and incessant begging, but we're trying to earn a fortune here. I suggest you keep the merchandise fit and slim! No feeding!"

He chucked the bar away from us, where it skidded across the concrete and fell through the grate of a storm drain with a wet *plip*.

Parker turned and began walking away, calling behind him, "Now, come on, I want her in her tank before people arrive."

Oliver gave his head a final colossal shake and then hurried me after Parker. As I was loaded up, I stared at my hand where the bar had been, just as confused as Oliver had looked when he had handed it to me.

People had sure been acting strange around me lately.

They seemed to do whatever I . . .

My brain stopped for a split second, and then my mind instantly went to my mother.

Could she . . .

She was always so good at convincing people to do what she said. Before I learned she was a naiad, I always thought it was just her beauty and bubbly personality that made people so obliging. She also had claimed that she'd always wanted to be a lawyer. She had made her arguments sound convincing, but was it possible there was more than logic to her words?

She wasn't a human who had grown up wanting to be a lawyer. She was a full-blood naiad. Could she actually *influence* people to do what she wanted? Was that a power naiads had? I didn't know much about my mother's side, but it made sense: naiads were well known for luring men into the water to drown them. And it made sense that I would inherit some of that power, being half-naiad and all.

My mind jumped to the odd interaction I'd had with Franco yesterday. His reactions to my tauntings were not normal, even for a meathead like him. Had Franco gotten so angry and tried to pry the bars apart because I'd somehow impelled him to? And afterward, he'd looked so confused, like he hadn't been aware of what he'd been doing. The same confused look that Oliver had had just now, when he'd handed me the protein bar, when he knew he wasn't supposed to. He was a *good* evil thug; he followed Parker's order's blindly. He wouldn't disobey a direct command.

And yet, he had handed me the protein bar when I'd told him to *feed me.*

I feared the rapidly increasing cadence of my heart against my ribs could be heard by everyone in the van.

This power of persuasion, if it was real, could be the key to my escape.

I bit down on the inside of my cheeks to keep any sound of excitement from escaping my lips as the van pulled out of the parking garage. The last thing I needed was to put Parker on his guard. If he knew I could influence those around me, earplugs would be worn in my presence, and then I'd be back to where I'd started: with nothing.

I would have to start slow, to see if persuasion was truly a power I possessed, though I would have to work quickly to escape once it was verified. I needed to practice, too. I needed to be able to control people without their hesitation.

I was quiet as we rode through the city, the breathless, jittery feeling of hope making me edgy. I didn't want to give anything away, but it was difficult to act beaten down when thoughts of escape were constantly barraging against my mind. But I would have to remain submissive if I was going to make this hope a reality.

For the first time since learning of my mother's heritage, I prayed I actually was like her.

Chapter Nineteen

We made it into the convention center without much problem, though people had come early tonight to catch a glimpse of me as we rolled into the room. Parker had Oliver make a beeline toward my tank, where I was lifted and lowered with their small crane without any incident. I never did find out what happened to the person who had tried to kidnap me, or if he was friend or foe, and I doubted I ever would.

The gawking began immediately. As I settled to the bottom of the tank to watch people gather around to stare at me, I had to keep from smirking at those who were nearly pressing their faces against the glass.

Here I was again, the freak in the tank.

But not for long. They had no idea what this freak was capable of.

My heart soared. This tank was a temporary prison that I would escape from. I would escape from all of them. I would find a way home, and I would get to my mother, and we would disappear forever, having outsmarted all these humans with their money and influence.

I would be free.

The evening passed much the same as the evening before. Parker once again had me on a magical tether powered by a kiss to my hand until I was put in the tank, worried about theft, I supposed, more than of me escaping. I knew here at the conference, escape would be impossible. I would have to wait until I was back at the office building, when Parker took off my tether and I wasn't sitting on full display in a giant fishbowl.

Parker was always busy, allowing himself to be led away by the rich and influential to sample foods or talk in crowded circles, leaving me alone in my tank to be oohed and ahhed over. I saw people of all nationalities and races pass by my tank. While many people were dressed in fancy evening gowns and tuxes, most others were dressed in blingified versions of their native dress.

It was mostly adults, but more than once I saw a child or teen ducking through the crowds. In fact, during a lapse of my guards' attention, one teenage boy, surrounded by a few friends, all dressed in lavish outfits, came up to the tank and began laughing and making faces at me. One of his friends handed him a handful of shrimp tails, and they began tossing the tails up and over into my tank.

Fast as an eel, I gathered the shrimp as they sank to the bottom of the tank and began munching on them, ignoring the squeals of disgust reverberating off the glass, just grateful for the food. I'd eaten worse things in the sea, my selkie instincts sometimes taking charge.

I thought my ravenous eating would've grossed the teens out enough to scare them away. However, the emboldened teens started throwing other—inedible, unfortunately—things into my tank. I watched as coins, chapsticks, and several chewed pieces of gum drifted to the tank floor.

I swam right up to the glass, making them jump slightly, and stared unblinkingly at them. They quickly laughed off their fright and began making rude hand gestures at me. I smiled at their snide expressions, elation flowing through me as I daydreamed about escaping right out from under their snobby noses. And maybe punching out a few for good measure. The thought filled me with sudden adrenaline, and I cast them one quick, innocent smile before I dove into a front flip, slamming the back of my tail with all my force against the glass, sending a deluge of water up and over the tank wall.

I closed my eyes, enjoying the muted screaming as the drenched teens, their silk suits and dresses now obviously ruined, were berated by my guards and chased away.

As I settled to the bottom again, grinning, I saw a man standing in front of my tank. He looked like he had just stepped out of a country-themed Vegas show, dressed in a ten-gallon hat, bolo tie, dress pants, and a bright red, bedazzled cowboy shirt. He was wearing so many rings it looked like he had on a pair of brass knuckles. The rhinestone cowboy was eyeing me appreciatively as he stroked his blond mustache. Goosebumps erupted on my skin at his intense stare, so I quickly turned and flitted to the other side of the tank.

For half a moment I'd forgotten that I was here to be sold, having spent the entirety of the evening relishing the thought of escape. I was anxious to practice my new gift, and soon.

I would never be able to practice controlling people here at the conference. For one, it was too loud and too conspicuous to get the attention of anyone to speak to them over the tank wall, and two, my guards were now on high alert after the water show incident.

To pass the time, I went over in my head ways I could get out of the office building. Both times I'd influenced someone, I had been feeling strong emotions of anger and fear. I didn't know if negative emotions affected the strength of my power, but I imagined it did. I knew my mother could probably do it effortlessly, but since I was only half-naiad, I would have to try much harder, and strong, negative emotions were my best bet. That would be easy. I had plenty to be angry about.

A few hours later, Parker returned, one hand hidden behind his back, the other holding a sandwich. He held it up briefly before me so I could see it through the glass, then he climbed the ladder just high enough to reach half his body over the tank and motioned for me to come to him, holding the sandwich down and out to me. My stomach quivered at the sight of the simple offering, and I quickly rose to the surface. As I reached for the food he was dangling, Parker snagged my wrist in a vise grip, dropping the sandwich into the water.

By reflex, I pulled back, hoping against hope to pull Parker into the tank with me, the darker side of me thinking to drown him for good measure, but he seemed cemented to the ladder. No matter how hard I struggled, trying to use my flippers to thrust myself away, he didn't budge. He simply stood still, holding onto the ladder, waiting for me to calm. After a few moments of thrashing like a fish on a line, I had to stop, winded easily due to my lack of food. My arm hung limply from his hand.

Taking his other hand, which had been holding onto the ladder, he quickly slapped a thick, dark bracelet onto my wrist. I tried struggling again, but he held me with both hands this time. A few lights on the plastic glowed blue where Parker's fingertips were touching the device. The bracelet seemed to shrink around my wrist as the lights dimmed, then he released me. I propelled myself backward until I bumped into the other side of the tank, water sloshing up the sides of the glass. After giving Parker a glare, I turned to the bracelet, studying it. It was two inches wide, made with heavy, dark gray plastic that looked like it had come off of some alien soldier's space suit.

I looked back at Parker, who was considering me from his perch on the ladder.

Bracing the bangle against my stomach and using my free hand, I tried to pry the bracelet off, but, like Parker on the ladder, it wouldn't budge. I couldn't slip, snap, or flex it off.

"I bought it for you," Parker said when I ceased trying to get it off and looked up at him, panting. "I got it in one of the tech booths here," he said, grinning. My heart sank.

Magic.

No doubt some sort of self-sustaining tether so that Parker wouldn't have to waste any more of his personal magic on me.

"It's a tracker," he continued, and my blood ran cold at his words. "So, should you get stolen, like almost happened last night, I can find you anywhere in the world. Blood tracking magic is useful, but it does expire. Don't bother trying to destroy that bracelet; it's reinforced with magic so you'll just end up hurting yourself. And only I can take it off you, with my fingerprints," he said, wiggling his fingers at me as he watched me with an evil look in his eye. With a flare of rage, I realized he was explaining all of this for his own sick pleasure of seeing me realize how truly trapped I was; that I had no hope of freedom or escape, now.

At least, that was what he thought. I still had my secret weapon, and I was going to fight with every ounce of determination I had left.

He skimmed the surface of the water with a few fingers in an arc, spraying me and bringing my attention back to him. "Now I can really relax and enjoy the rest of my time. Isn't peace of mind a wonderful thing?" He asked. Without another word, he winked at me, then climbed down and disappeared into the crowd, a few eager buyers following in his wake. I ducked beneath the surface and stared at my new accessory.

My hope soured. This tracker ruined everything! Even if I did escape, he could find me with ease. Something harder than my nails would have to pry it off. There weren't any rocks big enough in the tank to attempt smashing the bracelet.

I dropped my hand and sank to the bottom of the tank, where sand and ribbons of dying kelp littered the floor. I pulled on a piece of kelp and began to tear it into strips, braiding them as I anxiously nibbled my lower lip, watching viewers pass by.

The tracker had to be dealt with, but I had no idea *how* I was going to deal with it. Working any kind of magic was far beyond my scope, as I'd never really considered the magic in my life. My mother's lies were once again making my life harder. I had no access to any tools, and it would be impossible to try to influence Parker.

I didn't know if his shield also protected him from magical attacks, but I had to assume it did. Plus, Parker was so cunning, he would immediately know what I was up to.

But maybe his guards wouldn't. They didn't seem like the brightest bunch, and that could only work in my favor.

It occurred to me that maybe I could try to escape when I was with my new buyer, but waiting didn't seem like a good idea. I could always try that if escaping Parker failed. Besides, it would feel so good to outsmart Parker, to outwit him and take away something that was so precious to him. It was the best payback I could think of.

Considering the devil made Parker appear, accompanied by the urban cowboy that had been ogling me earlier. The two men weren't speaking, just staring up at me, the cowboy with a shrewd look on his face, Parker, an ecstatic look on his.

I didn't like either of their expressions.

The cowboy murmured something to Parker, who nodded and whispered something back to the cowboy, who frowned. After a few more minutes, they departed, and I spent the rest of the evening wondering if I had just seen my buyer. Parker hadn't brought anyone else up to my tank like that before. As I glanced at the evil bracelet on my wrist, fear began to poison the excitement and hope that had been flooding my body all evening, leaving me cold.

Just after one a.m., during the circuitous, paranoid ride back to the office building, Parker confirmed my fears.

"You won't believe the offer I just received!" he gushed as he leaned forward in the seat beside my wheelchair. He turned to me, his eyes bright. "He offered me one hundred and fifty *million* for you! Can you believe it? *One hundred and fifty million!*" he squealed, his voice cracking at the shrillness of his words. "I mean, while that oni sold in record time, it was purchased for only forty-five million. I know horses that are more expensive," Parker cackled.

My throat constricted as Parker babbled on about the amount he was going to receive, and what prices other items at the conference had gone for. If that obscene amount of money was the current top price for me, the buyer wouldn't be too pleased if their purchase escaped just after forking over all that cash. Who knows what lengths they'd go to to recover their lost prize.

"I mean, selkies usually go for several million or so," Parker continued, "because they're so hard to find and catch, either as humans or as seals, and for a while, even though I pitched your one-of-a-kind-ness amazingly, I thought you being a selkie sub-species was going to bring the value down. But no! He wants you for one hundred and fifty million dollars!" Parker thumped the seat in front of him with unsuppressed elation. He quickly stopped pummeling the seat and took several breaths, calming himself.

"Of course, I told him I would have to wait till the end of the convention tomorrow, when the rest of the bids come in, but I didn't reveal to him that his was far and away the highest bid I've received!" He paused, thinking. "Hmm, maybe I should spread the rumor about his bid. Or I can tell him I've gotten an even higher offer . . . he may up his price, and I may start a real bidding war!"

I sat quiet in my chair, but my mind and heart were anything but still.

Tomorrow was the last night of the convention. Afterward, I would be handed over to my new owner right there at the convention hall, and Parker and I would split ways. And if this person was willing to pay a hundred and fifty million for me, I had no doubts he had the means to keep me under lock and key better than Parker could.

I clenched my hands together to keep them from shaking. My time was running out.

I had to get out.

Tonight.

Chapter Twenty

I could barely sit still in my tub while I waited for the dinner that Parker had promised me back when I was being unloaded from the van.

"You shall eat like royalty! I'm sure any bloated tummy you get will shrink by tomorrow night in time for the convention. A spot of a midnight snack shouldn't hurt," Parker had said, his jovial tone almost kind, were it not for his barbed words.

But I didn't care. I didn't care if Parker called me stupid or ugly or fat, because I would be having the last laugh. The second my meal was over and I knew Parker had retired to his soundproof room for the night, I was getting out of here.

Fear made it hard to swallow as I considered practicing controlling the guards. The best time would be when the guard brought me my food. I could practice on him, hopefully without raising suspicion. I assumed I would have to be confident in my ability for it to fully work on them, but fear kept dampening my courage. What if I failed? What if this didn't work? No, I was determined to get out of this place within the next hour. I would also have to find some way around this bracelet.

Smashing it seemed my best bet, and I would have to find something hard enough to break magic-reinforced plastic. It wasn't like it was steel. I could probably even get one of the guards to get it off, possibly after I'd eaten. I would convince him to take it off me.

There was a playful, four-note knock on my door, and then to my horror, instead of a guard bringing my meal, Parker entered, bearing a long tray laden with several small plates.

"What are you doing here?" I blurted out, my stomach shriveling. Parker paused, cocking his head at me.

"What? I thought I'd share a last meal with my pet before we part ways." His lips pouted at me as though the thought made him sad.

I swallowed, trying to wet my mouth that had gone as dry as the Nevada desert. "We've never shared a meal before; why start now?" I said through clenched teeth, trying to still my panicking heart. How long was he planning on this "last meal" to last? Parker could blather on for hours. I had to suppress the urge to vomit.

"I had some very special things sent up, just for you, my little golden ticket!" He winked at me, and I grimaced at how disgustingly thrilled he was acting. "I wanted to share it with you." He lowered the tray onto a mini table provided by one of the guards, and then the guard stood in the doorway, watching us.

Now I really was going to throw up. Could I never catch a break?

However, that feeling of nausea turned to ravenous hunger as I looked at the food set before me. Green olives, cheeses, salami, crackers, grapes, shards of chocolate, pickles, berries, bread, and nuts were arrayed on the tray.

"Dig—" Parker began, but I was already grabbing handfuls of olives, nuts, and bread and stuffing them into my face.

Parker laughed as he watched me with a slightly disgusted smile on his face. "Oh, you silly creature."

I ignored him as I stacked several salami rounds and cheese onto a cracker and shoved them into my mouth along with several grapes, not wanting to give away the method to my madness: the sooner the food was gone, the sooner Parker would leave. Hopefully.

Plus, I *was* starving.

I watched Parker out of the corner of my eye as he spread Brie over a thin slice of baguette and plucked a few grapes from the tray, popping them into his mouth with exaggerated slowness. He exhaled as he chewed, watching me. "I will miss you, pet."

I couldn't stop the snort of laughter that spewed bits of cheese and chocolate onto his suit. "Sure. You just happen to all of a sudden get swept up in sentimentality that doesn't exist."

"Nonsense," Parker said, blotting at his suit with a grimace. "You're the first creature to break my previous record of sixty-three million dollars. A true feat for me. Oh yes, I know it's small fry compared to what HAMMA cooks up," he said, gesturing to the wall beside me, where Angelina was no doubt sleeping on the other side, "But then, I don't have to share all that wealth with my thousands of followers. I get to keep it all for myself. Not bad for a couple of weeks' worth of work, if I do say so myself."

"Is there a point to this speech you're making? Can't you rehearse it to yourself in your bedroom?" I snapped, feeling goosebumps shiver down my spine, recognizing the hypnotizing power rising within me. I inwardly cringed and snapped my mouth shut.

Easy, I rebuked myself, willing the feeling to settle. I could see the very faint ripple of the magic around him, still protecting him from any influence, and I didn't want to blow my hand just because Parker was being more pretentious than usual.

Thankfully, Parker didn't seem to notice anything, because he just laughed. "Oh, I have. This is the performance."

I rolled my eyes as I slid more salami slices into my mouth. I stopped chewing for a brief moment, an idea popping into my mind.

Swallowing, I grimaced and then began itching around the bracelet.

"Ugh, this thing is so itchy!" I complained as I tried to stick a finger beneath the band. "I think the saltwater is getting trapped under it and giving me a rash."

"Oh, I'm sorry about that," Parker said, not sounding sorry at all as he bit into an olive.

"Can't you take it off, if just for a little while?" I asked, violently scrubbing my nails over my arm, causing large red welts to appear on my skin.

"Hey, hey! Careful," Parker said, sitting up and finally sounding concerned. "Don't hurt the merchandise!"

"Well, this thing is hurting me," I moaned, trying to sound pathetic. After a moment of watching me dig around the bracelet, Parker clicked his tongue.

"Very well, maybe just for a little bit." He took my arm and pressed his fingertips into the bracelet. After a few seconds, the bracelet made a whirring noise and disconnected, opening on a magical hinge.

I sighed in relief and rubbed my wrist, hoping to hide the "rash" that didn't exist.

"Thank you."

I considered asking him how the bracelet worked and if it had an alarm or something to alert him when I was getting far away, but I didn't want to blow it. I would just pray he'd forget to put the bracelet back on me.

Parker nodded and leaned back into his chair, snapping a piece of chocolate with his teeth. Hiding my "injured" arm in the water, I continued eating with my other hand as we fell into silence. I tried to ignore the studious looks and the way Parker's eyes raked down my body as I continued to eat. We finished off most of the tray in silence, and I prayed that Parker would find me boring and go to bed. However, he sat for several minutes, no longer eating, just looking at me and snapping a few photos of me with his phone.

The dinner platter was now basically clean, and I had to stop myself from licking the crumbs off it, yet Parker stayed, staring at me while humming dreamily to himself. After several minutes, the anticipation of escape curdled in my now-full stomach. I was never going to get away. For some reason, Parker was feeling overly sentimental, probably because the price on my head was so high, and so he would sit here with me all night and maybe all day tomorrow, reveling in his victory. I would never get the chance to even try making a break for freedom. Parker's magical protection made sure of that.

I swallowed convulsively, trying to keep down all the food that I had just gorged myself on.

I wouldn't be able to escape.

I bowed my head, trying to hide the welling tears in my eyes.

"You're tired," Parker said suddenly, and I jumped, looking up at him through misty eyes. "Yes, you are, I see that. Well, we best get to bed."

"What time is it?" I asked hurriedly, praying that Parker sitting here had only *felt* like hours, and that it actually hadn't been that long.

Parker shook back his sleeve. "Oh my, it's nearly two-thirty. Yes, we best get some shut-eye. Well, this was a lovely chat. I will miss you." He stood, and hope flared again in my chest so much that a gagging gasp escaped my lips. I hurriedly covered it with a fake burp.

Parker wrinkled his nose, then said, "And I must say, if you weren't an animal, you'd be very attractive."

I bit down hard on my tongue before giving him a weak smile. "Thank you."

He smiled. "You're sweet. When you're not behaving like a beast."

I could taste blood, but I smiled again, unable to hide the sarcasm. "Funny, I was thinking the same thing about you. Except the sweet part."

Parker laughed. "Don't I know it, darling."

He bent down to pick up the tray, and I reached to snag the very last piece of chocolate on the tray. Parker diverted from the tray and quickly snatched my hand, slapping the bracelet back on.

"Ow, hey!" I cried as the bracelet snapped shut around my wrist. "What are you . . . ?"

"You didn't really think I'd let you have this off while out of my sight, did you?" he asked as the blue lights glowed under his fingertips, and then he pulled away.

I wrestled with the urge to scream and thrash and rage at him for replacing the bracelet, but the thought that I just needed him out of the room so that I could get on with my escape forced me to sit still. I took several calming breaths disguised as yawns and then shook my head.

"I suppose not," I replied, forcing my tone to be calm. Before I could flinch away from him, he patted my cheek and then hefted the tray. Just before passing through the door, he turned back to me.

"Good night, pet. You probably won't see me until just before the conference," he said, stifling a yawn. "I'm not used to these late nights, and I've been hibernating like a bear these past couple of days in that comfortable bed." He chuckled at his joke, then exited the room, oblivious to the venom-filled glare I sent after him.

The door closed, and I was left alone with a newfound hope beginning to swell inside me.

A laugh bubbled up out of me. "Yes, maybe it will be a good night, indeed, Parker."

Chapter Twenty-One

In the minutes after Parker's departure, my hope deflated. Why did he feel the need to tell me I wouldn't be seeing him? Was it a trick? Or was he just flaunting the fact that he had a comfortable bed so he was able to sleep for sixteen hours straight? He had to know I didn't have that luxury. But was he suspicious of an escape attempt?

After a half hour of mulling and waiting and agonizing over his words and the fact that my bracelet was back on, I slammed a fist down into the tub water. It didn't matter! It didn't matter if it was a trick. I was going to get out. Now. This fear-driven procrastination had wasted enough time.

I only had to hope that Parker was asleep by now.

Licking my lips, I looked toward the door. "Hey, hello? Hey!"

At my call, one guard unlocked the door and stepped inside the room. He was fairly young, dressed in the navy blue uniform of Parker's colors. He didn't have a gun, but there was a radio strapped around his waist.

"What?" he demanded, frowning at me, a lit cigarette in his hand. I took a deep breath, the acrid smell of the smoke burning my nose.

"Put that out," I commanded, my heart hammering against my ribs.

He glanced at his cigarette, then scowled at me. "No."

Anger and fear flooded me, and I let them envelop me as I tried again. "It stinks. It's bothering me. *Put it out.*"

The man stilled, and then, with a vaguely blank look on his face, dropped the smoldering cigarette and put out the glow with the twist of a foot.

"*Can you tell me how many guards are out there?*" I asked as the man looked down at his ruined cigarette with a miffed expression on his face.

"Just me, why?"

"Isn't there supposed to be two of you out there? Where's your partner?" I breathed. I prayed he was the only one on duty. Having to influence only one person would be much easier than two. "*Tell me.*"

"I owe Erikson a favor. Don't tell Parker. Parker said he always wanted two guards here, but Erikson wanted to get some quick shut-eye. I'm supposed to wake him in an hour."

My pulse quickened in excitement. "Don't you get bored?"

He looked at me with narrowed eyes. "Why are you asking me all these questions?" he asked.

"I'm bored. Aren't you?" I paused, then with a rush of fear, asked, "*Tell me if you get bored.*"

"Yeah, I get bored."

I calmed any excitement that tried to bubble to the surface as a smile.

"Is Parker in his room? *Tell me.*"

"Yes."

My breath seemed to flutter in my lungs. Now was my chance. My fear was solidifying to anger and commitment. No more idling around. I could influence him well enough, and I was wasting time.

"*Tell me when the guard changes,*" I demanded, confidence rushing through me.

"I just got on half an hour ago, and I have a three-hour shift," he replied, his voice almost monotone.

"Okay, okay, okay," I breathed, thinking quickly. "*Listen, I need you to get me a set of towels and one of your clean uniforms. With underclothes if you can find some. Right now. Don't let anyone know what you're doing, and if they ask, say you spilled something,*" I commanded, putting all the force I could muster into the command. I had no idea if I was making the persuasion more effective or not, but it was all I could do right now.

The man nodded and left, shutting the door behind him, and I hoped it wasn't to report to Oliver how weird I was being, my odd requests, or that he was feeling strange when he talked to me.

As quietly as I could, I hefted myself up and out of the tub, landing on the floor with a wet thud. I scooted toward the bench, which was bolted to the wall, and with a lot of grunting and heaving, I got up off the puddled floor and seated myself on the bench. I began using my hands to wipe the water that clung to my fur, hoping to speed up my metamorphosis. After getting out as much seawater from my fur as I could muster, I sat, waiting with a hitched breath at every sound, wondering if I was about to get caught.

After a longer time than I had wanted, the guard finally arrived with a stack of towels and a folded uniform on top, complete with a folded set of boxers.

"*Tell me, did anyone see you?*" I asked, turning my anxiety into anger to channel the magic.

"No one," he replied.

I exhaled in relief. "Hand me the towels and uniform."

The man didn't move. He frowned, his eyes unfocusing, and he shook his head. My heart leapt into my throat.

"I said, 'hand me the items, now,'" I commanded, my voice firm. Still he hesitated, and I saw a hand reach for his radio at his side, his eyes losing their fog.

"*Stop!*" I gasped, truly angry and afraid now, and the adrenaline rushed into my blood, the influence singing through me. No, I was not going to choke here, not when I had come so far! "*Do not touch your radio,*" I commanded. A wave of something surged through the room, and the man's hand dropped away from his radio.

"*Hand me the items,*" I repeated. "*And give me the card key and passcode for the elevator.*"

"I do not have a key or code," he replied, his voice again blissfully empty as he placed the stacked items in my arms.

"*Can you sneak a card? And casually ask for the code,*" I asked, heart pounding. "*Without getting caught?*"

He paused, but not because he was coming out of it. I could see that he was considering my question. "Yes," he finally replied.

"*Good, go do that.*"

Without a word, he left, and I began to dry my fur with a vengeance, wrapping the towels around my tail and wiping down my damp hair and torso. I wanted to take off the damp corset top, but I didn't have a bra, so I left it on for support, putting the dry uniform top on over it.

I glanced at the tracker again, my stomach squirming anxiously. It wouldn't matter if I got away scot-free if I had this tracker on me. I would just have to find a way to destroy it enough that the device would be useless. I had debated jumping into the nearest canal and swimming far away before trying to get the bracelet off, but I figured that my best chance at finding some way to get it off would be here in this high-tech city. Afterward, I could jump into the water and disappear forever.

Soon I was dry enough that the volts began surging through my body, and within a few seconds, my legs were back. Standing on the bench, a little shaky, I slipped on the boxers and pants, both of which were too big. I tucked and folded them to keep them up as best as I could, then waited for my unwilling participant to return, feeling more terrified now that I was so close.

I didn't have to wait long for the guard's return, though.

He wasn't alone.

Oliver was accompanying my current guard, who was stuttering and blithering out excuses, looking dazed. Blood roared in my ears at the sight of the herculean man, and panic threatened to make me lose focus. But I was too close to freedom to get foiled now, and anger filled me, giving me power.

Seeing me through the doorway standing on my bench and dressed in a uniform, Oliver stopped in his tracks, still gripping the muttering guard by one arm.

"What is the meaning of this?" Oliver asked, hand racing to his radio.

"*Don't you dare touch that radio, Oliver,*" I thundered, and waves of goosebumps erupted over my skin. I was relieved to see that I wasn't the only one: I could see the hairs standing up on both men's arms, as though a sudden gust of glacial wind had whipped over them. Oliver stopped dead, staring at me with a dumb expression.

"*You have charge of the keys, Oliver. You will accompany me down the elevator and out to the street. Carry me out of the cell, Oliver, and don't let me get wet. Now,*" I commanded. I'd never really tested if touching any amount of seawater, no matter how small, would change me back, and I wasn't going to take any chances now. Dropping the first guard's arm, Oliver strode forward and picked me up so fast I felt dizzy. Within two seconds, I was outside my cell, and on solid ground, on my own two feet.

"*You, what's your name?*" I asked the first guard, who stood about, looking confused.

"Adrian."

"*Adrian, open this door,*" I said, gesturing to Angelina's door, which the guard hurried to unlock. Angelina lay on her cot, but sat up, bleary-eyed, as the door banged open.

"Angelina. Come on," I said. I had been considering it while I had dried off, and I knew releasing her was the best thing to do. Even though she had betrayed me, there was no way I was going to leave her here. Besides, it would put me in her debt, should a situation arise where we would meet again.

Also, it gave me plausible deniability. I didn't want Parker learning about my ability in any way, even if I never saw him again, so this was the best way to throw him off any suspicion that I'd gotten out under my own power. He would immediately suspect the missing HAMMA girl.

Angelina rubbed her eyes and stared at me with a stunned expression.

"What's going on?" she breathed, looking between the two blank, motionless men. "Are they helping us escape?"

"*Shh*," I commanded, having no time for questions, and Angelina fell silent, her eyes glazing over as I turned to my two mindless minions. I could understand now why Parker liked having so many men to order around. It felt good being in control.

"*Now, Adrian, go find me a hammer or something to smash this bracelet with. Quietly, and hurry back.*" Before Adrian had disappeared from sight, I had turned back to Oliver.

"*Oliver, can you get this off me?*" I asked, holding up my wrist. "*Tell me.*"

Oliver shook his head. "Only Parker can. It's programmed to his fingerprints."

"*Is Parker asleep?*"

Oliver nodded.

"*Could I get into his room to use his fingerprints to take it off without waking him?*" I asked.

Oliver shook his head. "He has his own set of alarms he sets up in the rooms he stays in, for his own protection, no matter where he's at. Not even the crew knows all of them."

I shook my head. It had been a long shot, but I figured I might as well ask. Good ol' Paranoid Parker.

Adrian returned, bearing a hammer, and I tucked it into my pants. A thought struck me that gave me pause.

"*Tell me, Oliver, are there cameras in this building?*" All my preparations to have Parker think I hadn't gotten out myself would be useless if he saw me on a security feed commanding his personal guards.

Oliver shook his head. "The entire complex is owned by friends of Parker. They don't want records that could implicate them concerning the things that go on here."

Friends of Parker. Criminals. I shuddered at what other things had been done here, things probably worse than what was happening to me, but I kept my resolve and looked at Oliver.

"*Okay, Oliver, I want you to accompany us to the nearest exit, where no one will see us, and where we can access the street. Got it?*"

He nodded.

"*Adrian, return to your post. You will forget what I said to you and what you did to help me escape, do you understand me?*" He nodded, glaze-eyed, and sat in his chair between the two cell rooms. Angelina stared at me with an incredulous look on her face as I turned to Oliver.

"*Oliver, Angelina, let's go. Quickly and quietly. Remember, the least trafficked way out.*"

With a nod, Oliver led us down the hall to the elevator, where we hurried inside and Oliver compliantly inserted the key card and entered the code. Instead of going to the parking lot, Oliver pushed the first floor button. He led us down a dingy hallway to a door that read *Exit, door locks when shut* in small English letters below large Japanese ones. He pushed it open, and tears stung my eyes as fresh air hit my face. I was *standing* outside for my first time in days. But I wasn't in the clear yet. Under the shadows of the building, I turned to Oliver.

"*Can you break this, Oliver?*" I held out the hammer and my arm with the tracker. "*Carefully! Don't break my arm.*"

He took the hammer, and after a moment's deliberation, he gently twisted my arm and braced the tracker against a corner of the doorway to separate my arm from the bracelet as much as possible.

"Curl your wrist away," he instructed in a monotone. I bent my wrist inward, then held my breath as Oliver began firmly striking the hammer head against the edge of the plastic bracelet. I winced at the jarring blows, but it didn't hurt too much.

His hits were always on the mark, but I was still nervous, especially since every blow seemed to echo across the quiet street. The bracelet itself made no sounds that it was being damaged. After several minutes, with Oliver's hits getting harder and harder, I called for him to stop and inspected the bracelet. There were a few small dents, but there was no way to know if it was still functioning. After a moment of trying to wriggle my wrist free, the dang thing still wouldn't come off.

"Ugh, this isn't working," I breathed, looking at the dinged plastic with growing alarm and hatred. The bracelet weighed me down more than anything that had happened to me so far This was the symbol of Parker's hold on me, and I would get it off first, or die trying. I would probably find better ways of getting it off in the city. Maybe a tech store would have something.

I had no idea how long my persuasion would last on these men once I was gone, or if commands given to them would continue to take effect once my influence had worn off, but I figured I would try giving them commands that lasted, just to cover my bases in case it did work.

"*Do you have money?*" I asked. "*Japanese money? Or American dollars? I want all you have.*"

Without replying, though his movements were jerky, as if he were a robot having trouble computing a command, he pulled out a wallet, where an obscene amount of cash resided, no doubt because Parker didn't want to carry money on himself. I took all of the cash, giving a few of the different bills to a still-silent Angelina before stuffing the rest into my pants pocket.

"*Oliver, you will not remember what I told you to do. You will not remember what I can do, and you will not tell Parker. If he asks, say the HAMMA girl broke me out.*" I ignored the indignant look from Angelina, but continued to stare Oliver down. "*Do not tell him I influenced you in any way, okay?*" The fewer people that knew about my gift, the better. Especially Parker.

"Okay."

"*Good. Now go back. Don't tell Parker how I got out when he asks,*" I commanded as loudly as I dared, the goosebumps erupting on my skin again. The eagerness to get away was evident in my pounding heart and twitching muscles. Oliver charged back into the building, and, with a quick nod at Angelina, we took off into the night.

Chapter Twenty-Two

We ran until we came to a more brightly lit street where there were finally signs of life from early risers, or perhaps very late night owls. I figured I had limited time until Parker got an alert that I wasn't in his vicinity anymore, and I wanted to get as far away as I could before trying to get my tracker off. For that, I would need to get to the most crowded part of the city I could find. And for that, I would need a cab.

We turned and ran toward a street that was even more lit up, but I felt myself lagging. Being stuck in that tiny tub, not being able to sleep or eat or even *move* much had drained all of my endurance.

"Cor, wait, what happened back there?" Angelina panted as we ran onto a busier road.

"I got us out of there, that's what happened," I gasped over the sound of cars passing by. "And now, this is where we part," I said, waving my hand to hail a cab.

"What? Why?" she wheezed, her mouth falling open. Glancing at her, I had to stifle a laugh. She looked terrible; hair greasy, clothing mussed, with bags under her eyes. I knew I looked completely different, the magical makeup and hair products keeping me looking fresh. For a moment I was glad of Parker's makeover. Looking like a ragamuffin wouldn't ingratiate me to people when I needed to ask for help.

"Because you'll slow me down," I said as an occupied cab passed, and I began to wave down another. "This thing on my arm is a tracker, and I have to get it off before Parker is alerted that I'm gone so that I can disappear properly. I can't drag you along, you'll slow me down."

"But . . . what am I supposed to do?" she demanded as a black cab pulled over to the curb.

"Run back to HAMMA, go home, go free your mom?" I asked as I opened the cab door and glanced back at her with a stern look. "Do whatever you want for all I care. Just know, should we meet again, you owe me."

"Cor, wait! I . . . I really do want to be your friend!" she insisted as I turned my back to her. "I want to help you. I can help!"

I exhaled then shook my head. "I really wish I could believe that." Without a backward glance, I slid into the cab and slammed the door shut. "*Take me to the Osaka city center.* Maybe to a tech store? Hurry, please," I said to the driver, taking care not to look out the window at Angelina. With a nod, the driver pulled out into the street.

Though I was breathing easier now, my nerves were frayed as I watched the buildings pass by. For now, most of the structures were apartments or office complexes, but the farther we got into the city, the buildings grew, and the city lights and crowds began to multiply.

Seeing all the people talking or staring at their phones brought a sudden idea to mind. I leaned forward toward the driver.

"Excuse me, may I borrow your phone?" I asked, pointing at his phone attached to the car's dash.

He glanced at me in the rearview mirror.

"*Your phone, let me borrow it, please,*" I intoned, pointing again. He unhooked the cellphone and handed it back without a word. Everything on the screen was in Japanese, but I was able to pull up the phone app and type in actual numbers. I dialed my mother's number. As I pressed the phone to my ear, tears filled my eyes.

Please answer, please answer, I chanted in my mind. She had to be sick with worry.

There was a squealing tone, and a woman's voice said, "We're sorry, the number you've dialed cannot be reached. Please try again." I bit back a scream. I redialed, but got the same message. Why was my mother's phone disconnected? Was being in another country throwing something off? I couldn't even leave a message on her voicemail, telling her of my plight or where I was!

As I handed the phone back, I realized that this knowledge made it more imperative that I get away. Maybe HAMMA had discovered my hybrid status by now and had already gotten my mother, and that meant that no one was coming to help me.

I sat back in my seat, nearly nibbling my bottom lip to nothing in anxiety.

By the time I got into the city where there were actual skyscrapers and buildings to hide in, I was practically dancing in the back seat. If the tracker hadn't been damaged at all by Oliver's hammering, Parker would be aware that I was gone, and hot on my trail. I was, after all, a one-hundred-fifty-million-dollar asset.

Though it was just after three in the morning, the streets were just as busy as they were during the day, but more beautiful. Lights upon lights blazed in the city, the waterways reflecting the neon jungle as we drove through the crowded streets.

Finally, I couldn't take it anymore. For all I knew, this guy was just going to keep driving until we reached the other end of Japan. I called to him, and, in English, told him to stop. He immediately pulled over, and I quickly paid him and hopped out of the cab, my nerves jangling.

I ran the city streets, dodging cars and bikes, the lights blazing overhead. I occasionally popped my head into stores to see if they sold electronics. My hope was, as this bracelet was electronic as well as magical, maybe someone who knew about phones could stop the electronic mechanisms somehow.

Finally, I found a tiny corner shop where phones and tablets were on display in the front window. I dove inside and ran straight to the counter, where an older man was examining a customer's cracked phone. I had no time to be polite. I was going to be the pushy American.

"Excuse me, I need to talk to this man now," I said, trying to force the magic inside me out, to get them to understand. Both men turned to me and stared. I felt my cheeks grow hot as guilt and embarrassment flooded me, but I pushed on. It was an emergency.

"Listen, I need help," I replied, turning to the man behind the counter. I reached up and slapped a wad of money onto the counter. "*Please.*"

Both men looked at me, then at each other, and the first customer bowed out of the way.

"*Thank you,*" I emphasized to the now-waiting customer as I turned to the man behind the counter. I quickly held up my arm, pointing to my wrist.

"I need this off. *Off*," I said, pointing to it and pantomiming taking off the bracelet. The man frowned at me in utter confusion. I held out my wrist to him, this time motioning for him. "Do you have tools to unscrew or cut this?" I asked, gesturing to untwist or clip off the bracelet, using my fingers to mime scissors.

With a frown, the man inspected the bracelet, pulling a mini screwdriver out, but his frown grew more pronounced when he couldn't find a seam or clasp to open the bracelet. The man turned away and went through a door, coming back with some scissors. He handed them to me, where I took them up so fast I almost cut off one of my fingers, and began to saw at the plastic with the scissors. It made some shallow marks, but otherwise no harm was done to it. It wouldn't cut.

I cast the man a helpless look, and, now aware of my desperation, he held up a hand and again disappeared into a back room. I panted and drummed my fingers on the counter, looking back at the store entrance, expecting black ops to come bursting in at any moment.

The store clerk came back with some heavy-duty wire cutters, took my wrist, and very gently began to snip at the plastic.

His frown seemed to become permanently ingrained as the wire cutters made just as little damage as the scissors had.

But he also looked curious, and I didn't wonder. A high-tech piece of never-before-seen equipment like this was probably intriguing. I was starting to get really desperate now. I couldn't stay in one place for very long.

I had no doubt the tracker still worked. If cutters couldn't cut through this plastic, then there was no way a hammer would've damaged the workings inside.

If Parker pinpointed my location, they would be on me in minutes: nowhere in the city, in the entire world, was far enough away from Parker. I growled as the bracelet refused to be cut. The owner now looked concerned, and I had no doubt he probably thought I was either crazy, or by my reactions to my bracelet, that I had a ticking time bomb on me. Which wasn't far off.

It was time to go. They would be no more help to me. Thanking the man, and bowing slightly, I ran out the door, leaving the confused looks behind. I ran into the street, panicked. I considered the honking, rushing traffic, and for a brief moment contemplated putting my arm under the wheel of a passing car, but I quickly dismissed it. I wasn't behaving rationally: I was acting like a wolf in a trap. I shouldn't have to chop off my whole arm to be free of this horrid thing. I was smarter than that. Besides, knowing my luck, I'd break my entire arm, and the dang bracelet still wouldn't even budge.

I ran down the street and saw an open doorway. Hoping for something to be of use here, I dodged inside it. My mouth fell open and I came to a full stop just within the doorway.

Inside the gigantic building, it looked like I was in an enormous outdoor market. Neon lights flashed in every direction, each one screaming for attention. People flooded the place, and after getting over my awe, I plunged into the crowd. I ran past shops of all kinds: stands that were selling vegetables or meat or sweets, booths offering little knickknacks, and food being cooked on open fires behind counters lining the thoroughfares.

Fire.

Seeing the flames, an idea sparked in my mind. I could try melting my bracelet off somehow. I grimaced at the thought. I would most likely get extremely burned in the process, but it was worth a try. And better than the alternative.

Over the shouting and chaos behind one counter, I snuck behind the bar and half hid myself behind one of the stovetops that spurted open flame. I grabbed a nearby knife and gingerly stuck it into the flames, trying to keep out of sight. One of the cooks turned, and, seeing me, began shouting at me in Japanese, but I stood my ground, staring him down. He stopped his shouting and forward trajectory toward me and stared back in confusion. I wasn't going to run. There was no where I could go, no way to be truly free, if I couldn't get this off.

Desperation took over as I looked the man in the eye.

"*Please ignore me*," I ordered, and I felt the powerful force of persuasion flow from me. The man's eyes glazed as he lowered the arm he had been pointing at me and turned away.

Relief seeped through me. Magic seemed to help the idea I was trying to convey pass through the language barrier.

I turned back to the knife, which was getting hot in my hand. I grabbed a dry, folded towel near the counter, using it to hold the knife handle. After several more moments, I pulled the blade out of the flames. The metal glowed a dull red, and I could feel the heat of it just looking at it.

Taking a deep breath, I pressed the flat side of the heated knife to my bracelet, hoping to soften the plastic. I bit my cheeks to keep from screaming as the heat radiating from the blade instantly began to burn my skin. The plastic sizzled and hissed, but it wasn't making much progress. Twisting the knife blade down, I made quick sawing motions against the bracelet, which seemed to do a little better in making marks on the plastic, but it wasn't enough.

I quickly pulled the knife away, eyes watering at the smarting on the back of my red wrist, and inspected the tracker. Melted gouges marred the dark plastic, but it was barely even enough to notice. I stuck the knife back into the flames, keeping the towel wrapped around the handle. After several agonizing moments, I pulled the knife out of the fire again. I shuddered when I thought about putting it near my skin again.

Think smarter, Cordy!

I looked around the bustling stall, searching for something to help. At that moment, one of the cooks dropped another towel on the floor, and before he could notice, I pounced on it. I quickly wrapped the towel around any exposed, burned skin near the bracelet, tucking it under the bracelet as best as I could to hold it in place.

Feeling a little better, I began sawing at the bracelet again in the same melted furrow as before. The bracelet began to heat up, and my skin began to smart and sting despite the towel, but again, not much damage was done to the plastic.

Biting back a scream of rage, I threw the knife down. This would take too long. It would take up all my precious time to take it off, and I would get third-degree burns or worse before ever getting it off! I was running out of time, I had to find a smarter way!

Ducking out of the food stall, I began running down the crowded thoroughfares, holding my burned arm, looking for something, anything, that would shine a light on my dimming hope. People passed by, everyone intent on their own business. Even though I felt alone in the sea of people, there was no hiding until I was freed.

As I was passing another lively food market, something strange on the air tickled my senses. It wasn't the smell of smoky food from stalls or the sounds of people and music. It was a shivery kind of feeling, resembling the sensation I felt on my skin when I persuaded people.

Magic?

If magic made this bracelet, magic could destroy it. I turned, searching for the source of the magic, and could somehow feel it coming from down a path between some crowded carts. I blindly followed the familiar feeling that was flowing out into the market and streets beyond, hurrying down an alleyway, passing laden stalls and carts until I came to a small storefront where herbs and vegetables sat in organized displays in the front window. The magic was almost tangible as I stood before the front door. Choking down a cry of relief, I flew inside the tiny shop. An aging Japanese man with graying hair and a clean-shaven face was helping an even older-looking woman at the counter, showing her something wrapped in a cloth.

Both turned to me as I entered with a wild cry of, "Please help me!"

The moment their eyes fell on me, they both gasped. Within an instant, the woman began hissing and spitting at me. Shouting in Japanese, she charged at me, making odd gestures with her hands. I jumped away, making a basket of some round, odd-looking fruit tumble to the ground in order to avoid her clawing fingers. After spitting in my face, the woman ran past me, out the door, and out of sight.

"*You*," the man barked in English, and I whirled to look at him, hope bubbling in my chest. It was short-lived, as the man was glaring at me. "You're *zasshu*! Hybrid! Get out, get out! You drive away my customers!"

"No, please!" I begged, stumbling forward, making the man retreat several steps. "I need your help!"

"I can't help you. Get out!" he said, waving me away as he moved toward a door back behind the counter.

"*Please!*"

The man paused, and I hadn't realized I'd used my influence without meaning to. I would make him help me. Calling upon the desperation pumping through me, I looked him in the eye. "*Help me!*"

He didn't speak for a moment, but looked at me with a careful expression. "What do you want, hybrid?"

"I need your help getting this off!" I pleaded, shaking my burned wrist at him, the bracelet glinting dully in the dim light. "It's magic. I need it off! *Please get it off.*"

"Do not try and use your influencing magic on *me*, mixling," the man snapped, and my mouth fell open. I quickly collected myself.

"Oh, I . . . I'm sorry," I stammered. He didn't move, just glared at me. Taking a deep breath, I looked at him again. "Please, I don't mean you any harm. Bad people are after me, and I need this off me. Please." My voice unexpectedly cracked on the last word, and I saw the man soften. But not by much.

"I don't like hybrids. Too unpredictable."

"Please. Just get it off me and you'll never see me again! I promise!" I insisted, thrusting my arm at him again.

After an agonizing pause, he smacked his lips in annoyance and came toward me. "Let me see."

I held still, my arm still extended as he approached, and he gingerly took my wrist, glancing up at me when I hissed in pain as he touched my burned skin, then looked back at the bracelet.

"Yes, magic is woven in this material, making it very durable. It also contains a tracking device powered with magic." He fell silent, studying the bracelet, and I nearly cried out in frustration as he took his time. He glanced up at me as if he knew my thoughts, giving me a reproving look before turning back to the bracelet. He ran a finger over the melted grooves and cracks along the plastic. "The tracker is still active, despite your obvious attempts to destroy it."

"Please, please destroy it!" I begged, my vision swimming, my head feeling lighter than air. I paused a moment to take several deep breaths. The man wrapped both hands over the bracelet and closed his eyes. I gasped as the plastic grew hot, stinging my already burned skin. Just when the heat was growing unbearable, the bracelet made a sharp, clicking *pop*, and the man pulled his hands away. The bracelet had cracked in several places, one chunk falling to the floor.

With a breathless cry of victory, I ripped the defunct manacle off and threw it on the floor in elation. The man gave me an annoyed look for the mess of plastic chunks I'd made on his floor.

"Sorry," I breathed, stooping to pick up the cracked pieces.

The front shop window shattered in a hailstorm of glass, dried herbs, and spraying tinctures, and there was a whistling, pattering sound of several things hitting the wall behind the counter. With a cry, I dropped fully to the ground. The old man shouted as he fell next to me, his body bristling with several tranquilizer darts as screaming erupted in the marketplace outside.

My heart froze as I checked myself. Finding myself free of darts, I glanced toward the ruined window. There was no sign of shooters between the panicked stampede of people running for cover, but I knew Parker's men would be coming.

The man beside me moaned, and I crawled over to him, glass shards cutting into my hands and knees.

"I'm so, so sorry!" I cried as I leaned over him and began ripping out tranquilizers, but, gurgling over the sounds of running and screaming outside the shop, the man grabbed my hand to stop pulling darts out of him. Tugging me close to his face, the man whispered, "A window, room behind the counter. Now go."

I was up and running, dodging into the doorway behind the counter just as I heard more gunfire and the peppering of tranqs in the wall behind me. I entered a tiny living space, where a narrow window was placed just above the sofa. I jumped onto the sofa and wrenched open the window, punching out the screen. Wriggling, I got my head and shoulders through as shouting emanated from the front of the shop. I tried pulling the rest of myself through, but my hips became wedged in the frame.

With a muffled feral scream, I pushed on the outside wall with all my strength. My hips burned as they, and the rest of my body, squeezed through the small window, and then I was falling through the air. I banged my elbow against the wall as I hit the ground on my back, nearly knocking the wind out of me.

Not taking a moment to catch my lost breath, I got to my feet. Gritting my teeth against the stinging cuts on my hands and knees—my blazing lungs screaming for air—I was up and running. I sprinted through the cluttered alleyway and back into the crowds of the marketplace, searching for an exit to the streets outside. I had to get to a waterway!

After passing flower stalls, food carts, and hundreds of people, I finally burst out of the market complex and into the busy street, where cars and lights and even more people passed. I could lose my pursuers in the crowd, make it to the waterway, any waterway, and escape. For real. Without any worry of being tracked.

I bolted into the street, nearly getting hit by cars and smashing into slow pedestrians as I blasted my way through the city streets, searching, feeling for any nearby water. In a city full of water, how was there none nearby, now that I needed it most?

I skidded to a stop, backpedaling as several people in Parker's yacht uniform weaved through the crowd toward me. I turned and went to duck down another street, and a scream of relief escaped my throat as I saw water glinting in the city lights.

I could make it!

As I ducked around the crowds, heading toward the lights dancing off the breathtaking water, a uniformed man jumped out from a car passing in front of me, tackling me to the ground. I screamed, picking up road rash as I tumbled to a stop. Before I could get to my feet, the man jumped onto me, pinning me to the ground. He tried to put a hand over my mouth while he fumbled for his gun, but I bit down hard on fingers that had gotten into my mouth. With a cry, he reeled backward, clutching his hand.

"*Get off me!*" I screamed, heart thudding in my ears, my whole body jolting with heat. The man's eyes instantly glazed over and he fell sideways off of me. I scrambled to my feet, and turned to swerve away from an oncoming crowd, when something pierced my elbow. A numbing sensation swirled up my arm. Horrified, I groped for the dart as I pushed through the crowd, pulling it out, but keeping it as a weapon.

My vision flashed, but the water ahead flashed brighter.

I would make it! I had to. If I could just get to the water, I could swim until I was completely knocked out, and sleep under the water, untrackable in the deep expanse. Safe. I shoved people out of the way, but I was slowing, and I heard several pairs of running footsteps on the concrete behind me.

I stumbled as another dart got me in the calf. I tried to reach behind to pull it out, but I stumbled again and almost fell. A few people stared at me with confusion puckering their faces as I staggered through the crowds; however, most ignored me, not worrying about things that weren't their business.

I didn't care—no one could save me but me.

The water beckoned a few yards away.

A third and fourth dart pierced my back, and the feeling left both my legs as I tried and failed to leap over the first of several railings that separated the sidewalks from the canal. I collapsed to the ground, gasping, the water just a few feet from me. I tried to roll over, to crawl, but my body wasn't responding. As I tried rolling again, I saw a towering, vibrant electronic sign on one of the buildings a ways down. The man on the sign was running. His arms, which seemed to be raised in victory, felt like a slap in the face, a taunt, while my body lay below in a useless, floppy mass.

A crowd of curious people gathered over my fallen body, their features blurred as my body finished turning into jello. Was no one going to fight for me? It was obvious I was being attacked, the darts visible on my body, yet no one tried to help me. They just stood there. Spectating. I wondered if I had cried for help if anyone would've done anything.

The lights of the city dimmed as several more, taller, dark shapes appeared before me, their voices authoritative as they shooed the crowd away, but as the tranqs took me, the dark shapes, too, dissolved into the blackness.

Chapter Twenty-Three

The telltale pain around the middle of my back was all I needed to figure out where I was as I started to come out of the sedatives. I didn't even have to open my eyes. The tub felt smaller and harder than ever before. My head throbbed, my body ached, and my wrist burned. Cold metal bit into my wrists, but I was unfortunately getting used to the feel of handcuffs. Though I was now shackled to the tub, my scalded wrist was suspended out of the water.

I lay still, not wanting to open my eyes to reveal the nightmare before me, so instead, I dwelt on the horrors inside my mind. At least I could escape from those when I wanted to, just by opening my eyes.

I had imagined that Noah pulling out his pocket knife and stabbing me was the worst thing that had ever happened to me. He was my boyfriend, the love of my life. I'd had stars in my eyes for him. I would get butterflies just thinking about him.

And he had tried to kill me.

I thought I would never recover, that my heart would never be the same. It had been the worst feeling I'd ever felt. Thinking about the overwhelming sense of betrayal and hurt and unrequited love left me breathless sometimes when I had dwelt on it. Nothing could top it.

Then I'd learned of my mother's lies, her deception, her failure to explain to me what I truly was, and that in the eyes of everyone I could relate to, I was a monster. I thought then that that was the lowest I could possibly feel.

Until I'd gotten kidnapped.

Being with Parker, and seeing his greed, his barbarity, as well as the cruelty of the human world as a whole, I felt I'd reached the bottom rung into the depths of the well of brutality, fear, and inhumanity. I was alone, forsaken with the worst creatures on earth.

All of those emotions paled in comparison to the horrible, dead feeling I had inside me now; a helpless, forsaken sensation, combined with the torment of fault. Self-blame pulsed through my body with every heartbeat. I had failed. It wasn't anything Parker had done. I could've easily escaped. A million new scenarios of escape now ran through my head, options I hadn't taken that would've allowed me to get away, or to get the bracelet off sooner.

I could've headed for the coast and swam for miles and miles, putting more distance between myself and Parker, making him have to take his boat out of port, which would have given me more time. I could've swum to the bottom of the ocean and worked on the bracelet until I'd gotten it off. Back in Maine, I had been able to dive down thousands of feet in the ocean, more than any human ever could without scuba gear. I could've stayed down there for weeks, eating fish and working on getting the bracelet off.

I could've taken more drastic steps, like actually cutting off my hand. Or at least cut off a couple of fingers so that the rest of my hand could've squeezed through. Or better still, I could've broken my hand so that the shattered bones could easily slide through the bracelet's grip. The hand would've healed. I should've put my arm under that passing car.

But no, I had played it safe. I had been trapped inside a box for so long that my mind had stayed inside the box. I'd been so focused on getting the bracelet off, I'd failed to realize that all my talents could've been used to aid my escape, that the bracelet wasn't as big of a problem as Parker had made it seem. Parker had gotten into my head, put fear in my heart that the bracelet was the key to his power over me, and so I had to take it off to show him he didn't own me.

My desire to throw that small victory in his face had been my downfall.

Gritting my teeth, I opened my eyes to escape the torrent of guilt building behind my eyelids. My burned wrist had a bandage around it and was dangling outside the tub to keep it from getting wet. A handcuff was clicked over the bandage. I could feel a cooling salve beneath the dressing, working on my ruined skin. My other wrist was also handcuffed to the other side of the tub. The cuts on my hands had been cleaned and were starting to scab over, but they still stung. My knees had morphed back into my tail, but I could see gouges in the fur of my tail where the cuts on my knees would have been.

The next thing I noticed was Parker, sitting beside my tub, watching me with a pale, furious expression.

With a groan I closed my eyes again, but snapped them open immediately as Parker kicked my tub hard, jolting my tub and causing water to slosh out the sides. I slowly turned my head to stare at him, too drained to feel anything but annoyance.

"Do you realize how much you almost made me *lose*?" he seethed.

I blinked once, keeping my face blank. Did he realize how much I didn't care? I'd lost more than he ever would. When I didn't reply, he clasped his shaking hands together, his knuckles growing white.

"How did you get out?" he rasped.

I blinked. "I really have no idea."

"Stop playing innocent. I want to know how you got out of here!" Parker demanded. "No one seems to know how you or that HAMMA girl escaped!"

"For your information," I spat back. "That HAMMA girl got me out, and I escaped from her," I lied. I was sure he would work out I was lying, especially if Oliver and the other man worked past my instructions, but I didn't care. There was no way I was going to tell him. Let the question torture him.

"Did she?" Parker sneered, "Well, lucky for us, HAMMA won't be able to bother us. They don't have support here in Japan; they're just an American and British institution for the time being. That's something to be grateful for, I suppose. Any attempt at a raid will be futile, even if one HAMMA agent is loose."

Parker glared at me, then stood so suddenly I jumped, sloshing more water out of the tub.

"However, you listen to me, and you listen good," he breathed, pointing a quivering finger down at me, his face blotchy with anger and, no doubt, anxiety that he had almost lost me, "I don't know how you got out, but I know it wasn't HAMMA. That girl may be Regina's daughter, but she's not crafty enough to be able to get the keys from my guards and sneak you out without anyone seeing. But

I'm going to get to the bottom of this. And tonight, I'm going to sell you for over one hundred and seventy five if I can."

The increase in price didn't scare me, and I just scoffed and looked away.

Parker paused, then his voice got a bit of his oily tone back. "And then, since I know you're not just a subspecies, but a *hybrid*, your mother must be a creature of some kind too."

I whipped my head back to face him, sweat beading on my forehead. He knew I was a hybrid?

"I'm going to track her down and sell her to the highest bidder. Callista, I believe is her name? It'll be easy to get her," Parker said, his pale face breaking into a sly smile at my gaping expression. "I'll just pretend I'm one of your friends' fathers and that you've been injured. She'll be leaping into my possession in no time."

The air left my lungs in a rush, and the burn on my arm seemed to blaze hot as my blood grew cold.

"*You—*" I choked back the desire to influence him. I would need a solid plan before attempting to use my gift on Parker himself, as I'd only have one shot at it. "Don't you touch her!" I snarled, straining against the handcuffs holding me down. I wanted to claw his face off, to take him and drown him in the tub. My mother would have no idea what was coming for her. "She didn't do anything!"

Parker's eyes screamed fury and determination, and I shrank into my tub.

"No, but you just did," he hissed with bared teeth. "Remember, I said I was nothing if not petty, and with your little escape attempt, you've just ensured your mother's capture."

I stared at him towering over me, and fury bubbled up in me. As he shifted, I realized he wasn't wearing his shield.

In one swift movement, I braced my hands on the tub rim and thrust my tail to the bottom of the tub before heaving it back upward. A wall of seawater crashed up into Parker's face, my tail slapping him under his chin. Parker slipped sideways, falling to his knees as he braced himself against the edge of my tub.

Fury spurred me on, and I brought my tail down on him again and again, knocking him face-first into my tub. As I pummeled him, for the second time in my life, the fire to kill came coursing through me, and I tried to keep him under what water remained with me in the bathtub.

However, after several moments, he managed to get the upper hand and slip out from under me. I continued to slap him as many times as I could until he fell backward and crawled out of range. Coughing and sputtering, he got to his feet through the torrent of my continued splashing.

With a roar, he lunged forward through the deluge and grabbed onto the very end of one of my flippers, digging his fingers into the fin and twisting it so hard pain shot up my entire tail. My hands slipped on their grip on the tub and I fell back against the tub bottom, pain raking across my nerves. Over my screams of pain, Parker shouted, "YOUR TEMPER WILL NOT SAVE YOU OR YOUR MOTHER!"

His eyes were savage, and his usually slicked back hair was sopping, clinging to his face. His manic expression sent jolts of fear through me as I tried to yank my tail out of his grip. He continued to shout over my shrieks of pain. "Now you listen to me, missy, I am not to be trifled with, DO YOU HEAR ME?" he bellowed, wringing my flipper harder, and I screamed out in agony again. His teeth were bared in a vicious smile. The terrifying expression filled my vision, and fear and rage pushed to get out of me as he crushed my fin with more pressure.

"*Stop hurting me!*" I bellowed, the mesmerizing influence in me bursting out before I could stop it, and I saw Parker pause, nearly letting go of my tail.

However, in an instant, Parker shook his head, his expression clearing. Parker straightened, staring me down. After wiping water from his face and straightening his soaking bedclothes, he exhaled.

"So that's how you did it," he breathed, leaning in closer to me, but remaining out of reach. "Nymph."

His expression sent a chill across my skin, and I felt the blood drain from my face. How was he able to shake off my influence so quickly? I stared, panting at him, my skin growing cold at the realization of what I'd done.

"No, no," I stammered. "*No, you will forget what you just learned!*" I demanded.

Parker half-paused, his eyes almost going foggy, but then he raised his hand and slapped himself across the cheek, hard enough to leave a red mark. His eyes cleared a bit.

"Don't. You. Influence. Me," he said through clenched teeth, his eyes coming back into full focus as he slapped himself with each word.

"*Forget,*" I commanded, sitting up in my tub, hoping to capture his attention fully, but he quickly stuffed his fingers in his ears as he retreated out of the room, shouting for Oliver.

"*Forget! FORGET!*" I screamed, the handcuffs biting into my skin as I pulled against them, but the door slammed shut behind him, cutting me off.

I sat back in my tub, my flipper throbbing, my heartbeat roaring in my ears.

What had I just done?

After just a moment, Parker returned, still sopping and disheveled, but I could see the shimmer of his protection around him. He didn't bother to shut the door as he came right up to my tub, leaning over me as he shoved his face right up to mine. His cheery expression was back.

"Thank you for giving me what I needed to know. I kept my protection off to entice you to show your hand, and I'm happy to say it worked. My men will now be protected, from both you and your mother, when we catch her. I'm assuming some type of water nymph. It would explain some of your attributes for fresh water. Naiad, perhaps? Now, naiads go for a pretty price," Parker said, his grin wolf-like. "Many billionaires like to use any type of nymph as trophy girlfriends, once they're sufficiently tamed. And if your looks are anything to go by, I can assume your mother is a stunner."

I sat in my tub, staring at nothing in paralyzed horror that I'd inadvertently given up my secret, my one advantage.

"Well, I'll definitely make sure to tell your new buyer these details. I wouldn't want to get a reputation that the items I sell can easily escape because I didn't know all the details of what I'm selling. I mean, how embarrassing would that have been? A man shelling out a hundred and fifty million dollars or more, and he can't have a guarantee that his new purchase won't escape?" He gave a shaky chuckle, a little color coming back into his wan face. "Also, I'm definitely asking the top bidder for more money: a selkie-naiad mix will certainly intrigue people."

Parker then pulled a walkie-talkie out from under his sodden robe. "Oliver."

Oliver appeared, looming in the doorway, a thick pair of over-ear headphones perched on his head. "Keep those noise-canceling headphones with the radio frequency on, keep me updated on any move she makes, and don't take your eyes off her for a second. I'll be gone for a few hours, buying more protective barrier pins for the men so none of them can be influenced again. I'll be able to breathe easy once this evening is over." With that, Parker left the room, and Oliver pulled up a chair in the doorway, settling down, his eyes trained on me.

I sat in the few inches of water that was left in my tub, numb. I couldn't even feel the pain in my tail anymore. Parker didn't bother to have the tub refilled, and it didn't matter if my legs came back. I wasn't going anywhere, not handcuffed to this tub, inside a cell, guarded by a man who I could no longer influence.

Parker knew my secret, and he would tell everyone. Everyone would know to take precautions around me for the rest of my life. Not that it would be much of a life.

I couldn't even cry, despite waves of despair, anger, and sadness battering against me. I had blown it. I had blown any chance of escape I'd had. I hadn't been fast enough, or smart enough, or daring enough. But I had been stupid enough to give Parker what he needed to know.

Disappointment and fatigue welled up inside me. Those feelings were replaced momentarily with fear, not only for myself, but my dear, wise, helpless, unsuspecting mother, who, thanks to me, would be rounded up and treated no better than cattle, as I had been.

I closed my eyes, feeling more tired, more drained than ever before. I just wanted to sleep. To sink beneath all these emotions that battered and crashed through me. To escape the failure I was, and hope for a better tomorrow. But tomorrow wouldn't be any better. I would be in another prison, with another owner, who would have an even better hold on me than Parker had.

All my emotions crumbled to nothing at that realization, and, feeling empty, I curled up into a lopsided ball, wishing to just fade away.

Chapter Twenty-Four

It felt like no time at all had passed when they came to load me up in my wheelchair for the final time, clearing out the rented apartment of everything Parker had brought. I barely noticed when Parker and a contingent of men came into my cell, all shimmering with their newly acquired magical protection bubbles. I stared at nothing, my mind empty as I was lifted from my tub and wrapped in the wet towels, tarps, and blankets. This time, Parker handcuffed me to my chair and covered my hands with extra blankets to keep any prying eyes from seeing the strange sight while out in public.

I didn't even flinch when some blood was drawn, no doubt for Parker's peace of mind now that the bracelet was gone, and then we were off.

Parker chattered on as we drove, but it was all background noise as I stared, unseeing, out the van window. I felt Parker elbow me once, as if trying to get some sort of reaction out of me, but I couldn't even feel annoyed.

I felt lost, adrift in my mind. I hadn't cried since being re-captured. I hadn't even been angry since Parker learned my secret.

I hadn't been anything. I knew I should feel scared at how I was feeling, or rather not feeling, but I couldn't muster up any sort of emotion. I didn't feel scared about being sold, worried about my mother being captured, sad about my future. I didn't think of who would be buying me, or what they would do to me. Nothing.

I was just empty.

Time passed in a blur, and when I came to myself again, I was in my tank. The glitzy gowns, lights, and exotic sights all seemed dulled as I stared out through the glass.

Sinking to the bottom of my tank, I sat on the scattered sand, and stared at the pathetic, lifeless scraps of kelp, limp and brown. Dead. Broken.

Without the energy to look at it any longer, my mind drifted back into the quiet nothingness.

Muted voices pulled me out of my emptiness for a moment. I hadn't noticed them before, and I realized it was because they were louder than usual. Flashes of light caught my attention, and I turned my head to look out the front of the tank. Parker was standing before my exhibit, a man standing beside him. They were shaking hands as camera lights flashed.

My new buyer.

I felt nothing. This was who I'd be leaving with. It didn't matter. A cage was a cage, it didn't matter where that cage was, or who was holding the keys. However, I did recognize him as the flashy cowboy from . . . yesterday? Was it yesterday? It felt like a lifetime ago. For half a moment, part of me wondered if Parker got the higher price for me like he'd wanted, before apathy swallowed any further questions in my mind. I watched with dazed disinterest as a table and chairs were brought up to my tank.

The two men sat, and Parker produced a piece of paper and a pen. Both men signed the paper amid more flashes from cameras. Once both signed the bill of sale, they took out their phones, watching the screens intently. After a moment, they raised their clasped hands, and there was the faint sound of applause as they stood again and shook hands, then turned around to look at me. I felt a jolt of disgust at the gleeful look on Parker's face, but it faded as soon as it appeared.

The cowboy was looking at me, an expression I couldn't place on his face. It definitely wasn't pity, but then again, it wouldn't matter if it was. I couldn't and wouldn't trust anything that came from a human ever again; they were always putting on a show, lying, trying to win you over for their own designs. So even if he did pity me, it didn't matter.

Nothing mattered.

Parker and the man moved away, no doubt to prep for moving me out of the tank once the party was over.

I turned away as more flashes of light lit up the tank, and the babbling crowd dissolved as my mind went back to its quiet place. A place where I didn't have to think about now, or tomorrow, or about anyone; not those I loved, and not those I hated. I could be selfish, and for once, not care about anything. It was safer. If you didn't care, you didn't get hurt when everything in the world failed you, disappointed you, betrayed you. The blank void was a place where I could reside forever. It was more tranquil, comfortable, and reliable than any place, or any person, in the entire world.

Something rippled across my skin, breaking the blankness. At first I didn't bother to see if someone had thrown something in the water. They wouldn't get a reaction out of me, no matter how many things they threw. Another surge, as tiny as it was, made me shift my shoulders in an attempt to dispel the feeling of pinpricks on my skin. I looked up.

There wasn't any debris in my tank, no shrimps, no beach balls, no coins. I looked around as the ripple echoed across my body again, and I realized it wasn't the rippling of the water around me. It was something else, dancing through the water, across my skin.

Something much more powerful than water. It tingled across my nerves and made my hair stand on end. I looked out at the crowd, and for a second, didn't see anything out of the ordinary . . . until I saw him.

He was wearing what looked like traditional Japanese robes, but he wasn't Japanese. He was tall, with dark hair and beard. At first I thought he was just another pretty face in the crowd, but while he was very handsome, it wasn't his looks that truly caught my attention for the first time that night.

It was his expression.

His eyes.

They were angry. No, furious. But confused as well.

It was an odd expression from someone who looked like they belonged here. It broke me out of my empty shell, and I stared at him, a ripple of curiosity skipping over me. As he looked at me, I realized his expression was a mixture of emotions: awe, confusion, anger, sadness, pain, exhaustion. I knew those looks, because I'd felt all of those emotions during my time here.

With wide eyes, he stared at me, his eyes so intense I felt as though they would punch holes into my tank. He stood with a ramrod straight back, but his fists were worked into knots at his side. Did he know what I was, and found me offensive? Did he know I was considered an abomination in the mythical world? Did he want to hurt me? The thoughts should've put fear into my heart, but they didn't.

We locked eyes for a brief second as he slowly walked past my tank before the booth next to mine caught his attention, and he wandered over to it, eyes drinking in everything on display before him. His expression was sick as he stared at the stacks of cloth and leathers made from the hides of mythical creatures.

I watched the pretty man with the angry eyes for as long as I could, until he disappeared in the crowd, and a flare of bewilderment echoed in my mind. Only those who knew about the magical convention would be here, so he obviously knew about magical creatures and the big selling hubs like this. Why should he be confused at what he saw? But it wasn't just confusion, I thought as I stared out at the crowd. It was as if he had been moving in a daze, dumbstruck. Like what he was seeing was blowing his mind.

My curiosity about the man fizzled after a few short minutes, my brain feeling exhausted by the emotion when all I wanted to do was sit in peace, and I was about to go back to the quietness when I felt something prod me in the shoulder. Instinctively, I looked up and through the water. I saw the rippling shape of Parker standing on the ladder above the tank. He was wielding what looked like a broom handle, swishing it through the water to prod me again.

I looked out of the tank, to the room beyond, and realized that the crowds had thinned somewhat. A few people were starting to pack up their booths and tables. The milling crowds of the rich and richer were slowly moving toward the exits, perusing the booths for as long as possible, with their purchases in tow.

The convention was over.

A jolt of anxiety zipped through my dulled senses.

It was time to go.

The large crane used to fish me out was being wheeled over to my tank. I watched as the net seat was lowered into the water, and, moving sluggishly, I floated over to it and settled into it. I didn't want to fight it. And that alone let me know I was broken. I would rather accept my fate quietly than fight and get hurt again. Especially from those heavy clubs I saw dangling from the guards of my new owner.

My head broke the surface as the crane lifted me out of the water, and all sound turned up. The crowds were just waves upon waves of noise. A few animals cried in their cages, and glasses clinked together as people chatted amongst themselves while observing everything being packed up. Several dozen people stopped to watch as I was slowly lifted out of the tank, water flowing off my body in a cascade. One more show for the people to watch.

Part of me wanted to fall out of the net, fall back into the tank. Being out of the water seemed to press down on me more than usual. I felt heavy, floppy under the weight of being out in the open air, of being out of my quiet, peaceful mind space, devoid of having to feel, or think, or be. I leaned the side of my head against one of the chain supports, feeling tired. I wanted to go back to my quiet place, but there was too much commotion out here that I couldn't find it.

I comforted myself with the knowledge that I would find it when I was settled into a different vehicle, driving away to my new life.

I was lifted up high over the tank edge, and lowered down onto a wheeled cart the cowboy had produced. Parker helped me out of the net seat and settled me into the overlarge cart which had rails to keep me from falling out.

I almost wanted to laugh.

I was literally an item in a shopping cart.

Parker placed something around my neck, some sort of jeweled necklace, but I didn't bother looking at it. They wheeled me to the front of the tank, where my new buyer was waiting with several large bodyguards. The bodyguard business must be doing pretty good nowadays. Everyone seemed to have them.

Parker began speaking with my buyer and I was hoping to zone out, but that was when I heard the shouting. If I'd been in my tank, which shielded me from a lot of pesky sounds, I would've been able to ignore it, but habit had me glancing over to where the ruckus was emanating. There were so many people milling about that I couldn't see who or what was making the disturbance. I was turning away when, suddenly, a name rang out above all other noise.

"CORDELIA!"

My head snapped toward the name. I knew that voice.

My mother's voice. But it was impossible . . .

"CORDELIA!" The call came again.

"Mom?" I croaked, sitting up in the cart as my name was called again. "MOM?"

"CORDELIA!"

And then, I saw her. Briefly, through the undulating crowd of people, but I saw her. Her eyes were boring into mine, and I thought my heart would burst.

"Mom! MOM!" I screamed. "MOM, OVER HERE!" I raised myself, trying to flop out of my cart, but I was restrained. "MOM, HELP! MOM!

I could see my mother fighting against the crowd, and I saw several men dressed in security clothing moving through the room toward her.

"Well, well," I heard Parker breathe, and I whipped around to see him looking between my mother and me as my mother battled through the crowd toward me.

"MOM!" I screamed, my heart plummeting at Parker's greedy expression. I didn't know how she had gotten here, how she had even found me, but I realized there was no way she would be able to get out. She was surrounded by security, not to mention all those willing to collect creatures like her. Mom had put herself in serious danger, and she had no idea.

To save me.

I had got us into this mess because I lied to her, went behind her back and didn't trust her. Right now, it didn't matter how she had found me, she had to get out, she had to escape. Without me.

"MOM, GET AWAY! GO AWAY!" I tried again to squirm out of the cart, but again I was pinned down by multiple hands. For several moments, my view was blocked by a crush of bodies, and I couldn't see where she was. I shoved one man out of my way with my flippers, screaming, "MOM! RUN! PLEASE! NO!" I shouted, watching helplessly as the guards reached her, about to put their hands on her.

"COR—"

The convention hall exploded.

A burst of light illuminated the middle of the room, blinding everyone in the vicinity, and most of the lights on the tree chandelier above us popped in fiery sparks, glass raining down.

There was silence for less than a second, and then the chaos was immediate and deafening. People screamed and rushed for the exits, booths were torn down or trampled in the ensuing pandemonium, and more explosions echoed off the walls.

My mother couldn't cast explosions like that, could she?

My blood went cold as gunfire cracked throughout the room.

"You better get her out of here!" Parker shouted to my new buyer, then cried, "Oliver! Contact the ship to prepare for immediate departure, *now*!" as he and his own bodyguards rushed away, disappearing into the seething crowd headed for the parking lot.

"*MOM!*" My voice cracked at the force of my scream as I too was wheeled crazily toward the double doors that led to the parking lot. As they hauled me through the doors, I caught one last glimpse of my mother, who was crouched down as a guard swung a fist at her, and for a brief second, I saw the strange man in Japanese clothing standing over her, casting a crackling streak of yellow lightning at another oncoming guard.

"MOM!"

Then we passed through the doors, and the explosions and din of fighting was muted as my cart was charged down the parking lot. Without hesitation, I was picked up out of the cart and thrown into the back of a bright yellow van that was idling in the thoroughfare, and the door was shut in my face. With many shouts, my buyer and the bodyguards piled into the van, and before the side doors had been shut all the way, the van's tires squealed and we raced toward the parking lot exit.

My mind no longer wanted to be in the quiet spot. It was racing, faster than the van's acceleration.

My mother was here! How did she find me? Was she safe, or was she being captured at this very moment?

I slapped my tail uselessly against the floor of the van. *Think, Cordy!* She's here to rescue you! You have to do your part to get rescued!

As we swerved, I fell against the doors then bounced back, hitting the back seat, and the idea came to me. I could open the door and fall out into the road. It was early morning, not very many people would be out. But anyone that did see me, I could convince to forget what they'd seen; a girl with a seal tail. And if my mother was near, she would help me. Maybe she could make whole crowds forget about me. She might even be strong enough to influence people through protective magical barriers. She could make my buyer forget about me.

And we could get away together.

Hope surged through me, and I hauled myself against the back door, reaching for the handle, praying it wasn't locked. Just then, someone grabbed my arm and wrenched me away from the handle. I looked up just in time to see a man reach down, syringe in hand. With a scream, I slapped my tail across his face. An earbud fell out of his ear, and my power surged as I realized he was unprotected from my influence.

"Don't give me a shot!" I screamed. *"Let me go!"* The man paused as the van swerved again. I bucked against his hand and he released me, and I pounced on the door handle. The door swung open, revealing a fairly empty road, with buildings crowded in and only a few people walking the street. I rolled toward the opening, but before I could fall out, several hands grabbed onto me, pulling me back into the van.

"MOM!" I cried out the open van door, but my mother wasn't anywhere in sight. She hadn't been able to keep up.

I felt a prick as the needle was plunged into my shoulder, and my vision instantly went hazy. I struggled to get out of their grip, but someone came into the back of the van with me and shut the door.

"Mom," I moaned as I fell limp against the ground, all sight and sound fading into blissful silence and darkness. My last conscious thought was that I hoped my mother had at least gotten away. What a waste it would've been for her to come all this way, to somehow find me—by our blood connection or just pure grit, I didn't know—only to be bound to the same fate as me.

PART IV
CALLISTA

Chapter Twenty-Five

One Week Earlier

Sunlight spilled through the trees, the day hot and bright. A day perfect for sunbathing. My sisters and I would never miss a chance to soak up the bright sunshine, and, hopefully, attract some foolish young men lost and wandering in the woods.

However, the woods were silent. The animals had been driven underground. The usual splashing of our lake was quieted, and a breathless fear seemed to seep through every leaf and branch, through the water to my sisters and me below. The silence of the landscape seemed to throb with one message: Danger. Danger. Unseen danger.

I peered up over the water's surface. Fear—a sensation that wasn't often felt by us—palpitated in my chest. The day looked perfect and serene. But I knew better. The unknown threat lurked, waiting for my sisters and me to flee the pond, where we would be easily slain with impunity. My sisters begged me to let them leave, to run, to find safety in human company until the danger passed, but I knew it was impossible. The danger would find us.

The crack of a branch echoed through the deserted forest, and my eyes sought the place from which the sound had originated, my heart nearly bursting. The woods fell silent again. But I could feel eyes on me. Angry eyes. My neck prickled. A screech broke the tension and the silence, and blinding pain hit me before I could even turn my head.

With a ragged gasp, I sat up in bed, the darkness an oppressive blanket around me. I gulped air, the fear still thrilling over my skin, my face hot, my feet and hands cold. I fumbled in the dark for my phone as the memory-dream faded. I hadn't meant to fall asleep while waiting for Cordy's call.

I stared at the phone in my hand, stomach dropping. It was well past midnight, and I didn't even have a notification for a missed call. Cordelia should have called hours ago. I suppressed the rising panic, trying to think the best of the situation. Maybe her phone died, or she forgot it in her room. I had called earlier, but it went straight to voicemail.

I knew she was still mad, but she had called me every night regardless while she was gone on her band trip. I'd said a lot of things that hurt Cordy when she had found out about her naiad side. I never wanted that, but it was hard for me, living this life.

It was one thing traveling the world as a naiad with my sisters, connected to my lake. Everything had been so simple, so fleeting, so inconsequential. Even the dangers we'd faced back at the lake, like the one in my dream that had really been a memory, had been soon forgotten. Nothing more than a thrilling adventure.

But now, I had no refuge to run to. No support group. I was trying to survive in a world without that connection, that safety.

My sisters had betrayed me. They had abandoned me. Cut me off. Cordy was the only person who hadn't forsaken me, and she didn't deserve how I had treated her. My lies had driven a wedge between us. It made my soul ache to think how selfish I had been, but it was difficult to fight against my baser instincts.

It was time for me to realize that this was my life now. She was my life now. I'd taken a lot of precautions in this new life, but hadn't really accepted that I would never be able to return to the lake. I had been holding out ridiculous hopes, just like my hope that Cordy's father would return. But Cordy's father wouldn't return, and I wouldn't be returning to my lake. Just as Cordy never would. In that, we were the same. Outcasts.

But we didn't have to punish ourselves. She deserved to know everything about her heritage, and the possible magical talents she could acquire now that she knew about her naiad side. I'd noticed that her selkie talents became more pronounced once she had learned about her father, but any traits she could've gotten from me had remained dormant. Now that she knew, more of her magical abilities were sure to start coming out.

The moment she got home, we would move out of this desert. I would find us a beautiful, lush, remote location near a lake, where I would teach her all about my side of the family, where we could live with water in our lives. Cordy deserved that, and more. We would have to be cautious, but we didn't have to live in fear.

To soothe my instincts that were screaming something was wrong, I took a deep breath, trying to calm my nerves, telling myself that my dream had made me jumpy.

The slight crunch of gravel from the driveway sounded outside, probably indiscernible to human ears.

I whipped my head toward my bedroom door as I heard multiple crunches follow.

In an instant I was out of bed.

I tiptoed over and peered through the crack in my bedroom door, the stairs and part of the front door visible below.

My night vision was ten times better than a human's, so I was able to clearly see the horde of armed men entering through my front door.

I clenched my jaw.

Cordy *was* in trouble. Her not calling was proof of that, not to mention the mob of gun-toting thugs currently storming my house.

My instincts, though dimmed, had never been wrong, but lately I'd been pushing them down, trying not to be as territorial, not as "naiad-like." For Cordy's sake. I should've listened to my gut.

Fury blazed inside me, and my fingers gripped the aluminum baseball bat I kept hidden behind the door.

These men had come calling to the wrong house.

With as much finesse and silence as a herd of buffalo, a small contingent of the men hurried up the stairs as I placed myself directly in front of the nearly-closed door. I bit back a smile as I decided that I wasn't going to try to influence them. Some physical activity would help me release some of the tension I'd been carrying since Maine. It would be nice to finally be able to crack some skulls. For Cordy.

The first man swung open the door and entered my room, his light shining on me. With my height of six-one, I nearly towered over him. He gave a startled yelp that was quickly followed by my heel slamming into his chest. He collapsed backward into his comrades, and then I started swinging my bat.

Being a naiad that was cut off from my lake, my strength and powers of persuasion weren't as strong as they used to be. At my strongest, I could sway whole crowds.

When I had to make it out in the world on my own with diminished abilities, I realized I had to find strength and skills of my own. I took self-defense classes, including all of the different types of martial arts. Because of my quick reflexes and inhuman strength, I excelled in all styles.

I knew I would be able to fend off all of these intruders in quick order. I wasn't afraid of a bunch of cowardly men in flimsy body armor who felt they had to ambush a woman while she slept.

Two more men filed into the room as I swung my bat, the shouting deafening as the bat cracked against bone. I knocked the guns out of their hands, then gripped one man and flung him into the panes of my bedroom window. With a crash of glass, the man fell through the second-story window and out of sight, hot desert air immediately filling the room. The second man tried to grab me around the waist, but I whirled away, grabbing his arm as I spun, and twisted it behind his back. I heard gunshots, and the wall behind me began to be peppered with red, feathery darts. Using the man I still held as a shield, I pushed him sideways into my bathroom. The entire front of my human shield bristled with tranquilizers, and when I finally released him, he fell to the floor, unconscious.

A fourth man charged into my bathroom, and, discarding his gun in such close quarters, began swinging an armored fist toward me. I grabbed his arm, turned, and heaved his body over my back, slamming him downward onto my toilet. The commode shattered, and the man slumped, motionless, to the flooding floor.

Straightening with a small groan, I heard more thundering footsteps coming up the stairs. Flicking my hair out of my face with a sharp exhale, I scooped up my bat, which had fallen to the bathroom floor, and charged.

My bat connected with a couple of faces, which successfully cleared my bedroom doorway, before I launched myself into the hallway, cracking knees and kicking men over the banister. The hollering started up again, and I was grateful for the distance from my neighbors. No one could hear these men scream.

I charged down the stairs, using the banister to hold my weight as I smashed both my feet into the oncoming men, slamming them back down the way they had come. Their shouts cut off as the men's bodies all dogpiled below, and I danced over the crush of men. At the bottom of the stairs, I whirled, facing three men who had come from the back door. I'd lost my bat on my way down the stairs, but that didn't matter.

"*Stop!*" I commanded, persuasion flowing from my heightened emotions. The men stopped where they stood, still as statues, their eyes glazed.

"*Lower your guns,*" I demanded, and they complied without complaint.

"*You. Who sent you?*" I barked, pointing at the man in the middle.

"HAMMA."

I frowned in confusion, but didn't bother with the semantics. I knew the "why," and I would understand the "who" soon enough, once I found the head man. These lackeys wouldn't know anything of real importance. I had to go to the top.

"*Where is your boss? The one who sent you?*" I demanded

The man struggled, as if reluctant to speak. I glared and pressed harder.

"*Where is your boss' center of operations located? Exactly.*" I thought I could hear the feedback from their earpieces, and could barely make out a commanding voice coming from those earpieces, but I smiled. These men were helpless, and no amount of commanding from their captain would make them disobey *my* orders. Even though I was cut off from my lake, my powers of persuasion were still more potent than what most humans could withstand.

"At a casino in Las Vegas." My heart constricted. I knew Cordy had been going to Vegas a lot. I just didn't realize . . . but the man continued speaking. "It's called The Lucky Clover. He's the CEO. He sent—"

I whirled as I heard more crunching footsteps on the driveway beyond the open door. In one swift movement, I yanked hard on one of the guns the spellbound men held and whipped it around, pointing it toward the door. As the first man entered, I fired the gun at the ceiling in warning, then pointed the barrel toward him.

"*Stop right there,*" I commanded, as two more men entered behind him.

They didn't stop.

They continued forward, advancing on me. My mouth went dry.

"*St—*"

The first man fired. A dart whistled and embedded itself into my shoulder. I glanced down at the stinging barb with a snarl. I ripped it free and hefted my gun again.

"You stupid humans think an ordinary tranquilizer will work on me? You don't know anything," I spat, an odd pressure mounting in my head. I fired back, but before the dart hit him in the neck where I'd aimed it, it pinged away and fell to the floor, harmless. I fired again, and the dart ricocheted off his body, as if he was wearing more than regular body armor. Blood pounded in my ears and sweat prickled my forehead as the three men slowly advanced upon me.

The front man fired another dart into my other arm, and I plucked it off with a hiss.

"*Get out of my house!*" I raged. Dropping the gun, I ripped a wooden spindle free from the banister with a *crack*. Raising it, I lunged forward and rammed the thick, bristly end into the flimsy mask of the front man.

The banister spindle glanced harmlessly away from his face as if on a slippery surface, though the force of it jarred my wrist and arm, making it go numb. With a feral scream, I leapt away from the man as he fired again, my movements sluggish, and another dart hit me in the side. With numb, heavy fingers, I tried to grip the dart, but my vision blurred as the men surrounded me. I threw a punch that I knew went too wide, and one of the men grabbed my arm, while someone lifted me at my waist. My vision began to stretch near and far like a bungee cord. I kicked out a marshmallowy leg but it merely flopped sideways. The heat from those evil darts was creeping along my veins, my vision spinning as if I were on a merry-go-round.

I . . . had to . . . keep fighting. I tried to throw another punch, but my arm didn't respond.

Before losing consciousness, the feeling of failing Cordy hit me hard. I hadn't protected us. These people knew exactly where and how to find us. We were out of our depth. We didn't have a chance. I was useless as a mother and protector; I couldn't safeguard my own flesh and blood. They even had darts that could put me out of commission. And if they had that, what else did these demons have?

The guilt of failure was too much, and I was grateful when the blackness put me out of my misery.

Chapter Twenty-Six

When I came to, it took a while to clear the fog in my brain. My body bounced around, but I was having trouble focusing on what was causing the movement. Whatever they were using to drug me was potent stuff, leaving me murky-minded. When I could finally open my eyes, I found that I was seated in the back of what looked like a police van, armed guards on either side of me. My mouth was gagged, and I was bound hand and foot. I tried to press the gag down with my tongue, but it was tied too tight. I raised my head and looked around. There were seven men surrounding me, all dressed as if they were going into battle.

I couldn't understand how these men could stand the heat. I was sweating, and I was only in my pajama shorts and a t-shirt; my bra, which I'd forgotten to take off before I fell asleep waiting for Cordy's call, was digging into my ribs with every jounce of the truck. I groaned at the uncomfortable jolting of our vehicle as it blazed through the desert. I knew we were still in the desert because I couldn't sense any water in the stale air.

"She's awake," one of the guards grunted.

"Put her back under. Nymphs can be tricky; we don't want any slipups. And call HQ. Tell them ETA is twenty minutes. They said they want to start working on her the moment we arrive."

I felt a prick, and before I could fully comprehend what they were saying, I was enveloped by darkness again.

When I woke up the second time, I immediately noticed the difference. I wasn't baking to death, for one, and for another, I wasn't bouncing around like a sack of jelly on a trampoline. A bright spotlight was shining down into my face from the ceiling, casting the rest of the room in shadow.

I was stretched out on a padded table, naked save for a hospital gown, my arms and legs tied down. They had taken my relic off my neck. I would never see that again. I was still gagged, but with a more refined, clean gag than the dirty one I'd had in the truck.

At that moment, I was being inspected by two women who were giving me a medical exam. Both women were in scrubs and wore face masks as they worked. After I made sure neither woman was holding sharp instruments to my skin, I jumped against the straps with a muffled roar, making both women shriek in surprise, stumbling away from me. They obviously hadn't noticed I was awake. I grinned against the gag. Now they knew.

"Oh, gracious, gracious, she's conscious," one of the women panted, rubbing her heart.

"Good thing we got all of our tests done, or I have a feeling she would've been a horror to draw blood from or perform the pelvic exams on while awake," the second replied, her tone wry.

I snarled against my gag, fury at their invasive disregard coursing through me. Who were these people? What could they possibly want from my medical exam?

"Well, we can inform Mr. Mendoza that she's awake now. He's eager to see her," the woman who'd first spoken said to her associate.

"I still can't believe that he arrived earlier than he told us," the second woman replied, the complaint clear in her tone. "We were in no way prepared for his arrival."

"You'll get used to it. He'll say he's coming tomorrow, be prepared to expect him today."

There was a whirring sound, and the table I was on began to tilt my whole body forward until I could see everything that was going on in the room. It was a sterile room with a counter containing a sink, a table holding stainless steel instruments, a wide mirror across the room from me, and a few stools placed around the table.

"Well, I suppose I'll go show him in."

I watched as one of the women exited the room, leaving the second behind. She turned to see me staring deadpan-yet-hostile at her, and she averted her eyes. I continued to stare, letting her feel the hatred boring into her until she finally coughed and muttered something about going to go get a drink.

The moment she disappeared out the door, I began yanking on the restraints on my wrists. The chains seemed so thin, I was sure that if I had enough time to work on them, I could weaken the metal enough to snap the cuffs free.

I strained one arm, sending all my strength to work on just one of the chains. As I struggled, I heard the feedback of a microphone, and a deep male voice said over an intercom, "They're reinforced with magic. Don't hurt yourself."

I snarled toward the voice, my gaze falling on the mirror before me, and I immediately stopped moving. Who was watching me, and how long had they been there?

Come out and face me, you cowardly bastard, I wanted to shout, but the gag prevented me from making anything more than awkward gurgling noises. Instead, I glared into the glass, willing the man to come out, to show himself, this Mr. Mendoza.

After several minutes of a showdown, those behind the mirror obviously got tired of staring at me doing nothing, and the door opened. The woman that had left to get their special guest accompanied a tall, handsome man of hispanic descent. He came up to my examination table, and I held very still, not wanting to give him a reason to harm me. I didn't know what his intentions were, but I had a feeling he wouldn't have any qualms about hurting me should he desire it.

After slowly circling the table twice, he came to a stop, meeting my gaze with narrowed eyes.

"Yes, yes, you're right Mrs. Galkin. She's been cut off."

"Will that make her less valuable?" Mrs. Galkin asked, holding up her clipboard, ready to scribble down whatever Mr. Mendoza said.

The man tilted his head from side to side. "Possibly. Best not spread that information around, keep it between us for now. But I'm not interested in selling her. Not yet."

"Then . . . why did you have us give her exams?" The woman asked, her voice heavy with confusion. "I thought you wanted healthy specimens for—"

Mr. Mendoza cut her off with a wave. "This naiad gave birth to a healthy hybrid. I'm interested to see if she can do it again."

After a brief pause, the woman nodded.

"Ah, I understand, sir."

My eyes widened as I, too, understood his meaning. Horror filled me. Why on earth did he want to breed me like a prized horse? What did he want with Cordy? What was his interest in hybrids? Whatever it was, I knew it didn't bode well for anyone, magical or otherwise.

"It'll be interesting to see if her outcast status will affect anything in a hybrid," the man continued. "It would be so much easier and cheaper if I could just breed them myself instead of hunting the world for them."

"But it would take longer, sir, with the gestation—"

"I have time," the man said, cutting her off again, his eyes boring into mine. "At least to experiment with this. There may not even be enough hybrids in the world at this time. But this will ensure that we'll have what we need, even as we scour the world to try and speed up the process. She, and the children that she will produce, are the key to everything we've been working toward."

My knuckles ached from clenching them so hard as I fumed at his cocky expression, and the nurse cleared her throat, trying to break the tension.

"Well, we have plenty of healthy male specimens here at the facility, sir. Would you want to make the rounds and see what catches your fancy?"

Mr. Mendoza nodded, finally breaking eye contact with me. "Yes, that would be nice. And if I can't find anything here, I can check the facilities near my home."

Where is your home, you witless swine? I thought. *I want to pay you a visit when I get out of here. If this monstrous human wanted to see a mythical creature in action, I would give him a show that would haunt the rest of his living moments, few as they would be.*

"Very good. Well, here are her stats, as you wanted, sir," Mrs. Galkin said, handing the man a clipboard filled with papers of charts and reports. "She's healthy and fairly strong in magical signatures, even though she is in a banished state. Her womb is healthy, and her blood work is normal."

Mr. Mendoza flipped through the report, nodding as he perused the pages. "Very good. I'm glad to hear it. Well, let's keep this little lady a secret from Mr. Banwell for the time being, if you wouldn't mind, Mrs. Galkin," Mr. Mendoza said, slipping a fat envelope out of his jacket pocket and handing it to the woman along with the clipboard.

"Of course, sir," Mrs. Galkin said, failing to hide her pleasure at the exorbitant bribe she'd just received.

"Excellent. I'll keep her here for the time being, until a suitable stud can be found, and then I'll have her transported to me in New York."

"Very good, sir. We have plenty of room for her."

I clenched my jaw as both humans turned to admire me for a moment, and I felt my blood burn hot. If they would let me loose, I would give them something worth staring at. The strength of my fists, for one.

"Beautiful creatures, aren't they, sir?" the woman asked, and I jerked my attention to her. She took several surprised steps back at my venomous glare.

"Yes, quite," Mr. Mendoza chuckled at Mrs. Galkin's reaction. "Too bad they're so dangerous, or I'd take one for myself. I kid, of course, Mrs. Galkin," he said, his tone light at Mrs Galkin's scandalized expression.

"Oh, yes. Of course. I knew that, sir." She gave a fake, airy laugh, then fell silent, avoiding my gaze. I looked back at the man, who was studying me, and I narrowed my eyes, staring into his soulless ones, not blinking. I poured all my hate and rage and wishes for violence into the look.

A small smile quirked at Mr. Mendoza's mouth, and he spoke to Mrs. Galkin, not taking his eyes from mine. "Yes, I am very pleased with this one. She's strong, and will make strong hybrids."

"Excellent. Well, sir, if you'll come with me, I can show you the males? We have a Scottish selkie, if you want another one of those, or a German nix. We also have two very handsome, healthy boto encantados from Brazil that could work nicely. But if you want to try non-water creatures, we do have a dzedka from Belarus, a haltija from Finland," the woman said, opening the exam room door. Mr. Mendoza waited only a half heartbeat, staring at me, before following her out the door as she continued to speak, "Or a giant Azerbaijani div that could be very promising, kept in an underground facility nearby."

Mr. Mendoza made an interested sound, and the woman continued, "Or, we also have several yakshas . . ." Her voice and list of mythical creatures tapered off as the two disappeared from view.

I took a deep breath through my nose, the gag drying out my mouth, and shook off the conversation that these monsters had right in front of me, as if I couldn't understand what they were saying.

They wanted me to make more hybrid babies, that much was clear, but I didn't know why, or what they were doing to my current baby, but it explained why they had targeted Cordy. They had no doubt followed the trail of rumors from Cordy's idiot ex-boyfriend back in Maine.

The why didn't matter. All that mattered was that I got out, found where they were holding Cordelia, and smuggled her away.

I began struggling against the restraints again, but in a few short minutes, the doors opened, and an orderly entered, bearing a syringe.

I growled and hissed as he approached, furious that they wanted to put me under again. I didn't have time for it! Struggling didn't help, though. My vision became blurry once more as he administered the sedative. I was getting really sick of being knocked out.

I felt myself coming out of the darkness yet again, and bullied myself to wake up, to push through the fading tranq and become lucid as quickly as I could. Something, not a smell or a sound, but a sensation, seemed to surround me. I forced my eyes open, despite the pull to keep them closed, to remain in the soothing blackness.

I sat up, bleary and dizzy, and took in my surroundings. A cell with bars. A cot. A small toilet and sink. I was dressed in a gray jumpsuit, barefoot. I rose unsteadily to my feet. Supporting my sagging body with a hand on the wall, I walked slowly to the bars and peered out. The cell block was large, but quiet. The amount of magic pulsing through the room was impressive. I could feel a flow to the magic, as if it were a surging stream, being sucked somewhere beyond this chamber.

The cell directly across from me was occupied, but the man in it was lying quietly on his cot, staring up at the ceiling, ignoring my obvious presence. I couldn't see any other occupants, but I could hear lots of breathing and people shuffling on cots. Many occupants meant many opportunities for help on escaping. I tested the strength of the bars. They didn't budge as I tried to pry two of them away from each other. I apparently wasn't getting out by pure strength. I looked around the cell block again. Time to get to know my neighbors.

I shook out my hair, fluffing it up with my fingers as best I could, then rubbed some color back into my cheeks.

Normal, lake-bound naiads were flirty, sensual, and extremely frivolous. We could also become vicious in an instant if provoked. Getting cut off from the lake had given me more sense and made me more able to relate to the humans around me. But flirty would probably get me further with these people than sensible. I squeezed my lips through my teeth to plump and moisten them, then I cleared my throat.

"Hey," I called, keeping my voice light, hoping to get an eager reply to a pretty voice. "Anyone there?"

"Yes. Now shut up," came one response, a male voice further down the block. He sounded young. There were a few chuckles. All sounded male.

"Friendly bunch," I replied with an arched eyebrow.

"Well, we *are* planning a welcome party for you when they let us out for rec time," the same male replied.

"We get rec time?" I asked, doubting.

"No."

There were more chuckles.

"You don't even care to see who your new fellow prisoner is?" I asked, standing on my tiptoes, trying to see any occupants in the cells. All were hidden from view, except the one across from me, but he didn't even move to glance at me.

"We already know. A baby-making naiad," a second man, this one sounding much older, almost elderly, called.

"Is one of you going to be my lucky mate?" I tittered. There was no response. I ground my teeth to keep from letting out a growl of discouragement. The creatures in here were so apathetic. If I couldn't rile them to help with a jailbreak, getting out of here by myself would be much harder.

"Wow, you guys really are dead," I said with a sigh, hoping to pique interest. "Not one of you is interested in the thought of getting with a smoking-hot naiad?"

"Who said you're hot?" the young voice snorted. "Hey, Santeri, you can see her easily. Is she hot?"

The man in the cell across from me lifted his head off his pillow to look at me. He was attractive, older, with salt and pepper hair, solemn eyes, and a strong jaw. He glanced at me for a brief moment, no emotion on his face, then rested his head back down on his pillow.

"Yes, she's very beautiful," he replied, his tone soft.

I giggled, ignoring the rising embarrassment inside me. "See? It's common knowledge that we're irresistibly gorgeous. Come take a look for yourselves." I flicked my hair back and put on a flirty expression, waiting for the curious eyes to peer through the various cells.

There was a pause, then a slow, collective response of. "Nah."

I frowned as not one occupant came into view. I could not believe the level of disinterest. What had happened to these poor beasts? I knew I could try to force them to help me with just a few hypnotizing words, but it didn't seem right to influence creatures that were in the same position as me. If worse came to worst, however, I wouldn't hesitate to force them to help me escape. But at the moment, there was no advantage to coercing them.

"Well, you all sure know how to make a girl feel welcome," I pouted, trying to get a reaction, any reaction.

"Listen, honey," a voice across the aisle to my left said, and I turned to see a man leaning against the bars of his cage. It was impossible to guess the real age of a magical creature, but he looked like a human man in his late forties. He was extraordinarily handsome, even in his plain gray jumpsuit, with golden tan skin, silky black hair, and a slight accent, but I couldn't place what kind of creature he was, especially since all the magic was being sucked out of the room.

"Well, hi there, gorgeous," I gushed, giving him a wink.

"Look, I get you're trying to butter us all up. It's in your nature, we get that. But here's the sitch: none of us want it. You naiads are notoriously immature and fairly simpleminded, so let me lay it out to you straight: these monsters that have locked us up want us to do something that is vile; making a hybrid child. It's repugnant. Hybrids aren't meant to exist. No one *wants* them to exist."

Heat flared in my gut and I bit back a snarl, thinking about how much these creatures didn't know anything about anything. Cordy was the light of my life. She was a thousand times more amazing, more exceptional, smarter, braver, more important than all of these dead-brained animals combined. What made them so special, so arrogant about their pure-blood status? They had no idea what hybrids could be, because they never gave them the chance.

I knew that wherever Cordy was, she was surviving, and not only surviving, but fighting. That was who she was. These creatures couldn't hold a candle to what Cordy was capable of, and had no idea what she was worth.

"But you see, they're watching us," the gorgeous man continued, pointing upwards, where a small black dome bulged from the ceiling. Several others were spaced along the length of the room. "To see if we'll take to you so they can mate us. Which wouldn't be good, especially for you. These guards like to chit chat; we hear you've already made a hybrid before. If one of us gets in there with you, we'd probably tear you limb from limb, not mate. And we don't want that either, cuz we don't want to be put in solitary."

"Why, because you'd miss all the enlightening conversation you get in here?" I asked, my tone more savage than I meant, and I heard someone chortle quietly.

"The point is, we don't want some mixling child. Try to get that through your air-brained skull."

I hid a fierce smile, my knuckles turning white at my grip on the bars. Well, if they wanted an air-brained dummy like I used to be when I was attached to my lake, I'd give it to them. It would be easier to fool all of them and escape the human monsters if they thought me incapable of intelligible thought.

"So please, stop trying to flirt with us. You're stunning, it's true," the man continued, and I gave a fake, girly laugh, pretending to blush. I inwardly cringed at the remembrance that I would always be so happy, so proud, whenever some foolish young human would praise my beauty. Naiads lived for it. I had lived for it.

"Well, you're pretty gorgeous yourself, hot stuff. What say we make a baby with all this hotness?" I murmured, batting my eyes at him. I thought I saw the hint of a smile cross his face before he exhaled and turned away.

"I tried," he said, tossing his hands up and disappearing from sight.

"Wait! Where are you going! Why don't you want to talk to me?" I pouted. When he didn't reappear, and no one else came into view, I sighed and moved back to my bed, my arms and legs feeling shaky. Those sedatives were taking their time leaving my system, but I couldn't show weakness.

I sat, deliberating what to do. Inciting a riot seemed out, and my brain felt so fuzzy it was hard to think.

I exhaled, looking around my cell, realizing I would need more planning to get out of here. I fluffed my limp pillow as best as I could and laid back onto the cot with a sigh.

When did we eat in this place?

Chapter Twenty-Seven

My answer came a half hour later, when the doors opened and I heard wheels squeaking down the hallway. I hopped up from my bed and hurried to the bars. Two men backed into the room, pulling a service cart loaded with trays of food. As they entered, I saw the glint of keys hanging off the pockets of the taller, skinnier guard. I also saw a faint, shimmering barrier around the two men. The same type of barrier the elite force of cowards had used back at my house.

My vocal mesmerizing wouldn't work on either of them, but I had a plan. I backed into the shadow of my cell and quickly unzipped my jumpsuit. It was a good thing they'd put my bra back on. The bra wasn't as sexy as one would think. It was actually fairly sensible, but did have a touch of lace. It would serve its purpose. And it would be more effective this way. Were I to be bare-breasted, it would make the guard more inclined to run away in shock or embarrassment.

I unzipped the jumpsuit down to my navel, and then quickly pulled my arms out of the sleeves and tied them low around my hips, exposing my entire torso. I then hurriedly stepped back into view and leaned up against the corner where the bars and cell wall intersected, trying to look as relaxed and sensual as I could.

If I couldn't incite the animals in these cages, maybe I could tempt their keepers, and I didn't always need my magical voice to influence men.

Thankfully the guard with the keys came up to my cell, ready to slide the tray of food under the thin gap in the cell door, but paused as he saw me standing there, my eyes smoldering and full as the moon.

"Hi," I murmured.

The man's mouth dropped open slightly, and I smiled shyly at him.

"What's your name?" I cooed, trailing the end of a lock of my hair across my collarbones, drawing his eyes there. The man made a dry gasping sound, then swallowed several times, stepping closer.

"Um . . . mynamessherrne," he slurred.

I slid my body across the bars so that I was standing right in front of him. I grabbed onto the bars above my head, leaning my head against my bicep, and gazed into his eyes, fluttering my eyelashes.

"I like that name."

He laughed nervously and looked around.

"Who are you looking for?" I asked with a hurt, accusatory tone. "Your friend?"

His fellow guardsmen had thankfully stepped out of sight, down another aisle to feed other occupants. The tall guard's eyes immediately snapped back to mine.

"I don't like him, but I like you. You don't want to share me, do you?" I pouted.

He quickly shook his head.

"Good. I don't want you to share me, either," I whispered, leaning against the bars. As I took in his face, I hesitated. He looked barely twenty. He was just a kid, like Cordy. How did a kid get into an organization like this? Did he even know what was going on around him?

"Step away, boy," came a call. Both of us snapped to look at who had spoken. The same caged, gorgeous man who had talked to me earlier was leaning against his bars, watching us.

I immediately shook away my reservations, realizing some humanity had rubbed off on me during my time out of the lake, and it was showing through at the most inopportune time.

It didn't matter if this guard was a mere boy. He had made his choice, to work for those who imprisoned human-like, thinking, talking creatures. He was my captor, and I wasn't going to let his age take away my edge, or my will to do anything to escape.

"Don't listen to him," I purred, although I wanted to reach through the cell bars and strangle the gorgeous prisoner. What was he thinking of, warning one of our captors away from the danger he was so foolishly stepping closer to?

The guard turned back to me as I clicked my tongue. "He's just jealous that I'm talking to *you* and not him," I said with a breathy exhale. The guard stepped closer, and while his eyes traveled down me, I did the same, scanning his uniform, looking for anything that could be holding the magical shield in place. There. On his lapel, a small golden circle. I could feel the magic of it.

"That's a pretty trinket," I said, gesturing toward his lapel. "Can I have it? Then I'll give *you* something in return." I slowly bit my lower lip, raising an eyebrow.

Without even looking, without even considering what he was doing, the guard fumbled for the circle. The second it left his clothes, I could see the shield around him evaporate.

"*Give it to me*," I intoned, losing my breathiness. I thought for a moment since the magic was being sucked out of the room that my magical influence wouldn't work, but the guard reached the gold circle out toward me, just as his friend rounded the corner again.

I heard the gorgeous man in the cell whisper, "Fool."

"Evans!" the second guard shouted, running toward us, "What are you—" *Too late.* I grabbed the unprotected guard's arm and yanked him hard into the bars. Over his cry of pain and the shouting of the inmates who had now pressed themselves against their cell bars to see the show, I threaded the guard's arm back through the bars. I twisted the guard around and wrapped my arm around his throat, snarling to the oncoming guard, "Stay back, or I snap his neck!"

The second guard stopped in his tracks, and instead backed away as my other hand searched my captive's jacket for the keys I had seen dangling there.

An alarm blared as I found the keys. I wrenched them off the jacket and shoved the hostage guard away from the door. He collapsed to the ground as I began jamming keys into the lock, trying to find the correct one as the guard gasped on the floor. After several breathless tries, I found one that entered the keyhole with ease. I whipped open the cell door and turned to the second guard who was on a walkie-talkie, calling for help.

I couldn't touch him, so I put on my most ferocious expression and, shrieking, I charged him. Shouting, he ran to hide on the other side of the cells. Without slowing, I turned to head for the door, but it was already opening, and a contingent of men were filing in, guns at the ready. My bare feet squeaked on the floor as I swung around and sprinted down the opposite side of the cell block. I heard the men open fire, and I threw myself into the breath of a space between two cells, exhaling as all the barbs missed.

There was another door. I sprinted for it. It opened as I reached it, and the man behind it rapidly fired his tranquilizer gun before I had a chance to even turn around.

Three darts hit me in the chest. I stumbled backward as more darts entered my body. I looked down at my front, bristling with tranqs, and I brushed my hand over one dart as I fell to the floor. The jeers of prisoners and the shouting of armed men drowned out all other sound as I laid my head back onto the concrete. I closed my eyes as my vision started going loopy.

This escape had failed, but my resolve was only bolstered. There would be more opportunities. I would try anything and everything to get out and find my daughter. It was difficult to know what escape attempt would work because I knew nothing about this facility, so I would just have to keep trying; every moment I could get, I would take. I was going to find out just how far I could push them until they decided I wasn't worth it anymore, or I escaped.

I struggled, straining against the void that greedily slurped at my consciousness, but I lay completely still.

A few more seconds, just a few more seconds. I could last a few more seconds for revenge.

I heard several booted feet surround me as I lay slumped on the floor. I felt a boot walk across my hair, and I struggled to crack an eye open. Through the slit between my lids, I could see a foot beside my curled fist.

With the last burst of energy I had, I half curled upward, and with a feral yell, I plunged one of the tranquilizer darts I had hidden in my hand into the calf of the nearest booted leg. I heard a strangled yell as my floppy hand ripped out the dart. I turned and stabbed it into the boot that had stood on my hair, and then into a nearby shin and ankle, and there were more satisfying screeches of pain before I passed out completely.

When I opened my eyes next, it was as if I hadn't opened them at all, it was so dark. I sat up in my cell, but I wasn't in the same cell block full of wearied males anymore. At least from what I could see. Or couldn't see, in the pitch blackness. I could sense my breath turning to frost as I exhaled, it was so cold.

This must be the dreaded solitary that the gorgeous man was talking about. I dragged myself to my feet, my body stiff and sore. I felt along the walls, but I only felt icy steel. I did manage to find a slim slot about shoulder height, where food was no doubt delivered, and the metal seams that outlined a door, but that was it. I traveled in a circle, almost tripping over a metal bucket bolted to the floor—my toilet—before I came to the slot again. I was in a freezing steel tube about ten feet in diameter. No metal bars for me to try to seduce stupid human men through.

The arms of my jumpsuit were still tied around my waist, so I quickly untied them, slipped my arms into the sleeves, and zipped up my jumpsuit, trying to stave off the cold.

Were I still attached to my lake, the cold wouldn't have bothered me as much. I was still fairly resistant, but it was uncomfortable. I curled up on the cold concrete ground in what I imagined was the middle of the room, away from the cold steel walls, to try to get some sleep. No cot for me. But I'd slept in worse places.

I woke up just a few hours later, burning hot. Light streamed in from an unshuttered grate high above me. I was sticky with sweat, and I quickly shed my jumpsuit, using it as a barrier between my backside and the hot concrete ground.

So this is what they did with those in solitary. Played games. Made the prisoners not only suffer from lack of interaction with others, but also small comforts, like a bed or a standard temperature. Not only that, they didn't keep regular daylight or nighttime hours. They shut the overhead grate after a few hours, plunging my cell into darkness, while it was still blazing hot. After a time, they adjusted the temperature to freezing while light streamed in, switching something up every few hours, to disorient and torture us.

However, being a child of the moon, I could feel the slight pull of the great celestial satellite, and so I figured I could generally keep track of how many days I'd been in this hole.

Food was delivered every few hours, a simple gruel of rice, oats, or beans, and a plastic pouch of water. I slurped everything down without complaint. I would need my strength and as sharp of a mind as possible, despite the harsh conditions these monsters kept throwing at me. But while I waited, I used the time to plan out exactly what I could do once I got out of here.

Getting out, however, was proving a challenge. I'd tried several times to scale the walls during the cooling or heating up periods, but the walls were too far apart, and too slick. I tried, and failed, to talk to those bringing my food. Obviously all were shielded and ear-plugged.

I would have to wait to attempt another escape when they released me from solitary. Unless I was in here for months, then I'd try something more drastic, like grab a guard who slipped up and got too close feeding me or something. I didn't think they'd keep me in here forever, and I'd try to escape once they let me out. And if that didn't work, then I would try again when they were transporting me. Surely I would build up a resistance to the sedatives soon, they used them on me so often. All I knew was I would never stop trying to escape, and never stop trying to find my daughter.

While I spent my time doing rigorous exercises during the cold bouts and hot yoga during the heated bouts, and sleeping in between, I thought about Cordy. It helped my mind feel alert, wondering, worrying about where she was and how she was doing—when I wasn't thinking about escaping or doing terrible things to those who had imprisoned us.

On roughly my fourth day, the room around me started heating up, so I stripped my jumpsuit to my waist and began a yoga routine, starting with Sun Salutation as my mind went to Cordy.

Cordy was strong. But she was also trusting. Too trusting. Sure, she was a bit of a naïve teenager, but that wasn't the reason she was so innocent. She wanted to believe the good in people, that people would be accepting.

She had shown Noah her selkie side after only a few short years of knowing him. And then, back in Moapa Valley, she had been all ready to trust, to be hurt again, after only a year. And I was sure, should she ever get free from this mess, she would be willing to trust again. My Cordy was too precious, too good, to have this happen to her.

Me, I could take the imprisonment, the vitriol, the poor treatment. I was used to all the judgment because of my naiad reputation. I could handle it. I was willing to do anything to get out of any current situation. But Cordy was not only more cautious, taking time to think things through, she also had morals that I lacked.

I'd murdered, stolen, slept around indiscriminately, and influenced people out of their hard-earned money. Even in Maine and Nevada. That was how I had kept us in comfort all these years without having to work a job. And Cordy hadn't known it. For years, she'd thought her mother was honest and naïve and kind. A good, truthful human with a lavish trust fund.

Sweet, guileless Cordy.

There were a lot of things she didn't know, like anything about the Ever—though I almost let it slip when I was telling her about what I was—and I was determined to never tell her about it. There was no way I would let Cordy step foot in—or even know about—that deadly place. She wouldn't last thirty seconds before something would want to rip her apart. It was hard enough for her here in the human world, where her good, sweet disposition was still a danger, despite it being what I loved most about her.

I fell into the different warrior poses, panting as sweat dripped from my face. I smiled. My daughter *had* to have inherited much of her goodness from her father. He *was* a good man. Well, selkie. I'd only known him for a week, but I fell head over heels for him because I could see goodness in him, something I inherently lacked. That didn't happen often with naiads. And I thought he'd seen something in me too. It was true that opposites attract, I supposed.

When he disappeared, it had hurt me. Had broken me, for a long time. He had been honest, funny, gentle, and just *good*. I supposed I liked him so much because he had reminded me of another man I had met, decades and decades before. But I didn't like to think of him, either. It hurt. He had left, too, but his reasons I had understood. Though it didn't make it any less painful.

I turned my mind back to Cordy, to focus myself.

She was learning a lesson someone as artless and gentle as her shouldn't have to learn: that in this world, and especially in the Ever, being good made you an easy target, that people would take advantage of you in a second if they wanted. It was a lesson that could break her, turn her bitter and hard. I didn't want that for her.

I needed to save her from becoming me.

A distant cracking noise broke my concentration, and I fell out of Downward Dog, listening hard. The cracking noise didn't come again, but I thought I heard a distant shout. I got to my feet and hurried to the steamy door, trying to peer out of the slot. The hallway was empty, but there was no mistaking the very, very distant sound of shouting. Had those dead-eyed males in the cell block been inspired by my escape attempt and tried a coup of their own? Maybe I would get some company down in this block after all.

A door opened somewhere, and footsteps and a male voice approached my cell.

"Aye, aye, there's the occupant in number three. No, no idea what it is. No, I heard it's been several days, I'm sure it's been beat down," an accented voice said, coming toward my door, but I couldn't see anyone through my food slot. The footsteps stopped before my door, but still I couldn't see anyone. How short was this guard?

"Aye, I can handle opening it. No, don't tell me how to do my business, lass," the man's voice came again over the rattling of keys. He must be speaking on a phone, I realized. His voice, a thick Irish brogue, was loud and nonchalant, as if he was on a social call, not in a place full of dangerous criminals. Were these idiots really going to open my door without sedating me first? And they only sent one very short guard to handle me?

I crouched, ready for the moment the lock on my door disengaged.

"Lass," the man was saying, his tone annoyed as I heard the scratching of the key in the hole, "why do you have so little faith in my metho—" The lock clicked.

I heaved against the door, and it swung open, catching the incredibly short man in the chest. He went down with a bellow, and I leaped out of the room, my eyes searching the hallway for more men. It was just the one guard—was he actually a guard?—who was sprawled on the ground. Seeing the keys in his hand as he lay spread eagle on the floor, I leaned down and snatched them up. The man hung onto the keyring, yelling incoherently, but I ripped the ring out of his grip, shouting, *"Get out of my way!"*

I locked eyes with the man for a heartbeat as he gaped up at me, his jaw slack as he took me in, shiny with sweat, only wearing my bra, my jumpsuit unzipped. He was fairly attractive—I couldn't help noticing, it was something I almost always noticed first about a person—with a full black beard, piercing blue eyes, and a rugged face. He wasn't dressed like a guard, looking fairly muscled under his sports jacket and trousers, and he looked about three feet tall. The man's stunned expression changed into anger as he leapt to his feet with fluid grace.

Humans couldn't move that fast.

I recalled his Irish accent as I beheld his short stature. Magic emanated from him, and an incredulous laugh burst out of me.

"A leprechaun? Really?" I chortled at his affronted expression. He straightened his jacket, giving me a glare.

"Oh, that's rich coming from some flutey nymph," he shot back, looking ready to spring for the keys in my hand. But I needed these keys if I was to get out, and I wasn't going to let some over-confident leprechaun get in my way.

"Flirting won't get you anywhere with me," I replied with a smirk, attempting to throw off his concentration.

His jaw went slack, his face blooming red. *"Flirting?"* he sputtered, but before he could say more, I leapt clean over him, kicking him in the shoulder and knocking him off his feet once more for good measure.

"Thanks, love," I called as he hit the ground with a curse. I laughed, barreling down the hall toward my freedom.

Chapter Twenty-Eight

The rest of the facility was in chaos. I had no idea what was happening, or how it had happened, but I was immeasurably grateful. Guards ran, trying to escape from the creatures that were out of their cages and had now turned on their captors. Several guards were lying unconscious in the hallways. I hurried through doors that had been left open, avoiding the groups of stampeding creatures, both humanoid and animalistic, running loose as I hurried down corridors that echoed with shouts.

I clotheslined a guard running past, sending him spinning to the floor. Standing over him, I then persuaded him to hand over his phone, wallet, and his tactical boots. I had to have a means of knowing where "here" was if I wanted to find my way back to Vegas. According to his phone, we were in the middle-of-nowhere Arizona, just past six in the evening. There were no windows and no clocks in this place; the exact time had been a mystery until now.

Through the crowd, as I finished lacing up my boots and tucking my new phone into my jumpsuit, I saw the gorgeous man from the male cell block taking a cell phone off of a guard he'd just body slammed into the concrete floor. Upon seeing me, he gave me a saucy smile and raised brow that made my stomach flip.

I marched over to him and slapped him squarely across the face.

"Hey, what was that for?" he complained, rubbing his jaw, though a small smile curled on his face.

"For calling me stupid in front of everyone. And for what you said about hybrids." I bared my teeth at him.

His smile widened as he quirked an eyebrow at me. "I believe I called you 'air-brained.' And I don't like hybrids, but I know you have a hybrid child, so I guess I'm sorry about offending you. I didn't realize what I said would affect you, most naiads don't usually let things get to them. In fact, I didn't know naiads could be so serious about anything."

"Well, I'm full of surprises. Not that you would care to know more about me." I gave him a vicious yet sultry look.

He grinned back. "You're a great actress. It was smooth, you playing the guard like that to escape. That was the closest anyone's ever gotten."

I slapped him again. "And that's for trying to warn him away from me."

His smirk never wavered as he touched his reddening cheek. "Sorry."

"So, what happened here? *How* did this happen?" I asked, looking around the quieted room for an exit. I bit back a smile as I looked at the unconscious guards scattered about.

"I'm not quite sure," the gorgeous man replied, pursing his lips. "Some crazy *moça* let us out, and took out most of the security too. A lot of us stayed behind for scavenging and payback before we left. I don't know who she is, but I've heard that they're gathering outside the building, if you care to join us."

I shook my head. "I'll accompany you outside, but I'm not sticking around. I have to get going. My daughter was captured too, and I'm going to find her."

I sauntered past him, searching for an exit. He fell into rapid step beside me. "I have no doubt you will. I mean, you had us all fooled here, you were able to talk a guard out of his own protection. Sorry again, for warning him away from you. I knew he didn't have a chance, so I tried to even the playing field a little." He winked at me, then his expression turned pensive. "You know, you're not like any naiad I've ever met. You seem . . . more put together."

"Maybe you don't know as much about naiads as you think," I teased, glancing down a hallway. I saw a sign for stairs, and the gorgeous man gestured toward it at the same time I pointed it out. Smiling at each other, we hurried toward the stairway.

"Well, maybe you could teach me more about you . . . and your kind." He gave me a knowing look as we began charging down the stairs.

I smiled and shook my head. "Sorry, don't have time. I just wanted to say good-bye, and to let you know that if you knew my daughter, you wouldn't have anything to fear from hybrids. They're not monsters. Cordelia is the kindest, most caring being I know." I kept eye contact with him, letting him see the earnestness in my eyes.

His face took on a thoughtful mien, but then he shrugged. "If you say so."

We came to the bottom of the stairs, where a hallway was brightened with natural lighting from an open door at the end. Several people were dodging out of it into the sunlight.

"Well, I gotta run," I said, as we reached the exit. "Stay out of trouble."

He grabbed my arm before I could fully exit into the sunlight that was pouring in through the open doorway. I glanced back at him, and was flattered to see him blushing. "Hey, if you're ever in the Amazon, look me up."

"Ah. A boto encantado?" I gave him a raised eyebrow, an arch smile growing on my lips. "So, you *are* trouble, then."

"Boto-cor-de-rosa, but I've heard it both ways." He winked at me. "Call me Luan."

"Callista."

"A pleasure, Callista." He bent forward and kissed my hand, his warm lips lingering on my skin, an electric pulse dancing along my blood. I could see the slight indentation of the blowhole hidden under his hair.

When he looked up at me, I gave him another slap on his cheek, this one more playful.

"Too bad you're so disgusted with the thought of being with me," I sighed, biting my lip. He opened his mouth, but before he could say another word, I darted through the open door, bursting out of the building into the late afternoon desert sun. Gratitude for the fresh, hot, dry air welled up in me for exactly five seconds, then I went back to cursing the wretched heat.

I studied my surroundings. Wide swaths of sand rose up into craggy desert hills in the distance, the desert pockmarked with sun-baked rocks and spiny vegetation soaking in the unrelenting rays of the sun. Nothing but stretches of sand for as far as the eye could see. I saluted Luan as he slipped by me and ran around the building.

I needed to get out of this place. I had to find Cordy.

I'd been stewing over my capture for nearly five days, the words of the man who had come into my house echoing in my mind like a mantra. He had said that their boss was back in Las Vegas.

My mouth curled into a snarl. I knew that Cordy had been going to Vegas, but I had no idea what she'd been doing there. She had insisted it was just harmless fun, and I believed that she thought that, but if HAMMA's head honcho was quartered there in Vegas, I now knew they had taken her there for ulterior motives.

I would have to get back to that casino, The Lucky Clover, and weasel out every scrap of information on where and what they had done with Cordy, all directly from the jackass's mouth. All the running, screaming fools back inside the facility wouldn't know anything. They were paid grunts, that's all.

An arid wind was blowing, whipping my hair in my face and causing pinpricks of sweat to pop up all over my body. I didn't bother to untie and zip up my jumpsuit, instead grateful for the fresh, albeit hot, air on my skin. I quickly braided and twisted my wind-whipped hair in a knot on top of my head as I considered my options. I would never get back to Vegas without a vehicle. These HAMMA monsters needed some sort of transport to get out here in the middle of forsaken nowhere. They had to have a garage somewhere.

I ran around the building, where a large domed airplane hangar filled with cars came into view, about half-a-football-field distance away. Growling, I started jogging across the sand, leaping over jutting rocks and scraggly bushes. The white hangar was open on one side, showcasing several armored trucks as well as a few regular vehicles.

I'd always wanted a Jeep.

I found a magnetic hide-a-key for the vehicle under the back bumper. As I climbed into the driver seat, I saw several other vans parked on the far side of the prison, opposite of where I'd exited. There was a crowd of figures gathering around the vans, several dressed in prison jumpsuits.

I ignored the growing crowd. I wasn't going to stay and find out who had led the revolt and what they were going to do now. I had a car, and I didn't want it stolen from me when there was no doubt going to be a mad dash for freedom. Slipping on the pair of sunglasses I'd found in the console, I peeled out of the hangar, kicking up desert sand as I left the facility behind.

Using the GPS on my new phone, I discovered I was several hours southwest of Phoenix. I considered driving to the Phoenix airport and waltzing onto a flight, but not knowing what flights were available, it could take me too long, not including the backtrack to actually get to the airport. The GPS said it would take me about five and a half hours to drive to Vegas. I stepped on the gas.

I would make it in three.

CHAPTER TWENTY-NINE

The sun was just setting as I entered Paradise.

The irony of such a town name made me snort aloud as I passed the *Welcome to Fabulous Las Vegas* sign, lit up in the sweltering dusk.

Yes, it was paradise, for the rich and for those like me who preyed upon the rich.

But this paradise was secretly full of vipers. I was smart enough not to get bitten, but most others were not so lucky, taken in by the flashing lights and promises of dreams come true. Naïve and young. Like Cordy.

A jaded person like me, however, could earn plenty of money making the rounds at many of the big-ticket casinos. I'd done it plenty of times during our stay in Moapa Valley.

The casinos had been gold mines. Enough to keep us comfortable for decades. There was always some old, rich beau monde with an empty brain, eager to have some hot young thing hanging off his arm while he paraded his wealth at the poker tables. All that was needed was some good looks and a dress that showed just the right amount of skin, and you could hang out with the old fools for an evening. You just had to simper and fawn all over them the entire night, and then ask them to hand over all their winnings as you headed up to their hotel room, and they did. They always did. For me, at least.

But I'd never been to The Lucky Clover. It had seemed so inconsequential. Little did I know, it held some of the wealthiest, most dangerous players I could ever imagine.

The thought made adrenaline flare through me as I pulled into the porte cochere with a screech.

I hopped out of the jeep, not caring that I left the car idling in front of the casino, and sauntered up toward the doors, ignoring the stares at my jumpsuit and exposed bra. I entered through the doors, passed an bronze fountain of a leprechaun, which did no justice to leprechauns like the one I'd seen just today, and went straight to the women dressed in green at the reception desk.

Keeping my voice light so that those around me wouldn't get alarmed or suspicious of my demands, I addressed one of the women, fluxing my persuasion. "*Take me to your CEO, please.*"

"Certainly, right this way," the woman said, coming around the table and gesturing for me to follow her.

"*Faster*," I whisper-demanded, and the woman picked up her pace considerably, practically running through the room with slot machines to a door in the back.

The woman slid the key card from around her neck into a slot and the door opened. We entered an elevator, and the woman took me to the top floor.

The woman led me to the door of the CEO's office, but before she opened it I stopped her.

"Leave us, and don't let anyone disturb us, understand? Also, you'll forget seeing me."

She nodded and departed, relaying my orders on a walkie-talkie. I turned to the door and took a deep breath. I didn't know what kind of security this man would have on him up in his tower. I would try to take out as many guards as possible, and then find a way behind the magical barrier he would no doubt have on him.

Loosening my shoulders and flexing my hands, I took another deep breath, and burst into the room, ready to take down several guards. The spacious office was empty save for a heavy-set man who swiveled his chair to face me. He sat behind a gigantic desk backdropped with floor-to-ceiling windows that allowed the neon lights of Vegas to dazzle anyone who walked in.

"Well, hello," the man said, looking me up and down. "I don't think I've ever seen you here before. You must be new."

I was surprised but relieved that there were no guards. It would make things much easier. And though my skin crawled at the thought of this man, I would have to play it cool, even though every instinct screamed at me to run over to him and wring his neck. I was still far enough away from him that should I make aggressive moves toward him, he could push an alarm.

"Yes, very new," I murmured, jutting out my jawline and puckering out my lips. He twirled his finger, gesturing for me to spin in place, and I complied, swaying my hips and flicking my hair as much as possible, hiding the rolling of my eyes when I had turned away from him.

"Well, my dear, I'm glad they hired you," he said, loosening his tie. "I haven't seen a showgirl as beautiful as you in a long, long time. Come, come."

I started to strut toward him when his smile of expectation faltered.

"You look familiar . . ."

Relief filled me as his eyes widened in recognition, no doubt from the surveillance they'd done on us. Playtime was over, and I could now get to the interrogation. Horror filled his face, and he turned to press a panic button.

I beat him to it.

Leaping over the desk, I yanked his hand away as I landed hard on his lap. He let out a cry of alarm, but I leaned toward him, bearing my teeth. He snapped his mouth shut and cowered in his seat.

"You obviously know who I am," I snarled into his face, "So if you want to keep this arm *attached* to your body, you will tell me what you've done with my daughter." I gripped his wrist and tugged hard on it until he whimpered.

"I-I don't know where she's at." He was shaking, his face turning a delicate shade of sage green.

Okay, physical manipulation wasn't going to do it, which irked me. I was looking to release some of my anger. Persuasion would have to do it, but I would still make him hurt.

"*Tell me where my daughter is*," I hissed. "*You're the founder of HAMMA, you must know!*"

"No, no, I'm not the founder of HAMMA," he replied, his voice shaky. "I just run this casino."

I paused. "*You're not the boss who took my daughter?*"

"I just got orders—orders to make an extraction plan from my bosses back on the east coast," he blubbered.

I cursed. The east coast? How far reaching was this organization? The man continued speaking in gasping breaths. "They heard about the incident in Maine and they followed up. They got your information from the boy that was attacked in Maine, and when you turned up in Moapa Valley, I was brought in to form the extraction plan, along with several others, as well as some of the yokels in the area. But Houston Banwell is the head of HAMMA."

"*What is HAMMA?*" I demanded. The more I knew of my enemy, the easier it would be to get Cordy out.

He began spilling his guts, sweat beading on his face and soaking through his clothes as he talked about who Banwell was and how HAMMA worked. It functioned like an anthill: workers would go out and collect magical animals, and the higher-ups would take the creatures and use them for their own gain. And Cordelia had been caught in one of their traps.

The more he talked, the sicker I began to feel. From what he was saying, this wasn't some small organization just in Nevada and Arizona. They had real estate all over the place, spanning the entire United States as well as a few pockets in Canada and the British Isles, with plans to spread around the world. They had communities and members all over the country. They owned banks, casinos, hotels, convention halls, stores, and even a university. Their members were regular people, living their lives but aware of the secret magical world around them. And they were enslaving those in the magical world, taking them for their own benefit, all under the false premise of rescuing them.

As he began to go into detail of how the communities were divided by chapters, I held out a hand. "Okay, okay, *enough*, I get it. This doesn't matter." It *did* matter, because it felt like we were surrounded, and when I got Cordy out, we would be hard-pressed to remain hidden, but I needed to get to the matter at hand. "*Where did you take my daughter? Was that band trip even real?*"

"No. The asset made—"

I wrenched on his arm, and he yowled.

"*Don't you call her that*," I breathed, and he nodded, sweat beading his forehead.

"Y-your daughter made that story up. Angelina, one of our specialty members who was pretending to be my daughter, told your daughter it was her birthday, and they were going on a trip to California. Your daughter made up the lie about band camp so that you would allow her to go."

I ground my teeth.

I knew it. Something about the whole trip hadn't felt right.

After our fight, and Cordelia's rightful anger at what I'd held back from her, I was determined to never use my influencing power on her again, or on her friends, which I didn't do often. I wanted there to be real trust between us, not coerced confidence. Cordy was so trusting, she hadn't realized that over the years she'd been with me back in Maine, I would sometimes make her promise me things, all without her realizing what I was doing.

I was still trying to learn how to shake off the old me, but Cordy's anger had opened my eyes at how wrong I had been to do that to her.

I didn't have to do it very often. Before the incident in Maine, Cordy had been so honest; she had no reason to lie to me, and here I didn't think she was capable of lying, thinking her fear was enough to keep her safe. I had been amazed that she'd been able to sneak past me and do lifeguarding without my knowledge. That had been impressive, as were her lies involving her friends.

Now I realized how far we had drifted apart, all because of lies; we no longer confided in each other like we once did. I'd wanted that back, but to earn trust, I knew I had to show her trust, so I'd believed her when she told me about the band trip, not coaxing out the truth from her, or from any of her friends. I wasn't mad at Cordelia for lying. I deserved it. I'd done much worse to her. I just mourned the fact that my selfishness and dishonesty had caused this. This was my fault. Cordy hadn't trusted me, couldn't confide in me, and had found trust and confidence in others. Others who were even more underhanded than I was, which I found incredible.

Cordelia's friends had seemed like nice kids, but I'd still felt uneasy. She had made these friends so fast. I should've listened to my instincts. I was losing my touch. That, or Cordelia was better at manipulating me than I thought.

So, though I had my reservations, I had let her go. I thought, for once, everything was going to be okay. I trusted her. I was striving to be a better mom, and moms had to learn to let their children go out in the world, despite always wanting to protect them.

But I'd failed in that too.

My heart twisted when my hostage said the kids had gone to California.

Ocean water. They'd wanted her near an ocean so she would be tempted to let her guard down and possibly reveal herself, so they could learn her secrets. And she was far from me, the only person who could truly help her.

"None of us knew she was a hybrid until word came down from the bosses, when they found out that your daughter had been poached, and they needed—"

"*Wait, what? What do you mean she was poached? You no longer have her?*" My stomach roiled. These freaks had competition? How deep did this industry go?

The man shook his head. "She was taken from our team by a loner who we've had trouble with in the past. Parker Colton. He's been known to sell to buyers all over the world."

"*How did you find this out? Where did he take her?*"

"Our team leader, Regina, was able to get aboard his ship, the *Elusive Fortune*, and put a tracking device onboard. The last place he was anchored was at the Osaka North Port in Japan. I have the coordinates here." He gathered several papers from his desk drawer, and I snatched them from his hand. There were indeed coordinates, a few more pages of information, and even satellite images of the docked ship in the Japanese harbor.

"He was docked there for quite a while before the tracker was turned off. We assume he discovered it, but we don't think he's moved his boat. We know he's looking for buyers. Japan is known for its magical black market, so he may be there for several days more, rubbing elbows with buyers. He knows we can't do much. We were waiting on the go-ahead from my bosses before we gathered a team to try to extract her, but some of the other higher-ups told us to wait, some losing their eagerness to go after her, wanting to cut their losses. My bosses had been rather unwilling to share the information that she was a hybrid. They desperately want her for some reason."

I snarled. How dare these humans think they can take Cordy for their own means. She was *mine.* "*Why do they want her so badly? Why do they want hybrids?*"

"I d-don't know," he stammered, the sweat now rolling down his skin, his shirt damp and pungent. "They only told me about her being a hybrid just last week, when they ordered me to get a team ready to capture *you* instead, while a decision about what to do about your daughter was being made."

"*How long have you known about me?*" I snapped.

"Well, since they knew your daughter was a hybrid, they knew you were a mythical creature as well, and we were going to capture you once we had your daughter in hand, but the timeline was moved up after she was poached. I have yet to hear anything more from my superiors, after I told them you had been captured successfully just a few days ago."

"You're a little behind the times," I replied with a smirk. Well, these HAMMA chumps might be waiting, but I wasn't.

Keeping the coordinate papers the man had handed me, I stood.

"*You will give me all the money in your wallet, and all that is available to you at this moment.*"

Without hesitating, the man stood, took out his wallet, and handed over a wad of hundreds. I gripped the bills, exhaling in relief. It felt good to be in control again.

He then went to what looked like a thermostat, pushed several buttons, and half of the wall off to our right slid back, unveiling an enormous silver safe that took up half the wall. I came up behind him, watching the door with interest.

With a few twists of the dial, the man opened the vault door, revealing varying sizes of leather duffle bags, stacks upon stacks of cash and other papers, several bars of gold, and a few hanging file folders. He began loading bundles of cash into a walnut brown leather bag, the largest duffle of the bunch. I should've thought about this money-making strategy months ago.

"*I want everything. The files, stocks, gold, and all the cash,*" I snapped. He slipped all of the files and other papers into the bag, including several bundles of other countries' denominations, effectively emptying the safe. He struggled to lift and pass me the bulging bag, which I took with one hand.

"*Now, you will buy me a plane ticket to Osaka. The earliest one available, most direct route, least amount of layovers.*"

He did so without hesitating, hurrying back to his desk, his fingers typing furiously on the keyboard of his computer as I lounged in the seat, waiting, though my heart was thundering in my chest.

I would've gone without a ticket, but it was going to be hard enough to convince the airport security that I didn't need a passport. It was harder to control what people saw when you placed multiple suggestions in their mind, and sometimes things got sticky, people got confused, and then time was wasted.

After a few moments, he printed out the boarding passes and handed them to me. I looked them over. He'd bought me a first-class ticket—force of habit, no doubt. It was nearly nine-thirty at night right now. My flight left at six-thirty this coming morning, so I had about nine hours to endure before I could really get going. Scanning the boarding passes, I noted that after a thirteen-hour flight, I would arrive in Osaka around eight-thirty the following evening.

I looked the man in the eye. "This is acceptable, I suppose."

The extra cash I had in the leather bag was for buying another set of plane tickets and another life, somewhere where no one would find Cordelia or me ever again.

"*Now, HAMMA owns this casino, you say?*"

When he nodded, I smirked. "*Well, you will call me one of your finest personal cars to take me to the airport. You will then pull the fire alarm after I leave the building. You will make sure everyone has evacuated, and then I want you to burn this place to the ground.*"

He nodded.

In a former life, I would've told him to burn the place down *now*, not caring if the people were still inside or not. I was a shadow of that self, and I had learned empathy, sympathy, and compassion. In a word, I had acquired humanity.

Naiads drowned people because we thought it was funny, not out of cruelty or malice. Everything was a fleeting joke. Humans knew full well how their actions would affect others, and they just didn't care. Selfishness was just one trait in a long list of major flaws in the human race, and, unfortunately, I was learning more from humans than I had bargained for. I now knew there were such things as innocent and guilty, good and bad. And these guilty ones that took my daughter? I would make them pay. After all, though I had learned compassion, I had also learned cruelty.

"Very good." I turned to leave, opening the office door and slinging the bag over my shoulder. I then paused and glanced at him with a sweet smile. "Oh, and one more thing. *You won't remember any of this conversation or that I was here at all.*" I closed the door as he bobbed his head in agreement.

I was just stepping into my requested limo when the fire alarm blared to life.

Chapter Thirty

The plane finally jolted to a stop at the jet bridge, and I was up and out of my seat before the captain had even flicked off the "fasten seat belt" light.

I charged down the aisle, not caring about people's annoyed mutterings as I shoved past them. My second layover to Osaka had been delayed, so it was nearing ten p.m., and I was not in the mood to deal with stupid humans.

I didn't have anything but my leather carry-on bag, and I was determined to be the first one off this plane. Some idiot brayed, "Hey, where's the fire, lady?" as I bulldozed past, but I ignored him; I ignored all the angry people. No one was going to mess with me today. I was going to find my daughter, come hell or high water.

I expected both.

I charged out of the airport, hailing the first taxi cab I saw by stepping right in front of it, despite the honking and yelling. A man was driving. I smirked.

That was good. Men were usually easier than women.

I slid into the cab and looked at the romaji words I'd translated out on my phone.

"*Take me to the Osaka North Port Marina via the most efficient route*," I recited in choppy Japanese over the driver's continued shouting at me, hoping my influencing magic would work as I pushed it hard toward the driver. It didn't matter if my Japanese was basically incomprehensible, the persuasion would take care of the rest, as long as the driver mostly understood what I wanted. Not even naiads connected to their lake were powerful enough to be perfectly understood through language barriers.

The man stopped berating me and nodded, turning back to face the road. He would get me to the marina without dallying like I knew taxi drivers did with naïve passengers. My phone calculated that it would take around half an hour to get to the port from here.

Those people holding my daughter captive had thirty minutes left to enjoy the rest of their lives.

As the cab pulled out into the street and began crossing onto the considerable bridge that spanned over the jet-black water, I looked out at the cityscape illuminated against the starless night sky. I'd forgotten that you couldn't see stars in heavily populated places like this. That was one beautiful thing about Nevada: we could look into the heavens and see the heavens looking back. I leaned my head back onto the seat and took a deep breath, trying to calm my mind. It felt like my first breath since finding out something had happened to Cordelia.

Even though I could easily brush off incidents, this was the first big personal situation I'd dealt with in a long, long time.

I hadn't had time to really process the last week. My incarceration had seemed a run-of-the-mill capture, and I had shrugged it off with relative ease. But I knew Cordy's imprisonment would affect her. Anything that happened to Cordy, I took very seriously. She was my purpose in life, even though I didn't often act like it, to my shame. She had only been on this earth for sixteen years. I've had at least twenty times that amount of living to learn and smarten up. She was just a baby. My baby.

The crazy events and the danger I'd faced to get here didn't matter. I was here now, on the brink of finding her. I only hoped that I was in time.

I snapped out of my thoughts. I needed to focus.

If this poacher had been docked in Japan for three days, he might already have a buyer lined up. He might already be gone. My stomach clenched at the thought.

The car slowed as several boats, many of them mega yachts, came into view, anchored on their own private wharf, their windows dark because of the late hour. I searched the names of the boats as we drove by, meticulously scanning for any sign of a boat resembling what I had seen on the satellite photos I'd studied during my flight. An elated gasp escaped my lips as I saw *Elusive Fortune* scrawled on the side of a particularly gaudy hull. The sheer tackiness of such a stupid name made me roll my eyes.

I threw a wad of Japanese yen at the driver, then stepped out of the cab. I waited until the vehicle had pulled away and was out of view before I turned my sights to the extravagant yacht before me.

I didn't have a concrete plan as I marched toward the darkened ship, but even from here, I could feel the magic flowing from the vessel. Cordy's odd signature felt very faint, but that was probably because her magic was being collected. I knew that she was here.

She had to be.

I paused beneath the shadow of the ship, considering how I would get my daughter out. If this Parker Colton guy knew about magic, it was more than possible that he and all his staff would be wrapped in magical barriers. However, it was midnight. Everyone would probably be asleep, except for the few people manning the yacht.

I would just sneak on, grab her, and sneak off. Maybe strangle a few people along the way for good measure. I shook away the idea. No, it was better to just sneak away without causing a scene.

And while it would be easier and more gratifying to kill everyone on board and then swim away with Cordy to find a new life, I had my giant bag of money to consider; which we needed to buy our new, even more hidden life. We couldn't run and live peacefully among the humans if we left a grisly scene in our wake and got caught by the law. Besides, Cordy had been through enough. A quick getaway, without any stress or violence, was what she needed, even if it wasn't what I wanted. So, in and out like ghosts it would have to be.

I studied the ship. The gangplank wasn't lowered, but that wouldn't be a problem. I stowed my money bag in the shadows of the wharf, and turned toward the glimmering waves. Taking the dock line that tied the ship to the pier, I lowered myself in the inky water and began climbing up the line. As I neared the ship's hull, I almost laughed. For a moment, I felt like a pirate. I'd known a few pirates back in my day. I'd have to tell Cordy that story after we were in the clear.

Reaching the hull, I grasped the railing and heaved myself onto the deck.

Shaking out the burning in my arms, sore from the constant workouts and insufficient food of the last week, I hurried down the deck, following the trail of magic like a hungry man followed the smell of food. I hid whenever I heard voices, but didn't run into anyone. I crept down two flights of stairs, finally coming to a closed door that pulsed with magical power.

I opened the door and glared around the room. A few magical creatures huddled in filthy cages, and the smell that hit me was nearly as powerful as the magic. With a wrinkled nose, I stepped inside the brig.

The strongest signature in the room came from the feathered serpent, but my heart fell as I realized Cordelia was not here. However, there was someone I recognized in one of the larger cells.

Angelina had been lying on a bench in one of the cages, and she sat up as she heard me enter. Upon seeing me, her mouth fell open in pure shock. I felt my lip curl in satisfaction.

"Ms. Jones?" she squeaked, her expression relaying more fear than confusion. "How did . . . how . . . why . . . how did you get here?" she babbled.

I let her stammer for a few more moments, before I cut her off with a swift motion of my hand. My voice was calm, but fiery anger burned through my veins and I stared down at her. "I suppose I'm the last person you expected to see. Thought I was captured too, no doubt. Funny, how does it feel to be the one in a cage? Seems an appropriate fate for the scum that tried to set a trap for my daughter and me." Angelina dipped her head in shame, but then looked back up at me, her jaw set.

"Ms. Jones, please, I didn't want to capture Cordelia! I had no choice! But I tried to help your daughter escape," Angelina began, her voice trembling, "Both me and Joshua, we tried—"

"*Tell me the truth*," I commanded, my influencing words visibly striking Angelina.

"Joshua and I tried to help your daughter escape," she repeated, her voice strong and clear, and for the first time since I had learned of my daughter's capture, I felt genuine surprise. Angelina was actually telling the truth.

"*Where is my daughter?*" I demanded, my tone only slightly more gentle.

"Parker was holding her in a special building somewhere in the city. I was there with her."

"*If you were with her, how did you get here?*"

Pain spread over Angelina's face, tears filling her eyes. "Cordelia made an escape attempt last night. She got me out too, and I thought we were going to escape together, but she left me. I don't blame her," she replied hastily, not meeting my eye. "She wanted to escape on her own. But I didn't want her to be alone, I wanted to help her where I could, so I followed after her. They put this magical tracker on her, and she was trying to get it off before really escaping, so she went deeper into the city."

I shook my head. Oh Cordy. She thought too much sometimes. She should've headed straight for water. It was her biggest advantage.

"I lost her for a time in the crowds," Angelina continued, "but when I found her again, she was being captured. I saw it. She was trying to reach a canal to escape, but then they sedated her and brought her back to the building where we were being held."

"*Why didn't you go to her aid?*" I snarled, and Angelina cowered away.

"I-I wanted to, but I realized I would probably get caught as well. Besides, Parker has been taking her to this convention of rich people, trying to sell her, and I thought maybe that would be a better place to try to break her out."

My worst fears were confirmed, but it sounded like there was still hope. "*So, where is she now? At that convention?*"

"Yes, they run till like one or two in the morning. At least that's always when Parker would return Cordelia for the evening." Angelina paused, considering me. "I realized that I could follow Parker to the building he was selling her at, and maybe try and get her out of there. I followed them in a taxi to the convention hall, which was actually more of a challenge than I thought, because Parker is paranoid. But my driver was able to keep up without being detected. When I saw the place, I realized I would need help." She paused, twisting her hands in her lap. "I-I didn't know who I could get to help me, then I remembered where Parker's ship was docked, so I took a cab here, hoping to break out Joshua, or maybe even get my mom to help me at least get Cor out of Parker's hands, but I got recaptured by Parker's men when I got on the boat. Parker must have warned them I would try to come back for my HAMMA companions." She lowered her head in embarrassment. "They must have moved the HAMMA members to a new cell, because it was empty when they put me back in here. This was the room where Cordelia was kept too, before they moved us to the city," Angelina babbled on, wringing her hands anxiously. "I think they wanted me in a separate cell from everyone else because they didn't want my mom to know that I'd escaped Parker, afraid I'd make trouble if I was with—"

"*Is Cordelia still at the convention center?*" I interrupted her, having heard enough.

"I think so, yes."

"*Okay. You know how to get there from here?*" I demanded, my heart a rapid cadence in my chest. I was getting so close, but I was short on time.

Angelina nodded. "I pickpocketed someone's phone while I was following Cordelia, and used the maps to mark and follow where Parker had been. The guards didn't bother to check me for a phone, so I still have it."

"Good. *You will—*"

"Wait," Angelina interrupted, and I glowered at her. "Please, don't force me to hand over the phone," she pleaded, and I raised an eyebrow. She knew I was influencing her? Impressive. "I won't be able to resist handing over the directions, but I have a feeling you'll leave me here, and I want to come with you. I want to help you get Cordelia out. Please."

I snorted. "*Oh, so you can hand her back to Mommy?*" I asked.

Angelina staunchly shook her head. "No. I will never do that again. Ever. I want to help Cordelia escape from HAMMA, the poachers, even humans in general, if she wants."

I narrowed my eyes. "*Why?*"

"Because I owe her that," Angelina insisted. "I need to help get her out, to help repair the damage I've done. Please." She stared at me with wide, beseeching eyes.

"*Are you telling me the truth?*"

"Yes. Please. I want to go with you."

Suspicion still rippled inside me. If Angelina knew I was influencing her, it was possible she could actually withstand the magical influence, and was just telling me what I wanted to hear. There were humans out there that had the ability to do so, and it could be learned with training.

"*Tell me something that you wouldn't want Cordelia to know,*" I said suddenly, trying to catch Angelina off guard.

"I like Joshua, and I got very jealous when he told me about kissing Cor," Angelina said immediately, her face blooming bright red as the words left her mouth. The body couldn't lie, and Angelina's burning red face was proof that she was telling the truth.

"*And you still want to help her get out, even if it meant Joshua might get back together with Cordy?*" I asked. I doubted very much Cordy would ever take Joshua back, even if he did break her out, but I wanted to hear the words.

"Cordelia is my friend. I want to get her out, even if they do get back together," Angelina replied, her tone serious. There was no hesitation, and the conviction and honesty in her voice erased any final reservations I had. I was still angry with her and would still keep my eye on her, but I believed her to be genuine.

I exhaled. "Fine."

"And Joshua. I want him to come with us." Her expression was resolute as she folded her arms, glaring at me.

I chortled. "Oh sure, anyone else?"

"I'm serious. Joshua wants to help, and he needs just as much redemption as I do."

I couldn't argue about that.

"He's coming with us to break her out," Angelina pressed.

I huffed again, staring at her in wonder. Humans were confusing, but teenagers were the most bemusing of them all. One minute they were gung-ho on capturing my daughter, the next, they were wanting to help her escape. Not to mention, all the drama with this teenage love triangle was sure to make things difficult.

And people said naiads were fickle creatures.

I shrugged. If nothing else, a pair of kids could provide a distraction for me at the convention center while Cordy and I got away. "Very well." I looked at the bars of her cell. I was strong, but not that strong. "Where are the keys?"

"Um . . . Usually Parker's giant bodyguard has them, but I think he gives them to one of the sailors when they're off-ship," Angelina replied. "The guy that locked me up is named Martin, or something."

"Have you noticed if they've had magical protection barriers around them?" It would be just my luck that they all had on protection that I couldn't get around. "The barriers look like that," I said, pointing to the cages occupied by magical creatures, the slight shimmer around them.

"Uh, no, not that I've noticed . . ." Angelina said, frowning.

"Perfect. I'll be right back."

I made my way up a flight of stairs, following small signs that directed me to the staff's kitchen. A couple of men were in the galley, eating and playing cards. Their jaws barely had time to fall open at my entrance before I'd said a few quick words and they were under my influence. As I munched on a shrimp taco I'd taken from one of their plates, I demanded the keys, then hurried back down to the brig and let Angelina out.

"Let's go," I replied, polishing off the last bite of shrimp.

"Wait," Angelina said, glancing at the other occupied cages, "Shouldn't we open those cages and let the animals out?" she asked.

I laughed as I wiped my hands on a napkin and threw it on the floor. "There's no way we're opening those. That feathered serpent is highly intelligent, and extremely venomous. The duende can be mischievous and would hinder our escape more than help, and the cadejo can bite, causing hallucinations. We're not opening them."

The reproachful look on Angelina's face made me pause, frowning back.

"What?"

"We can't leave them here," she demanded.

"Where was this conscience of yours when Cordy needed it?" I muttered. When Angelina stood staunchly, not moving from the room, I clicked my tongue in annoyance. "No," I replied with an eye roll. "I suppose not. But we're going to have one of the men open them, after we leave. Okay? Let's go."

Angelina led me to the door where she said Joshua was being held, and we quietly opened the door. This room was dark, filled with half-built cages. By the light streaming in through the open door, I saw two groups of people stuck in two smaller, completed cages. All were asleep. Angelina hurried to one of the pens and stuck her arm through the bars, prodding a sleeping figure awake.

"Joshua," she whispered. "Wake up."

He groaned and rolled over. I clenched my jaw as Angelina tried to wake him again without success.

Exhaling in exasperation, I marched to the cell door and un-locked it. Not caring that I was trodding on sleeping people as I picked my way over to him, I grabbed the unconscious Joshua like I was picking up a very large toddler and heaved him up onto his feet, giving him a few bounces to wake him.

"Ahhh! What? *What?*" Joshua cried out, bleary-eyed, as he found himself in a standing position. The moment his eyes focused on me, his face drained of all color. "M-Ms. Jones—"

The others inside the room had woken up to his yelling and my stomping feet, and they were looking around, moaning in confusion.

"Come on," Angelina hissed, her face half illuminated in the dark room by the open door, and Joshua whipped around to look at her.

"Angie?" he slurred.

"We're getting you out!" Angelina said as I dragged Joshua out of the cell, stomping on multiple body parts, triggering another chorus of grunts and yelps. I quickly shut and locked the cell behind us amid the babble of confused and angry voices.

"*Angie!*" A woman screamed, and we turned to see Angelina's mom standing at the cell door, staring wide-eyed at us through the bars. "You're okay?" Her voice broke in a sob. "How did you get free? How did you get here—" Her eyes slid to me standing beside Angelina, a towering shadow in the dark, and her voice died out, mouth falling open.

"Regina, I presume?" I growled, giving the woman a black look as I pushed Joshua and Angelina toward the door. "Be glad I don't have time to give you a proper greeting. Come on, kids."

"Angelina! You stop right there!" Regina demanded. "Don't you dare walk out that door. You let me out right this moment!"

Angelina paused, taking a bracing breath, then turned to face her mother, her expression resolved. "Mom, I'm quitting HAM-MA. Effective immediately."

Regina opened her mouth, but no sound came out, and Angelina turned and marched out the door. I hurried after her, pulling a still-groggy Joshua along with me. After casting a venomous smile at Regina, who paled, I slammed the door shut behind me.

We headed back to the galley, where I instructed one sailor to lower the gangplank, and told another to release all the creatures after we'd safely left. I didn't bother telling him to be careful around the mythical creatures he would be releasing. It was a hazardous line of work, being a criminal. If he got poisoned or kicked in the head, he had it coming for not respecting magic.

We practically flew down the lowered gangplank, then I gathered my money bag and we hurried to the nearest street to find a taxi. When one pulled over, Angelina relayed the coordinates to me, and I translated them with my phone to the cab driver. Just as the cab was pulling away from the curb, Angelina gasped. She was looking out the window, and I followed her gaze in time to see a group of people running from the direction of the marina, toward our cab, Regina a prominent figure leading the shouting group.

My lip curled in disgust. "That idiot sailor must have let *all* the beasts out," I growled. Sometimes, feeble human minds could get confused by persuasion. But there was nothing for it now, and our cab was already down the street and turning the corner. The HAMMA monsters wouldn't be able to find a cab in time to follow us.

Angelina turned back to face the front, her lip trembling. Though pity for her was wasted on me, I could understand the hurt she must be feeling. Mothers and daughters were always complicated.

I shook my head. I had to get back on track and steer my vindictive emotions toward those truly responsible for Cordy's abduction.

I couldn't wait to make this Parker Colton's acquaintance.

And end his existence.

Chapter Thirty-One

After about an hour, I went rigid in my seat.

"We're almost there," Angelina reported, looking at her phone. Joshua peered at her screen over her shoulder.

No kidding. It felt as though we had entered into the shallows of a magical sea, and a tidal wave of power awaited just ahead to engulf us. I hadn't felt magic this diverse in a long, long time, if ever.

I had no doubt the people at this magical convention were collecting what magic they could from all the magical creatures in the building, but there was no way they would have enough relics to collect it all; from what Angelina said, it sounded as though there were more magical creatures gathered in this one location than there ever has been before. Even one hundred relics wouldn't be able to draw in all the power they exuded; the dregs of magical signatures seeping out into the street were almost overpowering.

"It's that building there," Angelina said, pointing to an gigantic, glass-lined edifice, the windows reflecting the city lights. The entire block seemed to ripple with magic.

I told the cab to stop on the next block over to avoid attention, and we hopped out, my mind debating on whose throat I'd be ripping out first.

We hurried toward the building, then hid in the bushes near the front entrance. One towering guard was standing beside the double doors. He seemed almost too tall and burly to be human. No other guards were in sight, and I realized the people who had organized this convention wouldn't need much more than this formidable guy. Just looking at him would deter most troublemakers or convention-crashers.

"I'm leaving this bag here in the bushes for now," I said aloud, just so the kids wouldn't think I'd left it behind on accident, burying the leather bag of cash deep into the foliage. "Now, what do we do about that guard?"

"You can see why I needed a little help getting in," Angelina said, glancing at me. "The back of the building is similarly guarded. He asks for invitations, and if you don't have them, you get the boot. I saw it happen to a couple of people. He's not gentle with them. I knew I would need an accomplice, and the only one I trusted was Joshua."

I narrowed my eyes as I peered through the bush. Now that I knew what I was looking for, I could see the nearly indiscernible shimmer of a protection barrier around the man. I wouldn't be able to incapacitate or influence him. I wasn't sure I'd be able to even if he didn't have magical protection to begin with, he was so immense.

"What I wouldn't give for one of you to be an Unmarked," I murmured.

"A what?" Joshua asked. I ignored him.

There was only one thing to do.

I turned and shoved Joshua out of the bushes.

"Go harass that man. Get him to chase you away from the door." I heaved Angelina out after him.

They turned to me, panic twisting on their faces. "W-what?"

"Well, you kids wanted to come along and help out, right? Now's your time to shine." I knew they'd come in handy.

Angelina opened her mouth. "But I had an id—"

"Go!" I interrupted.

"What are you going to do?" Angelina asked.

"Get my daughter, by whatever means necessary," I murmured through clenched teeth.

They gave each other a look, then, nodding in resolved agreement, they turned and charged toward the man. I snuck along the bushes toward the building, watching as Joshua and Angelina reached the guard and began doing various annoying teenager things; pretending to punch and kick him, taking selfies, and mocking how big he was. I could see him bristling from my position in the bushes.

I was impressed. They were good. But then, teenagers usually were when it came to finding someone's weaknesses and exploiting them. Shouting, the man swatted at them, trying in vain to drive them off.

Finally, one of them must've said something truly stinging, because the man bellowed and charged at them. The teens screamed with delight, and probably fear, and fled around the corner. The man didn't follow them, but it didn't matter. I was already slipping inside the front door before the man had even turned back to his post.

As the door shut behind me, I hurried across the wide, long hallway to the rows of double doors that lined the wall.

Stiffening my resolve at what ghastly things I might see, I stepped through the doors.

I was assaulted, not only by the overpowering waves of magic, but the smells of cooking food, music, chatter, and all the colors and shapes of the gathered people and mythical beings.

Mobs of people congregated at the variety of booths, buying pelts, enchanted elixirs, creatures great and small, books of spells, relics as old as time, or the teeth and hair of mythical creatures. Many of the booths were empty, and several were being taken down, though the crowds were still impressive. Other people were leaving the hall through other doors, taking purchases with them.

Queasiness flared within me.

I wandered through the crowds trying to ignore the people—mostly men—stopping to stare at my face. Usually I was flattered by such displays of admiration, but at the moment, I was nauseated. These disgusting human beings were gawking at someone they would sell or purchase in a heartbeat if they knew what I was.

As I watched the sellers behind the booths cheerfully selling those of the Ever, I felt unsure of my next step for the first time after breaking out of the HAMMA compound.

What if she had already been sold?

I pushed the horrible thought away. No, she had to be here. She had to be. But that brought up another problem. If my daughter was in here, there was no way I would be able to get her out without drawing attention to us. There was no way I would be able to hypnotize all these people at once. Most, maybe, but if they had barriers, it would be impossible. I could cause a commotion, and in the chaos, slip away with her. Or I could just wing it. I just needed to find her first.

I was just climbing some stairs to a small, empty stage in hopes of spotting Cordelia in the chaos when I heard my name being called just as someone crashed into me. Joshua looked up at me from his prone position on the stairs he'd tripped over, dazed, with Angelina trailing behind.

"What? How did you get in here?" I demanded as Angelina helped Joshua to his feet. I couldn't guarantee they wouldn't get hurt, and I thought the guard would've kept them safely outside. "What about the guard?"

"I'm a well-trained HAMMA agent," Angelina said, shaking back her hair. "I know how to handle myself, and that guard, with a little help."

"She was so cool," Joshua said, casting Angelina a grin.

Angelina blushed. "I needed Joshua's help, though. He's really good too."

I waved away their teenage twitterpation with impatience. "And you couldn't have shared your plan with me?" I demanded, annoyed. They'd gotten in so easily, for humans.

"I can't give away all my secrets," Angelina replied with a knowing look. "We brought your bag too, in case you needed to make a quick escape." I raised an eyebrow, irked at how this human continued to impress. And also how she seemed to know I would've taken her tactics and used them to my own benefit, rendering her useless.

"Okay, well, I suppose you can help me look—" I stopped mid-sentence, my heart constricting in my throat.

Across the room, I saw a large crane rising up, and slumped in the crane seat, sat Cordelia. Her face was devoid of emotion.

Catatonic. Water flowed off her seal tail in a cascade, and my heart constricted further. All these people had seen her. They knew what she was.

But her expression. I put a hand over my mouth, choking back the bile rising in my throat.

Her vacant look nearly broke my heart: it was as though all the life had been sucked out of her. She sat, limp, not fighting, not trying to escape.

What had they done to her?

Was I too late?

Joshua and Angelina followed my gaze, and I heard Angelina gasp. We watched in silent shock as Cordelia was lowered onto a cart and wheeled to the front of the tank, a huddle of burly guards surrounding her.

"Okay, time for sneaking is over," I growled, fury roaring inside me at the sight of my baby, *my baby*, in such a state. "Get out of here, kids." Before they could say anything, I was leaping off the stage with a feral scream.

"CORDELIA!" I shouted. Hitting the floor at a sprint, I dashed toward the tank on the far end of the convention hall, my blood burning. My progress was immediately slowed as I hit the congested middle of the room. I tried shoving people out of the way, but the crowd was so dense it didn't help much.

Through the press of people, I saw Cordelia perk up as my voice reached her.

"CORDELIA!" I called again. I needed to wipe that dead look off her face. I needed her to just see me, to see that I was here for her, that I had, and always would, scour the world for her. I didn't care if

I was calling unwanted attention to myself. Together, we might be able to get out of here in one piece.

"MOM?" I heard the returning shout, and I nearly choked on the tears that flooded my eyes. She sees me. She knows I'm here.

"CORDELIA!"

For an instant, our eyes met through the milling crowd, and I felt a jolt in my belly as I saw recognition in her expression.

"MOM! MOM, OVER HERE!" Her voice cracked, and I saw her try to squirm out of her cart, but several men surrounded her, breaking up any escape. "MOM, HELP! MOM!" came her plaintive cry. The fury surged up around me again as I fought through the crowd. They weren't getting away with my daughter.

"*Move!*" I commanded those around me, and a few in the crowd near me stepped out of the way, but others just gave me insulted looks as I tried to press through. I cursed inwardly at whoever it was that had created these magical barriers. I glanced around, and, to my annoyance, saw several men dressed in security clothing moving toward me. People got out of *their* way faster than they ever did for me. I ground my teeth. Humans.

Suddenly, Cordelia's screams became more frantic. "MOM! MOM, GET AWAY! GO AWAY!"

I knew she was worried about me, but it was these security guards who needed to be worried about me right now.

I squared up, ready to knock some human's lights out as the first wave of guards reached me, when I heard Cordelia shout, "MOM! RUN! PLEASE! NO!"

A guard lunged at me, blocking my view of Cordy.

"COR—"

Behind me, the room exploded in a burst of light and sound. People around me were knocked to the ground, and with lightning fast reflexes, I crouched to stop from being blasted off my feet as most of the light bulbs above us shattered, glass showering down on us. The second the shock wave had passed, I turned to see what had happened. The room around us was still for half a moment, and then the crowds erupted into pandemonium as more explosions echoed around the room. Had Angelina set off a bomb somehow?

For a moment, I was more afraid of getting trampled than of what had caused the explosions, but then someone grabbed me. I looked up to see a guard, stun gun in hand, holding it in my face. I twisted out of the way as he fired, and, seeing his barrier, I dove toward another oncoming guard. Both guards cocked their fists to punch, and I ducked as they swung at me. The guards instead punched each other, their fists bouncing off each other's barriers, the energy of the impact throwing them backward several feet, taking out several other people around them.

Another guard faced me, menacingly whirling a baton tipped with a hissing arc of electricity. I bared my teeth at him, crouching low, coiled for the moment of his attack. He lunged forward, the blue of electric sparks aimed at my heart, and I danced clear, ducking under and spinning toward the guard. I popped up and ripped the baton free from his protected hand. Taking a chance, I whirled in place and smashed the electric tip into the barrier of the baton's owner. The barrier around him evaporated, his pin smoking. I felt a victorious smile curl on my face.

The barriers weren't infallible.

I slammed the electrified tip onto the guard again, and he went rigid, falling to the floor. Suddenly, another explosion echoed right beside me, and a headache buzzed in the back of my skull. I spun around, ready to swing my recently acquired baton at this newest incoming threat, but paused. Through the blinding light of the explosion, one man stood tall, the lightning bursting from his hands in golden, crackling bolts, taking out several security officers who had been heading in my direction. I crouched as another guard took a swing at me, then I met eyes with the young man shooting lightning.

My breath caught in my throat, my mind reeling. How?

He gave me a slight nod in recognition, and relief flooded through me as he dodged to stand beside me, but before I could process everything, my mind went back to Cordy.

I would be getting my daughter back now for sure.

Somewhere, a gun began firing again. Back-to-back with my new, old ally, I knocked guards' barriers out with my baton while he fired back at those shooting at us, stopping bullets and casting shields to deflect any debris.

My ally cast another bolt of lightning, and as I crouched to dodge the punch of an unprotected guard, over the noise, I heard a faint, "MOM!"

I turned to catch a glimpse of the group of men that were taking Cordelia away, disappearing through a pair of swinging doors.

"CORDELIA!" I screamed. I looked at the group of guards whose barriers I'd vaporized, and raised a hand, summoning as much influencing power as I could.

"*SLEEP*," I roared, and the whole group around us collapsed.

The destroyed convention hall was nearly empty now, except for us and the remaining guards.

I bolted toward the exit where they had taken Cordelia, bursting through the doors just as several cars and a yellow van began speeding out of the underground parking lot. Other people were rushing to their cars, but none were toting my daughter. The van!

"NO!" I screamed, sprinting after the yellow vehicle. Heart fluttering like a panicked bird, muscles pumping, I dodged into the street. The roadway was quiet and empty, save for the squealing van careening away into the dark. I raced after it, gaining as the vehicle struggled to accelerate. I ran up beside it, punching the van's side, hoping to alert Cordy and scare the driver, but then the van swerved, knocking into me and sending my body skidding and tumbling to the concrete. Gasping, I raised my head just as the van gained a burst of acceleration, sped down the street, then turned onto a busier road.

With a feral howl, I surged to my feet. Ignoring the burning in my knees and hands, I sprinted after the vehicle, my legs screaming, feet barely touching the concrete as I burst into the lighted street. Several people walking the sidewalks gave me strange looks as I bolted to the corner and scoured the intersection, panting hard, my eyes straining for sight or sound of the vehicle, for Cordy's magical signature, for any hint of their direction.

I felt nothing. Heard nothing. Sensed nothing.

The van was gone. My daughter with it.

I stared into the gray morning light on that street corner, not seeing the cars pass me by as shock roared in my ears.

I had lost her.

Again.

Savage rage erupted inside me. I wanted to scream, to slaughter every single human that I came across, to make every human being pay, pay for the sins of their brethren, but I held myself in check. Those around me were innocents.

I squeezed my eyes shut, panting hard to shake off the raging fury that could kill those passing me on the street. I took several deep breaths, desperately trying again to hear her, feel her, smell her, to get any inkling of what direction she'd gone. I'd never listened or focused my mind harder, trying to sense her, her magic, her trail, but it was lost in the lights and sounds and smells and wind.

The street seemed to fill with an influx of humans in the few moments I stood there. The traffic of all the people walking through the scent soon obliterated any possible trace of her with their odors: their hair sprays and deodorants and perfumes, even their individual body odors; each human smelled of twenty different smells. And the sounds humans made; it was all so deafening.

I realized that those barbarians that had my daughter also probably had some sort of relic or magical signature dampener on her. It would explain why I hadn't been able to sense her unique trace at all in the conference hall. How would I be able to find her? My knees threatened to buckle beneath me, but my mind caught onto one hopeful thought.

No, all was not lost. He was here. After all these years.

Hope cooled the fury in my veins. He would help me.

I turned and sprinted back to the convention hall.

He had to.

Chapter Thirty-Two

When I returned to the convention hall, the place was deserted save for the unconscious guards littering the floor. I had to stop myself from kicking their motionless forms as I walked by. It was a difficult temptation to resist now that I'd lost Cordy a second time.

A lone figure paced around the hall, picking up items and throwing them back down in disgust. He was dressed in traditional Japanese clothing. His brown hair was longer than I remembered, and his beard was a wild mess, so long it was nearly tickling his collarbones.

I marched over to him, my headache returning with pressurized buzzing.

He turned at my approach, a smile on his face. "Well, well. Callista. It's been—"

I cut him short as I flung my arms around him and hugged him to me. He was more densely muscled than the last time I'd held him. The magic on him was almost blinding, an ancient, deep smell-feeling, like caves and dripping stalactites, but underneath all of that was the smell of *him*. It brought back memories of warm summer days with my sisters, of feeling safe.

He choked, frozen for several heartbeats, then gave me a tentative hug back. I released him with a short exhale, wincing at the strange pressure in my head.

"Brennan Lennox. I never thought I'd see this day," I breathed, my face flushing. He was just as handsome as the day I'd met him, even with that tangle of a beard, and I felt that same girlish excitement I'd felt when he had come to our lake home. He looked just as flustered.

Brennan ran a hand through his wavy hair, nodding. He looked me up and down, cocking his head, and I knew he could feel the difference about me, the less-ness that came when I was separated from my lake.

"And, I never thought I'd see you . . . *out* of your pond. Is it . . . permanent?" He gave me a sideways look.

"Does it show?" I asked, half-teasing, half-saddened.

He shook his head. "You're as beautiful as the day we met. Though maybe not as dangerous." He gave me a hesitant smile.

I shrugged, making a face. "I suppose. A little older, and though we do age slower than humans, *you* haven't changed a day."

His beard quirked in a sad smile.

I brushed my breathlessness away. "Okay, okay, re-acquaintances aside, I'm so glad you're here," I said. Acting like a giddy school girl wouldn't help rescue my daughter. "I need your help."

Brennan laughed. It was a brittle sound.

"You're not the only one, apparently," Brennan said, waving a hand around the ruined convention hall. "The whole world needs my help."

"Uh, yeah, where have you been?" I demanded. "How could you let all of this go unchecked? I thought your whole *mission* was to protect those of our kind who were in danger! This looks like danger to me! There were people buying magical creatures from all over the globe!" I huffed, gesturing to the smoldering fires and wrecked booths. A few chittering messenger squirrels from Norway were climbing up the rubble, searching for a tree to hide in. I was surprised that so many merchants had left their belongings, running from the man with the lightning. Then again, Brennan was a force to be reckoned with. "The world has gone crazy in your absence, if you couldn't tell," I pressed.

Brennan sighed, shaking his head, pain pinching his features. "I . . . I know. I'm sorry. I've been underground. And not in the metaphorical sense." He took a deep breath, rubbing a hand over his bushy beard. "I've been a diplomatic envoy for the last eighty-odd years, trying to make peace with the oni. Very closed society. They take a very long time to make amends, and I haven't been above-ground since I started. I didn't imagine that something like this . . ." He paused, surveying what had moments before been a den of magic traders. "I had no idea this was going on. How much the world has changed."

"You couldn't have come up to check on the world every once in a while?" I snapped.

He gave me a look. "I told you, I was underground, and you have no idea what I've been through to protect the world from the oni. It takes over a month of climbing down a cave just to reach their gates. No magical transportation allowed, even if you wanted to. And now, I'm pretty sure all of my hard work there has been for nothing, because the oni have been offended again. I promised them I would help, which is why I came up here."

"What's so important up here that they would take offense to?" I demanded, shaking my head as the headache creeped deeper in my skull. I could hear the blood pounding through my ears, and I tried to shake the pain away, but it wouldn't shift.

"An oni prince was kidnapped. Out from under our noses, in his own kingdom," Brennan replied, the disbelief coloring his tone. "The oni are beyond infuriated. I offered to track him down, since I had finally earned their trust, but it's puzzling. Whoever kidnapped him was smart enough to take an oni from his own kingdom, but wasn't bright enough to mask his magical signatures. I was able to follow his trail here."

Brennan sighed, moving over to a seat around a table where shattered glass sparkled like sharp little constellations. The glass moved out of the way on its own as Brennan sat down with a short burst of breath. "Apparently he was purchased in a hurry, and whoever bought him was keen of mind and cloaked his magic, because the trail went cold here. Not a hint of him to be found. The trail just ends. I'll need to start over. I'll have to search the entire world." He put a hand over his face with a soft groan. I could at least understand how he was feeling. I was in a similar boat.

"Everyone who could've given me information on him is long gone by now." He looked morosely around the deserted convention hall, a chagrined expression pinching his hollow cheeks. "I was stupid to drive everyone away, but when I saw you, fighting by yourself against so many, everything about this place just made me snap." He paused, then laughed in a rueful way. "It might not have been the best idea. I've scared away anyone who would have been helpful in finding the oni prince. I'll have to start tracking down those who kidnapped him and learn who bought him—"

"No, you need to help me, now, to find my daughter," I demanded, stepping up to stand over him. "They took her. They *took* her, and sold her here too! But she's still in the city, we could catch up to her—"

Brennan leaned back into the bench to look up at me. "You have a daughter?" Brennan chuckled, the sound emotionless. "You didn't have one when we first met."

"Like you said, things have changed." I stared at him, concerned about how tired he looked.

"Is she the reason you were cut off . . ." He caught a look at my face and grimaced. "Sorry. Never mind. So your daughter, is she like you?"

"Yes. And no." I shook my head and threw my hands up in the air, not sure I could trust him with an explanation of what she was. "Look, it's a long story, I'll have to tell you all about it later. For now, I need your help. Some scumbag kidnapped her and sold her here, and . . . " I fell silent, resolved to go back to that yacht and torture the man who took Cordy before sinking his ship into the harbor.

"It won't work," Brennan said suddenly, and I looked toward him, frowning. "I'm sure that man that took your daughter is already long gone, after seeing you."

I grit my teeth, suddenly recognizing the strange pressure on my mind, and I shied away from the feeling.

"You don't get to read my mind," I snapped, shaking my head at the pain. He raised his hands, his expression chagrined, and the pressure inside my mind disappeared, my thoughts my own once again. "Sorry. The oni are impervious to mind reading unless I concentrate tremendously on one mind, so I'm just used to my mind being open all the time. I forgot that most others are easy to read. It wasn't intentional, forgive me," he murmured. "I'll have to practice closing my mind again so as not to intrude . . ."

As great as it was to see Brennan again, I didn't have time for any more small talk.

"Brennan, please, you *have* to help me!" I insisted. Brennan stopped talking and stared at me, a sorrowful expression on his face. At that moment, I was extremely annoyed that my manipulations wouldn't work on him. He was too strong, and would never do as I commanded.

"We have to track her *right now*. She's still in the city somewhere, but she won't be for long, and I can't seem to sense her signature at all! But you can!"

"Callista, I lost track of an *oni*," he said, his tone grim, "whose magical signatures are colossal. Do you understand? If I can't even find Prince Fukayama, I won't be able to find your daughter in this city, especially without knowing what she feels like first, *especially* if her signatures are being blocked. Trust me, I want to help you, I really do. But . . ." He looked around the ruined building, his expression hopeless. "I've been gone too long, I can see that now. It was easier to be underground, and that might be my failing. It was peaceful, quiet. I could forget . . ." He cut himself off with a sharp exhale as he stood up from the bench. "But I have a prince to find before the oni decide to take matters into their own hands, *and* I have this world to straighten out. I can't do all that and find your daughter right now. I'm just *one* man. I mean," he growled, running his hand through his hair again in anger, "I was fighting against technology I've never *seen* before. I couldn't understand it! I'm out of touch." He dropped his hand, shaking his head as he looked out over the wreckage.

"No, you don't really think that, do you?" I asked, alarmed. If he was so defeated, feeling so lost in this world that had grown so much in his absence, he wouldn't be able to help me track Cordy.

"I'm rusty, Callista. I'm an old man in a new-magic world. I'm to blame, which doesn't feel great, but when I left, most people didn't even believe in magic. I never expected it to explode like this in less than a century. This was an open market for magic, and I had no idea how to stop it." The fury was evident in the tendons standing out in his neck. "I stood like a numpty, watching this place clear out of items that I've never even seen before, and I almost did nothing. Until I saw you." His tone softened as he met my eye. "You made me snap out of my stupor and do something."

We stood, silent for a moment, until a humorless chuckle burst out of him. "I didn't seem to help much, though, did I? I made a mess of things. I have so much catching up to do. If I hadn't been gone . . ." He sat back down and buried his face in his hands, taking deep breaths. "The world used to be a much smaller place. Fewer problems."

I knew it was wrong to push him when he was reeling from the awareness that he was so out of his depth, but I needed him.

"Well, you have me," I replied, sitting down beside him, placing a gentle hand on his forearm. He sat up with a sigh, then gave me a tight smile.

"A two-man army against a worldwide trade," Brennan laughed, "The odds don't sound so great."

"Speak for yourself," I teased. "We took on this entire building and won. Sort of." My heart still twinged at the thought of Cordy.

"Now multiply that with a thousand more," Brennan huffed. "I don't think we could do it."

"Even with your amazing amount of power?" I quipped, half-worried about how despondent Brennan was.

"Even then." He gave me a half-hearted smile, but I could see the strain in his jaw. "I don't know if my magic can combat all the new ways magic is being used. So many things I saw here were being powered more efficiently with smaller amounts of magic, to greater effect. Not to mention, the amount of magic users that were here was more than I've ever seen in one place. I'm greatly outnumbered."

Something rustled behind us, and we turned to see Joshua and Angelina making their way toward us through the rubble, my leather bag still in Joshua's hand. Brennan stood, turning to face them. His hands at his side began to glow threateningly, but I quickly put a hand on his shoulder.

"Easy," I said.

"Who are they?" he asked as they approached.

"Well, they're with me, but they're also sort of responsible for my daughter's kidnapping," I replied, the latent anger bubbling underneath my exhaustion. "They've been taught to believe that humans that use magic are evil."

"That's not a new philosophy," Brennan murmured, his voice heavy with sorrow.

"Yeah, but it's more twisted now. They have all these weird ideas about magic and mythical creatures, and they torture and steal from people who have magical items or creatures," I said, recalling what Angelina's fake father had told me back in Vegas. "I'll explain more later, not in front of them."

"They're just children," Brennan breathed, the glow of his hands dimming as he watched their progress toward us.

"They start them young nowadays. You've been gone, remember?" I shot back at him.

Brennan shook his head, his jaw clenched.

We were silent, watching as they finally reached us. Joshua and Angelina glanced hesitantly between Brennan and me, and, after a pause, Angelina finally spoke.

"Did Cordelia escape?" she asked, her voice timid.

I shook my head, my jaw aching from keeping back the biting words I longed to shout at them. "Her buyers got away, *with* Cordelia." I took the bag from Joshua more forcefully than I meant to, and Joshua gave me a frightened look. Angelina looked down, tears filling her eyes, and Joshua put a gentle hand on her shoulder before regarding me earnestly.

"We're . . . we're so sorry," he said.

"You should be," I replied, unable to keep the acid out of my tone. "I've lost her for the second time, but this time, she's in the wind. And I can't find her alone." I looked at Brennan pointedly.

He sighed. "Callista, I told you, even if you joined me, it would be very difficult. It's a whole new world out there that I'm unfamiliar with. Even working together I'm not sure it would be enough to—"

"We know of some people who could help," Angelina said suddenly, her attention snapping to Brennan.

I snorted. "Oh, yes, I'm sure HAMMA would *love* getting their hands on my daughter again, as well as Brennan and me to boot." Brennan's bad mood was souring my own, and Joshua and Angelina glanced at Brennan in curiosity.

"What's HAMMA?" Brennan asked, looking between me and the kids.

"I'll explain later," I sighed.

"No, it's not HAMMA," Angelina continued, "I . . . I heard my mother talking a while ago. There've been problems—a group of people have been causing HAMMA a lot of trouble lately. They've rescued numerous creatures and raided several of HAMMA's warehouses."

"Doing it for their own benefit, no doubt," I sniffed. There seemed to be no safe place for people like me and Cordelia nowadays. Brennan looked inquisitively between me and the two teens, his face puckered in a frown.

Angelina shook her head again, her expression earnest. "No, they're the real deal. HAMMA *pretends* to capture animals for the good of the animal, to release them into the wild. They preach magic is bad for humans to use, and they punish humans who use it, or who have magical animals in their possession. But this group, HAMMA calls them The Menace, truly want to help magical beings. They steal animals from us and actually release them into the wild, and they save a lot of humans too from the . . ." Angelina swallowed. ". . . the torture that awaits them for owning or using magic."

"*Tell the truth*," I surged.

"It's true," Joshua said immediately. "This group is working against HAMMA, and if you guys need help, I'm sure you could find it there. They're big enough that HAMMA spends a lot of their time trying to track down and quash this group and its leader. They're really causing HAMMA a lot of trouble."

"You kids were a part of this HAMMA group that kidnapped Callista's daughter?" Brennan asked, his expression hardening as he stared at Angelina. "Involved in the torture and kidnapping of humans because they use magic?" he raged. I knew some of Brennan's story, so I knew that would hit home for him. I watched as Angelina's face burned bright red and she looked down at her fingernails.

"Well, yes," she finally stammered out, tears evident in her voice. "I was a special agent for HAMMA, but . . . but—"

Joshua stepped forward. "HAMMA is cruel and manipulative, and we didn't know it when we joined. And now, after learning the truth, we've abandoned their organization," he said, glaring at Brennan, putting an arm around Angelina's shoulder. "My family had joined HAMMA at first to free magical animals from what we thought were evil human beings, but now we've seen what they truly are."

"They're hypocritical and barbaric," Angelina said, her voice catching as tears filled her eyes. "What they made us do to Cor proved that."

"We want to help you find Cordelia. And we think this other group can help you," Joshua continued. "They say it's a group led by a leprekin, but that's just a rumor."

"A leprekin, you say?" Brennan asked, his expression softening into interest. "I've read about them, but never met one. They're rare. And powerful." He paused, something seeming to lift off his shoulders. "Well, if anyone can help, it's a leprekin and his allies." Brennan turned to me, his expression brightening further. "Maybe there's hope yet in finding your daughter, the oni prince, and taking down this abominable trade once and for all."

I smiled, the pain around my heart loosening. I wasn't alone. And soon, my daughter wouldn't be either. But I hated the thought of giving up on the chase of Cordelia. Tracking down the leprekin would take me away from the scene of Cordy's second abduction. I was about to open my mouth to ask Brennan one more time to at least go back to Parker's boat, but he was turning back to the teens, already speaking. "So, young lady, where can we find this group?" Brennan asked, looking at Angelina, who blushed.

Frowning, I looked at Brennan, who had nothing but polite curiosity on his face. Joshua was also staring at Brennan with narrowed eyes as he glanced between Brennan and Angelina's pink face. I hid a smirk as I detected jealousy coming from Joshua, even though I knew Brennan would never be interested in a child like Angelina. He was too honorable.

I shook my head. Teenagers.

"That's the hard part," Angelina admitted, avoiding looking at Brennan's face. "We know they're back in the United States, but HAMMA has been having a really hard time tracking them down."

"I'm sure the four of us can find them soon enough," I replied, smiling at Brennan, hoping to goad him into a more hopeful—and helpful—mood. He tried to hide a smile, but I caught a glimpse of it at the corners of his mouth.

"Perhaps. With these children's help," he finally said.

I saw Joshua and Angelina give each other a look at the word "children," as Brennan only looked a few years older than them, but Brennan didn't notice.

"And I've got the way home. I have plenty of money in here to buy us plane tickets. Courtesy of HAMMA," I replied, holding up my brown bag, where the stacks of cash still resided. It had taken quite a bit of power to hide the contents as I went through airport security, but I was able to scrape by, and by my calculations, there was about three quarters of a million in my bag. "Or, wait, Brennan. You can travel a quarter of the way around the world in a blink . . ." I pointed out, hoping to encourage him with peer pressure. We all looked at him.

Brennan chuckled nervously, his face going red. "I . . . I haven't used that style of magic, or much of any magic, in a long, long time. Decades. Like I said, I'm pretty rusty, and I would hate to mess it up trying to jump *all* of us that incredible distance." He ran a hand through his hair, making Angelina blush even more. "I've never even gone that far just by myself. Besides," He perked up, "I've never been in a plane before. I remember hearing about their invention and how they were used in the World Wars, but I've never actually flown in one."

Joshua frowned in outright confusion at Brennan, with Angelina looking just as bewildered, but definitely more intrigued. I stifled a laugh.

"We'll explain later," I told them. "For now, let's see if there's anything of use for us here." Brennan turned to regard me, an almost rebuking expression on his face, and I held up my hands in question. "What? It'd be better to have these items in our hands than anyone else's right? Besides, we need all the magical help we can get."

Brennan nodded, his face softening to weary consent. "You're completely right. I'm sorry, this place and what it represents just put me a little on edge." He glanced at the teenagers beside him, who also looked affronted at my suggestion of gathering up items for use. Brennan turned to them, and I could tell he was about to put on his "teaching about magic" voice. "It's not a sin for humans to use magic, so long as you do it respectfully. It's here for us to use as well as anything else."

The pair slowly nodded, but doubt still clouded their faces.

I turned to the kids, feeling a little more callous toward them. They were fresh off the HAMMA juice, so while they were still learning, I didn't completely trust them yet. "Don't touch anything. Brennan and I will go gather some things."

We left them standing, mouths agape in offense, as Brennan and I split up and spent the next several minutes going through the conference hall, gathering several useful-looking items that hadn't been destroyed in the fighting.

I found a relic, similar to the one that Mendoza's doctors had taken from me, but this stone was pure red beryl. It would hold centuries worth of magic. I slipped the priceless pendant over my head, then something round and shiny caught my eye. I moved to pick up several of the small shield talismans. It would be good to level the playing field a little with these cowards who used magic but shielded themselves from the consequences of using it.

I was also able to skim a few unbroken phials of medication and tinctures before I turned back to see how the others were getting along. While not much was left, I had found enough to save, and so had the others, it seemed. Brennan was slipping several bottles; a handful of acorns; a long, bright blue feather; and a leather book into his robes. He also opened a crumpled cage, hidden beneath a fallen tarp that housed a pair of bright pink crabs. He picked them up, then suddenly gave a faint yelp, straightening. Seeing me staring at him, he cast me a sheepish smile.

"One got my thumb," he called. I laughed as I moved toward the others.

The teens, who hadn't listened to me, had instead gone ahead and started touching everything. They had gathered someone's money pouch filled with gold nuggets, some new high-tech phones, and a bag filled with items they were reluctant to share with us. I was just about to force them to open the bag when voices echoed across the room. Several figures emerged through the doors on the far side of the convention center, their exclamations of distress echoing across the destroyed scene. Someone spotted us, and, with angry shouts, a few began to move in our direction.

It was time to go, and I wasn't leaving here without at least trying to find the one last connection I had to Cordy. As we hurried out the doors into the underground parking lot, I grabbed Brennan's arm with an uncompromising grip.

"Brennan, you can transport us to the harbor, just to see if we can get a lead on Cordelia. I would go myself, but I don't have the means to get there before Parker does. He won't have reached his ship yet. I could wait for him there to get answers, and I won't have to start from scratch. Any lead will be enough," I insisted. Brennan's pause of unease made tears of frustration spring to my eyes. "Brennan, you can do this. I just need this meager chance. Please."

Brennan searched my face, then exhaled. "Very well. But only because I saw the image of the harbor from your mind, and it's fairly close by. I'm not going to aim for the ship, because even the slightest swell moving the vessel could be disastrous." He stowed the crabs into a pocket inside his robes and gestured for us to come nearer. We all gathered in a circle around him. His expression grew more stern as he looked at me. "Promise me you'll keep your killing to zero, no matter how much those there may deserve it. We need them for information."

"I promise," I lied, thankful he was no longer reading my mind.

Concentration etched into Brennan's features as he closed his eyes just as shouting human voices echoed around the parking garage. Fear hitched in my throat, but the clamoring of voices suddenly ceased. The smell of brine was sharp in my nose, and the sound of water lapping against ships' hulls and creaking rigging filled the air as we appeared in the midnight-quiet port.

"It's this way," I called, heart pounding as I hurried down the darkened wharf, searching the ships in the early morning gloom.

"No . . ." My eyes found the place where Parker's ship should've been, and I sprinted down the dock, skidding to a stop at the empty space. Disbelief coursed through me. "It's gone . . . " The empty stretch of dark water echoed the horrifying truth.

How could he have disappeared so fast? We were only at the convention center for about twenty minutes. It took longer than that to drive to the harbor, let alone prepare to sail!

I strained my eyes and my senses, trying to pick up any signatures, or any hint of the ship sailing out of the marina, but there was nothing. I was sure a man with Parker's resources had ways to cloak his ship. My one last connection to my daughter was gone . . .

Brennan came up beside me, placing a gentle hand on my shoulder as I stared out at the moonlight reflecting on the pitch-black water. "I'm so sorry, Callista. I should've helped you here sooner. I'm sorry for my reluctance. But I promise, I'll help you get your daughter back, no matter how long it takes. I'm with you."

I glanced at him, the anger at him flaring for a moment before settling. Brennan had a lot on his plate, I knew that, so I was grateful for his pledge. And now at least Cordy knew I was coming for her, that I'd always come for her.

Squealing tires echoed across the deserted port, and we turned to see a van rounding the corner with jerky motions, barreling toward us. My heart leapt. Was this Parker? Did his own crew leave without him?

The van peeled to a stop before us, and the driver jumped out, running toward the place the ship had been. "Wait, wait, wait! Please say they waited!" the man was calling, dashing toward the wharf. His expression became more horrified as he skidded to a stop before the empty dock.

"No, no, no, no!" he screamed out to the open water, not seeming to notice we were standing there. "I can't believe they left me behind!" He took off the cap he was wearing and threw it on the ground in fury, his vibrant red hair visible even in the dim light of a nearby streetlamp. "WHY? How could he do this? What am I supposed to do now?" he raged. He looked young, wearing the same colored yacht uniform Parker's men had been wearing.

I glanced back at the van, but I couldn't see anyone else inside, nor anyone exiting the van. So no Parker, obviously. He was long gone with his ship. This kid would have to do.

Brennan and I shared a glance, and Brennan held up a hand to me, probably because he could see I was ready to rip the kid's throat out. Brennan turned and walked up to the young man who was gripping his hair, staring in disbelief out at the dark, open water.

"Excuse me, lad," Brennan said softly, and the young man jumped, whirling toward Brennan with a strangled yelp. "You seem distressed, can you tell me what's wrong?"

"Oh." The kid glanced behind Brennan, finally noticing the rest of us, and his face bloomed bright red. "Oh, uh, my employer, he . . . he left me behind, and . . ." The driver finally caught a glimpse of Angelina and Joshua, and the adolescent's face immediately drained of blood, leaving him looking like a corpse.

"You . . . you were prisoners on the ship!" he stuttered, backpedaling away from us. In two heartbeats I lunged at the kid and had his upper arm in my grip as I snarled at him.

"Yes, and you are going to tell us where your employer is!"

"I don't know," the kid stammered, looking close to fainting. Brennan pried my hands off the driver's upper arm with a reproachful expression.

"I'm sure he'll tell us without us having to hurt him," Brennan said to me before turning to the kid. "*Won't you*, lad?"

I was at least happy to hear a slight threatening note in Brennan's voice.

The kid just stared at us, fear trembling through his body as he remained silent.

"Your employer abandoned you," Brennan reminded quietly. "He left you like you were nothing. You don't owe him any loyalty. Surely you can tell us where he's going."

When the kid continued to remain quiet, I rolled my eyes, and, knowing Brennan didn't care for my influencing people, I opened my bag with a flourish. I dug out several bundles of cash and flashed the stacks of bills at the kid.

"Maybe money will get you to talk? You're going to need it," I said, gesturing around at the empty, quiet dock. "How did he set sail so quickly, and where is he going?"

The kid's eyes lit up as he gazed at the stacks of cash in my hand. "I don't know where he is. Parker and his bodyguards came running to the van outside the convention center, and instead of getting in the van, they told me to drive as quickly to the marina as possible, that they were going to transport ahead, then they each pulled out a little glowing ball, and they like, squeezed them, and then disappeared. I drove here as fast as I could, but . . ." He gestured to the empty pier.

"*And where are they going?*" I demanded, no longer caring about Brennan's disapproval. The kid cowered from the venom in my voice, and he shook his head, trembling like a leaf. "I don't know. I swear, I was just their driver. Sometimes I would help clean up and wash dishes in the galley, but that's it, I was never told anything important. I have no idea where they're headed next!"

Brennan pulled me back a little bit, his soft touch fighting to calm the storm inside me as he forced me to look at him, his expression earnest. "This boy can't help us anymore, he doesn't know anything."

I snarled in protest, but Brennan's pacifying voice continued. "This Parker Colton seems intelligent enough not to share his plans with underlings, and had contingency plans for quick escapes. We were thwarted before we even knew what we needed to do."

"So even if we'd left when I first asked, he probably would've already been gone." I cursed, gnashing my teeth. I hated clever humans, rare as they were.

"But I promise you, Callista, we will find her," Brennan asserted, the streetlamp behind him wreathing him in a slight glow, but casting his earnest face in shadow. "The leprekin will help. They're some of the most powerful beings in the world."

"Well then, let's go find us a leprekin." I threw the bundles of money back into my bag, ignoring the cry of indignation from the driver at my deception as we left him behind. We hurried toward the street to catch a cab to the airport, as Brennan did not know the location well enough to transport us all there.

As we climbed inside the hailed cab—Brennan giving our destination to the driver in perfect Japanese while tucking an escapee crab back into his robe pocket—hurt and hope twined inside my chest.

Hold on, Cordelia. I thought as I stared out at the city just starting to wake. *You aren't forgotten. I will scour the world for the rest of my existence until I find you.*

I'm coming.

PART V
CORDELIA

Chapter Thirty-Three

My face hurt.

With a grunt, I pried my eyes open, wincing at the intense brightness. The reason for my pain immediately became apparent.

I was dangling in the air, wrapped in a heavy net. My face was smashed up against the bristly mesh, my lip snagged open. No wonder my mouth was so dry.

Wincing at the pounding in my head and the disgusting taste of morning mouth, I tried to pull my face away from the rope, but I couldn't move much. Fear spiked through me. Why was I netted like this? What was happening to me? The last few . . . hours—days?—were fuzzy. I couldn't be sure how long I'd been out, as the last thing I remembered was my final frantic escape attempt from the van, and even that was hazy.

Not only was I netted, I was shoved up against a very white wall of some sort, so that my vision was blocked. It was also extremely bright, like I had a spotlight on me. After my eyes adjusted to the brightness, I realized it was not artificial light, but the warm, healing rays of the sun. I stopped wriggling. I was outside. I noticed the crashing sound of surf behind me, and I could feel the humidity in the air. Where was I?

I shook against the net, but my arms and tail—wait, my legs were back—were pinned by the heavy ropes. I couldn't even move my jaw. I grunted loudly, praying someone would hear me and hopefully let me go. Terror lapped at my mind. Had something awful happened? Was I stuck like this with no one to help me?

Somewhere above me, I heard a voice say, "Mr. Whitfield? Yeah, she's awake now . . . Very good, sir. Yes, I have my earplugs. Very good, I await your whistle."

I tried to shake off the groggy feeling in my head, and again made the grunting noise, trying to signal to the man who had spoken that I wanted out. My arms and legs ached with numbness, and my dry, swollen tongue was desperate for a drink of water.

Voices were growing louder somewhere below and to my left, and as they got closer, I could finally make out what they were saying.

"Okay, now keep your eyes closed, my love, no peeking."

"Oh, Carson, I can't wait! I'm too excited!" a female voice piped up. Over the sound of the waves, I could hear footsteps crunching off to the side, and then I heard them stop below me. I rocked, trying to see what was going on, but the net was like a full-body straightjacket, and the wall blocked my view.

"My precious Min-Ji," I heard the man begin, "I know I've had this part of the house cordoned off for a long time, but I wanted to do something special for our five-year anniversary. I know you've been having to deal with those insufferable ladies at your book club, with their special sitting rooms and spas, so I thought I'd create for you the most luxurious place to bring your friends; you can sit here and bask in their envy."

The woman squealed, and the man laughed. "Okay, now before we go inside, I want you to see it from the outside. When I count to three, open your eyes, but don't look up, not yet. Happy anniversary, my love."

He counted, and then there was silence for a split second before the shrieking below renewed, this time more shrill and drawn-out than before, causing my already pounding head to throb in double time.

"Oh! Oh, Carson! This is incredible! It is so beautiful! This patio is perfect! And that tank! How did you do this? You brought the entire ocean to me!"

The man was laughing over the woman's shrieks of elation, but I still couldn't see anything, and I struggled to keep the panic from totally enveloping me.

"It's the largest private tank in the world! I made sure of it! I had Adus magically strengthen it, to help keep it healthy. And that's not all. Wait until you see inside. I wanted a real special centerpiece, not just for your new spa and sitting room, but also for the tank. A real jewel in the crown. So I scoured the globe, and I have found the rarest creature in the world to grace your new sanctuary, my love. Here, come inside to sit in one of these massage chairs, and watch the tank." The voices faded, and there was just the murmur of soft waves behind me before a sharp whistle broke the calm.

Suddenly, the net—chafing against my skin—began unraveling. I bumped against the wall as the net loosened, and for a brief moment as I rotated, I could see sunlight glinting off of the water beneath me. I considered hanging on to the ropes and ruining whatever surprise the man below was hoping to give his wife, but my arms were too sluggish, and I wouldn't have had the strength to hold on long anyway. I was freed from the net and fell a few feet into the waiting water below. When the bubbles and tingly sensation from my transformation cleared, I could see my surroundings. My mouth fell open.

An artificial coral reef spread ten feet below me, extending far enough that it was difficult to make out the glass on the far side. Tropical fish of all species, sizes, and colors darted between the rocks that were flourishing with live anemones, kelp, and seagrass. A few striped sharks the length of my arm from fingertip to shoulder rested in pockets of sandy bottom. Several rays glided through the water above the reef.

I swallowed a bunch of seawater in alarm as a shark longer than I was tall swam past me. It was a dull yellow-brown color with dark brown spots and an elongated tail like a sail. For a moment, panic jolted through me, then I noticed that its mouth was small, nothing like the razor-filled jaws of a great white. So it wouldn't be able to eat me in one bloody bite. Just in smaller bites, if it wanted. The shark's beady eye stared at me as it glided by before dipping down and settling into the sand, where it lay still. I put a hand to my chest, feeling my heart thundering beneath my skin. Okay, it was one of those sharks that rested on the bottom a lot. Hopefully it wouldn't bother me if I didn't bother it.

I whirled around to see if there were any other sea monsters creeping up behind me, and I saw that the tank continued on for dozens of feet behind me as well. But no other sharks were in sight. I exhaled, my tense muscles loosening.

The tank was huge. Around fifteen feet deep, the entire length and width of my house back in Moapa Valley could have sat comfortably in the middle. Half of the tank faced outside—toward a white sandy beach and the ocean beyond—and the other half made up the entire wall of the room inside this building, curving to follow the shape of what had to be a huge mansion. My view into the house faced an opulent sitting room and spa. Two people stood before the glass several feet below, staring up at me.

The cowboy who had bought me—his shirt now a different color, but no less florid—had a contented look on his face as he stared at the short Korean woman standing beside him. She looked barely twenty, and had a gnarly scar across her neck. The woman was staring at me with a rapt, almost sly, look on her face.

Seeing her scar reminded me of my own injuries from my ill-fated escape attempt, and I looked at my wrist. The burns were almost completely healed, along with the cuts on my palms, with barely any evidence I'd been injured. How long had I been unconscious? Or had it been fixed with magic? Whatever it was, I was grateful. Nothing burned wounds more than saltwater.

I flitted a few feet away from the side of the glass, then glared at the cowboy. He was an idiot to put a hundred-and-fifty-million-dollar tourist attraction in with a shark, even if the shark did seem harmless. You never knew with wild animals, but the dumb cowboy didn't have to worry about it. I did.

I couldn't hear anything else the couple was saying, as their voices were drowned by the acrylic glass and water, but from the couple's expressions, the cowboy had just asked the woman what she thought. The woman replied, clapping and jumping up and down, and no doubt squealing, and then they embraced, kissing passionately.

Grimacing, I turned away to inspect the whole of the tank. I swam the length and breadth, taking care to avoid the large shark and any dark crevices where who-knows-what was hiding, studying the terrain of my new home.

Dozens of fish darted in schools, and an orange octopus with white dots speckling across its skin like the night sky pulsed nearby. It quickly squeezed between a pair of coral-crusted rocks and disappeared. I swam along the glass, emerging out from the indoor portion of the tank, entering into a section that sat outside the house proper, overlooking the beach. Bright sunshine streamed in through the clear acrylic lid that covered the outside portion of the tank to protect us from the elements.

Outside my tank I could see a pristine, sprawling sandy beach, enclosed by towering, lush, green-covered cliffs extending into the water. The sight looked familiar, like something I'd seen in a movie or nature documentary, but I couldn't pinpoint where I'd seen such distinctive pinnacles of verdant-covered rock surrounding a beach. I saw a figure swimming in the calm waters of the sheltered cove, but they were so far away that I couldn't get a good look, let alone signal for help. But it didn't matter if they saw me anyway. Clearly I was meant to be on display without fear of discovery from outsiders who didn't know about mythical beasts.

I continued swimming, circling back around to where I'd started. The woman was still giving the man a long thank you, but they broke apart as I swished past them. When I circled the tank and came back around again, the couple were no longer admiring the tank, but were trying out the amenities of their new spa.

So, this is what I was bought for. I was to be an ornament, an exotic pet, kept in a tank. I didn't know what I had been expecting from my buyer, but now that I was here, it made perfect sense. Why buy a creature that could breathe underwater and *not* have it on display?

I didn't shy away from the horror of it, I was getting used to being ogled by now. It was something else that hit me that made my stomach drop.

I was going to get so bored.

Back at the convention, I had barely endured the boredom, but I'd also had fear and mulling over means of escape to occupy my mind, giving me purpose. Here, this was my final destination. This was my life now.

I was going to be a permanent part of this aquarium, with no way out. I would literally watch the world go by, people living their extravagant lives, and I would remain inside, stunted, growing old, accomplishing nothing in my own life. No college, no vacations, no more human food, no career, no family, no new hobbies, no friends. Although, at the moment I was fine with going without the last item; my friends of late had all been betraying desert rats.

I settled to stare out toward the beach and sea beyond. The figure was still swimming, and my heart hurt as I looked at the foamy waves. I was already dreaming about getting out of the tank, running the fifty yards to the breaking water, and making a dash for freedom.

With a jolt, I noticed that my bout of mindless, emotionless depression was gone, which I found interesting. I thought I would feel more depressed now that I was actually sold, but I supposed I had accepted my fate. Or if not accepted, then resigned to it. The worst had already happened. But that didn't mean I wasn't going to try to escape. I had a glimmer of hope. My mother was looking for me. And if she had come all the way to Japan looking for me, I knew she would continue to search the world. I wasn't forgotten. I had no idea how she had made it to Japan, to the conference center, even, but I knew she was resourceful and smart, even before I had learned she was a naiad. Which brought another thought to my mind that caused a rush of love to surge through me: she learned that I had been kidnapped, and came after me. She didn't see it as an opportunity to go back to her sisters, like I imagined she might have done. She came for me. And now I knew she wouldn't leave me to my fate. Maybe she'd even find Parker and give him what for. I smiled.

The thought not only gave me hope, but had jarred me out of the emotionless void I'd been sucked into. I didn't want to go back to that place ever again. Sure, I would die of boredom, but not because I shut out the world. I would concentrate on my mother, and consider what she would do, what she had done, to try and find me. And I would use that to try and save myself, too.

I suddenly realized that I didn't really know much about my mother. She'd kept a lot of secrets from me, but I supposed I was just as guilty as her, just not to the same extent. I hoped that when we reunited, we would be much more open with each other.

But right now, now that I seemed to be at my final destination, I had much more time to consider everything, and find a way to escape.

I would find a way out.

Chapter Thirty-Four

The sun was nearing the horizon when I noticed that the man and woman were nowhere in their spa room.

Wow. One hundred and fifty million dollars spent and already they were bored of their new toy. I tried not to feel insulted, but it was difficult. I had been kidnapped and sold, and they knew nothing of my feelings. They didn't care. To them, I was just an obscenely expensive addition to their lifestyle. To vent my feelings, I took several high-speed laps around the aquarium, frightening fish and whipping up sand, then fell back to the aquarium floor. Was this really going to be my life now? Just sitting here, nothing more to do than float around like one of these mindless fish in this exotic underwater prison?

I would go crazy long before I died of boredom.

Something disturbed the water and I glanced upward. A rope with a loop on the end was being lowered through the water. Cautious, I swam up to it, giving it a suspicious prod. Instantly I felt silly. I mean, it wasn't like I could be captured *again*.

I looked up, and through the rippling surface, I saw the waving shape of the young Korean woman, the cowboy's wife. She held the rope in her hand, and gestured at me to sit in the loop.

Bored and intrigued, I shimmied my hips into the rope ring. When I tugged on the rope, I was heaved upward and out of the water. The woman hoisted me up past the lid and then guided my body to rest on the sun-warmed acrylic top of the tank.

"Whoo, you *are* heavier than you look," the Korean woman panted, her voice colored with a laugh as she closed the large clear trap door. "And you look pretty heavy."

I took a moment to close my eyes and take several deep breaths of crisp air. It was clear, smelling of the sea and palm trees and fruit.

Wiping my wet hair out of my face, I looked up at her, realizing she was all alone.

"Wait. You pulled me up by yourself?" I asked, amazed. She wasn't wrong, I was a lot heavier in my selkie form, and I was about two feet taller than her.

"Looks like my personal training sessions have been paying off!" she replied, giving her raised arm a flex. I snapped my slack jaw shut. Even if she was a world-class bodybuilder, it seemed impossible she could pull a soaking wet selkie hybrid through the water and into the air without additional help.

"So . . . you're letting me out?" My heartbeat quickened. I didn't know why she had lowered the rope. I thought maybe to feed me. But to let me out? That had seemed impossible.

"Of course! I'm not heartless. I can imagine it gets extremely boring in there. Here, dry yourself off. My husband, Carson, said he was told that's how you get your legs back." She handed me a towel, and, after giving her a shrewd look, I quickly dried my face, then wiped down my fur. The sun helped speed along my transformation, and soon my body convulsed a little as it changed back. When the metamorphosis ceased, I blushed. I still had on the corset bodice from the convention, but I was now naked from the belly down. I quickly covered my nakedness with my towel, but the woman laughed.

"Oh please, no need to be embarrassed. I've seen my fair share of bare bodies. People are so weird about being clothes-free. Here you go." She handed me a pair of panties, shorts, and a soft t-shirt. Thanking her, I stood and quickly slipped everything on.

"I'm Min-Ji."

"Cordelia," I replied, pulling my darkened silver hair out of the collar of the shirt, leaving a damp trail on the cotton fabric.

"Nice to meet you Cordelia. Come on, we leave this way." Min-Ji gestured to a hanging ladder near the edge of the tank that led upward, to the second-story balcony above. I frowned, wondering what was going on, but realized anything was better than having to go back into the tank.

Climbing after her on shaky legs, I made my way up and onto the balcony above that overlooked the beach and sprawling jungle. Min-Ji was already looking out over the foaming seashore, and I turned to follow her gaze. I gasped. The sky was starting to turn different hues of orange, pink, and purple as the sun began to set beyond the cliffs and the glimmering horizon. The water crashing onto the sand was turning into a kaleidoscope of colors reflecting the sky. I sighed. Gorgeous. But it wasn't enough to distract me from my dozens of questions.

"Where's your husband? Does he know you're letting me out?" I asked, still feeling wary. Maybe there was more to my incarceration in the tank than I thought. Maybe they would have me be a maid or something in my time off from the tank. "Are you putting me to work?" I asked. I hadn't considered having to pull double-duty in my new gilded cage.

Min-Ji laughed. "My husband has taken the helicopter to the mainland. He was gone for a week to that conference, so he says he needs to catch up on work at the office. He'll be gone for hours, and he won't know that you've been out. And no, I'm not putting you to work." She cast me an amused look.

So, not a maid. What, then?

"Does this mean you're letting me go?" I asked, looking sideways at her, holding my breath.

She fully turned toward me, an apologetic expression on her face. "I mean, my husband did end up paying one hundred and eighty mil for you; I can't just let you go. He would ask questions, and then suspicion might be put on me, and I don't want to be found out."

Despair billowed up, threatening to overtake me, but I pushed it down with a resolved huff. It's okay, I couldn't give up. After a moment, I gave a humorless internal chuckle. So Parker *had* been able to up the price, and it was paid. I almost couldn't believe it myself.

"Come," Min-Ji said, interrupting my thoughts. "I've ordered dinner out on the patio."

Though disappointment continued to roll through me, I conceded that I was starving and dying of thirst; food would help. I followed her down a set of sweeping spiral stairs to the spa room I'd seen from inside my tank. We exited the spa onto a spacious covered patio outside with a perfect view of the beach, complete with comfortable couches and lounge chairs, dining table, fire pit, outdoor bar, and spouting water features.

A sumptuous meal of fish, rice, fruit, and vegetables was set up on the table, and the woman gestured for me to sit. Suspicious but ravenous, I decided to eat before trying to think of anything else, including an escape.

As I dug into one of the best meals I'd ever eaten, I studied the woman sitting before me.

"What did you mean, 'you don't want to be found out?'" I asked, shoving fish and mango into my mouth.

Min-Ji swallowed her mouthful, then in a flash, she was gone. Sitting on her seat was a small white fox, a plumage of nine tails with flaming red tips wreathed behind it like a peacock. Another flash, and Min-Ji was back, a calm look on her face.

"You're a magical creature?" I gasped, coughing as rice fell out of my open mouth.

"I'm a kumiho. A Korean nine-tailed fox."

My mind spun so much I had to grip the tabletop. "And you're keeping *me*, another mythical creature, as a hostage?" I demanded.

Min-Ji wrinkled her nose. "My husband meant well with giving you as a gift to me but, well, he's a little naïve." Min-Ji laughed as she turned back to her meal. "I mean, you are kind of a tacky gift, given what I am, but he's not at fault. He doesn't know that I'm magical. He doesn't care to know, and I'm happy not telling him."

I paused, trying to compute everything she'd just said along with her unbelievable revelation. "He doesn't know about you?"

"Nope."

"But he knows magical creatures exist?" I affirmed, frowning.

"Yep. You sitting here is proof, isn't it? I'm sure that if he knew I was magical . . . well, he might freak out. But if he knew, I don't think he would've gotten a hybrid magical creature as a decor item." She shrugged. I stared at her in amazement as she sipped her tea.

"But *you* know!" I insisted, stunned by her blithe attitude. "You should let me go!"

Min-Ji shook her head. "Like I said, it would put suspicion on me, and I'm very happy where I'm at," she said, giving me a warning look. "I don't feel like ripping out my husband's liver and eating it right now, so please, keep my true nature to yourself."

"Oh yes, of course," I replied sarcastically, pushing away my half-eaten plate of food. "Anything else I can do for you?"

"Hey, I got you out, didn't I?" Min-Ji pointed her fork at me, her tone offended. "I'm letting you have your legs back and serving you human food. My husband has the idea of feeding you chum like everything else in that tank. I'm going to let you out for meals, and treat you like a human being while he's not here, which is nearly all the time. I'm treating you with respect, even though I know you're a hybrid, and I know it's custom to kill beings like you, but I find it a silly custom, so I won't."

She turned back to her meal, not acknowledging how I tensed in my seat when she'd mentioned killing hybrids. Despite her assertions that she said she wouldn't kill me, there was no way to know what she really would or wouldn't do. She might be playing a long con. She might find thrill in getting me to trust her and then killing me. I had no idea what a kumiho's temperament was. Were they malicious?

"Why did you let me out, then?" I demanded, the fish and rice sitting heavy in my stomach. "And why did you show yourself to me? I had no idea what you were, I can't even feel your magic."

She gestured to a gaudy gold ring on her finger set with an obscene pink diamond. My mind flicked to my mother's necklace.

"It hides my magic. But I showed you who I was, to prove to you that I'm your friend. And I'm pretty confident you'll keep my secret. I got you out because I'm not a monster. I understand you've probably had a horrible time, so I want you to be happy here. You'll be able to stay in the mansion, and watch movies, and swim in the pool and talk to me, basically live a normal life except for when Carson's here. It's a pretty sweet deal. And in return for all this, you're going to keep my secret, and not expose me to my husband. If you do, you'll never leave that tank again."

We stared at each other for a moment.

"You're pretty confident that I'm going to go along with your plan," I finally said, keeping my tone and expression aloof, though my heart pounded. Waiting and overthinking had been my downfall with Parker. Min-Ji's threats and terms were clear, but there was one thing she'd overlooked. I had no tether on me now. "But what's to stop me from doing . . . *this*?"

I leapt up from my seat and bolted from the patio. I surged over the sand, preparing to dive for the foaming surf just feet away when I ran headlong into an invisible barrier. I careened backward and landed hard on my butt, rolled back onto my neck, my legs flopping over my head as I somersaulted backward. I came to a stop and lay in the sand on my back as the fine white granules rained down on me, my ears ringing, my head throbbing, my eyes vibrating in their sockets. When everything stopped reverberating, pain began pulsing through my body. I clenched my eyes shut against the enveloping pain as it ebbed and flowed through me.

Soft footsteps approached on the sand, and I cracked open one eye, blinking away the gritty sand that had gathered in the hollows of my eye sockets.

Min-Ji stood over me. "My husband has several magical creatures roaming our property, and so he put up a barrier around the entire perimeter of the island to stop them from escaping." Min-Ji gestured toward the innocent-looking foaming breakers. "He uses blood magic to bind each creature to the barrier, which is why *I* can do this." She left my side. With a groan, I sat up, spitting out sand, and watched as she sauntered past the place where the barrier was, and dipped her toes into the frothy swell. "He never took my blood to bind me here, because, again, he doesn't know what I am." There was a threatening note in her voice.

With a groan, I collapsed back to the sand. Min-Ji came to stand over me again.

"So, even if I wanted to release you, I couldn't. I'm sorry. Anything broken?" she asked.

I took a moment to rotate my wrists and ankles, and I tilted my neck from side to side while lying in the sand. Everything felt okay, nothing too painful now, besides a headache. "No."

She held out a hand to me. "Come on, let's finish our meal before you have to get back into your tank."

I allowed her to help me up, and she stayed by my side as I hobbled back to the patio. By the time dessert was served—a coconut ice cream garnished with dark chocolate shavings—the dizzy feeling in my head had abated. But my determination hadn't.

I took a deep breath and looked Min-Ji in the eye.

"*Release me*," I demanded.

Min-Ji smiled at me. "I admire your tenacity, young lady, but I'm naturally immune to magical persuasion. Foxes are wilier than naiads. Sorry."

I slumped into my seat, feeling truly stumped.

She gestured at me with a spoon. "Eat your ice cream. It's my favorite."

"Can you at least tell me where we are?" I asked, twiddling my own spoon in my fingers. Knowing my location on a map would at least take away some of the feeling of disorientation and mystery.

"A private island off the coast of Thailand. I'll have to take you on a tour sometime."

Thailand. Another place I had wanted to visit with my mother. Now the location was ruined for me. Not that I was going to be making any vacation plans anytime soon. But now I had a semi-concrete idea of how far away from home I'd ended up, and would use the information for planning a jail-break in the future. A gilded prison was still a prison, and I was determined to do all I could to break myself free.

Chapter Thirty-Five

After dessert, which had been irritatingly delicious, Min-Ji offered for us to move to the enormous horseshoe shape of comfy couches surrounding the fire pit as dusk settled.

A snappy little fire was lit in the pit, and a pitcher of lemonade and some bowls of nuts and fruits were set out on the coffee table by a few servants while the dining table was cleared.

Occasionally Min-Ji would talk at me about things like what the weather was usually like here, and how Carson was frequently gone so I wouldn't be in the tank a lot. I stayed mostly silent as twilight fell around us, hugging a pillow to my chest as I stared into the dancing flames of the pit, considering everything.

Even if my mother did somehow find me again, would she be able to get me past that magical barrier? I had no idea how it worked, and so I didn't have the first idea on how it would be able to be taken down.

"Does Carson know how to use magic?" I asked, interrupting Min-Ji as she chatted about a party in Singapore she had recently attended.

"Yes, a little, but he also employs a true sorcerer to cast the barrier spells and make potions and act as his bodyguard while on the mainland and the like. He also takes care of the magical creatures—Oh look," Min-Ji said abruptly, pointing, "there's a few of our al-mi'rajes. We're very lucky to see them. They don't often come out onto the beach."

I turned and saw several rabbits, each with a golden horn spiraling out of their heads, hopping across the sand near the patio. One paused and raised itself up on its hind legs as it stared at us, then hurried after its fellows into the darkness.

"What other mythical creatures do you have? I asked, settling back into the couch.

"Not much. We have two alicantos, birds that eat small amounts of gold and silver, then their feathers turn to precious metals when they molt. The birds are actually very useful for finding gold deposits in the earth too. We also have a flock of chickens running around that lay multiple golden eggs during a full moon, and, oh, this is a definite surprise. Here comes another creature right now."

I turned again toward where she was pointing. Out on the night-darkened sand, a pair of shining eyes stared at me from the shadows. I squinted, unable to make out what it was, it blended in so well with the gathering darkness. With a yowl, the creature leapt out of the night and into the light of the patio. It landed onto the couch beside me, snarling and hissing. I leapt up with a scream as an adolescent black jaguar gave me a hiss before springing onto Min-Ji.

Min-Ji screamed, and I stood rooted to the spot, horrified as the jaguar began mauling her. My horror turned into confusion as Min-Ji's scream turned into a shriek of laughter, and she tackled the jaguar back, laughing as they tussled on the couch. Min-Ji transformed into a fox, and the two began darting from couch to couch to couch, upsetting cushions and flinging pillows as they gave each other chase. Finally, after several minutes, Min-Ji reverted to her human form and collapsed onto the disordered sofa. The jaguar pounced on her and tried to reinitiate play.

"No, enough! Luciano, stop! You'll spill the lemonade!" Min-Ji cried out as the jaguar knocked into the coffee table, the lemonade jug teetering dangerously and sloshing lemonade onto the teak surface. After a final playful tug on Min-Ji's shirt, the jaguar released her blouse and flopped onto her lap, panting.

I stared at the pair with an open mouth, and Min-Ji laughed as she ran a hand over the winded jaguar's head, ruffling its fur.

"You eavesdropping little scoundrel," Min-Ji sighed, fanning her pink face. "Cordelia, this is my son, Luciano."

"Your . . . what?" I asked, my brain reeling, trying to catch up with everything that had just happened and connecting that to what she just said. "He's not a fox."

"Well, he's my step-son. Come on, Luc, be polite. Introduce yourself."

The black jaguar instantly turned into a twelve-year-old latino boy. He gave me a big grin and a cheery wave, flicking his long black hair out of his eyes. "Hey, I'm Luciano. You can call me Luc."

"You're a jaguar?" I asked, dumbfounded, and Luc and Min-Ji laughed.

"Well, technically he's a Yucatec nagual," Min-Ji replied as Luc helped himself to the pitcher of lemonade, which had miraculously not shattered during their tussle. "Carson is his biological father. His mother, who was also a nagual, was married to him until she abandoned them six years ago."

I glanced at Luc with a sorry expression. He was busy chugging lemonade, and he shrugged at me as if speaking about his mother abandoning him was no big deal. I frowned.

"So wait, Min-Ji, if Carson doesn't know you're a . . ."

"Kumiho," Min-Ji supplied.

"Yeah, a kumiho, then does he know about Luc being—"

Min-Ji shook her head with a quick, "Nope."

"How is that possible?" I asked, incredulous, as I dropped back down onto the disheveled couch. "His own child?"

"Carson doesn't know a lot of things. Like how he is attracted to many mythical creatures," Min-Ji replied, laughing. "I'm actually his third wife. Luc's mother was second. I met his first wife once, and she's actually a sprite or nymph of some kind, I can't remember. She's a very popular celebrity in the human world, which is why the marriage didn't last long. He just doesn't seem to notice that he attracts, and is attracted to, mythical beings. But Luc's mother taught him to never tell his father what he actually is, to keep it a secret, because humans can be . . . well, you know."

I stared between the two of them, still frowning. "And neither of you care that you're just lying to this Carson guy?" I wasn't going to call him my owner. I at least had some dignity left.

They both shook their heads, and I stared at them in amazement.

I didn't care much that the man that had bought me was being lied to by his family, I just couldn't believe they were all living their lives like this. I would be so lonely and upset if I couldn't talk to my mother about what and who I was. In fact, her lying about half of myself was what drove us apart in the first place, and probably caused most of the mess I was in now.

"Why?" I asked.

"He's happy living in ignorance." Min-Ji shrugged.

"But he keeps magical creatures; doesn't that bother you?" If I couldn't convince those like me to let me go, I was never getting out of here.

"Well, it didn't before he brought you here, because we've only had actual *animals*, like the chickens and rabbits and reptiles and stuff. Nothing humanoid before now."

"And now? Me being here doesn't bother you?"

"You seem nice. I like you," Luc piped up. "But you feel funny. That kind of bothers me." He looked to Min-Ji for an explanation. She gave him a kiss on the head.

"She's a hybrid, sweetie." Luc turned back to stare at me, his eyes wide.

"Is she dangerous?" Luc whispered to Min-Ji, shrinking slightly into her.

"No, I don't think so. A little unnatural, but not dangerous," she said consolingly, giving me a pointed look. Annoyance curled in my stomach.

"No, I'm not," I spat, standing again. Here I was in the presence of people who had captured me and were holding me hostage, and they were worried *I* was the dangerous one? "I'm not nearly as dangerous as you!"

I turned and stalked out into the darkness, hurt crawling up inside me.

As I stomped across the sand, I had to remind myself that I couldn't let the faux freedom, the luxurious environment, and the magical creatures surrounding me fool me. I wasn't on vacation, I couldn't leave when I wanted. I was a prisoner, and not even my magical captors would let me out.

I walked toward the water with a hand outstretched in front of me so I could feel the boundary before I ran into it again. When my fingers met resistance, I gave the water one quick wistful look before walking alongside the barrier, trailing a finger along it, wondering how to get out. A waning crescent moon rose over the cliffs, turning the sea foam into liquid moonlight.

Over the beaching waves, I heard splashing, and I turned to see the shape of a jaguar following in the shallows behind me.

"Luc, stop it," I snapped, realizing he'd probably been hoping to scare me. I was not in the mood to be pounced on, especially by an animal that had claws. And with the ill humor I was in, I would probably take my anger out on him and accidentally injure him. "I don't want to hurt you!"

The jaguar growled, and I realized it was a much deeper pitch than Luciano's had been.

"Luc?" I asked hesitantly, fear curdling in my belly.

Silently, too quick to react, the jaguar charged out of the surf toward me. In the moonlight, in the half-second before the beast leaped on me, I could see this cat had the regular golden coloring, its black spots starkly visible on its fur.

I screamed for help as the jaguar slammed me into the sand and pinned me down, snarling in my face. The air was knocked out of me so I could only stare, mouth gaping, lungs paralyzed, in horror up at the massive cat. Its hot breath filled my nose, its glistening fangs mere inches from my face. After sniffing and growling at me, the jaguar instantly turned into a young man, his hands pinning my wrists to the sand.

"What are you? How do you know my little brother?" he snapped, his face drawn up in a horrific snarl. "Did you hurt him? Have you come to capture him?"

Relief washed over me that the jaguar was actually another shape-shifting person, and the realization helped my lungs to relax and function. I drew in a ragged breath and began coughing. When I was able to breathe normally, my relief quickly heated to anger as the outraged young man glared down at me.

"How many more of you are there, just so I can be aware?" I demanded, my voice a rasp.

He glared down at me. "What are you?" he asked again. "You smell unnatural."

The anger inside me boiled over at being called *unnatural*, again, and I shoved against his grip with all my strength, cuffing his chin with the backs of his own fists. He let go of my arms in surprise, rolling off me to his feet.

"I am not unnatural!" I demanded, sitting up and rubbing my wrists where his claws had pricked my skin. "And why would I want to capture your little brother?"

He stared at me with narrowed eyes. The moonlight reflected off his black hair. He looked like he was just a couple of years older than me.

"If you're not here for Luciano, then why are you here?" he demanded.

"I'm your father's new house ornament, didn't you know?" I snapped, wincing at the pain in my body. I had really taken a beating this evening. This was going to be my life, now. Great.

"What are you talking about?"

"That giant tank your father built?" I retorted. "I'm the 'main attraction.'"

He turned to look toward the house, where the lights shining in the tank were barely visible.

"He bought a humanoid for the tank?" he asked, sounding amazed.

"You live here, don't you?" I asked, my tone scathing. "You didn't know that?"

"My brother and I have been away for several months," he said, still looking toward the house, his tone blank. "We just got back today. I knew he was building that tank as a present for Min-Ji, but he didn't say anything about . . . you." He looked back down at me. His face was shadowed, so I was unable to read his expression.

"Yeah, I was a wonderful surprise," I snapped as I got to my feet, brushing sand off my bottom and elbows.

We heard running paws, and a fox and jaguar materialized out of the darkness, popping into their human skins when they reached us.

"Oh, Bastian! Hi! You're back," Min-Ji replied, her expression pleased as she took in the young man. "Luc had told me you cut your vacations short."

"Did he tell you why?" Bastian asked, giving the twelve-year-old a steely look.

"No. Should he have?" She glanced between him and the young boy, who stuck his tongue out at Bastian.

"*No.*"

"He also said you sent him ahead of you," Min-Ji replied with a careful tone. "Why? Where were you?"

"Nowhere," Bastian snapped. "I'm going to bed."

"Wait!" Luc interjected, coming to stand beside me. "Did you meet Cordelia?"

"We've met," Bastian replied, brushing past me. "Goodnight." We watched his retreating figure as he stomped away.

Min-Ji chuckled and shook her head as Bastian disappeared into the dark. "Teenagers with their mood swings. Are you okay, Cordelia?"

"He certainly gave me a memorable welcome," I said, wincing as I rubbed at the bump on my head where it had hit the sand. For a second time today.

"Let's get you some painkillers and disinfectant for those scratches. Who knows where that boy's claws have been!" Min-Ji tittered, leading me back up the beach to the mansion. Luc ran ahead of us, disappearing through the open patio door. "Oh, also, Carson called."

My stomach sank. Back to the tank I go.

"He said he's staying on the mainland tonight. He owns multiple apartment buildings and hotels in Bangkok and other countries, so he has no shortages of places to stay. He'll be back tomorrow afternoon, so you can sleep in a guest bedroom tonight if you'd like, as long as you don't slit our throats during the night."

I turned to her, aghast and angry, and Min-Ji paused to look at me with a cool expression on her face.

"I would never do that!" I vented. "I'm not a monster."

"I know that, dear. But just know, *I* won't hesitate to become one, should you threaten my family," Min-Ji replied with a cheerful smile that sent a chill down my spine.

"I won't," I insisted, still insulted but wary.

"Good." She led me inside, through the spa room, and into a sweeping entry hall. We went up yet another set of grand stairs and down a wide corridor. She brought me to an opulent bedroom with a king-size bed, a private bathroom, and windows that looked out at the ocean. "I'll get a maid to lay out clean clothes for you while you shower. Breakfast will be at eight. I'll see you in the morning."

"Wait, wait."

She paused at the door, looking back at me with a patient expression. I debated asking, but then I decided it was better to know all I was up against here, and what doors were closed to me.

"So, I've seen your servers and maids and things around here, and you freely turn into magical creatures with them around. Aren't you afraid they'll tell your husband about you? Tell the world about you?"

"Oh, they won't be telling anyone anything. Since Carson has several valuable mythical creatures and valuable items here, he can't risk word getting out, because then our house would be a target for thieves. My husband has the staff drink a potion or something every morning that keeps them docile and ignorant of anything magical going on around them. And I'm sure he's had his warlock add something to help the staff withstand your persuasiveness."

"Wow, your husband has thought of everything," I replied, sullen. I wouldn't be able to ask the maids for help, or even force them. And, if they didn't notice a jaguar turning into a boy, they wouldn't care about helping a kidnapped person.

"Yes. That's why he's so successful, and why I was attracted to him in the first place. I like clever men. The money helped me stay. Goodnight, dear." She left, closing the door behind her.

"How clever can he be if he doesn't even know his own children are magical creatures?" I asked the closed door. I turned back to the bedroom.

It was the nicest room I'd ever been in, and I would definitely want to be clean before I slipped between the obviously expensive sheets. I quickly entered the bathroom, an outrageously large room decorated in gold and crystal to match the bedroom. I found a clean, fluffy towel in a cabinet and quickly stripped, stepping into the roomy shower.

The news that the staff wouldn't be able to help me escape made discouragement pulse through me, but I didn't feel totally hopeless. My circumstances were not so dire anymore, so I had time to think of the perfect escape plan. While I would never attack anyone outright, I could play my cards right, and act innocent and docile, and Min-Ji would let me roam about. That was the key. Once I earned enough of their trust, I would be able to snoop around and search for a weakness, or a phone, or something, anything, to help me out of here.

I exited the shower after a long soak and scrub and found painkillers and disinfectant on the bedside table, along with clean pajamas and a set of new clothing on the foot of my bed. Once I'd dressed in the jammies, brushed my teeth, and combed out my long silver hair, I couldn't help feeling relaxed.

My feet sank into the plush carpet as I went to the panoramic windows and slid open the panes, allowing fresh, humid air—and the sound of the sea—to fill the bedroom. I stood at the windows for a few moments, breathing in the smell and wondering where my mother was, if she was safe. She had risked everything to come for me. If she was safe, I knew she wouldn't abandon me.

"I love you, Mom," I murmured to the night air, wishing my words could be carried on the breeze to her. I turned off the lights—the moon sending slashes of pearly light across the room—and clambered under the covers of the cloud-like mattress. I realized with awe that this was my first time in a real bed since my kidnapping.

My discouragement from earlier had vanished. I would find a way out of here. It would take some time, but I would never stop searching and plotting. My numbness back at the convention was a state I never wanted to enter into again. My mother was looking for me. That gave me life and hope again.

And who knew? Maybe after a while these people would let me go. I wasn't counting on it, but as I snuggled into the comfortable mattress with a full belly and clean body, with the knowledge that I wouldn't be constantly stuck in that tank for the rest of my life, anything seemed possible. Tomorrow was another day, and I wouldn't stop trying to get back to my mom. For now, I could rest. Eyelids heavy, I fell asleep, soothed by the sighs of the sea.

EPILOGUE

The chains rattled as the strung-up man was slapped again, then punched in the gut. His weak cough turned into a disdainful laugh as he turned, spat blood onto the floor, then faced his interrogator again as he dangled by his arms from the ceiling, his ankles shackled to the floor.

"I'm going to ask you again—" the questioner thundered.

"By all means, do," the prisoner interrupted.

"*Where* is she?"

The shackled man licked his bloodied lips and winced. "You know, your methods of persuasion aren't helping me remember. In fact, I think I feel a concussion and amnesia coming on. What a shame that would be if I completely forgot everything."

"You enjoying this?" The interrogator asked, raising a threatening fist.

"Nothing gives me more pleasure than angering you HAMMA people," the prisoner drawled.

"Phillips, enough," came a female voice over the intercom. "We have other ways to get the truth." The big man, Phillips, backed away, popping the knuckles of his bloody fists as the door to the interrogation room opened, and a woman bearing a small metal briefcase entered. She was very pretty, dressed in a business skirt suit, her chestnut hair pulled back into a ponytail.

"Ooh, are you going to take over questioning me, pretty lady?" the captive asked, looking her up and down.

The woman smiled and set her case on the table. "Would you like me to?"

"I think it would certainly be more enjoyable."

"Oh, I'm not so sure about that. My methods aren't as *exhausting* as Mr. Phillips'."

"Are they physical, though?" the prisoner asked with a suggestive raise of his brow.

The woman laughed. "You know, for someone who's been through hours of torture, you sure do have a sunny disposition. I'm hoping a few minutes with me will change that."

With some clicks, the woman opened her case and reached inside. When she withdrew her bare hand, a scorpion the size of her palm rested on her knuckles.

"The Jwalakhna is a very rare species of scorpion found in the Himalayas. Have you heard of these, during your many travels?"

"A pet of yours, is it?" the prisoner asked, his expression no longer brazen.

"We have a healthy respect for one another." The woman tickled a finger down the scorpion's back, then met the shackled man's eyes. "Its name roughly translates to 'the fire that crawls.'"

The prisoner went still, the arrogant grin slipping from his bloodied lips. The woman returned her gaze to the scorpion. The body of its shell was a glossy, chocolate brown, with vibrant orange legs and tail that ended in a live-coal red stinger.

"Pretty, isn't she?" the woman asked brightly. "She's very sought after for the magical properties of her venom. One sting will start to slowly eat away at you: flesh, muscle, bone, marrow." She studied the scorpion as it began scuttling up her arm. "And it's very painful while it happens too. The nerves are nearly the last to die," she replied, giving her prisoner a warm smile.

The chained man was no longer smiling. In fact, he looked pale, like he was about to be sick.

"So, to show you I'm not lying about the virtue of Anala's venom here, I'm going to let this little darling give you a kiss. That's what you wanted, wasn't it, Mr. Colton?" she asked, stepping closer toward the shackled man, the fear growing in his bruising eyes.

"No, no, no, we can just be friends," he stammered, swallowing shakily, tossing his limp blond hair out of his eyes, sweat beading on his forehead and upper lip. "I believe you, she looks very pretty and very dangerous, and I'll tell you everything you want to know."

"Oh," the woman replied with a click of her tongue. "I wouldn't want Anala to be disappointed. And you seemed so eager for things to get physical with a female."

She slipped the scorpion onto Parker's chained hands above his head as he began struggling, shaking the chains and trying to fling the scorpion free. Agitated, the scorpion scuttled further down Parker's arm, coming to a rest in the crook of his elbow. The woman took a thin stick out of her briefcase and gave the scorpion a sharp thwap on its head.

Threatened, the scorpion raised its tail as Parker began shouting, jerking against his restraints, and he briefly shook himself free of the arachnid. However, the tumbling, airborne scorpion caught itself on Parker's pant leg with sharper-than-normal claws. Parker struggled to shake it free, but was hindered by his chained ankles. The scorpion dug its grip into the fabric of his pants and arched its tail over its back. The woman gave the arachnid another tap, and the scorpion sank its stinger into the top of Parker's knee.

The woman watched with a satisfied smile as Parker began to scream.

Acknowledgements

Acknowledgements are probably one of the hardest things for me to write, because it's so difficult to truly express how grateful I am to every single person that has helped me put this piece of heart work out into the world. It's beyond humbling to know I have so many wonderful people that are so willing to help and support me. What seems like a small question ends up having a large impact on my book.

As always, I must thank my Heavenly Father and Jesus Christ, without the knowledge of Their love and patience for me, nothing I accomplish in this world would feel worthwhile. They truly give me hope, joy, and peace, both in tumultuous times and out.

I would like to give special thanks to Jyoti Kumari for being so patient with me as she helped me with the Hindi language for a mythical creature I made up for this book, and just for being an amazing friend! Love you, Jyoti! I would also like to give special thanks to Barbara Fortunato Alves for her help in getting the Brazilian Portuguese language and mythical creatures right! Thank you so much, Barbara! You're wonderful! Thank you both for helping me get your beautiful languages correct!

I also need to thank to my brothers-in-law; Jacob Burnham for help with some Japanese words, your knowledge was very helpful; as well as Matthew Burnham, with his help on some medical questions I had. Thank you for helping me even as you were busy prepping for your boards. I will probably be coming to you for more of your expertise, especially if I need to write about the more gruesome aspects of medical procedures. (And no, I did not model Oliver the ex-Orthopedic-surgeon-bodyguard after you, haha.)

Big thanks to my critique partners that read this story years ago, Mary Locke Jolley and Sarah Lowe, I know it was a long time coming, but you made it possible with your incredible help and expertise! Also to my Beta readers, Katherine Kitchen, Gayle Burnham, Camille Woodward, Emily Warner, and Nicole Burnham, your feedback and encouragement and excitement for this book was so incredible! Thank you!

I also want to thank my discord and critique groups and all my writer friends, you are all incredible writers. It's so fun to get on and chat with you about writing, and I love the atmosphere of kinship, encouragement, and writing advice. I know it's a lot of names to write down, but I'm going to do it anyway; Kailie Ward, Nikki Siegel, Mary Locke Jolley, Amanda Tullis, Kristine Allan, Katelyn Yates, Miranda Day, and Lori Hadley. You and the others that pop on occasionally are so wonderful to chat and commiserate with, and it's so fun to be part of your writing community!

Also, a huge thanks to the author community on Tiktok! The future of TT seems uncertain (as per usual,) but for those of you who have bought my books, cheered me on, recommended my books, and been kind enough to like and comment on my posts, and that have given me inspiration by your hard work and dedication to your stories, and been incredible internet friends, (you know who you are) thank you so so much! Your dedication and love, not only to your writing craft but to marketing and video-making, is inspiring!

More thanks need to be handed out, and this one may seem odd, but as music is such a huge inspiration and conduit for me, I cannot write without the perfect music to set the mood. I want to send a specific shoutout to Brandon Flowers and The Killers. While I was writing this book, their music was very influential for me, and it was particularly special for me, as they are from the Las Vegas area, and so their love of the desert rang true for me as well, (despite some characters not loving the desert so much.) If these books ever get made into a movie some day, I will require several of The Killers' songs to be in it. (Especially, "Have All The Songs Been Written," which is the quintessential essence of the relationship between Cordelia and Callista. I have the entire scene in question to accompany that song planned, complete with music breakdown and choreography in my head, and have had it planned for years.)

Of course, I need to thank my amazing editor, Rebecca Bird. You are incredible, and you've helped me learn how to be more concise and to the point (I'm still learning, lol) but your edits are always so beyond amazing, and truly polish up my words! Thank you!

I also want and need to thank my cover artist, My Lan Khuc, for her incredible artistry, you truly make my covers pop, and your patience with me is so so admirable! I can't wait to continue working together on this series with you in the future!

There needs to be a shoutout my dear friend, McKell Parsons; all those author brunches over the years have been so so fun and important, thank you for putting those together! You're a rockstar!

I also need to thank my family, for being a wonderful support, my parents and siblings, in-laws and niblings, you're all amazing for supporting me! I love you!

And as always, I must thank my incredible husband. Without you, none of this would be possible. Your patience, love, encouragement, help with all the small and big things, and your belief in me has made me grow into the author I am. Thank you for being my first fan. I love you to infinity and beyond.

I also need to add a special note here, in case some people from Moapa Valley read this book and feel offended by the viewpoints of some characters: I love the desert. Let me say it again, louder, in case you didn't believe me: I LOVE THE DESERT, *especially* there in Logandale and Overton. I know that several of my characters complain about having to live, not only in the desert, but in a small town, but they are not of my opinion.

I've spent almost half of my childhood in Southern Nevada, in Logandale, riding the dunes, swimming at Lake Mead and the Res (the reservoir for those not fortunate enough to know the nickname), and climbing the rocks there at Valley of Fire, and my all-time favorite smell in the world is the desert during a rainstorm.

Most of my formative years, happy memories, and especially story ideas, have been made in that special place with special people. I promise, I don't hate Moapa Valley or the desert; both have my heart, and they always will. And while it may not seem like it, this book is a love note to the desert and those that have made it wonderful. (If in doubt, see the description of the desert sunset in chapter eight: That is how I truly feel.)

And finally, last but never, ever least, thank you dear, wonderful readers! I became an author because I wanted to share the stories trapped in my head, and you reading them have helped me set the characters and adventures free! You're all heroes, and I will always sing your praises.

About the Author

Chantel Burnham is a writer of Young Adult Fantasy and Sci-Fi, as well as a movie quoter extraordinaire. After spending some time as a film major, she discovered that her true passion is creating worlds of her own through writing.

When she isn't procrastinating writing her next book, Chantel can be found crafting decorations for Spooky Season, listening to music non-stop, reading from her ever-expanding TBR list, or snuggling her dog, cats, and husband, usually all at the same time.

Chantel lives in Northern Utah even though snow isn't her thing, but mountains, forests, and lakes are, so it evens out.

Check out her website at www.chantelburnham.com or scan the QR code.

9 781962 158046